are invited to relax and enjoy the mess he has made of so much of his life without a reproving dear-dear or tut-tut. What a huge relief. The book begins in mid-hangover. Alcohol runs through it as his never-failing companion and undoing. As he entertainingly describes, he has wrecked several promising careers with its help - in journalism, photography, television . . . Most alcoholics, I hear you say, are bores. Not Farson . . . the book is rich in cameos . . . His tolerance is total - and for someone who passed so much time in a haze, his memory is piercingly vivid . . . despite having already written Bacon's biography, he has more fascinating observations to offer us here.'

PETER LEWIS, *Daily Mail*

'It is a tribute to Farson's spirit and his good humour that he has survived to the age of seventy, still hale and hearty and able to tell the tale. He is a good old trouper who deserves our approval - at least so long as he is sober.' RICHARD INGRAMS, *Evening Standard*

'One suspects, despite all the hangovers and débâcles, he has had a whale of a time.' MARTIN GAYFORD, *Sunday Telelgraph*

'Farson, now seventy, has a life of alcohol-tinged bohemian colour to recount, and he does so with charm and rueful vigour.'

STEVEN POOLE, *Guardian*

'A rattle-bag of gossip, entertaining and lively.'

IAIN FINLAYSON, *Independent on Sunday*

'A captivating piece of writing. It not only gives an insight into Farson's life but also that of his famous friends, such as Somerset Maugham and Francis Bacon . . . Farson is instantly likeable because of his childlike honesty and self mockery. He charms the reader with his wit and his ability to vividly paint every scene, even those of his childhood.' FIONA ROBINSON, *Manchester Evening News*

'So winning is Daniel ████████ ography that one is soon thinkin ████████ his Soho cronies . . . it's the off ████████ out both the famous and the inf████████ eers.'

m & High

DANIEL FARSON

NEVER A
NORMAL MAN

An Autobiography

HarperCollins*Publishers*

For those who don't belong

HarperCollins*Publishers*
77–85 Fulham Palace Road,
Hammersmith, London W6 8JB

This paperback edition 1998

1 3 5 7 9 8 6 4 2

First published in Great Britain by
HarperCollins*Publishers* 1997

Copyright © Daniel Farson 1997

The Author asserts the moral right to
be identified as the author of this work

ISBN 0 00 638326 2

Set in Postcript Bembo

Printed and bound in Great Britain by
Caledonian International Book Manufacturing Ltd, Glasgow

Contents

Illustrations

My great-grandfather, General James Negley.

Christmas 1930. Aged three, in Cossack costume brought back from Russia by my parents.

Bohinsko, 1935.

My mother and pigmy during the journey across Africa in 1939.

A 'minor ambassador', evacuated to Canada in June 1940.

As a private in the US Army Corps in post-war Germany.

The ruins of Munich.

Somerset Maugham, Christmas 1947.

Photographing a model for *Picture Post* (Hulton Deutsch).

The double exposure of Salvador Dali. (Hulton Deutsch)

My parents at the Grey House in North Devon.

Martin Seymour Smith, Robert Graves and Robert Kee at a bullfight in Palma, Majorca. (Hulton Deutsch)

Brendan Behan. (Hulton Deutsch)

Colin Wilson.

Cliff Richard.

The French Pub became my second home.

John Deakin.

On board the *Orcades*.

The nudists in *Out of Step*.

Caitlin Thomas gave me my first taste of notoriety when I had to fade her off the air. (Photograph by John Deakin)

Playing myself in the film *The Angry Silence*.

The beggar in Barcelona.

Noël Coward.

Trevor Howard.

Barbara Cartland.

Richard Burton.

Miss Carrie James, the old lady of Tasmania.

Boy at Barnstaple Fair.

On my balcony in Narrow Street overlooking the Thames at Limehouse.

Graham Sutherland.

Francis Bacon.

With Bacon at the fair in Soho Square.

At Charlie Brown's in Limehouse with Deakin and Bacon.

Gallery, the art quiz I devised for Channel 4. George Melly, Maggi Hambling and Vincent Price.

Henry Williamson.

Jeremy Thorpe.

Crossing the Caucasus in 1992.

Gilbert & George at the opening of their exhibition in Moscow.

Peter Bradshaw by the pool at the Grey House.

In the peaceful backyard at Appledore. (Photograph by Karen Lamey, 1996)

Acknowledgements

Paying compliments to editors can be an awkward matter of lip-service. Not in this case. I owe much to Richard Johnson for his careful perseverance, and to Robert Lacey, whose final editing was tough yet sympathetic. Care, perseverance and tough sympathy, with scarcely a cross word: all an author could hope for. Thank you.

I am grateful to Century and Vintage (*The Gilded Gutter Life of Francis Bacon*), and to Michael Joseph and Penguin (*A Dry Ship to the Mountains*), for kindly allowing me to describe in this book events which I have previously written about elsewhere.

Daniel Farson
Appledore, November 1996

The Horns of the Moon

He ran against a shooting star,
So fast for fear did he sail,
And he singed the beard of the Bishop
Against a comet's tail;
And he passed between the horns of the moon,
With Antidius on his back;
And there was an eclipse that night,
Which was not in the Almanac.

Robert Southey,
'St Antidius, the Pope and the Devil'

One

The Tongueless Turk

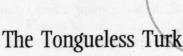

TWO NIGHTS AGO I flew into Istanbul to sort out my life. So far I have not done well. This is not the vanity of self-pity: you need to see me smiling as I write this to appreciate that I should not be taken too seriously. Yet, somewhere along the line, I have taken the wrong turning. Otherwise why am I drinking myself to death in a slow form of suicide? Why am I so consumed by guilt? I have never been able to forgive myself, but I do not know why; I am my own victim.

I need to find some of the answers before the end of this journey. After all, time is not creeping but rushing up behind me. At the age of sixty-eight, I suppose it is time to grow up.

I am writing this at one o'clock on a Sunday afternoon in May 1994 in the Pera Palas Oteli, built in 1882 for the first passengers off the Orient Express, who were carried up the hill by sedan chair. When I first came here, twelve years ago, I knew I had crossed from Europe to the East as soon as I saw the exotic inner hall which came from the Arabian Nights of my imagination: an orgy of baroque in brown, yellow and gold, with a high, carved ceiling inset with latticed windows where veiled beauties might have looked down on those below, dwarfed by the overwhelming chandelier. My bedroom was huge, with old-fashioned wooden furniture and a glimpse of the Golden Horn, the lift a graceful fantasy of open ironwork. Operated by a boy in brocaded uniform, it rose sedately like an elegant woman from a curtsey. The legendary bar was so high I had to climb onto my stool.

All these remain; but either the hotel or myself have lost our charm. I miss the owner, Hasan Süzer, who has flown to Gaziantep in his private plane to supervise his Hittite museum, a tough man who would kill for his hotel. We took to each other at once, partly because neither spoke the other's language so we could not quarrel, but sat there drinking and smiling with the occasional intervention of an interpreter. Once he took me upstairs and unlocked the room where Kemal Atatürk stayed when he was a young officer before he founded the Republic and dragged Turkey into the twentieth century. The room is preserved as an intimate museum, or shrine, with souvenirs acquired by Mr Süzer who reveres Atatürk. There are even shirts and underclothes, which look surprisingly pristine in view of Kemal's reputation, which suggested that no woman, boy or goat was safe from his rapacious advances. In that curious interregnum after the First World War when Constantinople was occupied by the Allies, a British general spotted the hero of the Dardanelles dining by himself in the Pera Palas dining-room, and sent a waiter with an invitation to join him.

Atatürk refused: 'No. You are a guest in *my* country. You come to me.'

Süzer was nearly in tears when he told me this. A huge photograph of Kemal Atatürk in the same dining-room hangs in the hotel today; it could be a film still of Bela Lugosi on a train to Stamboul.

But Süzer has flown and though I miss his company I feel so lack-lustre that I might anyway have avoided him. Yesterday it poured with rain, I seem to have hurt my knee, I have lost a substantial part of my money, and my train to Adana in the south-east has been delayed by twenty-four hours, so I am forced to linger for another unnecessary day. Though I am at a low ebb, I am not unhappy. I do not travel to enjoy myself, I dislike travelling, but for the change of scene, and if I were sober and able to explore as I have done before there would be no problem. Half-drunk, and my will-power, never too strong at the best of times, starts to crumble.

My horoscope last week advised me to look in the mirror and keep on doing so until I liked what I saw, but mirrors are not what they used to be. Today I was confronted by a cracked face with bleary, half-closed, piggy-red eyes which peer back at me reproachfully. The puffiness subsides as the day progresses, but why do I insist on capering into the early hours? My forte is a Russian whirl as I sink to my knees and just manage to rise again, a combination of Twist and Tsarism. After that first look in the mirror I did not dare to retrieve my camera case from reception to discover what is left in the inside pocket which serves as my safe. Where is my passport? I have a hazy image of the sardonic clerk behind the desk handing it back yesterday in my fury when they refused to let me take that bearded Turk to my bedroom though it was only six o'clock in the evening and I spoke loudly about kilims, to the Turk's bewilderment, to impress on the posse of porters that this was a business relationship. They were not convinced and descended on the young man with shrieks and threatening gestures as if they recognized a criminal. Perhaps they did, but he was my criminal. Had my money and my passport left with him?

At one point there was a bespectacled Englishman – now who was he? – less boring than he appeared and indifferent to my tantrums as if he were a contract killer instructed to ignore them. He led me to a Kurdish bar near Taksim Square, where a scissor-faced elderly American queen was indulging in an interminable argument with a handsome young Turk, or Kurd, who stared back impassively. Desperate for company, I attempted to join them but was waved away by the American, though the Kurd gave me a quick smile. The staff, with the liquid, submissive eyes of sheep served me with familiar lethargy.

There was a certain irony in my search for rough trade in Istanbul. The night before I left London I visited a pub known as the Elephants' Graveyard. I had started going back there after a gap of several years, unable to remember the way until the taxi-driver turned round: 'Excuse me, guv'ner, don't think me rude, but do you mean the boozer where young blokes go to pick up old geezers like you?'

'Exactly!' I cried, delighted.

Though some of the other elephants looked less than pleased to see me, the staff were kind and the new landlady, whom I knew years ago in the East End, gave me a friendly welcome. Encouraged, I seized the microphone on karaoke night for a vigorous rendering of 'Mack the Knife' – except that I started too late and never caught up, swinging the mike from hand to hand so that half my words were lost. I was fooled by the confidence which stems from drink, yet sober enough to recognize the horror as two hundred gays stared at me open-mouthed when I finished. I walked straight out of the Graveyard to a silence that chilled my heart, though when I ventured back a few nights later, a very young, very camp barman assured me: 'I thought you were absolutely gorgeous, and so brave!'

With that guilt expunged, I was chatting away to someone when a smart, stiff-backed queen in a blue overcoat swept in with the handsomest man in the world – coarse, squat, with a great round face and a shock of jet-black hair. Somehow I discovered that he was

Turkish. The smart queen shot me a nasty glance, knowing me of old, but he was distracted trying to cash a cheque so I seized my chance and asked where the young man came from.

'Istanbul!' I echoed, 'that's where I'm flying tomorrow.' I should have asked if I could deliver a message or bring him anything back, as a way of getting his address, but I thought of this too late. Instead, I asked if he had ever made love to a man.

'Only one time. Actor in Turkey loved me very much.' At this point the friend swept back and swept him away, and I have never seen the handsomest man in the world again.

Now I was in the bitter position of searching for such a Turk in Istanbul and finding none in my sights. Little wonder that I woke in my old-fashioned bedroom in the Pera Palas at four in the morning, close to howling in my frustration, wondering what I was doing here when I might have been meeting up with the London Turk. I knew I was deceiving myself into the belief that I would have stood the slightest chance, but there is no deceiver like the self-deceiver.

◆

I have fallen victim to the irresistible raki, the clouded silver poison which propels you into the vicious circle where you need another raki to start the day and continue to oblivion and obliteration. Raki seduces more than any alcohol I know: if you are approaching happiness it makes you delirious with joy; if verging on melancholy, it plunges you into the abyss. Either way, it leaves you disembodied and alarmingly horny. And if you drink so much as a sip of water when you clean your teeth in the morning, it sets you off again.

No drink should be abused, and if I drank raki more wisely, starting later in the day and accompanied by bits of melon and cheese as the Turks do, there is no drink I know to equal the ecstasy.

As for the final obliteration, it has the advantage that you pass out and remember little. The horror comes with the 'coming-down', those nights of the 'heebie-jeebies' when I lie in bed at home in Devon, hour after hour, not able to sleep nor daring to in case I fail to wake up, my dog peering at me anxiously as I twist and turn, trying to find the cool spot on the pillow.

Have I mentioned the lightly bearded Turk who kissed me in the street? I wondered if he picked my pocket as he did so, for kissing in the street is a new experience, but I misjudged him there. Opening the hotel's large leather folder in my bedroom I have discovered several substantial Turkish banknotes and twenty dollars which I must have hidden among the stationery and envelopes. Possibly my traveller's cheques are still in the safe at reception? I seem to remember shouting at the unfortunate, burly new under-manager last night until a charming young English couple led me to their bedroom where they plied me with miniature bottles of raki from their minibar. He had the looks, she the personality; and they could not have been kinder, explaining that they had come to the Pera Palas after reading my guide to Turkey, which made everything seem worthwhile again. Unfortunately they left this morning. I could have done with their company today. Instead I wandered aimlessly around, finding that even Istanbul can be triste on a Sunday morning, boring the barmen at the Sheraton Hotel as barmen have been bored by lonely strangers for years because that is part of the job.

There is no way I can retrieve the elation of that very first morning in Istanbul when I walked down the hill from the Pera Palas as soon as it was light to the hectic fish market at the bottom nudging the start of Galata Bridge across the Golden Horn, with the faint shapes of mosques and minarets beyond in the rising heat haze like a smudged watercolour. The Golden Horn – a name of such romance I did not admit it was a stinking sewer, nor that the view from Pierre Loti's café overlooks an industrial backwater. Today I decided to return to my favourite haunt over the years, Çiçek Pasaji, the Flower Seller's Alley, the wildest place I knew, much as the East End of London might have looked a hundred and fifty years ago.

The flowers were banked on either side of lanes in the covered market and the alley was not much wider, drab and grey with alarming and alarmed cats peering down from the overhanging corrugated roofs erected to protect the customers from crumbling masonry. The ancient houses had known grander, quieter days; sudden glimpses of someone moving behind a window are disconcerting, for the effect is that of façade with no substance behind. In contrast to this bleakness, the alley below exploded with drama, lined by restaurants with tables and chairs outside where Turks came from various parts of the country to celebrate. A few declaimed verse, with impassioned bursts of applause from their companions. Most had musical instruments, like the hideous, smiling woman with a contraption which looked like a giant colander and sounded no better. The singers, acrobats and orators fused together in a friendly cacophony except for the fat violinist Hasan who played with such intensity inside his restaurant that he might have been performing in Carnegie Hall, though apt to rush out to shoo away a rival who dared to strike up outside. A woman danced by herself, her mouth stuffed with lira notes which she had put there earlier, but no one wanted to follow her example; and a shoe-shine boy pirouetted in parody behind her. Another boy sold packets of chewing-gum and shamed the occasional tourist who refused to buy by presenting a stick for nothing, after which he was tipped handsomely to go away. He gave me a conspiratorial wink as he did so, realizing that I knew his game. An acrobat balanced precariously on a tiny plank, swaying on rollers, swinging a hoop around his neck, balancing a bottle on his nose, all surpassed by a double-somersault, watched open-mouthed by the chewing-gum boy. When the acrobat finished he poured cologne into our hands, accepting lira as payment, not as charity.

While his unsmiling father played the flute, a small boy beat a drum with such a powerful rhythm that his hands must have bled. When anyone gave him a note he seized a moment's rest and his father glared resentfully, especially when the child indulged in a sudden solo on the drum in a burst of independence.

A boy staggered past with a weighing machine, a baffling though common sight in Istanbul; if he found two customers it would save him for another day. Sadder was the boy who stumbled through the throng so pale and weak from hunger that I followed and thrust a note in his hands thinking how generous I was, though relieved that he gave me no thanks as he turned around, dazed. Far kinder were the Turks who made way for him at their table and pushed their unfinished dishes towards him which he devoured in silence. In the same way an old man, 'shabby-genteel' as the Edwardians would have called him, was invited with the utmost courtesy to sit down by those who had eaten with him when he knew better days.

Food vendors paraded past with crab claws, mussels and skewers of Adana kebab, yet the waiters did not seem to mind. The noise increased. Turks pushed away their plates and rose to sing to the accompaniment of the strolling players. A man from Kars on the Russian border danced with abandon, his feet shooting out with the speed of castanets – then commotion as a fight erupted near the acrobats at the far end and waiters rushed to their tables to whisk the plates and glasses away as the fighters pursued each other down the alley with people dancing out of the way like the young bloods in Pamplona from the bulls; though I noticed that when they were separated the men, now covered in blood, seemed relieved while making a few unconvincing lunges towards each other. All over in seconds, the glasses and bottles restored, the music recommenced. I loved this place.

Now, returning to Çiçek Pasaji, I found it spruced up for the benefit of tourists who might be shocked by such exuberance. The individual restaurants are there, but now all a uniform colour with no distinction. Hasan is dead. That is the penalty of returning, that both of you have changed. It is the curse of the travel writer that he destroys the place he loves.

Denied the cats and the acrobats, I soaked up the atmosphere that remained, watched by the owner of one of the new restaurants, pale and smart and less robust, with a few English words which proved less useful than my vestigial Turkish, though he kept on persevering. Finally, and astonishingly, he said: 'We make love – fuck. I have no family.' He said this as casually as if he were offering me a cup of Turkish coffee, and as he was half my age I felt extremely flattered until he added, 'You pay me five hundred pounds.'

'Oh no I don't.'

'You come back here at midnight. Maybe one hundred. We go my place. Near.' His English had improved remarkably and he had grown more handsome, but I shook my head regretfully as I knew that both sobriety at midnight and £100 were beyond me. Instead I headed back to the tiny restaurant at the end of the little street opposite the Pera Palas, yet almost invisible. This had a hint of the atmosphere I was craving for, the better for being unexpected, with Turkish music sung in that deep-throated chant by a man and woman separately, though they sounded identical. The owner, a small, worried man, insisted on placing me at a table on my own, not because he recognized a troublemaker but as a natural courtesy to a foreigner on his first visit. Within moments a group of young Turks waved to me to join them, immensely good-humoured as Turks invariably are, anxious to forge a rapport with anyone who seems to be enjoying himself, however drunk. When they departed, the owner shook his head nervously as another Turk joined me, and shot me warning glances which I ignored. Instead I burbled away to this inevitably handsome, tough young Turk who seemed to be struck dumb by my eloquence – until it dawned on me that he was literally speechless for his tongue had been cut out. I have no idea how or why, nor could he tell me, but for one, insane, raki-ridden moment, I thought how marvellous it would be to take him back to England where I could look after him and possibly arrange a tongue transplant, if such a thing is possible. Beware of pity. But he would have the advantage of being unable to bore me about sport or television. Suddenly tiring of me, he left.

'Very bad man,' sighed the owner, plainly relieved. I was about to protest until I noticed the face of the tongueless Turk pressed against the window, his nose squashed flat, and even through the steamed glass I could tell that he was manic. It is not often one escapes from a tongueless stranger possessed by devils.

Why am I discarding the last shreds of reticence? Because I approach seventy and have no family to embarrass. Why, when life can be so glorious, do I dwell on the indecencies as if showing off? Because all this is part of the life I lead and I make no excuses. My alcoholism is self-inflicted.

'No, you're not an alcoholic, you're just a drunk,' my local doctor assured me, which was good news. But that was three years ago and matters have deteriorated since then. If alcoholism is hereditary, it is sad that I have inherited my father's vice and so few of his virtues. Even as a child I understood his alcoholism and by God I do now, sympathizing with the agonies he endured when he was recovering, described in a recent letter from an old woman who was a nanny in the house where we stayed when I was a child, with friends of my mother. 'I do not think I have seen a man suffer more than your father.'

If only he had relished the binges that caused such mental and physical remorse, but I suspect he hated alcohol as much as I enjoy it. Waiting for one of his many 'cures' in a hospital in pre-war Munich, he wrote that 'Meteor lights flamed through the sky of my mind, and torn faces laughed at me.'

'Torn faces'! – the most haunting alcoholic image I know, for I have seen too many at four o'clock in the morning.

Many years later my father committed himself to the state asylum in Switzerland where the director told him, 'Keep your conflicts, Mr

Farson, it is better for you never to be a normal man.' My father seized on this advice gratefully and it helped to ease his residue of guilt, but he was a stronger man than I am, free from the taint of homosexuality.

Two

Negley's Boy

MY FATHER did the things that most men dream of doing. Not many people read his books today but those who do love them still. He retained an astonishing presence up to his death and one of the few pleasures I gave him was to introduce him to Colin Wilson soon after the publication of *The Outsider*. They forged such a strong if unlikely friendship that I might have been envious had I been excluded. It was proof, if proof is needed, that a loving relationship can exist between men of such disparate ages – Colin barely twenty-one, my father in his sixties. In his Foreword to my father's book on Africa, *Behind God's Back*, Colin described how we drove down to Devon in the summer of 1956 with the journalist Kenneth Allsop:

> Negley was sitting outside his house in the evening sun, his shirt open at the neck, his trouser leg rolled up to the knee, showing the huge hole in the shin he had received during the First World War. He was a big man, with an American accent and a strong, handsome profile; in spite of his size, he was light on his feet. And you only had to speak to him for five minutes to realise that he was interested in everything. This was the quality that made him one of the world's greatest foreign correspondents and – in my own opinion – one of the best writers of this century.

'Interested in everything' – that was it!

During that same visit, in notes shown me by his widow, Allsop made the disconcerting comment: 'Eve, not the tall, elegant woman I expected: dumpy and fat but charming and laughs a lot.' Why did he expect her to be elegant? She was nice-looking. The trouble was that my father was so extrovert that he eclipsed everyone around him, and I have the problem that in writing so much about himself, my father left little for me. Nor can I remember a single reference to his father. All I know of my grandmother is an impression relayed by my mother of an embarrassing woman with dyed red hair. All I have gleaned of my father's background comes from his auto-biography *The Way of a Transgressor*. I am fortunate to have such a legacy.

As my childhood was dominated by my father, his was inspired by his grandfather, General James Negley, of whom he wrote: 'All I knew was that he made other men around him look like mongrel dogs.' That, of course, was how I felt about my father. General Negley hoped my father would adopt his name but, as a token of respect, he kept his own father's name, becoming Negley Farson. My full name is Daniel Negley Farson.

If people's lives are predestined, my father's followed an extraordinary turn of the wheel. He embraced the curve of life as it should be, starting from champion athlete to become adventurer, foreign correspondent and big-game hunter, ending as a contemplative – and writing all the time. Of all the eventful chapters in *Transgressor*, those I return to with the most affection are the first and least familiar, growing up with the General whose photograph is in front of me now, standing stiffly in his creased tunic with epaulettes, sword, tassels, frogging, his plumed helmet perched on a stand beside him, like the Italian tenor in an operetta. The inscription is dated 1 October 1860, signed 'Jas. Negley Commanding 1st Brig 18 Div. Penn.'

He had been a great man, and perhaps he still was though nobody knew it. At the age of seventeen he ran off to the Mexican War; at the outbreak of the Civil War he raised the brigade which he presented to the North. He was made a major-general for his gallantry at Stone River, inspiring the war song 'Who Saved the Left?' and the citizens of Nashville expressing their gratitude with a golden sword. He was one of the generals who rode with Sherman's army of 62,000 men when they burned Georgia from Atlanta to the sea in 1864, leaving no living thing in their tracks. This past glory was followed by terms in Congress until he was broken by a powerful railroad baron whose bill he refused to lobby. Now the people who called on the General were creditors who refused to allow him the breathing space to pay his bills. 'I could not understand any of it,' wrote my father. 'He put me on the table and sank my hands into his curly head. I grabbed handfuls of grey hair. He roared with laughter when I pulled his goatee.'

My father told me that he preferred 'hurt people', meaning those who had known the crueller side of life, and he grew up among them. Negley's Folly, as the house was known locally, was largely façade. My father lived with the sword from Nashville hanging over the mantelpiece, an outstretched eagle with green emerald eyes on the hilt, and the escutcheon citing his bravery at Stone River faced him at the breakfast table, but things had gone wrong. To start with as a small boy he watched the General drive off in the carriage to catch the morning train, presumably in search of work, and then they had no horses. 'I watched for him around six o'clock, when I knew that in a little while I would see him come limping around those pine-trees by the graveyard where he had just left the trolley.

The General was unpopular on two counts. Ironically, the first was his zealousness in the Civil War. Disobeying his superior officer, General Rosencrans, who ordered him to withdraw at the battle of Chattanooga, General Negley held on and lost most of his men. Rumour added that he shot many of them in the back if they turned and ran. He might have inspired 'Who Saved the Left?' but did so at a cost which was considered excessive. He demanded a court-martial and was exonerated with full honours, but he never held a top command again. The military establishment did not forgive him. My father played in the stables with the old dispatch books which were destroyed by his aunts on the General's death. When a historian arrived to write *The True Chattanooga*, my father realized he had played with letters from Grant and Lincoln, using the General's franked mileage books as railway tickets in one of his games.

Among the detritus left in the stables were packets of love-letters between the General and his first wife, and this was the cause of his second offence. If he did something shameful at Chattanooga the truth will never be known, but his marriage to the second Mrs Negley was a public scandal. She was the same age as his eldest son, and condemned as 'flighty', alienating the church-going Thomas Mellon, father of Andrew, who had married the General's sister, Sarah Jane Negley. In the early days Thomas Mellon was a farmer's son who lived at Poverty Point in the shadow of the small village of Negleystown. The Negleys, who were the proprietors of the valley, had the upper hand then. Sixty years later, Judge Thomas Mellon wrote: 'I remember wondering how it could be possible to accumulate such wealth and how magnificent must be the style of living and what pleasures they must enjoy who possessed it. I remember also of the thought occurring whether I might one day attain in some degree such wealth, and an equality with such great people.' He did, with a vengeance.

The brothers-in-law could hardly have been more opposed: the reckless General Negley versus Thomas Mellon who 'begrudged every minute spent in solving other people's troubles' and dunned the widow of his brother who died owing him $3000. He was thriftiness personified, and, as a judge, was known as 'the embodiment of stern, unsmiling justice'. If a murderer committed suicide, he declared, 'this growing tendency to self destruction is not to be discouraged'. He conceded that it was disagreeable to condemn a fellow man to the scaffold, 'but it is not so hard if they clearly deserve it.' All the time he amassed the Mellon millions.

Of the two men, I know which I prefer: the maverick General. Except for the incident involving Billy, the snow-white horse without a single blemish which he captured from a Confederate general who came to Pittsburgh when the war was over to ask for him back, as he was entitled under the surrender terms granted by Ulysses S. Grant. With uncharacteristic meanness my great-grandfather refused because the new Mrs Negley used the horse as her own, riding in a habit made of regulation army blue with a white plume in her cavalry hat. That was bad enough. There was worse. One day after his eldest son came home, the General found him sitting in a trap with his stepmother's horse between the shafts. The General seized the whip and lashed his son across the face. Jim Negley walked out of the house and never returned. Two years later his name was listed among the passengers lost in a ship off Buenos Aires. Pittsburgh never forgave the General for that.

Despite all the vicissitudes, the swings between good and disastrous fortune, my father loved his life at Negley's Folly, thanks to the excitement generated by the old man, and to the servants Abner and his wife Rhodie, the cook, who had been born slaves: 'My grandfather kept his three negro servants by the simple expedient of not paying them. They did not seem to mind. They lived on the place, they ate about the same food that we did; and when good luck came to us, why, good luck came to them. They got paid.'

When Abner took him to Madison Square Garden in New York, my father wondered where he could take a large black man to eat, until he walked boldly into Sherry's where the head waiter took in the situation at a glance and showed them discreetly to a table behind a covered screen – he was French.

Throughout the reminiscences of his childhood there is a wistfulness for a decent life which my father never forgot. He hated the way in which it was *déclassé* to be poor in the United States. 'Glory had to have a bank account to back it up. That was the real trouble. We were poor. In fact we were worse than that; sometimes we were poor – and then suddenly we were not. My grandfather had hit it again. There was something mysterious about that family among the pine-trees on the corner.' Ruined after four terms in Congress, people said 'General Negley can swing only two votes now – his and his nigger's.'

Whenever I see John Ford's *The Sun Shines Bright*, with the Fourth of July procession joined by Judge Priest as the former general takes the salute, I have the image of my great-grandfather doing the same, down on the sidewalk as the Civil War veterans marched by. As my father wrote with unusual bitterness: 'Every year more and more of them marched on, never to return; and with them went many of the fine things that had made the United States. The cash registers marched in.'

The final lines of his novel *The Sons of Noah* convey my father's yearning for the innocence of his early, untarnished years:

> I'd like to feel some of the things that I used to feel. The simple, satisfying things of American life. I'd like to wade out into the creamy surf off the Carolina sands, and use that fine snakewood rod again.
>
> Sometimes, as I sit and stare at that rod, I think that *it* holds the answer. It is among scenes where that rod can be used that the human spirit can find peace and sanity again. I would like to get back to them.
>
> But I have burnt my boats.

❖

Though my father dominates these pages, my mother, Eve, was equally remarkable. She was born in 1898 in India where my grandfather Thomas Stoker was Chief Commissioner of the Northwest Provinces for twenty-five years, so she was brought up with the traditional colonial trappings of servants and an Indian ayah. When my grandmother, Enid, returned to England, they made their home in Egerton Crescent, where I was born in 1927, partly to be close to Harrods. Though looked after devotedly by my grandmother during my parents' absences abroad, I did not know Tom. I gather he became increasingly cantankerous after his blindness which may have been caused by those years in the glaring sun.

Early photographs show my mother with a gentle, wistful look which I knew so well in later years, as if she expected the worst from life and therefore could not be disappointed, almost a martyred look. This was misleading for it concealed a sharp sense of humour that could be frolicsome, tremendous sympathy, and a craving for adventure. At the age of eighteen she volunteered as a VAD nurse and was sent to Petrograd – her ornate passport embossed on a sheet of white paper: 'By His Britannic Majesty's Ambassador Extraordinary and Plenipotentiary to His Majesty the Emperor of All the Russias Etc, Etc, Etc . . . Miss Enid Eveleen Stoker of the Anglo Russian Hospital, Petrograd . . . Given at St. Petersburg . . .'

She described the opening of the hospital by the Tsarina with her usual jauntiness, for Eve was not easily impressed:

By two-thirty we were all standing there dressed up to the nines in starched everythings, and the priests began to arrive, and dress in their wonderful gold and silver and purple clothes. Then we heard a crowd moving slowly up the stairs, and a small dowdy woman in black, like a plain edition of our Alexandra, but with a very sweet expression came in, and behind her such a crowd of gold and medals and ribbons as you never saw – or certainly as *I* never did! The two little Princesses, Olga and Tatiana, came and looked quite charming and so pretty in little ermine hats with white ospreys in them and little low-necked rose-coloured frocks and ermine furs and muffs. Olga is the prettiest and is really lovely I thought, so jolly-looking and natural . . . All our embassy were there in full fig, and all the attachés and secretaries we used to dance with made us roar – all covered in gold lace and things.

Sir George Buchanan [the British Ambassador] looked very well, she is fat and rather common-looking though good at her job. The Empress [reputedly Queen Victoria's favourite grand-daughter] smiled so sweetly and Marie Pavlova [her sister-in-law] came up to me and talked and a strange and very beautiful Russian seized me by the hand though I can't remember who he is and said '*Zdrazwoite* Sister'. When she had been all round we went into the big hall to be photographed and dear old Colonel Fenton, who had on nearly all the medals in the world, seized me by the arm and said, '*Là – au pied de l'Impératrice*' and pushed me down, so I have come out larger than life, leaning against her knee. Then she and the two princesses departed and the rest of us went back and had the dickens of a tea off the hired gold plate!

On one historic night the Grand Duke Dimitri, who had loaned his former palace to the hospital, burst in with Prince Felix Yusupov, an effete aristocrat who was married to the Tsar's niece. They were so hysterical that the doctors assumed they were drunk until they saw the blood. They had just murdered Rasputin.

My mother returned to England earlier than she would have liked, to help my grandmother in nursing Tom, and was introduced to my father as he recovered in hospital from the crash when he demonstrated a sidecar as part of his job as an armaments salesman in Petrograd, which had nearly cost him his leg and was to land him in further hospitals in various parts of the world for years to come.

With their shared experience of Tsarist Russia, a love of literature, and their sense of wanderlust, they were drawn to each other and they married at the Savoy Chapel on 22 September 1920 though there was no reception due to Tom's illness.

The next morning my father wrote to 'Smee', as he called my grandmother, from Southampton, before the boat sailed for America:

Darling Smee,

This is just a short note, written while Eve is dressing, to tell you how happy we are. I never knew what love, real love, meant until Eve entered the church yesterday.

Eve is wonderfully happy and I am not quite sure I am alive – it is so like the dreams I used to have years ago.

I only hope and pray that you are happy. She cried a bit on the train about leaving you and she was so miserable that I gave her your letter then. It was well that I did so; at once, for whatever you said, it made her eyes light up with a wonder of love and happiness for you.

I shall not attempt to tell you how much I love you. You are *my* mother now. God bless you and make you always happy. Last night, at dinner, we drank your health and then we took a long walk in the moonlight, by the boats lying in the docks. For the only time in my life I felt the workings of another soul, and its sweetness – and I am too happy to tell you how I feel.

I will keep your Eve free from harm and the sordid things of life.

After such a letter, so full of confidence and decency, it is little wonder that my mother loved him throughout. Everything lay before her: adventure, romance, disaster and triumph, and ultimately 'the sordid things of life' he had vowed to protect her from and which nearly broke her. If she looked martyred in the photographs there was good reason. Writing to me before Christmas 1995, at the age of ninety-seven, Kathleen Hale, the creator of Orlando the Marmalade Cat, described my mother as 'a very gallant lady'.

Her loyalty was absolute. She lived with my father on a houseboat on a remote mountain lake on Vancouver Island for two years, followed by the din of Chicago where he struggled to sell Mack Trucks and finally succeeded. With promotion and security staring them in the face, they knew they could not endure it and spent their savings on a twenty-six-foot yawl in Norfolk which they sailed across Europe down the Rhine and various canals until the Danube emptied them into the Black Sea. The dispatches he sent back led to his job with the *Chicago Daily News* whose foreign service was considered the best in the world, and for six years he was never in any one country for more than six months.

It sounds high romance and it was. My mother coped staunchly with the rigours, hardships and constant travel. In her ceaseless struggle to defeat his alcoholism, she may have fought too hard, adding to his reservoir of guilt, but I doubt if he would have survived otherwise. She loved him with all her heart.

My father remained unspoilt by success because he knew it was not the end-all of life. He never lost his energy nor his remarkable looks. When he came into a room, you took notice. This is not merely the idolatry of a son. A woman told me how she followed him, walking up Fifth Avenue in his Royal Canadian Flying Corps uniform, and saw the number of people who turned round in admiration as he passed. He was as popular with men as with women. He had no conceit and only the vanity that any man should have. His dress sense was instinctive rather than calculated. The joy was that he was unaware of it all.

I realize I am dogged by my sense of failure because I could not compete, though he gave me a sense of adventure and a reckless optimism. He always knew what to bring back from his trips abroad to delight me: an elephant's tooth from Africa; an embryo crocodile (or was it an alligator?) from South America, a pair of brown and white co-respondent shoes from New York.

As for his drinking, I grew up with it. Reviewing *A Mirror for Narcissus* (1956), the *New Yorker* described the foreign correspondent as

> an interesting creature, who flourished most luxuriantly in the 1930s and is now almost extinct. The men of Farson's breed – if such a congeries of eccentrics and prima donnas can be called a breed – were not so much serious as cynical. 'I know,' Farson says, speaking of his job, 'of no profession more calculated to kill one's enthusiasm for the human race.' They were Americans, and Americans are apt to begin life as optimists, so this cynicism must have been an acquired one, from exposure to the hypocrisy and chicanery of high European politics. It was a shell that had to be constantly guarded against cracking, for most of these men were simply nice, healthy, eager, extroverted boys. But they were personalities (the titles of their books are indicative of the objectivity they brought to the world scene – 'Personal History', 'The Way of a Transgressor', 'I Saw . . .' this or that country fall – and they were all egoists and snobs – achievement snobs that is, the reverse of money or position snobs. And many of them ultimately became bored, and many became drunks.

Seldom was my father bored, but the drunkenness is undeniable. Yet the worst effect of alcoholism, apart from the anguish of the alcoholic, is other people's reaction to it. I would have accepted my father's drinking as a fact of life if it had not been for my mother's constant battle in which I was conscripted, party to the cover-ups, excuses and apologies, which burdened my father with additional guilt. Even then his drunkenness seemed more overwhelming to everyone else than it did to me. Once in the Savage Club a member led me aside to tell me not to judge my father, who was drunk at the time, assuring me that he was a 'good man'. I remember my indignation, for he had no need to tell me that. Drunk or sober he cut a romantic figure: I loved it when, walking up Exhibition Road one morning with my governess and passing the entrance to some political conference banked with hydrangeas, he suddenly shot out and pulled me inside to show me off. I enjoyed travelling: to Berlin where I played with a Siamese princess in the Tiergarten; to Norway, where he was a best-seller, photographed for the front page of a newspaper ('Negley Farson . . . little son Dan'); on the ferry to Denmark, pouring salt into his drinks in an effort to stop him. How long-suffering he was. Gandhi came to our house in Walton Street, two workmen's cottages put together; Hitler patted me on the head as a 'good Aryan child' when my father covered a speech at Garmisch and the streets of Munich were bedecked with swastika flags.

We set out to drive across Europe in the spring of 1935. Colonel Knox, the owner of the *Chicago Daily News*, had written: 'You have so thoroughly absorbed the English point of view that you no longer report the passing show from the viewpoint of a detached American observer' and instructed him to return to Chicago so as to be 're-Americanized' by working with the local staff. Also, reports of his drinking had percolated back to Chicago. My father resigned and took one of the few options left open – to cash in on the wealth of his experience and write his autobiography. Everything lay in the balance. His job had been taken away and his marriage was threatened by the persistent affair with his mistress Sybil Vincent, which I shall recount later. I was eight years old.

In those days it took weeks to drive across Europe, at least in our battered old Ford, which kept breaking down with eruptions of steam as we searched for water to fill the protesting radiator. We coasted on optimism and my mother's resilient sense of humour. I had a large and handsome Mickey Mouse, a Christmas present from my father's best friend, the American journalist H. R. Knickerbocker, who had persuaded a contact in the American embassy to issue Mickey with a genuine passport, photograph and all. I flourished this proudly as we passed through border controls. Some of the officials had the wit to enter into the spirit of the game, particularly the French, who saluted Monsieur Mouse and stamped his passport with imposing stamps and occasional sealing-wax. The Germans were suspicious. 'They suspect that Mickey is Jewish,' said my mother loudly, which almost had him confiscated and enraged my father.

Exasperated by the ritual of hotel forms as we zig-zagged across Europe, she broke the tedium by filling in imaginary names, from 'Señor and Señora Fernando Alvarez from Chihuahua, Mexico, and Master Ramon Alvarez' to 'Mr and Mrs Hirahoto Tagasi of Tokio'.

The clerks at reception never seemed to notice until we reached Munich where she signed us in as Dr and Mrs Rosenbaum of Jericho. I was master Reuben Rosenbaum. The foyer sported a large sign: 'Dogs are not admitted. Jews are not wanted'.

'What an unfriendly hotel,' exclaimed my mother, 'neither Jews nor dogs.'

'Dogs are allowed on a lead,' the concierge conceded.

'As I have a Jewish friend in Munich, could I bring her on a lead as well?'

My father exploded in the lift: 'Why did you have to say that? And that was a damn fool thing to do, signing us in like that, do you want to get us arrested?' Sure enough there was a knock on the bedroom door a few minutes later, with the unsmiling manager presenting us with new forms because there had 'obviously been some mistake'. Suitably chastened, my mother filled them in properly, watched by my irate father.

When we made it at last to Vienna everything was fine as my father met old journalistic friends and introduced me to Madame Sacher in her famous café where she gave me one of her cakes. Then he disappeared. For days we waited for news in the dark hotel bedroom with heavy crimson curtains and a big brass bed, my mother trying to find ways to distract me while she stayed by the phone. Suddenly we were roused by phone calls and knocks on the door, urgent messages and worried faces. In her desperation, my mother sent me to a chemist at the end of the street to collect some photographs which had been developed. I was agitated, knowing this was an excuse to get rid of me. Running back, I experienced a split-second of horror: my father was being carried into the hotel on a stretcher. I dodged the traffic, running to join him, oblivious of the scream of motor horns and passers-by.

I wrote to my grandmother: 'We are going now to Yugoslavia. Papa is very horrid. I don't like him.'

The journey seemed interminable. I crouched underneath a blanket on the floor in the back, pretending to be asleep – impossible with the arguments raging in the front, my father constantly wanting to stop, seizing any excuse for a drink, while my mother implored him not to. Occasionally he lost his temper, sometimes violently, followed by angry silence and the utter desolation of my mother's sobs, when I did not dare to move. Then there were whispers as they remembered

I was there. On such an occasion the car stopped and I looked out on a dull countryside with one forlorn shop and a twisting path leading up to it, which resembles a scene from Chagall in my memory now. My mother gave me some money and asked me to get a box of matches. I ran up the path and into the store. Ropes, equipment, kettles, sausages dripped from the ceiling, but no one was there. I banged on the counter and screamed until a young woman appeared. 'Streichas!' I yelled, having been told the word. This provoked a fit of giggles and she walked out again. Left alone, I experienced panic – should I return without the matches and be blamed, or risk the car going off without me?

When the girl returned she was accompanied by her entire family. They stared and smiled, for time was of no concern to them. The more I shouted for 'streichas', looking through the window to make sure the car was still there, the more they laughed until an older woman sensed my fear and gave me the matches. I thrust the money on the counter and bolted down the path into the safety of the back of the car. Then the worst part as I gasped my excuses for taking so long. Instead of scolding, they turned round and said how clever I was, with bright faces as if they were wearing masks. My father said we would stop at the next town to buy some tutti-frutti ice-cream. This was more alarming than their arguments.

Everything changed when we reached Lake Bohinsko in the far north of Yugoslavia. At last we were able to unpack all our gear, not just enough for an overnight stop. The cases and the duffle-bags, the trout rods and typewriter were carried into the simple SV Janez Hotel, named after the small whitewashed church opposite with a fresco of St Christopher carrying Christ on his shoulders across the water. In the morning Minka brought a breakfast of coffee and whipped cream, warm croissants, butter and wild honey. My father reckoned that a night's full bed and board for the three of us with two separate rooms cost the same as one double whisky in the Savoy. I cannot remember how long it took him to recover. In such surroundings I doubt if it was more than four or five days before he found himself again.

❖

Of all the images that come winging back, Bohinsko is the most peaceful, a wild part of Europe enclosed by mountains – the Julian

Alps – whose northern slopes were permanently covered by snow, bordered by the frontiers of Italy, Austria and Yugoslavia. There was an unrivalled freshness in the air and at dusk the clang of bells echoed across the lake as cowherds brought their animals down to the valleys. When the snows melted, they took the cattle up into the higher alpine meadows and you could hear the rattle of carts as they passed by.

The River Sava rose mysteriously at the far end beyond the lakes where the mountains started to rise, and poured out again beside the church, swirling around the rocks. The banks were so dense with lily of the valley that I picked them by the armful.

Blessedly, Lake Bohinsko was comparatively unknown. I do not know how my parents found it but they could not have chosen more wisely, for there was every incentive to start life again and few distractions, with no foreigners who spoke our language. Only Minka, the royal huntsman's daughter, and Josef, the smiling black-jacketed waiter who served my father relays of black coffee as he sat by a table on the gravelled terrace when the sun was shining, typing, typing, typing away until he completed his quota of ten pages a day, after which he put on his trousers. We were self-contained.

In the afternoons we rowed across the lake and he fished for trout which my mother cooked with spoonfuls of butter in a heavy frying pan on a fire made from the wood which I collected nearby. In the spring when the lake swelled from the melting snow from the mountains, I was able to look down and see carpets of wild flowers below the surface of the water, which I found magical. And there were nights when we rowed back in the dark, satiated by the day, and I fell asleep counting the shooting stars in the clear sky – never have I seen so many.

Once a fortnight we packed our rucksacks and climbed into the mountains with our alpenstocks, wearing the sturdy, studded leather boots made for us by the local cobbler. We passed peasants who murmured 'Grüß Gott' and doffed their caps, and primitive painted memorials where someone had been killed. If the little picture showed him upside down, he had fallen; if prone with an axe, it meant that a tree had struck him when he was logging. Away from the beeches near the 'Sweaty James', as we called the hotel, there were tracts of pine forest and unpeopled valleys. One was carpeted with yellow globe flowers, most exotic in the sun; and the valley of the Seven Lakes had one which was pink, another aquamarine blue, and a frightening lake seething with water snakes, as dense as in a fish-tank. They made the water ripple.

We left the beech trees behind, their buds still tight a thousand feet up, saw primulas among the higher rocks, the lovely blue gentian and the first crocus blossoming under the ice, soon to break free. Occasionally a wild chamois scuttled away; once the excitement of finding edelweiss. Wild strawberries in the summer.

Our aim was to reach one of the mountain huts by nightfall. Vogel was a favourite, looking down on the lake far below from a barren stretch of rocky ground, sleeping in the rolled blankets carried by my father as the pack-mule, now astonishingly fit in spite of the wound in his leg. We used our alpenstocks as ski sticks to slide down slopes, once colliding with a hidden ridge of rock which grazed my knees, which was part of the excitement. We climbed to the top of Triglav, the highest mountain in Yugoslavia, though a heavy mist hid the view which was supposed to embrace the Adriatic. As with all mountains, we thought we had reached the peak, but another loomed ahead of us, and then another. When we made it at last, we found a round little sentry box with a pointed top made of metal, where people had scrawled their names inside. We lost our way as we descended, hoping to return to the lake before it was dark, and spent the night in a barn, sleeping on hay next to huge round cheeses. On a distant rock-face we saw the zig-zag of Italian soldiers searching for refugees who had escaped from Mussolini.

Life on the lake might sound soporific but I cannot remember a moment when time lay heavily. My mother gave me basic English lessons during the week. I made a tree hut in the woods as a private retreat; played a game called Polet in which I stuck a peg in a hole and, if I were lucky, won a large, sickly chocolate. Apart from breakfast the food was invariably schnitzel and trout – nothing wrong with that, except we had them every day. I befriended a piglet at a farm nearby, bringing it scraps from my meals until I saw the farmer and his family watching me one morning, delighted that someone else had taken on the daily responsibility. As they stopped feeding it, my self-indulgence became a necessity until the day when I arrived to find my piglet was missing. That night, for the first time, we had pork for dinner; at least the others did.

As spring arrived the peasants held a service in the church of the Holy Ghost, all of them carrying umbrellas. With the approach of summer, the hotel stirred as guests arrived on holiday, including the politician Leo Amery who was to hasten the fall of Neville Chamberlain with his rallying cry in the House of Commons in 1940 – 'In the name of God, *go!*' A strong man came as part of a travelling circus, a squat hairy bear in baggy trousers who bent bars of iron as if they were toffee. I marvelled as he walked on glass and asked for rocks to be broken on his head. A swimming instructor was employed, a young, handsome man with black curly hair and flashing teeth, so tall that I scarcely reached his waistline. The wooden jetty grew so hot we splashed water on the boards before we could stand on them.

The inevitable happened – my father started drinking again. It was less important until one afternoon when people were relaxing on the lawn in the dying sunlight and my father started to taunt me, which was unusual, though the relentless repetition was all too familiar. He found some fault with my courage and dared me to climb a particularly tall pine-tree a few yards away. Probably he wanted to show me off, as he did when he threw me in the air with a cry of 'Allez-oop!' 'Come on little one, show us what you're made of.'

I started climbing and as the branches were dense it was easy. As always, it was the reaction to my father's drinking rather than the drink itself which alarmed me, and when I reached the top I clung there, sensing the commotion below as people clustered round the tree and my mother ran across the lawn and joined them. The swimming instructor climbed up and brought me down, carrying me over his shoulder with no difficulty. The incident was unimportant except that I had not been as brave as I should have been.

But nothing could mar the perfection of Bohinsko, my father writing all morning, fishing in the afternoon, or simply lying against a rock, having a smoke in the sunlight, contemplating. Using a fly, he would take a stream and work it as far as he could into the mountains, before the forest closed in. 'Up there,' he wrote, 'in those utter solitudes, I found pools that had something mystic about them: haunt of the trout that I often thought had better remain undisturbed. Staring into the pool, I felt now and then that I had no right to be there, and that there was something supernatural about the trout being there: they were spectral, possessed, part of the secret of this place. At any rate, that they seemed to be part of a thing that I was trying to find out – of something that I was trying to get back to.'

Though I have never shared my father's passion for fishing, and made my dams contentedly further down the river, I can remember the extraordinary abundance and beauty of the trout, with vivid scarlet spots and pale mauve backs. They were fighters too.

There is one passage in *A Mirror for Narcissus* which sums it up:

> Fishing those streams was my Nirvana. A short time after I was in the stream my mind was miles away from it, in another world. In this mood, letting my mind wander freely, I had moments when I was close to some of the intuitive truths as any Hindu practising yoga. There was the water, as pure as the snows from which it came: the beech and alder in spring bud as the world began to renew itself: the steady rocks ripping the flow into a dancing white rapid: and up above, where the dark pines stood over a deep pool, a bend, around which lay another infinitely lovely prospect. Here was the grace of life.

The grace of life – even at that age I was aware of it too.

As we drove away from Bohinsko for the last time, back to England, we could hear the hammering as they started to construct the first big modern hotel.

'They will ruin it,' said my mother.

My father nodded: 'We will leave nothing alone.'

❖

If my father was apprehensive over the reaction to his autobiography, I was unaware of it. I expect he knew it was good, and my mother gave him that vital confidence throughout. *The Way of a Transgressor* was published at the end of 1935 by Victor Gollancz who, with his genius for advertising books, took full-page spreads in the Sunday papers. In America it was hailed by Sinclair Lewis: 'I know of no international journalist of the last two decades who has written a personal chronicle so exciting, so authentically romantic, yet so revelatory of what forces have been surging through the world.'

The book became one of the top best-sellers of the 1930s and we basked in its success at a time when it meant something to be a writer. I was infinitely proud when I saw my father's photograph on the front page of the *New York Times* book section – how handsome he looked. Wherever we arrived he was interviewed. The columnist Drew Pearson wrote that 'Colonel Knox [the proprietor of the *Chicago Daily News*] has fired Negley Farson into prosperity.'

That was the trouble, as my father acknowledged: 'The success of the book did save my skin, and at a time when I had little hide left. It gave me almost too much freedom.'

Three

Minor Ambassador

I T SEEMS we were indestructible as children, because we knew no differently. We were fatalists, like dogs. Until you grow up and life is muddied with the realization that your parents are fallible, you do as you are told. At least we did then, when children remained children into their teens. Torn from home at the age of nine, sentenced to preparatory school – in this case Abinger Hill, a progressive institution surrounded by woods near Dorking in Surrey – I was popular during my first term as a curiosity due to my various travels. Years later I received a letter from the late John Gale, a fellow pupil: 'Does it annoy you that you were called "the trout" at Abinger because of your freckles? Outwardly, at least, you were one of the toughest small boys I ever saw: you kept coming in, even under fantastic punishment.'

I remembered that my nickname of 'trout' was given to me for my ability at swimming under water, but I had forgotten the 'punishment', presumably bullying by older boys. Was I tough? I may have been tougher than I realized, for I ended up as head boy, the last, as it turned out.

In 1940 the decision was taken to evacuate the school to Canada, in our parents' belief that Britain would be defeated after a Nazi invasion. Today I find that extraordinary, but it seemed logical then. One evening my father had taken me to the Savoy Hotel, as he was wont to do. Though I was scarcely thirteen, neither the Savoy nor the Café Royal and the various pubs along the way objected to my trailing in his wake, because I kept silent. Especially so this evening. I have an image of a large room on the ground floor of the Savoy, perhaps the foyer, which was darkened against the blackout and unnaturally still as a cluster of American writers and journalists surrounded a woman dressed in black and heavily veiled, who sat in an armchair sobbing. This was Geneviève Tabouis, the most distinguished

French journalist of the time. One of the men in attendance was H. R. Knickerbocker, better known as Red Knick due to the colour of his hair and his politics, who was the highest-paid foreign correspondent in the world for William Randolph Hearst, and my father's closest friend. Usually they made a fuss of me but tonight it was different – France had fallen.

I must have been affected by the emotion around me for I can still summon up that scene clearly, the tableau of desolation as these powerful men tried to console the frail lady from France. She was inconsolable, as racked by grief as if she had lost a son.

Perhaps it is not so surprising that our parents assumed that Hitler would invade us at our weakest moment, already demoralized by the evacuation from Dunkirk. Yet it was an act of cowardice taken on our behalf, for we were not consulted. I am sure we would have voted to stay, fiercely patriotic as boys could be. We were allowed to listen to the broadcasts by Winston Churchill in his capacity as First Lord of the Admiralty, shepherded to the housemaster's study in our woolly dressing-gowns, and did not believe that Britain could be trounced, not after hearing him.

One pretext for the school's evacuation was expedient: that we should return from Canada when we had grown into young men and join the British resistance in helping to free our country. Another reason, as the Germans massed their landing craft in the French ports, was our usefulness in persuading the Americans to enter the war as Roosevelt wanted to do, though opposed by the isolationist America First Committee. Cecil Beaton's photograph of a child wounded in the Blitz had great propaganda value when reproduced on the cover of *Life* magazine. Conceivably the arrival of little English evacuees might touch a few hearts. As we were told repeatedly, it was up to us to behave like 'minor ambassadors'.

Less romantically, our parents might have found it convenient to be free of the responsibility for us. Discussing this with my close schoolfriend Anthony West shortly before his death in 1994, we found it bizarre that his parents accepted evacuees from the East End of London while sending their own sons to Canada. Snobbery played a part, as well as the excuse of our safety.

Maybe I erased the experience from my memory as too painful, but I cannot remember my departure. This was odd, for when my mother drove to the school a few years earlier to break the news that she was going to join my father for a year in Africa, she did so in the most unfortunate way. I had spent most of my short life accepting my father's absences abroad; after all he was a foreign correspondent, so this was exciting news and seemed natural, almost a cause for pride, until my mother engulfed me in her guilt: 'Oh darling Danny, how I shall miss you, can you ever forgive me?' and so on. As I had been shunted off to boarding school at the age of eight, clinging to her at Waterloo Station until I was torn away, her emotion seemed belated, especially as I would be perfectly happy with my grandmother in the holidays as I had been many times before, but her crying was so infectious that it was not long before I was blubbing too. She had to stop the car on the way back to the school, blinded by her tears, and by the time I was handed over to Matron I was reduced to a jelly.

'I wish that woman wouldn't do this to him,' I heard the matron whisper as my mother left. I did not wet the bed that night but shat in it, and did so for the next few nights, though the shame was concealed so swiftly and skilfully by Matron and her assistants that no one was much the wiser, not even myself. So it is all the more curious that I have no recollection of saying goodbye to anyone when I left for Canada, not even to my doting grandmother who must have doubted if she would see me again. The excitement must have suppressed the dread of separation, but where were my mother's tears now?

In the last week of June 1940, approximately forty boys from Abinger and twenty-five girls, mainly sisters of the boys, sailed from Liverpool on two overcrowded liners, the *Duchess of Richmond* and the *Duchess of Montrose*. After the sinking of a later ship carrying more evacuees to Canada, confirming Churchill's suspicion that such a flight was both unwise and defeatist, no more were sent.

Abinger was an outstanding progressive school with an impressive list of names among the pupils when I arrived, including Nicholas Mosley and Peregrine Worsthorne. Also those mysterious names which denoted industrial wealth such as Melchett (steel), or the aristocracy, the curly-haired Drumlanrigg, heir to the Marquess of Queensberry. My father's friends sent their young sons – Knickerbocker, Fodor and Arlen.

Once at sea we raced around the decks upsetting the passengers, convinced we saw a polar bear on a passing iceberg, taking a midnight boat drill as a real disaster, until our exuberance was brought to heel by a moustachioed character called Major Ney who impressed on us that it was our patriotic duty to behave ourselves. I cannot remember a boy crying – to us it was a spree.

When we reached Quebec I looked down in wonder at the fresh, sun-drenched landscape as the *Duchess* edged her way slowly along the St Lawrence River to Montreal – at least that is how I remember it. The evacuation had been arranged with the speed of wartime emergency with Major Ney as the self-appointed go-between, cabling Mr Archdale, the headmaster of Ashbury College in Ottawa, with the suggestion that 'ABINGER TEMPORARILY AMALGAMATE PARENTS NOW BEING CONSULTED HERE IS GREAT OPPORTUNITY HELP US THIS CRITICAL TIME'. Archdale cabled back: 'DELIGHTED HAVE ABINGER JOIN US IF FUNDS AVAILABLE TO COVER BARE EXPENSES'. James Harrison, our headmaster, assured him: 'FIFTY SAILING VERY SHORTLY EAGER ANTICIPATION BELIEVE FINANCE ALL RIGHT'. This was far from the truth; barely $2000 was the total capital he could bring to Canada, and wartime restrictions prevented the transfer of more. Unknown to him, Ashbury – the self-styled 'Eton of Canada' – was on the point of liquidation with an overdraft of $20,000. Archdale was shrewd enough to predict that the influx of British boys would prove a patriotic fund-raiser with loyal Canadians. Ashbury was saved and Abinger, inadvertently, was the saviour.

Yet when we arrived, Major Ney vanished pursued by the police, while Jim Harrison and most of the other children were delayed in the following liner. There was no one in charge of our group except for ten kind-hearted ladies from the National Committee of Refugees who swept us up undaunted by the brashness of English schoolboys compared to the Dickensian waifs they might have expected and preferred. We were welcomed, cosseted, and interviewed. I kept the cutting from the *Montreal Star*, 4 July 1940, with the headline PER-FECTLY TOPPING HERE above a photograph of several children 'sit-ting laughing at the antics of the only one in the party who brought over his gas mask'. That was me. The caption continued reproachfully: 'The others left theirs in England as they were told that the children there might have more use for them than the lucky ones here.'

The interview reveals that I was insufferably vain even then: 'Poet, world traveller and chief editor of the Abinger Hill magazine, Daniel Negley Farsen (*sic*), son of the author of the book on the Russian

Revolution The Way of Transgression (*sic*) is caught taking a snapshot of his companions . . .' I hope the reporter had a sense of humour as I told him my life story. 'My ambition is to be a newspaperman because one can travel and do all that sort of thing.' The bug had bitten me that young.

We were fed like uncaged animals: Irish stew for lunch, to make us feel at home, though a curious choice for July, followed by strawberries and cream and cookies – 'every one of the poor mites had a second helping', the reporter was told, making us sound like the runaways from *Oliver Twist* they were hoping for. After games on the lawns, we had supper of tomato juice and cake, and were put to bed in two dormitories with milk and biscuits.

Wartime security prevented my family from alerting anyone to my arrival, yet it puzzles me that I had not been given addresses or phone numbers to contact on arrival, for I had two elderly aunts in New York and a godfather and a godmother in the Midwest. Instead I was claimed by a man who saw my name in the *Montreal Star* and said he knew my father. As this was a 'clearing house' where the children could be collected like parcels from Lost Property, he was not asked for proof of his identity or his alleged acquaintance with my father.

My benefactor was far from the Dickensian figure of a Mr Brownlow, but a short, perspiring man with weepy eyes behind the spectacles which he removed in his office, where it was plain even to my eyes that his secretary loved him to the point of idolatry. I cannot remember his name. He was a man defeated by life, a failure in his own eyes and certainly that of his family – unmemorable, except to the secretary. His tragedy was alcohol. Presumably he had made money in his time, for we drove to a pleasant country house on the shore of a lake with a cool welcome from his harassed wife and hunky, disapproving sons in their early twenties who looked at me with dismay as if their father had brought me to stay for the duration. But he was an exemplary benefactor in his way, finding in me another lost soul if not a kindred one. I never saw him touch a drop, although the atmosphere in that house was blighted by his alcoholism and the rowdy returns from the office. They did not worry me. He gave me my first taste of root beer and took me fishing in his rowboat with an outboard motor, crossing the lake until he found a favourite spot and cast away, telling me his life story and present troubles while I gave the occasional nod hoping that it was appropriate, my own thoughts miles away in

England. This idyll was interrupted by a furious relay of cables in reply to the man's assurance to my father that I was safe. Nothing could have enraged my father more than to learn that I had been collected without his permission by a fellow alcoholic whom he scarcely knew. I was shunted off to Montreal to stay with a friend of my grandmother.

Again the overriding asset of the child, that he knows no better. My new destination was bizarre: a shuttered house on a hill, well-furnished, though that was hard to discern in the half-light. I think there was a parlour maid who served us meals as we ate in silence. Perhaps the elderly woman suffered an intense personal grief which was worse than that of Miss Havisham, who at least spoke to Pip. This woman said nothing; she might as well have been dead. No affectionate cobwebs dared intrude into those curtained rooms, no speck of dust would have thought of falling there.

I assume she gave me pocket money for I was able to escape, running down the hill to explore the town and buy a newspaper. Each day I lavished my money on a glass of fresh orange juice and a caramel sundae, while I learnt what was happening in Europe. Newsprint and ice-cream became my daily treat until I was told to pack my few possessions. I do not remember who put me on the train to Chicago.

❖

My destination was the home of my godmother Janet Ayer Fairbank, who knew my father in the early days of his marriage, when he was attempting to sell Mack Trucks in Chicago:

> Janet Fairbank saved our lives in Chicago [he wrote in *The Way of a Transgressor*]. Her wooden house out at Lake Geneva had defied all the raucous progress of time and mass production. It was almost a museum piece. And her exhilarating house-parties would compensate one for purgatory itself. Janet, most sophisticated creature, who had seen more of the world and been deeper into her own country's affairs than most women, *loved* Chicago.

I may have met her on my first visit to America when we sailed on the old *Olympic*, but then I was too young for her to make an impression. At Abinger she once came to 'take me out' for the afternoon and I waited at the gates with two special friends until they gave up in disgust. As I did so myself and walked disconsolately up the drive, an immense Buick edged slowly down it driven by Mrs Fairbank. My mother got out hurriedly, explaining that Aunt Janet insisted on going her own way, and had got lost. The day was overcast by now and it was too late to be taken to lunch in a hotel so we made a reluctant fire in the woods with damp twigs and tried to make it fun with a picnic of delicacies brought from Fortnums, a treat for adults but baffling for children. Subsequently, Aunt Janet redeemed herself with the spectacular birthday present of an electric train – the celebrated Silver Zephyr that rode the Middle West. A boy would forgive a godmother anything for that. I wondered if I would recognize her, unaware that Mrs Fairbank would have been known anywhere, causing a fracas if she were not. She was as formidable as a galleon, not just the figurehead but the entire ship in full sail. She was waiting on the platform of the little station at Lake Geneva and was far from pleased.

'I've met two trains already!' she greeted me reproachfully. A harassed, bird-like figure behind her was introduced as Miss Cronin, who attempted a welcoming smile as I stammered my apologies, blinking in the August sun in my English tweed suit.

Aunt Janet's home on the shoes of Lake Geneva was one of the last of the wooden 'gingerbread' houses built in the style of a grandiose Swiss chalet. It had eccentric charm and I dread to think of what it has become today unless it has been preserved as the 'museum piece' described by my father.

I was startled by the large number of people on the veranda, for this was Sunday, and even more surprised by the unusual lunch handed round on trays by maids in black uniforms, all bits and pieces and bowls of warm popcorn while the guests knocked back their cocktails which Aunt Janet prepared herself. Once she had added salt instead of sugar, but no one dared to tell her and they drank it all the same. Ravenous by now, I ate as much as I could before the servants swept the canapés away and announced that lunch was about to be served. Before we went inside, Aunt Janet led me onto the lawn and clapped her hands. 'This is Dan, my godson and the son of Eve and Negley. He has just been evacuated from England and is spending the summer at Butternuts.' Everyone smiled at me pityingly and applauded her. I had become their token refugee.

After the wartime austerity of England, lunch seemed an orgy. I still yearn for the home-churned vanilla ice-cream which has never been surpassed. The afternoon respite was broken by iced tea with bitter cookies on the shaded veranda or in the spacious drawing-room before the guests changed for a dinner which was even longer and richer than luncheon.

Few boys today are so naïve as I was then, now that television pervades their lives. But even with my particular naïvety, the irony of the next few days was not lost on me: that of all the homes in all America I had to end up in Butternuts, where conferences were held for the America First Committee of which Aunt Janet was the vice-chairman. America First! even the name seems ominous now. Then it had considerable popularity, pledged to keep America neutral, and was blatantly anti-British in the cause of isolationism. Honoured guests at the lovely old gingerbread house included Colonel Charles Lindbergh, who stated that it was their 'first duty to keep America out of foreign wars'; Colonel McCormick, the rabidly anti-British owner of the *Chicago Tribune*; and General Wood the committee chairman.

Within days I was told to remove my British War Relief badge, which I did under protest. Then I was told I should never mention President Roosevelt's name in the house. 'We hate that man,' Aunt Janet explained through clenched teeth, 'more than the British can ever hate Hitler.' This was a shock; but it did not prevent me from creeping along the drive where I opened one of the car doors and listened to Roosevelt addressing the nation with one of his radio fireside chats as I crouched on the floor.

Occasionally an interventionist would be invited by mistake. One was a friend of my father who insisted that I watch him take his bath, drinking tumblers of whiskey while he gave me an alternative point of view as he inveighed against everything America First stood for. These are impressions, hazy with time. I believe that I spent three vacations with Aunt Janet altogether. Superficially, no child could have asked for more, racing down the blistering wooden boards of the jetty to hurl myself into the water, included in the family life even to the dinner-parties which I attended in my smart blue jacket and white trousers, part of the new outfit eventually billed to my father when Aunt Janet had had enough of me. Thirteen is an unattractive age, neither young enough to cuddle nor old enough to be taken seriously, and I was precocious as well as naïve, an unfortunate combination I have been unable to shed.

Aunt Janet was always in a hurry, dictating as she went to Miss Cronin who followed nervously in her wake. Her sister, Margaret Ayer Barnes, was equally formidable, the successful author of American historical novels and winner of a Pulitzer Prize. Aunt Janet wrote novels, too.

There were two strapping sons, married with small children. One son was in big business, which always seemed in trouble, the other was athletic, dumb and friendly on the surface but less so underneath, for the brothers and their families vied for Aunt Janet's approval, living in constant fear. Tennessee Williams would have been enchanted: this was Big Mummy on the lake. To this day I shall never understand the motives of the sons when they told me the facts of life. Were they being sadistic or did they really believe I should soak my private parts in a bucket of salted water after sexual intercourse? As I had no idea what sexual intercourse was, no lesson could have been more calculated to make me avoid it for as long as I lived. Even if their advice was well-intended, it had the usual effect of 'sex-talks' of transforming a pleasure one was looking forward to into an ordeal fraught with danger.

There was a daughter too, Janet Junior, who might have been difficult in any circumstances. A handsome, deeply tanned woman, she practised at the piano all day, for she was a singer, of modern, discordant songs rather than the classics. Her background and her demanding profession had given her a tough carapace, though I suspect she was a seething, terrified and lonely neurotic. It was my task to massage her back every afternoon when the accompanist had gone and her nerves were knotted by tension. I enjoyed the feeling as my fingers unlocked them and she grunted with relief.

I had a small bedroom at the top of Butternuts which provided the perfect hideaway as I wrote and produced a magazine called 'Panorama', seen by no one but myself. Otherwise I spent as much time as I could in the kitchen which was ruled by a fierce Swedish cook with a moustache, the only servant who was not intimidated by Mrs Fairbank. She was paid a salary beyond an English cook's comprehension, owned a Buick and a mink coat, and gave in her notice the moment she was crossed. She tolerated me as I helped to turn the handle of the ice-cream churns until my arms began to ache. There was a middle-aged maid whose expression implied a life of regrets, and an English butler. With a child's intuition, I knew there was something wrong there. Realizing that I saw through him he made it obvious that he would not take it out on me so long as I did not sneak on him. Nor did I, until the day he absconded with the silver and the housekeeping money, when I told everyone that I had suspected him all along – English butlers do not come from the East End of London and speak with cockney accents. It turned out that all his references were fake and he was being hunted by the police, which explained his sudden departure.

There were no children of my age apart from the gardener's son, a lively Irish boy with a gleaming new bicycle. I adored and envied them both, but Aunt Janet discouraged my friendship with the servants. The Fairbanks were snobs. Strangers taking advantage of their right-of-way around the edges of the lake were shooed off, though the neighbouring Wrigleys, of chewing-gum fame, made no such objection.

Rarely were the Fairbanks upstaged, but on one occasion they were betrayed by their snobbery, when an elderly man called Lasker came to stay, even richer than they were with an art collection of his own. He arrived grumpily and was more so when he left, due to a misunderstanding when a shabby little man walked up the drive with a small case and asked to see him. He, too, was shooed away, despite his protests in fractured English. As the morning progressed, the truth dawned as Mr Lasker phoned down repeatedly to enquire about his barber, for he was so rich that he was unable to shave himself and travelled with his personal hairdresser who would stay nearby – the shabby Italian who had been told to go away. I caught a glimpse of Lasker later, disgruntled and unshaven.

In spite of all this activity, there were afternoons of blank boredom and once I decided to kill myself by swallowing iodine. As I took only a few drops in a glass of water I felt the better for it. This was a moment of self-indulgence that could have happened anywhere. There was one surprise when I flicked through a pile of old visitors' books and was delighted to come across my father's name with that of a woman called Sybil Vincent as his travelling companion. When I showed this proudly to Aunt Janet, the book was seized and removed. Years later I discovered that the mysterious Sybil Vincent was my father's mistress, but it was baffling then. Where was my mother?

At the end of the summer we moved to Chicago, where Aunt Janet had an old mansion which looked tiny from the outside but was roomy within. I liked the position on North State Street, and was unaware of the rarity of such an old building in this setting. Once here, Aunt Janet was in her political element and changed gear to move forward at even quicker pace. *Life* dubbed her 'the first lady of Chicago', and she was actively involved in city politics. Her money came from Nathaniel Kellogg, who invented a soap and dined with the élite at the Millionaires' Table in the Chicago Club alongside men whose names are still remembered: Marshall Field; Robert Lincoln, the President's son; and George Pullman. The architect of the club had designed Butternuts. I was introduced as Janet's godson from England, and tried to look suitably grateful for her magnanamity, considering her hatred of the British.

I have met only two people who could make effective scenes: my father, who could be appalling but magnificent, and Aunt Janet who was just appalling. One afternoon she took me to be fitted for a pair of shoes, though I do not understand why she had to do so personally. The salesman was slow and somehow offended her. Apologizing profusely, he did his best to placate her and I made matters worse by taking his side. Inevitably and horribly, Aunt Janet knew the owner of the store – I think it was Marshall Field III; she called him to the telephone and had the assistant sacked. His terrified expression haunted me for days.

In spite of her hectic schedule, Aunt Janet found the time to keep me entertained. In view of her hatred of 'that man', as she called Roosevelt, I found it odd that she whisked me off to the Democratic Convention where Eleanor Roosevelt accepted the nomination on her husband's behalf. This jamboree is familiar today through television, but it was pageantry then as I looked down from our box open-mouthed at the razzmatazz below, while Aunt Janet fumed in silence beside me.

She took me to first nights of plays I did not understand, and I was disillusioned to see Lynn Fontanne remove her wig and eyelashes in her dressing-room afterwards. We went to newsreels in the cinema until I disgraced myself, as she explained in a letter to my mother:

I have been sorry about the Roosevelt business, as it has done Dan out of a certain amount of fun. When he goes to a movie he boos Willkie and cheers Roosevelt, so I don't take him any more. I suppose I can only make you understand my point of view when I say that my feeling about F.D.R. differs only in intensity from your feeling about Hitler – both men threaten the countries we love. F.D.R. has no shame and no standards. He is using the war to further his own ends, and I feel more strongly every day that if he goes back to the White House only a bloody revolution will save the United States. I believe that if Roosevelt is re-elected, the November election will be the last one held for President in the United States.

Now that you know all this, I hope you will not encourage Dan in what really is a serious breach of manners.

I was rescued by a warm-hearted woman who was passionately pro-British, though wise enough not to fall out with Aunt Janet who might have prevented me from seeing her. June Provines and her husband, Neil Cowham, lived in a smart apartment overlooking the fashionable Lake Shore Drive, and for a time I became the child she never had. She took me to lunch at an exclusive restaurant underneath a posh hotel near North State Street, with separate alcoves all in plush, which became our favourite. I assume I frequently stayed overnight at the apartment, remembering Neil in his pyjamas taking me aside to tell me gravely of the German atrocities in the First World War, such as bayoneting babies in Belgium. I have no idea why he thought this information necessary, especially when England was about to be invaded by the awful Hun.

During the day when June was busy preparing her column for the *Chicago Tribune* – 'Front Views and Profiles' – I walked the streets of the city, finding a total sympathy and an urban beauty which never failed to excite me. Using June's press pass I watched several films in the course of a day (George Brent seemed to be in most of them), and I was free to cheer and boo whom I pleased during the newsreels, though that was less fun on my own. It was in her column that my first work was published, a poem called 'Absence' by Daniel Negley Farson Jr:

> O, to have a little look
>   At England once again,
> To walk once more in London's streets
>   Or down a village lane.
> To see anew the little house
>   In which I used to live –
> O, only just a little look,
>   And anything I'd give.

This was the most pro-British sentiment ever published by the *Chicago Tribune*, and though he had no idea of my identity, Colonel McCormick entered the long editorial office one morning just as I lit a cigarette in the mouth of a face I had constructed from a giant ball of string as I killed time while June worked on her column. He studied it without a flicker of emotion as the typewriters stopped and everyone fell silent, and marched out again. June was unshaken; indeed, she hated the *Tribune*'s politics to such a selfless extent that she threw in her job a few weeks later, losing a lucrative pension, to join the new *Chicago Sun* which was more liberal, though they failed to exploit her and the column finally fizzled away. The price of integrity.

She was devoted, buying me an electric gramophone with several records and a rare recording of Edward VIII's abdication speech which I can still mimic today, but I missed the company of my schoolfriends. I was sent off by Aunt Janet to weekend house-parties, dances and prom balls, where I felt hideously out of place with the boys, all dressed in identical clothes and bringing corsages for the girls. A hopeless dancer and virtually tongue-tied, I found these occasions an ordeal, noticing that the brothers were nicer to me in a quizzical way than their sisters who resented the liability of such an English lump. Consequently, when I heard that young Fodor, one of the evacuees from Abinger, had arrived for a short visit to Chicago, I seized the chance to meet up with him. My godfather Tom Seyster phoned to invite me to lunch with Somerset Maugham and he seemed amazed when I refused, explaining I was meeting a schoolfriend. Though I doubt if Fodor and I did anything of consequence, for once I had my priorities right.

❖

Somerset Maugham collected me from North State Street a few days later, accompanied by his 'secretary' Gerald Haxton. We were on our way to visit my godfather Tom Seyster who lived in a sleepy town in Oregon, all folksy on the outside but seething with undercurrents. Seyster was an exotic fish in this small pool, who ruffled the water with his disturbing behaviour.

The trip put Mrs Fairbank in a quandary. She was against it but could hardly tell me why – that the three men were known homosexuals, and the younger two notorious for their drinking. At the same time, she was thankful to be rid of me for a few days, and Maugham's reputation provided a semblance of respectability. As she wrote to my mother:

'It was impossible for me to refuse to allow him to go to Tom's.'

Tom Seyster had the ageing good looks of a matinée idol in the mould of Tyrone Power. His mother, a celebrated beauty, was dead, but his father, with the crinkled looks and personality of a peanut, owned the local bank and at the age of ninety still went to his office each morning.

Why did my parents make Seyster my godfather? They knew all about him, for he had broken down one evening in Spain and confessed his homosexuality, saying how miserable it made him. Shamefully, their motive must have been money, for Seyster was rich and there was no family waiting to pounce.

The joker in our odd pack was Haxton. He was considered good-looking, too, in the style of the time, with a neat moustache, more Don Ameche than Tyrone Power. He made surprisingly little impression on me, probably bored by the company of a boy in whom he had no interest. If he was jaundiced with life it was understandable, for he must have yearned for the sweet temptations of Monte Carlo and the home he shared with Maugham on Cap Ferrat, the Villa Mauresque.

Willie Maugham was astringent, withdrawn, cynical and parsimonious, but I saw another side of him at a moment when he was homesick and befriended me with a gentleness which belied his reputation. Far from resenting my presence, Maugham sensed the loneliness of my position. Seyster had shown him some of my poems, and after my refusal to have lunch, which might have appealed to his dry sense of humour, he sent me a handwritten letter. It revealed an emotion which few suspected in him:

> I have read your poems. You must expect them at your age to be immature, but I who cannot write verse at all envy you the gift of being able to. I hope you will write more; you will find it a constant source of pleasure.
>
> I think the best of the lot you sent me is 'Absence'. That is very simple and very moving, I suppose one always writes best when one is impelled by a given feeling. But the others also have some very good lines.
>
> Bless you. W. S. Maugham

Far from shy, his reticence was due to his stammer which I took for granted though it marred his childhood. Looking back, I suspect that he felt at ease with me because I was not in awe of him.

Maugham adored Haxton. They were opposites, which was part of the attraction. Gerald Haxton was born in San Francisco in 1892, and though he was brought up in England by his English mother, I recall him as wholly American. When I met him he was nearly fifty, which explains why I did not find him so handsome as I was told, but rough and ready with immense vitality. An early photograph shows a curious but significant discrepancy: the right eye frankly mischievous; the left one threatening. What lingers most from the first impression in Chicago was a large ginger moustache and a violent temper when he was not mute from hangover.

Haxton was twenty-two when Maugham met him in Flanders in the First World War; both were members of an ambulance corps. Maugham's reference to this traumatic encounter was terse: 'I had been attracted to him by his immense vitality and his adventurous spirit. I had met him infrequently in the interval. I had found him a very useful companion.' It sounds as if he was giving him a reference to be used in court, and there was some truth in this. Their affair had been intermittent, and might have continued so except for a nasty incident in a Charing Cross hotel: Haxton had the bad luck to be found in bed with another man when it was raided by the police who were looking for an army deserter. On 5 December 1915 he and the other man appeared at the Old Bailey on no fewer than six counts of gross indecency – Haxton was not a man to show restraint. Well represented by lawyers, both men pleaded not guilty and were acquitted, but Haxton was under suspicion on other charges and the police had their revenge by deporting him as an undesirable alien when he returned to England four years later. This is why Somerset Maugham moved into voluntary exile in France.

By this time, Maugham was married to Syrie Barnardo, who became fashionable as the decorator of all-white interiors, though the marriage seems to have been loveless on his part if not on hers. At least she served as a cover for his homosexuality and when she became pregnant it was the decent and convenient decision to marry her. This makes his affair with Haxton an infatuation, for Gerald had no discretion. Was he as bad as people said? Syrie Maugham, who did not lack spirit, replied, 'He drinks like a fish and lies like a trooper and if one has any sense one doesn't leave one's bag out of one's sight for a moment if he's in the same room, but he *is* very attractive.'

Robin Maugham, the nephew, described Haxton's air of 'dissipation' while Beverley Nichols, a popular writer of the day, was vituperative: 'Although he was careless of the conventions (he used to pick his very white teeth with some ostentation), he was a gentleman and he was no fool. For example, he translated many of the Master's finest stories, and André Gide, who presumably knew what he was talking about, once told me that his French was impeccable. There was only one thing wrong about Gerald, and it can be put quite simply. He stank. He had about him an aura of corruption.'

This was the jealousy of a rival and helps to explain why Nichols took such exception to 'something very disagreeable' which took place after Haxton stumbled back from the Le Touquet casino where he had gambled with his usual verve but unusual success. Nichols put on his dressing-gown to investigate the moans coming from the next room and was outraged to discover Haxton on the floor 'stark naked, *covered* with thousand franc notes. Never seen so much money in my life', trying to be sick. At this moment, Maugham appeared 'as livid as his bright green dressing-gown' and screeched, 'What are you d-d-doing in G-G-Gerald's room? Did-d-did he ask you to c-come to his r-room?' (Nichols exaggerated the stammer for effect.) When he tried to explain, Maugham gripped him by the shoulders and told him to get out – 'leaving Willie, not for the first time, to clear up the mess.'

After a less successful night at the casino in Monte Carlo, Haxton was so drunk that he dived into the swimming-pool forgetting it had just been drained. As he was carried off on a stretcher, he regained consciousness: 'I knew I should have added water!'

It is not surprising that Maugham loved him, and if he was a rotter, as Maugham wrote to an American friend who was having problems with her younger man: 'You must expect to pay something for the amusement you get out of knowing wrong 'uns.' He also admitted: 'I have loved most people who cared little or nothing for me,' but Haxton enabled him to love even if it was not requited: 'I've never been good-looking and I know that no one could fall in love with me.' Haxton enhanced life immeasurably in those sensual summer days on the Riviera between the wars when the house was filled with guests and the pool was usually filled with water. One of the guests, the writer and broadcaster Arthur Marshall, related that Maugham's face lit up when he saw Haxton coming through the trees to the tennis court: 'Oh look, good, here comes Master Hackey.' Marshall added: 'It was said with love, you know, and deep affection.'

Haxton was the invaluable catalyst for Maugham's writing. Imagine the excitement when they sailed the Far East and Haxton burst into their cabin to recount the latest story he had heard in the ship's bar. Maugham's loathing of his fellow man meant that he retired early, unless he was playing a foursome of bridge, but Haxton was a man's man in every sense, with a gift for encouraging his fellow-passengers to bare their souls as they drank together. Some of the stories were common rumour in the East, like the woman who shot her lover – but there was this incriminating *letter*. Haxton passed the anecdote on and the Master immortalized it in his short story 'The Letter', one of his classics. Another is 'Rain', based on two missionaries and a tart who had sailed on a previous voyage.

Maugham acknowledged his debt to Gerald Haxton in *The Summing Up*: 'I was fortunate enough to have on my journeys a companion who had an estimable social gift. He had an amiability of disposition that enabled him in a very short time to make friends with people in ships, bar-rooms and hotels, so that through him I was able to get into easy contact with an immense number of persons whom otherwise I should have known only from a distance.' This was characteristically fastidious. He meant that Haxton got pissed and winkled out incidents in a way that he could not.

With the outbreak of the Second World War, they stayed on at the Villa Mauresque until Maugham had to escape on a crowded cargo boat, flying to America on 2 October 1940 carrying a phial of poison which he broke dramatically on his arrival. Haxton, with the immunity of his American citizenship, remained in France to hide and store their possessions, joining Maugham in December. I met them a few weeks later during my Christmas holidays when they were at a particularly low ebb. After a brief ride on the wagon, Haxton was drinking again, though Maugham hated drunkenness, disapproving if a guest dared to suggest a *second* cocktail before lunch. As he confided to an old friend, Barbara Back, 'I cannot spend the remaining years of my life acting as a nurse and keeper to an old drunk.' Yet he did so devotedly during Haxton's terrible, final illness following a collapsed lung a few years later, sitting beside his hospital bed enduring the railings of abuse and blame until his difficult and beloved companion died.

Like many experienced travellers, Maugham was easily fussed, convinced we would miss our train which, unless my memory is playing a trick, proved to my great delight to be the original Zephyr of the silver toy train I had left behind. With little idea that he was regarded as the most popular author alive, I chattered away over our meal in the dining-car before we returned to our first class compartment. As the train drew into the station, Maugham discovered he had lost his wallet and had hysterics. Haxton may have been suffering from a disastrous hangover for he seemed mute and motionless, so I was told to find it and raced back to the dining-car with the terror of the train leaving with myself still on board, no addresses to contact, no ticket, money or identification. At the last moment our waiter discovered the wallet on the floor and I jumped onto the platform as the train moved away. Much relieved, Maugham gave me a pat on the head in a rare display of affection.

Images are left: just as happiness is a matter of moments, a number of images stand out even if the whole is dimmed.

The town seemed clean and white with clapboard houses – no more than that.

Seyster billed himself as 'Landscape and Garden Architect', but Pinehill was an imposing though not a particularly attractive house. I have no recollection of my bedroom but do recall the staircase into the dining-room where Seyster and Haxton fought furiously as old Mr Seyster descended on his way to the bank without saying a word or acknowledging our arrival. But one image is as vivid as yesterday's: a rose-red porthole through which I stared enchanted at the neglected garden of shivering shrubs and a few brave winter roses in the snow. That view was magical to me, with the strangeness of a porthole in a landlocked house opening onto a peaceful world beyond, silent and white.

Presumably Seyster and Haxton were lovers and Maugham did not object. They did their best to entertain me, driving for miles to a cinema where they bought me popcorn and sat through a third-rate film while their minds and hearts were elsewhere. In my godfather's case, this was the bowling alley he had bought for a young man in the town whose embarrassment is another image as Seyster proudly displayed his famous guest. In this small Midwestern town our appearance must have been disconcerting to the point of shame – Seyster besotted with the young man; Haxton scarcely able to stand upright;

and the celebrated writer who must have looked desperately bored unless his professional instinct sensed a story. I trailed behind, totally uninterested in bowling. The tough boyfriend could hardly look us in the face, though he shot me a glance of fierce dislike, all too conscious of the stares from his friends who watched our entrance.

Maugham redeemed us all, retrieving Seyster's tarnished reputation with a signing session of his books the following afternoon. He did so with the humility of a long-suffering Christian martyr until one woman brazenly produced a bag filled with his collected works. 'My husband was furious with me,' she explained, 'when I brought these home even though they were a special reduced price. He accused me of wasting his money, but if you sign them he'll think I got a bargain after all!' Maugham rewarded her with a slight chuckle, signing every copy punctiliously with the stammered apology, 'I do hope your husband will f-forgive you for such a t-terrible extravagance.'

Otherwise he played patience interminably, hardly speaking to Haxton, though they might have raged and ranted after I was sent to bed. When we were alone at breakfast, I asked him why Mr Haxton hated my godfather.

'What do you mean?' Maugham asked.

'They're always fighting each other.'

He replied that I was too young to understand but grown-up people were frequently unkind to those they loved.

Maugham did not speak to Haxton on our journey back to Chicago, where he made an immediate call to Aunt Janet who invited him to dinner.

'I'm keeping it to family, just the Fairbanks,' she told me enthusiastically, 'I'm sure Mr Maugham will prefer that.' Knowing both the family and Mr Maugham, I doubted it.

When Maugham surveyed the Fairbanks his distaste could have accounted for his vindictiveness later. After telling Aunt Janet that I might become a good journalist if I were more observant, he took her aside to advise her that Tom Seyster's home was not suitable for a boy of my age, which she repeated to me with considerable satisfaction. And that was the end of the rose-red porthole.

❖

In between the holidays I went to school. At Abinger the terms seemed interminable while the holidays were over in a flash; in Canada, although I cannot remember an Easter vacation, the Christmas break was long enough to travel to America, while the summer vacation stretched over several months. School was secondary.

Ashbury College in Ottawa claimed it was 'the Eton of Canada', a sad case of wishful thinking. It was much like other schools except that the bullying was more refined: the masters were bullied by the Canadian boys, who were tough six-footers with a healthy contempt for authority. Yet they welcomed the boys from Abinger, clever little creatures in shorts, without the slightest resentment. We shared their rooms and, as the tough can afford to be, they looked after us with an instinctive chivalry though they were brutal to the masters.

Though Abinger took pride in being different from the usual run, the bullying there had been normal for an English prep-school, by boys of boys, particularly one day-boarder who aroused the hunting instinct of the pack. Afternoon showers after sport were his particular hell as the boys flicked him with wet towels, forming a crocodile, their hands on each other's shoulders, as they chanted 'Bait, Bait, Bait!' until he escaped, crimson, sobbing and half-naked, into the waiting car of his horrified parents who removed him at the end of term. He must have been spoiled for life.

The worst case of bullying at Abinger was that by a housemaster of a boy called Gale, a hero on the cricket field though hopeless in the classroom. His amiable stupidity was that of a friendly labrador dog, and the master set out to punish him for his popularity. We had no inkling of it then, but I can only explain his obsession as a sexual infatuation with sadistic undertones. The master and his hideous sister, a scrawnier version of himself, were thinner versions of the Murdstones and it is difficult to understand why they were allowed to be in charge of anyone. With an irony which may have been intentional, the master beat Gale with a cricket bat, determined to break his spirit, while the rest of us listened appalled to the daily ritual, though no one intervened. This continued throughout Gale's last term, yet he never cried aloud, which drove his persecutor to further violence. After leaving Abinger he joined the army, where I hope he knew some happiness. He was killed a few months later.

Ashbury's headmaster was friendly but 'fly' as I realize now. The Canadian boys knew this instinctively, sensing that the two masters from Abinger were made of a different mettle. Jim Harrison adjusted miraculously so skilfully concealing his problems and the lack of money that we never thought of ourselves as objects of charity. Somehow he managed to be generous. Ottawa was a cultural backwater so he seized the rare opportunity to take the older Abinger boys like myself to see any touring show, or the New Ballet which appeared at the local cinema when it was showing *They Died With Their Boots On*. Aware of our feelings, he encouraged the English boys to remember their roots.

Dick Sykes, the other Abinger teacher, had played cricket for Kent, which meant little to me but transformed him into an idol for young Michael Arlen, who was taken to various matches as Sykes's protégé. As Arlen recalled in *Exiles*:

> I think those Sundays were up to then the happiest I had been: meeting Sykes in front of the school, cycling down those great shaded avenues on the Governor-General's grounds; and then the whole ritual of the game itself, which must have been so extraordinarily colonial (this was wartime after all) – the Ottawa ladies in their flowing Bournemouth gowns, the men in Old School blazers, the little garden-party lettuce-and-tomato sandwiches passed around on trays between the innings.

Abinger saved Ashbury financially. Eighty thousand dollars were needed and two old boys with the pleasing names of General Charlie Maclaren and Nixie Newcombe asked people to stake $500 towards a boy's boarding fee or subscribe to a $20,000 trust fund, to be paid back if and when the war was won, though I doubt if this promise was fulfilled. With Hitler's U-boat war and air raids increasing, Britain stood alone and this was one way the Canadians could show their support.

Abinger's arrival meant more than dollars. We reinvigorated the Canadian boys and stretched their horizons. Ashbury's academic standards were so far behind that Jim Harrison needed to give private coaching in Greek to some of our boys to ensure their entry to Eton and Winchester, should they return. Also, our presence made the Canadians aware of the war as they had not been before. Michael Arlen shared a room with two Canadian and two English brothers, George Sargent 'a nice boy, about my age, ten, tousled blond hair, fair skin [and] Nicholas, a roly-poly little English boy, no more than eight. It was all in a way very friendly and lonely.' One morning they called George Sargent out of class and told him his father, who was in the RAF, had been shot down and killed.

For days and days he didn't say a word, didn't speak, cry, anything. He had told Mr Faircloth that he would be the one to tell Nicholas, no one else. Each evening, George would sit on his bed – he had a model airplane he was building, and he would lay all the pieces out, precise little slivers of balsa wood, and glue, and sit cross-legged on the olive-coloured blanket, and arrange and rearrange the pieces, and now and then take up the knife and cut a little slit in one of them, and fit two together. Then one evening he began to cry. Nicholas sitting at the foot of the bed as he usually did. George holding pieces of his model airplane, tears trickling down his face. Nicholas didn't know what to do. I remember George then holding Nicholas, all I can really remember is how Nicholas seemed, the back of Nicholas's head, curly hair, and Nicholas at one point saying, 'But was it really a Spitfire?' (which had been the plane their father flew) and George just holding Nicholas, eyes so tightly clenched, that English thing of fighting back the tears, nodding his head.

It seems sad, in view of the happy absorption of Abinger into a strange school, that we left no memorial at Ashbury, planted no tree, left nothing behind except the fading memories. But in 1995 a plaque was erected to the memory of Jim Harrison.

◆

With the arrival of the summer vacation of 1941 I was on the move again, an evacuee to be housed and endured. This time the destination was the home of one of my father's close friends, Ben Brinton, with the imposing business address of Number One Wall Street. He had a ranch in Montana and a colonnaded mansion in Virginia, with white pillars straight from a Hollywood film of the Deep South complete with sassy Negro servants.

Brinton was a severe-looking man, like the bespectacled farmer with a pitchfork in the painting *American Gothic* by Grant Wood. He seemed exhausted both by big business and by his hyperactive wife who was possessed by Moral Rearmament; she held 'quiet times' every evening when she asked God whom she should invite to her next dinner party, which struck me as an imposition he could do without, yet he never failed to give her the answers she wanted. I was conscripted into handing out M.R. leaflets outside the grandest hotel in Richmond, enjoying the pitying glances I received as I tried to look suitably abject for a cause for which I felt contempt. The sons were her dutiful converts; the teenage daughter a nymphomaniac.

Such cases are not supposed to exist, but she was striking proof that they do. Even before I arrived I was puzzled to receive passionate, almost pornographic love letters. Perhaps she was expecting an athletic hunk, for her mouth dropped open when confronted by a plump schoolboy with no knowledge of girls, but as we were misfits in our different ways a bond formed between us and we became conspiratorial friends. She was too scrawny to be beautiful, but she exuded sex-appeal because sex was her obsession. Her mother was too discreet to ask God's advice about her daughter and the whole family were unable to control her, though much of every day was spent in the attempt. The main purpose was to stop her going into Richmond, but she was as cunning as an alcoholic.

One day the two of us escaped from her brothers, who acted as chaperones, and headed for the public swimming pool where she was quickly enveloped by a crowd of lusty young men until her brothers arrived in pursuit, flushed and breathless, and took her away. Driving home I noticed that she was silent yet strangely satisfied. As the evening approached she became alert and soon there was the crunch of gravel on the drive as cars drew up in front of the house and young men knocked on the door. In those few moments of freedom at the pool, she had dated several admirers and now screamed with obscene frustration as one gigantic brother held her back while the other turned the startled studs away, explaining there had been a mistake and that she was ill. This was a regular distraction. Once more, I gravitated to the friendship of the kitchen, where I was fascinated by the brevity of her underclothes hung up to dry.

I was taught to drive, but I put my foot hard down on the accelerator and charged into a tree. I was so overcome with guilt about the damaged car that I never referred to it after I had been rescued, and nor, to make it worse, did they. I was taught to ride, but the horse bolted through the old town of Williamsburg as if I were a messenger in the Civil War while I clung desperately to the animal's mane, pursued by police cars with sirens which drove it faster until it came to a sudden halt as if bored by the whole affair. By now the Brintons were not too keen on me either, and I was sent to some friends in New York. The husband had been a successful stockbroker until he was wiped out by the Depression, while Brinton emerged unscathed.

By most standards he and his wife lived comfortably in a large house with a pleasant garden, but he was out of work and the atmosphere reeked of failure. His one relief was carving decoy ducks for his shooting expeditions with Brinton. Childless, they coped with me awkwardly, taking me to the right places like the top of the Empire State Building, to the Rockefeller Center to see the Rockettes with their deadly precision dancing, and to a nightclub where the husband rebuked me for not dancing with his wife. I duly galumphed around the floor, which should have explained why I was so bashful.

My visit ended in disgrace for I was far from bashful with the pretty little girl next door who knew Shirley Temple, which impressed me greatly. One afternoon there was a moment of fumbling and giggling, though I doubt if this went so far as a kiss. If there was anything more than natural curiosity, we were too innocent to recognize it, but she told her parents who complained to my new guardians who were 'appalled' and complained, in their turn, to Ben Brinton. So that was that. I was returned to Lake Geneva branded as a molester of small girls. If these various people had planned to turn me away from normal sex, they could hardly have done it better.

I still have a lingering regret for something I did not do, because no one told me to do it: I failed to visit my two great-aunts, the Misses Negley. They may have been old and slightly dotty, but they helped to bring up my father and doted on him as the pride and joy of their lives. In his second autobiography, published in 1956, which he dedicated to them – *A Mirror for Narcissus* – my father described one of his last visits to see them in New York, a city which he loved for its infinite variety, and hated for its corruption. 'Apart from living in the world of art and the spirit, I know of only one way in which to beat New York. This is the way followed by two maiden aunts of mine, last members of my family left alive in the United States, and, so far as I know, the sole surviving daughters of a Civil War general. They do not go down to the Bright Lights: they are too old and cannot afford it.' Instead, they indulged in the rare treat of stalls at the Metropolitan Opera, at a visit to their club to attend a lecture.

Of all the people in that great roaring city these two maiden ladies seem to have got the most out of it. They feed the neighbourhood's stray cats; they take in any mongrel which, they think, has been left out for the night (and what a row *that* has got them into once or twice!); and they feed all the starlings, sparrows and pigeons that circle down the shafts between the tall buildings, and get their breakfast on the fire-escape landing outside my aunts' window. Once they had a miraculous adventure: a grey squirrel (God knows how he did it) crossed two lanes of roaring traffic from Central Park, and arrived one morning on their window-sill. He was fed with nuts for two days. They are still talking about that squirrel . . . These two old ladies live in such small things: in their books and in the memory of the old country days, when they would ride through the changing colours of the autumn woods. They have beaten New York because they have made that city *small*.

Even if they had smothered me half to death, I should have visited them. If they knew that I was in New York, how hurt they would have been. I cannot understand why we were never put in touch.

There was a further regret: that I did not continue to the Brintons' ranch in Montana. How salutary that might have been, showing me America in the raw, untarnished by politics or causes like Moral Rearmament. Whenever I see a Western like *Shane*, I yearn for that missed opportunity, the foolish regret for something one never had and which might have proved disappointing – even the great open spaces.

Curiously, I grew fond of Aunt Janet's home at Lake Geneva and by now I felt at ease with her in spite of our differences. She had a devastating effect on everyone else, but she did not intimidate me. Then a new actor entered the stage and disrupted the play – Alexander Woollcott. After seeing a newspaper photograph of Aunt Janet on a platform with Charles Lindbergh, who had resigned his army reserve commission as colonel following criticism of his anti-war speeches, and who seemed to be giving the Hitler salute, Woollcott cabled my father that he thought Aunt Janet's was not a suitable home for young Daniel.

Woollcott, described by Rebecca West as 'the greatest journalist in America', had known my father since 1936 when he wrote: 'Here am I sailing for home tonight with no chance to tell you by word of mouth how absorbed I have been by "The Way of a Transgressor"' and how deep is my admiration for it and you.' There were plenty of chances to meet after that: they had breakfast in New York with Kerensky, briefly premier of Russia after the first 1917 Revolution, who lost his temper when the *New Yorker* mocked his assertion that he would return to Moscow and depose Stalin, just as he had been deposed by Lenin. On 25 November 1941, Woollcott sent me a letter after a further breakfast in London with my father who asked him to report to me when he arrived back in America that 'he and your mother were fit and mighty homesick for you. Your father wanted to find out if your arrangements for the Christmas holidays were all made and satisfactory. If not, let me know and I will confer with you about an alternative. Perhaps you would like to spend those holidays inspecting New York, in which case I could provide you with a room and latchkey and tickets to all the theatres and hockey matches you wished to see.' This was confirmed as late as 14 December, when he sent a handwritten letter from St Louis, where he was probably on a one-night stand playing his favourite part, that of himself as Sheridan Whiteside in *The Man Who Came to Dinner*. Jim Harrison took me to see the film when it came to Ottawa, and another astonished master fetched me from my bed when Woollcott phoned me at midnight and sounded annoyed that I was tongue-tied with sleep and unimpressed. 'Don't you realize who I am?' he snapped, and sent me a signed copy of *While Rome Burns* to give me some idea. My lack of interest must have been exasperating, but he persisted in his new role as my guardian in spite of my decision to spend Christmas Day with the Fairbanks in Chicago. On the 27th, writing from Saratoga Springs, he broke the news that my arrival in New York had to be cancelled: 'It goes against the grain with me to have to report all my mid-winter plans for you have gone to pot and the invitation must be withdrawn. This is what happened. When you elected to visit New York so late in the holiday season I foresaw that I might not be there to greet you, so I arranged for your shelter at Mrs Miller's.' This was Alice Duer Miller, whose poem 'The White Cliffs of Dover' caused an upsurge of sympathy for Britain. Plainly she would be a suitable antidote to Mrs Fairbank. Woollcott added that his secretary, 'a fine guy named Legett Brown who knows and admires your father, should play elder brother and guardian to you in the matter of hockey games, ice carnivals and the like. I no sooner arranged all this with magnificent ability than Mrs Miller was carried off to the Roosevelt hospital with pneumonia and Brown enlisted in the air force as a gunner. This is the effect you have on people.' I took this literally at the time and was dismayed until someone explained he meant it as a joke.

Privately, Woollcott explained to my mother with asperity that 'the plot I hatched with Negley did not come off. I gather that young Farson did not share his father's aversion to his spending the Christmas holidays with Mrs Fairbank.'

The reason I returned to Aunt Janet instead of risking a greater adventure with Woollcott was a case of 'the devil I knew'. I was tired of being handed around like a begging letter. Once in Ottawa, through a friend of a friend of my well-meaning grandmother I was sent to lunch with a young married couple and their small children in a rough wooden cabin on the outskirts of the town. To English eyes it looked unusually attractive but I could sense that they were ashamed of it, an ordinary family who were doing their duty resentfully, and we had so little in common that the long meal was eaten in miserable silence. It was not their fault that we had nothing to say. I had become a prig.

This mixture of sophistication and naïvety has never left me, though I had the excuse of gaucherie then. Unlike most children, who live for the day alone, I was immersed in the past and the future, homesick not for home, which was transitory, but for England. Always England. I appreciate now how infuriating I must have been to the Fairbanks when my patriotism overruled my loyalty to them and made me anti-American, writing to my grandmother later that 'a wave of hysteria has swept over her, they go into the streets and cheer for war, they laugh at Japan, who so far has made America the subject of laughter. They cry foul play and treachery about Pearl Harbor, when they were caught napping.' Aunt Janet was justified in complaining to my mother about a letter I was rash enough to show to one of her daughters-in-law who promptly sneaked. 'Overcome by the pride of authorship,' she wrote perceptively, 'Dan wound up his diatribe in a splendid burst which said "American men are so weak that they will not fight to defend their country." Startled, Ginny said "Dan, you know that isn't true." And he said, "Yes, but it's much more dramatic."'

Vexed by harbouring such an ungrateful child, she decided to Americanize me by taking me to the Todd School in Wisconsin. Reading Simon Callow's biography of Orson Welles, I realized belatedly that this was a missed opportunity. When Welles enrolled in 1926, though it might have changed by the time I was taken there, Todd sounded like my sort of school, with an abhorrence of interschool athletics and similar competition and automatic membership instead of the Literary Society. The enlightened headmaster, Roger Hill, who became Orson's mentor and idol, declared his belief that 'Boyhood is not a preparation for life. It is life itself in one of its most glorious aspects. At Todd we "expose" our boys to opportunities for expression of any inner urge. Let the boy hitch his waggon to a star. He'll never rise unless he tries.' A journalist described Todd as 'the most complete laboratory for self-expression to be found in the land'.

I am not sure if I met Hill on my visit but he sounds such a marvel that I believe I would have remembered him. He liked the theatre, so he built one. He loved dogs, so he started a kennel and the children learned about breeding and veterinary medicine. The boys wrote musical comedies in which they played the chorus girls, and they made films. 'I fell in love with Roger Hill,' said Orson Welles later. 'He has never ceased to be my idea of who I would like to be.'

Desperately in need of such a figure myself, Hill sounds like everything I needed — I imagine that even his sex-talks would have been sympathetic — but though I was tantalized by the knowledge that Orson Welles had been there, and was offered a scholarship, I refused it. Did I refuse my destiny? As Simon Callow concluded: 'It was a stroke of destiny that put that boy [Welles] into that school at that moment.' Can one change one's destiny, or do we revolve in much the same circle however different the circumstances? Could I have changed my life? I doubt it. And Alexander Woollcott had not given up. He invited me for the summer vacation: 'I have a proposal to make to you and one with which your father is heartily in accord. It so happens that here in Vermont I live on a seven-acre island in a lake eleven miles long, which is the best swimming I know anywhere in the world. We keep open house here all summer long and there is great coming and going of the kind of people your father thinks you would enjoy meeting. It was my idea that you would enjoy it even better if we offered you a job, such as putting you in charge of the vegetable garden, and also, if you think you can manage it, the boats. We have motor boats, sail boats, canoes etc., and you could be ferryman to the mainland. I think this would give you a good summer and that you would enjoy returning to school with money in your pocket that you had earned.'

It was an offer I would have pursued with all my heart a few years later, but I found the idea of working as a ferryman intimidating then.

Instead, I returned to the far cry of Ashbury, as hidebound as Todd was progressive. I can understand my stubbornness. America was still a foreign land to me, and at Ashbury I had friends. Above all, and this was the clincher, I had the yearning to return to England. That was my one objective.

On 19 April 1942 I sailed on a banana boat from Halifax in a convoy to Britain. It was our second attempt. The first day out we had been attacked by a U-boat which was sunk by our accompanying destroyer. Then we developed engine trouble and limped back to port. Now it was plain though eccentric sailing on the *Jamaica Producer*. The dozen passengers grew to know each other quickly and too well. I was in a cabin with three other boys from Abinger. There was a woman editor, smart and bossy, who analysed our dreams with sexual interpretations I failed to understand, and a slim young American woman with a mop of curly black hair and a languid drawl. Probably she was highly affected but she seemed the epitome of sophistication then. With long lashes, bulging cheeks and popping eyes, she resembled a comic strip figure of the time whose name, I believe, was Mopsy. She developed an infatuation for me and as we lay on the deck listening to the songs of Jean Sablon and Charles Trenet on her wind-up gramophone, I assumed that I was in love with her too. 'La Mer' was playing endlessly as the sea sparkled beside us. Meanwhile I was pursued by the Bishop of Hong Kong. In spite of this exotic appellation, he was a clean-cut Englishman which baffled me as I expected him to be Chinese. The Bish and his assistant were travelling with their wives, two faded and defeated women. In retrospect, it was all rather Somerset Maugham.

The Bish was a personality, dark, handsome and zealous, and though he never tried to convert me he took us for evening prayers as we were getting ready for bed. His timing was precise. One morning at breakfast another Abinger boy, R. Woodward, aged thirteen, announced: 'The Bish gave us a bath last night, all over,' which cut the conversation like an axe. The Bish giggled while the wives lowered their heads in mortification. He continued to take us for nightly prayers and was deeply distressed when Mopsy persuaded me to sleep on deck on an especially hot night. Pleading with me not to go, the Bish implied all sorts of nastiness; but I was saved by the rain.

I do not stress my naïvety in order to appear disarming. Far from being a virtue, it was and is ridiculous. Most children do and say dirty things behind the bike-shed, but even here I was different. Around the age of nine, I went into a shop in Brompton Road with the courage to ask for a catalogue of the corsets displayed in the window, which the assistants gave me with astonishment and such amusement that I could hear their laughter as I hurried out clutching it under my blazer. Back at Abinger, I showed it to another boy on a bank overlooking the cricket field, where we giggled so furtively that a passing master frowned at us, realizing that the cause was smutty. Later I was fascinated by the special hair-net worn by a Hungarian boy to keep his thick red hair in place. I stole it and wore it at night in the holidays, my mother finding it once in my bed though she made no comment.

During our last term, several girls joined us in the wartime 'emergency' and I stole a pair of regulation knickers and wore them in the 'rears', returning them afterwards. I had no inkling that these were fetishistic tendencies, for the word meant nothing, though I knew the pleasure of taking risks. There was one traumatic incident at Ashbury. A boy I admired wore ordinary Chilprufe underpants with an elastic top that I envied and which struck me as a symbol of masculine normality, simply because he wore them. In England I had been given longer, better quality though unattractive underpants with buttons down the front, cast off by the sons of a wealthy friend of my mother, so these Chilprufe pants were all the more desirable. I stole a pair from a laundry basket of dirty washing. That they had been used was an additional thrill and as I was not discovered, I stole again. Soon the unfortunate boy was so short of underwear that he organized a lightning search one evening. From room to room along the corridor, boys were made to drop their trousers as the search proceeded, and by then it was too late for me to take them off or make a sudden dash which could have looked suspicious. I stayed on my bed pretending to read, praying for something to prevent the discovery. At last the boys entered the room and the owner of the pants noticed the fear in my eyes. For a moment he hesitated. Then he turned away with a shrug, sensing that the search was over. 'Oh, let's stop,' he told the others. 'I probably made a mistake and they got lost in the laundry.' The other boys who were bored by now gave up readily and left the room while I continued to read intently. No mention of the incident was made again, and the boy's pants gradually made their way back to the laundry baskets.

As for sex, my ignorance was absolute, though that might have been usual then. When I tossed and turned in bed unable to sleep, the Canadian boys in the same room made jokes about masturbation I did not understand, which they found hard to believe. Once a younger Canadian boy and I romped about on a table, rolling on top of each other, jerking our bodies together, wriggling and alert as puppies. The instinct was there though we did not know why or how.

If you suspect that the 'infatuation' of Mopsy and the Bish was either a misinterpretation or a wishful illusion, I should add that it continued in London. The Bish sent loving letters, inviting me to the Hong Kong restaurant in Piccadilly where he ordered an extraordinary number of dishes considering it was wartime. The waiters were impressed by his dog-collar and fluency in Chinese, though I embarrassed him by taking a decayed lettuce leaf from the dustbin near the lavatory, slipping the sodden object on my plate and urging him not to pay. Sometimes I brought Mopsy, and he concealed his jealousy though insisting on a private kiss in the cloakroom to which I submitted with impatience. The Bish was a great one for kissing and though I thought this a bore it did me no harm. My parents were pleased that I had a bishop as a friend until my father found one of his loving letters and I was forbidden to see him again, which I regretted for he was a kind man and fun, for a bishop.

Mopsy was more acceptable. There was a mutual attraction of some sort and though my parents were surprised when I invited her to our house in Devon they took it in their stride. Puzzled when Mopsy refused to swim like the rest of us, my mother explained delicately that Mopsy had the 'curse' and that was the extent of my sex education.

In London, Mopsy and I wrote jaunty songs, and the friendship might have continued until I learnt with astonishment from my parents, who had been warned by a friend, that I was being cited by her husband, a monocled junior officer in the Welsh Guards with a plum in his mouth, and who was suing her for divorce. He hired a private detective to watch their house, who reported on my constant coming and going late at night unaware that we were composing our songs. Though flattered to be cited, I shied away afterwards. Her husband must have realized the absurdity of his suspicions for I heard nothing more.

Mrs Fairbank, isolated in her gingerbread stronghold on the shores of Lake Geneva, had written to me after I boarded the ship: 'I felt badly about not getting any word to you. It was too late to wire you, as of course I did not know the name of your boat.' After giving me news of her family, she wrote 'I have been unsuccessful in finding any war work which is of the slightest importance. Unless I do I shall go to Lake Geneva and try to finish my novel. It looks as if the coming year might be a good time to earn some money! It will be difficult to write about the Civil War in the midst of this one.' I was touched by her last words. 'Do write me from time to time. I should be greatly interested to hear what happens to you – what you do, where you continue school etc, etc. My love and best wishes for you. Don't forget us.'

Had I been happier at Lake Geneva than I realized? Judging by her letter I might have misjudged Aunt Janet, though her concern was diminished by the inclusion of a detailed account for my mother of everything she had spent on my behalf, starting with a round-trip ticket from Canada in 1940, $26.22, to travelling expenses in 1942. In between came shoes, swimming trunks, underwear, one tie, one shirt, dentistry and the railroad fare to Richmond in August 1941. I can think of little she left out except for my bed and board. The total came to $375.73 – hardly excessive, though I find it extraordinary that she presented it at all, considering that she was my godmother.

The *Jamaica Producer* docked in Liverpool on 3 May. When you look forward to something that desperately and for so long, it is bound to prove a disappointment. It had not occurred to me that my arrival in London could be so disillusioning. I scarcely recognized my mother, a fat woman with her fingernails bitten down to raw stumps. We were strangers and I looked out of the taxi with dismay, expecting the bomb damage but not the air of desolation – the streets almost empty, the shops boarded-up or shut, the public houses closed. And it was raining. My God, I thought – England is destroyed.

I forgot one thing: it was an English Sunday.

Arriving in Pelham Place, my grandmother looked older and I heard her whisper to my mother, 'Too bad on Danny's first night home.' I knew this referred to my father who was out drinking, but that was what I expected and I loved him drunk or sober. The next morning – Monday! – London was alive again, and my father lay in the basement, impressive as ever.

Four

Fleet Street to Pfungstadt

ABINGER AND ASHBURY spoilt me for conventional schooling on my return to England, especially as I was sent to Wellington College, known for its military associations. Tony West, who was sent there too, asked me once about this aberration of our parents in choosing such an unsuitable place for two fifteen-year-old boys whose main interest was producing a magazine as we had done in Ottawa. When we tried to continue *Panorama* at Wellington, it was forbidden.

After a year there, in 1944 I persuaded my parents to let me study Russian at the School of Slavonic Studies in London. After a further year, when I had mastered the alphabet and read *The Cherry Orchard* in the original, I realized I had no gift for languages. Then I had one of my lucky breaks: with an introduction from my father, I joined the Central Press Agency in Fleet Street. I might have stepped back to the Dickensian days of apprentices and quill pens, for the war was still consuming young men of call-up age, which accounted for the Agency's aged and skeletal staff headed by Guy L'Estrange, who was the wisest of men to be guided by. Now I suspect that some personal shadow clouded his life, which could explain why he gave up so much of his time to help me. He was dreadfully upset when his oldest friend was arrested for molesting a little girl as they sat together on a park bench, L'Estrange explaining to me that he had no doubt a terrible mistake had been made . . . and yet, such things happened. He was old, very old, with pale, rheumy eyes, a weak voice though a strong sense of humour, and a trembling hand. He dressed immaculately, if verging on the music-hall concept of the toff, with a white snowfall of cigarette ash on his lapels, and high wing collars.

The old-fashioned ornate letter-head declared that the Central Press was 'The Oldest Press Agency in the United Kingdom (Established

1863)'. I joined at its last gasp, but the agency was so long-established that it had access to institutions out of all proportion to its importance, such as the right to both a parliamentary and a lobby correspondent in the House of Commons. It indicates the age of all concerned that L'Estrange had not been in the House of Commons this century, while his 'Junior', Mr Varwell, had created a precedent as the first man to enter the place without a top hat. Varwell was referred to as if he were a 'lad', but in fact was an elderly gentleman who walked heavily with a stick and struggled up the stone stairs each morning, clutching the first editions of the London evening papers from which he compiled the stories for our daily News Letter which was sent to such provincial papers as the *Bristol Evening Post* and the *Cambridge News*.

I shall call the other senior member of the staff Miss Albertini, though she must be long since dead. She was sweet, wide-eyed and started nervously when spoken to as if expecting to be struck down by tragedy at any moment. She had dyed blonde hair with a broad centre parting which exposed the darker roots, and her whole appearance was out of date, like an English Blanche du Bois.

Her woman's column, with fashion tips so out of date they were almost back in vogue, was so eccentrically individual that none of the provincial editors dared dispute it. On the rare occasions when she left the office to attend a meeting at the Women's Press Club, my heart ached as I imagined her bizarre yet wistful entrance among her merciless female colleagues. Sure enough, she returned in a sorry state having drunk too much, her large, pale eyes tearful, the mascara smeared and lipstick smudged, to be comforted by Guy L'Estrange who remained devoted throughout, even when she had hysterics, nodding to me to leave the office. The rest of the staff consisted of three harassed elderly lady secretaries, loyal unto death.

As the only member who was mobile, I became the parliamentary correspondent, drama critic, film critic, art correspondent and general roving reporter. I could not have hoped for a finer, if eccentric 'breaking-in' as a journalist. It says much for L'Estrange and for the press corps in the Commons that I was never made to feel ridiculous in spite of my inexperience. With my hair peroxide blond I must have looked decidedly odd, but it is the genius of the House of Commons to absorb and accept; the only people who commented on my appearance were the notoriously 'queer' MPs Tom Driberg and Skeffington-

Lodge who pursued me down the corridors, curious to know if I was 'one of them'.

I had no idea who I was, but I was enthusiastic and relished the hard work and late hours for I had little else to tempt me in the evening; few friends, no sex, no pubs.

There were times when L'Estrange should have curbed my exuberance: writing about *The Captive Heart*, I told the readers of the *Sussex Daily News*: 'Once in a lifetime there comes a film of such magnitude that one is tempted to run into the streets and proclaim it to the world.' With free tickets for the second nights of the best shows, I declared of Ruth Draper: 'It is great acting, and we do not often see its like.' I must have been reading too much Woollcott. Perhaps L'Estrange, who resembled a desiccated matinee idol with his upright stance and translucent skin, preferred my rapture to the usual cynicism, forgiving the excessive emotion of my adolescence. More likely he hoped the shock of seeing it in cold print might make me more discriminating.

When L'Estrange promoted me as the Agency's lobby correspondent at the age of seventeen, I believe I was even younger than Charles Dickens when he arrived at the House of Commons. He described it as 'a conglomeration of noise and confusion to be met with in no other place in existence not even excepting Smithfield on a market-day or a cock-pit in its glory'. It was much the same when I arrived, but I loved the place – 'the best club in London'. Nor was I put off by my father's disillusionment with politicians; he had described Ramsay MacDonald, Stanley Baldwin and Neville Chamberlain as 'three duds in a row'.

It was fresh to me and I found it thrilling. The war was won and I followed the victorious Churchill as he drove from one election meeting to another, growing increasingly verbose. High up on a balcony in Marylebone, hundreds of cheering figures below, he received rapturous applause as he gave the V-sign and introduced the Conservative candidate Sir Wavell Wakefield – 'Whom we all admire so much' – except that he had forgotten his name. When an aide whispered it he rallied but misheard: 'My old friend, whom I have known for so many years, Sir Wavell Wake!' The crowd roared every time he mentioned the blushing candidate beside him, urging him on. But he lost that 1945 election and when I looked down from the Press Gallery, he sat on the Opposition benches. Contrary to general belief he was splendid in his rejection. Apparently slumbering through a suffocation of speeches, he would rise at the crucial moment and reduce the tangle to a single, salient point, exposing and exploding it. But even in my idolatry – I actually bowed when he spoke to me once in the Lobby – I was able to write in the *Sunderland Echo and Shipping Gazette*: 'And what of Churchill? Firstly, he is never less than magnificent in whatever he is doing. His command of oratory, his wit and passion, always dominate the scene. But he finds it hard to acclimatize himself to his new position. His startling excitement over trivialities often detracts from his unequalled wisdom in handling matters of real importance.'

What surprised me was the rough and tumble of the place. The Speaker's procession and the paraphernalia of the mace contrasted with the schoolboy chaos which reigned inside the Chamber, with ministers trying to control it, though there was instant respect for the Speaker.

I was puzzled to find the House barely a quarter full for most debates. When Churchill made a historic speech on foreign policy, he delivered it to a dozen members because it was Friday morning and most had left for the weekend. In a vital two-day debate with the future of Africa at stake, there were never more than forty-six members present. I saw members make an exodus, almost a stampede, when Clement Attlee rose to speak, though he was the Prime Minister. The speakers did not seem dismayed to see their audience evaporate – it was normal. As one newspaper put it when Quintin Hogg spoke for the opposition: 'Mr Hogg rose to his feet and emptied the chamber.'

Certain MPs played the role of buffoon deliberately. My favourite was a Tory with a resemblance to the comic actor Edward Everett Horton, who rose spluttering with rage, discharging such verbal sallies as 'We want deeds, not words!' which were greeted by cheers and counter-cheers, to the mystification of the strangers in the public gallery. Puzzled myself, I asked the veteran reporter for the *Daily Express* who sat beside me why such a buffoon was tolerated. 'He makes so much noise,' he explained, 'that we wake up from our afternoon nap and report whatever he says. The local papers copy it with the headline ANGRY SCENES IN THE HOUSE, taking the idiot seriously, and all his constituents think he's a helluva live wire, instead of an absolute cunt.' I looked down on him with new respect.

Cries of 'Withdraw!' and 'Shame' ricocheted from side to side, interspersed by an occasional 'Take your hands out of your pockets' or 'You cheeky crowd of beasts.'

It was an extraordinary turnabout in British politics, the wartime leader cast aside, dozens of new members swept along in the Labour avalanche seizing such safe Tory seats as Brighton in the case of Skeffington-Lodge, who was such a nincompoop that when he was swept out again at the next election he wrote to Attlee suggesting that he might be considered for the House of Lords. The party leader replied tersely: 'I hope you get what you deserve. Attlee.'

This was a rare example of Attlee's acerbic wit, otherwise he appeared as dry as a piece of Bombay Duck. When he addressed the lobby correspondents in our room, announcing the forthcoming freedom of India, I dared to ask a question and he slapped me down impatiently like a gnat. But he had the ability to delegate, and needed this skill with such a volcanic front-bench team as Stafford Cripps, Hugh Dalton, Aneurin Bevan and Ernest Bevin, the Foreign Secretary, who befriended me as we stood in the Central Lobby, a privilege reserved exclusively for Members of Parliament and the few accredited lobby correspondents. Once a week we were briefed on the next week's business by Herbert Morrison for Labour, chirpy and composed before the bitterness of thwarted ambition set in; and R. A. Butler, or occasionally Anthony Eden, for the Conservatives. Speaking to us off the record, they gave the alleged truth of a controversial story, to save us leaping to conclusions which would be to their disadvantage.

Once a year we gave the Lobby Dinner. It now seems bizarre that my two guests were James Callaghan and Quintin Hogg, a future Prime Minister and Lord Chancellor. I reminded Lord Hailsham of this in his high office in the House of Lords thirty years later, but he did not remember me. As Hogg he had been pleased to write the occasional article for the Central Press Agency and was jollier than the narrow man that he became. Realizing my ignorance, they helped me choose the wine for the Lobby Dinner and insisted on paying for it.

Gradually I realized it was all a game. I thrilled to the clashes late in the evening when Churchill raged against Cripps or Bevin. 'I will leave it to the House to judge who should be in the infants' school or the lunatic asylum,' Cripps shouted, using one of Churchill's phrases against him; later they passed pencilled notes across the table and smiled, ignoring the uproar surrounding them. After one brutal verbal combat, Churchill and Bevin passed me in the Lobby arm-in-arm, smoking cigars on their way to the bar.

Covering the House of Lords as well, I heard Maynard Keynes

interrupt a long-winded peroration by Lord Beaverbrook: 'In a long and rugged life in the statistical jungle I have never heard statistics one fiftieth part so phoney.'

Beaverbrook exploded – 'You think that *funny* . . .' Afterwards the Hansard reporter and myself checked with Keynes: 'I know I said "phoney",' he confirmed, 'but please put it down as "funny", he's upset enough as it is.'

If it was a game, it was a good one. Compared to today's ministers they were giants of integrity, believing in their cause, resigning at the first hint of impropriety, like Hugh Dalton who made a careless remark to a Parliamentary reporter before his budget speech which could have been misconstrued. Few would resign today for an action a thousand times worse.

In my role as roving reporter, I covered such boring events as the English Electric Company's War Activities Exhibition. By contrast, on 7 January 1946 I covered the opening of the United Nations General Assembly as Dr Zuleta of Colombia struck his hammer three times on the raised table in Westminster Hall and a new world organization was born. There was a rare moment of honesty when Bevin turned on the Russians with startling frankness after the usual evasions, accusing them of incessant propaganda against the British 'as if no friendship between us had existed'.

Eleanor Roosevelt gave me an exclusive interview which was so dull it was hardly printable, for I had yet to master the art of the interview. I suspect she expected my father. Best of all were the film previews, enjoying a conspiracy of critics as we sat in the comfort of the deep armchairs in the morning, bribed by a buffet of bits and pieces afterwards which served as my lunch, though I did not join the rush for the drinks table, then.

All this was left behind with my call-up for national service. One of the more bizarre aspects of my life is the way it has veered from triumph to disaster without my recognizing the difference. A year after reporting Churchill in the House of Commons, I was composing a paragraph in an army news-sheet in Wiesbaden announcing the birth of a staff sergeant's baby. That I brought the same enthusiasm to both can be seen either as my constant failure to put my life in the right perspective, or an astounding ability to adapt.

It is claimed that national service was an extension of school. Possibly this is true of the initiation rites of a crack regiment, otherwise I cannot conceive of two experiences so opposed. At school we were taken from our parents almost as soon as we could walk and incarcerated most of the year, but we were among our own kind. The immeasurable blessing of national service lay in finding ourselves in an environment, where everyone was different. Doubly so in my case, for I enlisted in the American Army Air Corps.

This followed various foiled attempts: first I tried to join Army Intelligence, then I applied for the Welsh Guards with a recommendation from Mopsy's monocled husband (before he saw me as a possible co-respondent). Attending the medical I joined a despondency of naked, shivering boys who looked far from fit, though most of them were passed. When it was my turn, I was rejected with the terse explanation that there was too much 'albumen' in my blood, which I found so alarming that I did not dare to ask the MO what it meant, nor do I know to this day. Then I was accepted by RAF Intelligence, encouraged by my father who thought I could be useful as an interpreter inside Russia. I am sure he loved me but a more appalling fate could hardly be imagined. This time I was accepted. Told that my call-up papers would arrive by the next post, I continued at the Central Press for the next two months when I received a letter from the Ministry of Labour informing me that I could not join any of the British services until I was twenty-one, because of my dual nationality. I continued happily with Guy L'Estrange until a year later when I received a 'Greetings!' from the President of the United States.

Reporting to the enlistment centre in Southampton, I walked vaguely down dismal streets until I asked a limping man if he knew the way to Hogland Camp. 'Do I know the way?' he exploded. 'I was stabbed in the back I was, stabbed and no compensation. Lost my job, spent two weeks in hospital, two to three inches of steel right in my back. Do I know the way!' With that he shuffled off, but I found it in the end.

My first and lasting impression of the American army was of laissez-faire compared to the brusqueness of the Officers Training Corps at Wellington College – even an 'about turn' was a casual slouch as if we had forgotten something, compared to the high steps and stamping feet of the British. My other lasting impression of the GIs was their ingenuousness; no malice was shown towards me, for all of us were misfits. At roll-calls, mine was one of the few names which sounded American: Hernandez; Fernandez; Schmidt; Muller; Fuccinia; Yamaha. Dual-nationals like myself contributed MacTavish and 'Taffy' Thomas. That first night I listened to the shunting of the freight trains in the distance and heard several of the recruits moaning with half-strangled fears in the horrors of the night to be forgotten in the morning, but I lay there smiling. I had been to an English boarding school.

Apart from the dual-nationals who lived in Britain, everyone was homesick. Deviously, I picked up scraps of rejected letters home: 'Dearest Lorrian, Will hony ive finally got started agen. this time im going to typ you one. Received a letter frome you yesterday was sure glad to hear frome you. Dont get much mail now most every body has quit writing except mom she writes every mail day. I'm back in Southampton with nouthing to do . . .'

He was right about that. Hogland (surely an unfortunate name?) was a far cry from Westminster. For a start, the little we did we did to music: we ate to music, slept to music, and when we wished to talk we shouted above the music. At the end of the week we had a barn-dance. The German POWs filled the hall with hay decorated in great bunches, with paper streamers hanging from the ceiling. The Southampton girls lined up outside the barracks, cooing in anticipation. How vastly different from those ritualistic balls I was forced to go to in Wisconsin where the girls were made of steel, and the boys brought them corsages and obeyed their every command. Here the GIs were lax and languid in our fatigue suits, gazing at them contemplatively as the German band, stony-faced in disapproval, played the latest tunes. A few couples danced properly, the rest jitter-bugged, inventing steps of their own, but the girls had invaded Hogland in such force that dozens of them had to dance with each other, laughing shrilly to conceal their discomfiture as the majority of the GIs, including myself, watched with melancholy stares. The girls held on bravely. With every dance they rose again, trying to attract attention, swaying and singing, their hips rolling, their jaws chewing with increasing intensity, their feet moving ever more rapidly, backwards and forwards, their skirts rising and falling, while a GI bellowed into the microphone the words of the only tune he knew, and he did not know all of that: 'It had to be you, it had to be you, la da la la . . .' The smoke-filled room revolved with the flexible bodies of Southampton's beauties who were looking anxious by now as they realized there might be no fulfilment at the end of the evening. The GIs drank Coke and watched them unsmilingly. I enjoyed it greatly.

During the interminable days of waiting, which I accepted as inevitable, I read the newspapers laid out in the recreation room. Surprisingly, these included *The Times*, and I came across a paragraph with my father's name at the head of it: American Writer Arrested for Drunken Driving. I managed to phone home and my mother told me sorrowfully, 'Oh Danny, we hoped so much you wouldn't see that,' though I was proud to see my father's name in print and the offence was hardly new. 'Such bad luck,' she explained. 'He had stopped the car to have a snooze, but the police charged him all the same. So unfair.'

After a week I was told by a recruiting sergeant that I had everything to gain if I enlisted on the spot rather than wait to be conscripted. Fortunately, I acted on his advice for this meant that I was able to go to any university in the world under the GI Bill of Rights when my service was over, one of the most generous and enlightened schemes offered by any government to its servicemen. After the charade of a medical, I took the next train to London to say goodbye to Guy L'Estrange who went into his office to write me a letter of reference in case I should need one, and returned with a typed recommendation and considerable coughing as he brushed the cigarette ash from his lapels. Miss Albertini wept openly. Even the dear old spinster secretaries and the elderly Junior seemed sorry to see me go – very Dickensian, with myself as Pip bearing great expectations as I stepped into Fleet Street with all the callow confidence of youth before life becomes muddled. It did not occur to me that I was saying goodbye to a rare experience.

Back at Hogland, my head was shaved by a German barber and I was fitted out for my uniform. The corporal who made me fill out the forms which dogged me throughout my service, took my fingerprints and ran through a list of likely complications: 'Fits, convulsions, sores, bed-wetting, venereal disease, typhus . . . ?' I shook my head and he looked dubious. 'Been to jail?' I shook my head again and he looked disbelieving. Finally, with a yawn, he asked the new recruits to raise our hands and we mumbled the appropriate words as the captain swore us in. The date was 12 September 1946, the next day would be Friday the 13th, and my number was Prvt. Farson, 10,602,600, the first of a new batch. 'Lucky number,' said the corporal as he saw me smile with relief.

Once I emerged in the outside world in my GI uniform, shaven head and peaked cap I found myself a stranger in my own country, and had my first experience of anti-American feeling in Britain.

On a train journey to London I shared a compartment with a tweedy, red-faced man and his equally pompous lady wife who talked about me as if I were invisible, running down America and the GIs as if we had invaded their country, which in their eyes was exactly what we had done. Their calculated abuse was vile, and directed, or so they assumed, at an ignorant young foreigner. As the train drew in to the terminus I said in my clearest English accent with a touch of Noël Coward: 'Thank you so much for making this tedious journey so interesting. I could not have believed that such prejudice existed until I heard your venom,' or words to that effect. Speechless at last, they stared dumbfounded as I snapped them a smart salute and stepped onto the platform.

Shops short-changed me shamelessly, explaining that I did not understand the currency. When I replied that I understood it perfectly, they became resentful. People picked quarrels on purpose. Another dual-national on a twenty-four-hour furlough took his girlfriend to a teashop and when he went to the lavatory he was followed by four British sailors who beat him up. At least they had a grievance for we were paid four times as much, infamously – 'Oversexed, overpaid and over here'. Yet the GIs were thousands of miles from their homes, while British servicemen in America were welcomed with typical hospitality. As a dual-national who could see both sides, now a member of the US Forces Overseas of whom I had written so contemptuously in my letter home from Lake Geneva, I became fiercely patriotic, this time on behalf of America.

Yet the GIs were capable of equal bigotry when it came to their black compatriots.

'If I get a gun I'll speak to them right between the eyes. I want to string several niggers up when I get home.'

'Do you think you're superior to someone like Paul Robeson?'

'Superior! Why I'm ten times as good as any dirty nigger. Give 'em an inch and they'll take a mile. If I see a nigger take hold of a white woman in the street, I'd take a sub-machine gun and shoot him straight through the head. Those in the North don't have to live with them, and they're not going to have the vote in the South.'

'Do you approve of lynching?'

'Well, it costs maybe $25,000 to be prosecuted in the States. Why spend all that money when you know a man's guilty? Why not lynch him ourselves?'

'Then you don't believe in fair trial?'

'Oh go on with you,' said the Southerner with a kindly smile, adding, irrelevantly, 'They're children, ain't they? You seldom see a serious nigger.'

I began to understand the Civil War.

By the time I was sworn in, the novelty of the experience was wearing off and I was pleased to be transferred to the American Army Air Corps at Bovingdon Aerodrome, though it sounded less romantic when my section – the European Air Transport Service – was abbreviated to EATS. Far from learning to fly, I punched air tickets instead.

We dealt with civilians as well as military personnel, usually celebrities on their way to Germany to entertain the men. One morning two elderly women came up and I sensed there was something wrong, though they looked as kindly as the sweet old dears in *Arsenic and Old Lace*. Then I realized who they were and called over a plump staff sergeant, asking him to look after the older woman while I took the other to complete some passport formalities in another office. When we returned I saw the sergeant marching the other lady up and down the corridor, subjecting her to one of his customary homilies. Handing her over, he gave a courteous little bow: 'Ma'am, I'd just like to tell you that I sure enjoyed our talk.' There was no reason to suspect that she had not been fascinated by his every word, her smile confirming that she took an interest in everything around her – as indeed she did.

'A good talk with the old lady?' I asked the sergeant later.

'It most certainly was, Dan!' He not only looked like Oliver Hardy but spoke like him too.

'You do realize,' I pointed out unkindly, 'that she couldn't see you, speak to you, nor hear a single word you said? She was Helen Keller.' He gulped and was quiet for days.

Mark Twain described Helen Keller as one of the two most remarkable women of the nineteenth century – the other was Florence Nightingale. Blind, deaf and dumb, stricken by an illness shortly after she was born, her achievement was partly due to the perseverance of a dedicated young teacher, Annie Sullivan 'the miracle worker', who struggled to convey to the unruly child not just the use of words, but the revelation that there was such a thing as a word. By constant repetition of putting the child's hand under a water pump and fingering the word 'water', she won through triumphantly. Helen Keller graduated from Radcliffe University at the age of twenty-four and became a respected writer and even a lecturer. Now she was seventy and her companion was a strong-willed Scot called Polly Thompson.

Knowing they were friends, I mentioned that Alexander Woollcott was my godfather, a whiteish lie of convenience which Polly Thompson relayed with startling speed onto Helen's hand, leading to an animated conversation. Drab though she looked, Helen Keller's face was radiant as she 'spoke'. Unfortunately, though she had learnt to speak after all these years, she mouthed the words incomprehensibly and Polly Thompson had to translate by hand. They had just returned from a tour of hospitals in the Far East where Helen Keller's example gave hope to the most seriously wounded. 'It was all right for her,' Polly confided with sudden asperity. '*She* couldn't see a thing – some of them had no faces to speak of. It was terrible for me.' She still looked shaken, but Helen smiled indefatigably as she tapped out the message: 'I have found such tragedy here, but over it all such triumph.'

My accent caused as much suspicion among the Americans as it did with the English. One officer was so startled when I saluted him politely that he came back to thank me. When he heard my voice and I explained my dual nationality, he sighed. 'I knew there was something odd. The other GIs never bother to salute me.'

I discovered that I was allowed to wear a fetching olive-green cap similar in shape to that later worn by Marlon Brando in *The Wild One*. Though intended for officers, a loophole stated that a GI could wear it if the badge was removed. I wore it on my visits to London, hitching a lift on the bus which left the base in the late afternoon. Wandering around Marble Arch I was arrested by the US Military Police for impersonating an officer, which was serious enough, but when I spoke my accent suggested I was an Englishman, probably a deserter, passing himself off as a GI. The CO at the base, a burly young man called Colonel Schott, proved extraordinarily patient when they phoned him, vouching for my authenticity. I was released with good humour and after several such arrests the MPs began to know me. Perhaps I became a curiosity, for Colonel Schott examined my records and asked if it was possible to arrange a visit to the House of Commons. A few days later, wearing civilian clothes, I met him in the Strangers' Lobby accompanied by the other kind of MP, possibly Jim Callaghan, who gave him a ticket for the Visitors' Gallery. When the policeman saluted me as he took the pass, I could see Colonel Schott blink with surprise. He had warned me that it was tactless to wear the olive-green cap, but after that salute he accepted me cap and all.

By this time I had made friends with another dual-national with an English background and a wry sense of humour. While I wore my officer's cap, Lockhart went further and bought a second-hand Jeep which we were allowed to travel in when transferred to Frankfurt, though we created confusion at every frontier post with our official papers which identified us as 'Privates First Class'. Though Paris and Luxembourg were intact, I looked incredulously at the devastation as we entered Germany: statues left where they had fallen, bridges still plunged into rivers, and an overriding hopelessness which hung in the air. Lord knows how our barracks in Wiesbaden had survived, long horizontal blocks which served as the headquarters for EATS. For the first time we were forced to drill every Saturday morning, but these were token inspections. 'About turn' was more a request than a command. No one shouted at us, and the food was excellent if bland. Always ice-cream.

What wistful conquerors we were! Disarming in our innocence, we must have been a mystifying contrast with our shuffling parades to the goose-steps that preceded us, yet a godsend compared to the threat of the Russian soldiers from the East. Our PX rations could transform the lives of a German family.

A first sergeant gave us a talk on VD, with the usual horrifying illustrations displayed on slides. After the general recoil, the sergeant taunted us: 'Why don't you find some decent women,' greeted with shouts of 'Where?'

'Just stop feeding your Frauleins from the PX,' he continued, 'and see how long they'd stay with you.'

'Stop feeding your wife, Sergeant,' someone called from the back, 'and see how long *she'd* stick it.'

Our theme song was, 'Was ist los in Deutschland, Alles ist kaput, Schlafen mit den Fräuleins, Das ist prima gut.' Though not for me.

We symbolized youth as we sped everywhere by Jeep – no GI liked to walk if he could help it – flirted with the *Fräuleins* or *Schatzis* and spent hours in the barber shop, anointed with aftershave and powder. Cum-Inn snack bars dotted the autobahn, vast advertisements for *Newsweek* plastered the backs of ruined buildings, and Coca-Cola stands heralded the new culture. The Germans disliked us, but we were their lifeline. A German secretary would bid an effusive goodnight to her American boss, but on the way home tell her friend that he was an impossible man and they would run down the Americans, contemptuous of our culture, or the lack of it. At home she would cut out fashions from the American magazines, waiting for the sergeant who was going to take her to an American film, turning on the radio to listen to the American Forces Network to make the time pass quicker.

The only open hostility I experienced came from an old lady who shook her fist as Lockhart and myself climbed through the rubble and shouted abuse.

'Madam,' said Lockhart with his usual smile, 'you seem to forget that we won the war!' I admired her hatred.

Generous by nature, the GIs shared their gum with the children and handed round their cigarettes to the old men. Such affluence was resented, reminding the Germans of their plight. On the outskirts of Frankfurt a GI played with the massive bulldog that belonged to an officer's wife. He held out a frankfurter (ironically), which the pampered dog licked suspiciously and dropped. A small boy in the usual peaked cap walked over, picked it up, backed away and ate it without expression. By the river a group of noisy, happier children returned from a boat ride organized by the 'US German Youth Activities', clutching their gifts.

From the army club on the main square in Frankfurt I looked down on the clusters of GIs in separate groups, white and black, while children watched hungrily, hoping for popcorn or candy. Above them on the balcony we sipped sodas and malted milkshakes under large umbrellas while the juke-box played incessantly inside.

Life for the Germans revolved around the black market on every level, with the railway station as the pivot. Every type congregated here: youths with long yellow hair; men in shiny black raincoats down to their ankles; men in short Bavarian lederhosen; a few well-dressed men with briefcases under their arms; and the occasional woman. Transactions were hasty, before the sirens were heard and the American police sped into the square on motorcycles followed by German police cars into which the suspects were bundled while the crowds looked on delighted, as crowds are by any distraction.

Thinking of those long-haired youths today, I fantasize over the opportunities I missed, but I was unaware of the undercurrents at the time, especially those within myself. Lockhart did better. He fell in love with a beautiful German girl whom he eventually married and brought back to England. Perhaps he expected eternal gratitude, for he seemed to regard her as one of the spoils of war and when their children grew up she left him to start her life all over again.

Meanwhile, I had another lucky break. Hearing of the annual 'School of Journalism' organized by the army newspaper *Stars & Stripes*, I applied and was accepted. It had been a vague ambition of mine to join the paper, which had a legendary reputation in the war. Pfungstadt, the *Stars & Stripes* headquarters, was one of the few villages which remained unscarred, unlike Darmstadt, the nearest town, where I climbed one of the few surviving buildings to look out on a scene of such destruction it was difficult to imagine how anyone could live there – yet life went on, if largely underground.

Pfungstadt was jaunty, almost Bavarian as geese strutted about like Nazis unaware that the war was over, and placid ducks floated smilingly on the stream which circled the few old houses. The course was opened on 4 August 1947 by a lieutenant-colonel who referred to the high professional standards of *Stars & Stripes* and our chance 'to enable unit papers' to benefit from the expertise, but I was determined that I would not return to my unit paper in Wiesbaden to report the birth of a daughter to Sergeant Schallenhoffer.

Not only was I asked to join the paper but assigned to the weekly *Weekend*, which must have been one of the first supplements to be published anywhere. It was run by hard-drinking, hard-living American civilians, both men and women, who may have been disenchanted with themselves, but to me they had the glamour of the expatriates in Paris before the war. Without the Coupole or the Flore, or any bar at all for that matter, they held parties at their homes instead which usually ended in tears and fist-fights. They were professionals. As the only GI on the staff, they adopted me. Looking back, I know they must have liked me, but it has always been my loss to realize this after the event.

In addition to the American civilians there was a middle-aged English secretary, to my bewilderment the only person to resent my arrival, and two Germans, literally hungry for their jobs, a writer called Werner Prym and a famous photographer for the Nazis, Hans Hubman, whose exuberance was undiminished by defeat. Hubman was more than prepared to offer his wife to the editor in the hope of advancement or some PX rations, and was totally amoral. I accompanied him to a private party held by the top brass in Germany in honour of their Commander-in-chief, General Curtis Le May. *Weekend* had wangled an invitation to this exclusive gathering, though we were there on sufferance. I followed Hubman discreetly, writing down the names of those he photographed, giving the wives charming smiles though the officers looked indignant when I asked who they were, especially when they heard my English accent. Suddenly there was a hullabaloo as Hubman hurled his camera to the floor, and shouted to me at the top of his voice: 'Every time I take photo, this lousy general's wife gets her face in the way.' We were arrested on the spot and taken by the military police to the nearest lock-up where it took the editor's considerable charm to have us released.

Tantrums were the norm with Hubman, who could be difficult. He, Prym and I set out in a splendid covered Chevrolet wagon to Munich where snow covered the ruined buildings, making them even more forlorn. I doubt if a young German today could conceive the desolation then. I remember it vividly because I have the photos taken with my first Rolleiflex after Hubman led me to the inevitable shabby back room where a crippled German sold me his gleaming, lovely camera for the usual cartons of American cigarettes, the hard currency then. My Rolleiflex was a beauty and it must have been guarded jealously and parted with painfully. It was my only sensible acquisition in Germany, for the Rolleiflex has a dignity beyond other cameras. It cannot do half the things that a modern Olympus or Konica can achieve with their built-in flash and multiple refinements, but I have found that when they fall apart the Rollei comes to the rescue. I took my first two rolls of film in the ruins of Munich, then joined Prym and Hubman who were beaming with their successful discovery of a cache of black-market sardines.

We returned to Pfungstadt in the late afternoon and I fell asleep in the back of the Chevrolet. I woke to hear screams in front and realized we were out of control, skidding headlong at increasing speed as Hubman wrestled to keep the car on the autobahn, away from the drop of several hundred feet into a valley. Then we crashed. Several hours later I recovered consciousness as I was wheeled into an operating theatre in Stuttgart and looked up to see the figure 22. As that is my lucky number it seemed a good omen.

I was fortunate in two respects, as I realized months later when I saw a photograph of the damaged Chevrolet, the two sides crushed together at the back. Because I was half-asleep and totally relaxed, I failed to tense myself against the impact. My left shoulder was broken at the joint between the humerus and scapular, and I had several broken ribs. Hubman had driven straight into the first pantechnicon of a long travelling circus – the alternative was the valley so he saved our lives, but while we were unconscious, the German circus people stripped us of everything we had, my uniform, watch and of course my new Rolleiflex. My other piece of luck was being found by some American civilians who drove me straight to the Stuttgart army hospital which specialized in fractures. Meanwhile, Prym and Hubman were taken by some Germans to their nearest civilian hospital. I learnt that when they recovered consciousness, Hubman's first word was 'sardines'. When there was no response he turned on Prym in the next bed. 'Where are the sardines?' Prym, who had just left the operating theatre, shook his head, which enraged Hubman who managed to get up, falling over Prym as he tried to strangle him, yelling, 'You stole the sardines!' As Hubman was dragged away, Prym, gasping for breath, managed to cry out, 'Yes, I admit it all. Unconscious and with my bare hands I clawed open every tin of those sardines, and they were *delicious!*' People said that Hubman was never the same again, but he seemed much the same to me.

For the next few months I was stuck in bed confined to a wooden cage with ropes and pulleys to keep me in a fixed position, unable to eat or shit for the first week and so having to endure enemas. My main regret, apart from the loss of the Rolleiflex, was missing my planned leave with my parents in Kenya. But the other GIs in the ward helped to pass the time. In the next bed was a black soldier (one of the few situations in the US army where such proximity was possible) called Sammy Roosevelt Mimms, who kept me entertained with his flow of stories. A gigantic man, he had broken both his legs when his Fräulein pushed him out of a window when she heard the military police searching for deserters. Unfortunately, she lived on the fourth floor.

Every evening Sammy Roosevelt got drunk by the simple means

of straining liquid boot polish, which had a high alcohol content, through slices of white bread brought to him by his friends. The kindly old German nurse could not make it out. Sammy tried to persuade me to join him in his nightly frolic but I was too prim.

Another distraction was the music. Woken every morning by the current hit on the forces radio, a wailing lament – '*So* tired, of waiting for you . . .', I shiver with recollection on the rare occasions that I hear it now. A group of German musicians attempted to cheer us up with 'There's nobody here but us chickens!' played loudly on squeaky accordions at the foot of our beds. Worse was the Red Cross lady who encouraged us to make dog leads and bracelets as occupational therapy.

Several of the Americans at Pfungstadt came to visit me. Though the Rollei had been stolen, the two rolls of film had been recovered and someone had gone to the trouble of having them processed. One of the prints was a stunner: the main square; a derelict building high to the left, a low line of skeletal houses in the background, slabs of stone lying in the snow, and a few black figures hurrying about their business on the wet street in the foreground. These were slightly out of focus as they moved, adding to the ghostly effect.

This was what photography was all about. I knew it at once, the antidote to beautifully composed prints of cherry trees in blossom with dew drops and frost on window panes. Instinctively, I knew that this blurred image represented everything I wanted to achieve as a photographer – my new ambition.

When I was lifted from my hospital bed after several months, I fell down again and remained so weak for several days that I could only walk with crutches. The photographs we took of each other, as we convalesced in the sun outside, reveal that I was thin for the first and only time in my life. A front tooth had been smashed in the crash and I needed to be fitted for a plate by the US Army dentists.

I returned to Pfungstadt and a warm welcome until I sought out the English secretary to let her know I was back. She looked at me, gap-toothed and cadaverous, and laughed venomously: 'Well, *you've* lost your looks and no mistake. No one will fancy you now.'

But it had never occurred to me that I had looks to lose.

When my army service was up, prolonged by my months in hospital, I was bursting with the excitement of going home. I could hardly wait.

'Don't look forward to it so much,' warned the editor at my farewell party. 'It's always a disappointment.'

❖

With the end of the war Somerset Maugham had re-established himself at the Villa Mauresque. He had found a new secretary, Alan Searle, a former prison visitor whose life was enhanced though consumed as Maugham's companion. If Gerald Haxton was the accident, Searle became the nurse. How appalling it would have been the other way round; Maugham had the luck of an old devil.

I met Searle for the first time at the Dorchester where dinner was served in their suite. It did not occur to me that my GI uniform might have been an embarrassment if we had dined in the restaurant. I never wore civilian clothes on leave except when I took Colonel Schott round the House of Commons, and I doubt if US Army regulations allowed us to wear anything but uniform.

Whereas Haxton was bristlingly abrasive, like a bulldog about to break his lead, Searle was more pussy-cat, and far more fulsome over me. I was no longer a child. Maugham was exceptionally gracious, signing copies of his books as if this was a new pleasure, including *Cakes and Ale* which he inscribed 'From your friend, W. S. Maugham'. When I transferred to Germany I wrote to him at the Villa Mauresque, sending him some luxuries from the PX stores in Wiesbaden. While admitting that he was not actually short of food, he accepted the gesture though insisting that I tell him the cost, explaining that it would spoil his pleasure if I were put to expense while he had 'plenty of money'. This must have been one of his rare moments of spontaneous generosity, as I was soon to learn. As I could buy the rations so cheaply, I refused any payment and received a further letter which was payment enough:

You don't tell me much about what you are doing and what sort of life you are leading. I hope at all events you are getting a good deal of experience. If you want to become a writer it is very necessary to expose yourself to all the vicissitudes of life, and it isn't enough to wait for experience to come to you, you must go out after it. Even if you bark your shins every now and then, that again will be grist for your mill. I don't suppose you have much time for reading or many books at your disposal but, you know, the more highly cultured you

can make yourself the richer your work will be. Few people know
how much industry and how much patience are needed to achieve
anything worth doing. I speak exactly like Polonius.

Good advice, and I tried to follow it – though I have barked my
shins too often.

Towards the end of 1947 Maugham invited me to spend Christmas
at the Villa Mauresque, and I hitched a ride on a US freight plane.
The flight was delayed by snow, so I phoned the Villa from Nice,
waking Searle who was dozing on the sofa and fell off, slightly chipping
a fingernail. He showed me the damaged nail on my arrival as
reproachfully as if I had given him a black eye. I could not understand
the fuss. Then Maugham had to see it when he padded into the room,
looking more fastidious than ever in a brown smoking-jacket as he
mixed a Bacardi cocktail before dinner, a monocle dangling to his
waist, and with that expression of slight distaste captured by Graham
Sutherland's portrait.

Over dinner in the curved dining-room lined with pretty pastels
by Marie Laurencin he became effusive, smiling broadly as he outlined
the treats in store – they would show me around Nice and introduce
me to so-and-so further down the coast, take me to a night-club in
Cannes which I might enjoy, and of course the Casino at Monte. A
cornucopia of fun. The meal was delicious, starting with mashed
avocado from the gigantic tree in the garden grown from a stone
smuggled out years earlier in a golf-bag from California, mixed with
lemon juice and hot pieces of crisp bacon. There was only one trouble
with the food – there was not enough of it. At the end I was so
ravenous that I made a second dive for the nuts and glacé fruits that
were whisked round the table, earning a withering glance from the
Master.

Somewhere along the way I failed. I doubt that it was my greediness
with the nuts; it must have been the embarrassment of that GI uniform
and the discovery that I had no luggage apart from an overnight bag
with a change of shirt, underpants, and a gaudy pair of nylon bathing
trunks which were laid out by the butler on a chair as if they were
evening clothes. My uniform was of good quality and fitted me perfectly. My army greatcoat rivalled a British 'warm'. Every item was
first class down to the khaki underwear and a pair of athletic shorts
which were cut so trimly that I nearly went back after I forgot them
in a back-street hotel in Marseilles a few years later.

But my uniform was not *comme il faut* for the Côte d'Azur. Beverley Nichols described the care with which he packed for a visit before the war: 'Dinner at eight with the Master *meant* dinner at eight, and a black tie *meant* black tie. Willie liked his young friends to be smartly dressed, and I was happy to oblige. There were new shirts from Charvet . . .'

I had never heard of Charvet. Naïve as ever, I had not anticipated the shame of taking an American soldier around the fleshpots of the Riviera where gossips would leap to the wrong conclusion at Maugham's expense. Expense! He went to no expense unless he could help it. How simple it would have been to tell the chauffeur to drive me into Nice where Alan could fit me out with a suit of clothes. That could have been my Christmas present.

Haxton would have coped, I am sure of that. When Godfrey Winn arrived in 1928, long before he became the highest-paid journalist in Britain, he wore a grey flannel suit. 'This is the South of France in August,' Maugham informed him scathingly, but he had the grace to tell Haxton, 'Get him some linen slacks, shirts and espadrilles at the Bon Marché, like yours.' Winn recorded ungratefully that he did not wish to resemble Haxton in any way, but at least he was bought the clothes, which was more than Searle did for me.

Everything would have been different if Graham and Kathy Sutherland, also invited for Christmas, had not cancelled at the last moment due to illness. They were sophisticated enough to have summed up the situation instantly – even in my uniform I could have been introduced as *their* friend. Instead, I was confined to the Villa Mauresque as if I was contagious.

It was more than that of course. I was a disappointment, and as Ted Morgan remarked in his biography of Maugham, 'Those who disappointed him were summarily dismissed.'

Reading Morgan's book many years later, I discovered an explanation for the change in attitude towards me. According to Morgan, from information contained in a letter written by Maugham to his old friend Bert Alanson: 'Alan had scattered his heart all over Europe, and there was hardly anything left for England. In December they went back to the Mauresque and spent Christmas with a lonely American soldier, recruited by Alan as their only guest.' *Recruited* – so that was it! I was intended to entertain Searle and was found wanting, or rather not only not-wanting but unaware. Realizing his mistake,

Maugham decided to punish me, for neither he nor Searle had the courage to speak the truth. The Sutherlands would have found it hilarious and could have laughed it away. Instead, bewildered by the *volte face* – what had happened to those jaunts to Monte? – I wandered around the Villa and went for walks in my army greatcoat along the coastal road which led to the pleasant port of Cap Ferrat. In my ignorance, I was surprisingly happy. The Villa Mauresque was beautiful, built in 1906 in the Moorish style – hence 'Mauresque' – with an open courtyard inside the house and the famous sign above the front door to ward off the evil eye which Maugham adopted for his books.

The garden was a tribute to thirteen gardeners employed before the war, though there were fewer now. There were steps and urns and statuary, pines and cypress lining the pool where Haxton had dived when it was empty, now with water gushing from the mouth of a cardinal's head which proved to be a faun by Bernini. Most sensationally for me were the orange trees with fruit upon them, even at Christmas, and the famous avocado which yielded hundreds of pears each year. Several were stolen by Cyril Connolly on his visit; he was caught out when the butler searched his luggage and, even worse, made to give them back.

Remarkably, apart from the absence of the beloved dachshunds left behind in the war, and allegedly killed and eaten by the starving French, life had resumed much as it had been before, with the delicious though tiny meals still prepared by Annette who had cooked for Maugham in the thirties.

If I expected a Scrooge-like transformation of Maugham on Christmas Day, I was disappointed. He seemed crustier than usual. Foolishly, in my eagerness to please, I had given all my presents on my first evening, including the tins of American chocolates which were Maugham's favourite, and as we had never driven into Nice or Cannes there was no chance to buy anything else as I had hoped. In my turn, I received no presents from either of them. As we went into lunch after our solitary cocktail, for Maugham kept to this discipline throughout, he made the bleak pronouncement: 'I'm afraid the price of meat is so s-scandalous in France these days that I cannot afford t-turkey.' Then, as if I had been responsible, he turned on me with a nasty gleam. 'At least we're not reduced to eating d-dog.'

Afterwards I walked in vain in search of a simple bar where I could buy a large cheese sandwich, or something coarse and filling. Now it seems peculiar that I accepted everything with such docility, though I remember wandering through the garden that night in a mood of dramatic self-pity. I was conscious of the honour of being Maugham's guest, perhaps the first at the Villa after the war. It would have been preferable if he had told me off, argued or abused me, but that was not in the nature of the beast. Maugham was a grand old man, submitting grimly when I photographed him in the garden with my small camera which went off like a revolver every time I pressed the trigger, for this was before I bought my first Rolleiflex. Flinching every time, he remarked, 'I'm afraid this is how I look. That's how it is.'

At mealtimes he made caustic comments on everyone mentioned, and I wrote them down in my bedroom afterwards: Alexander Woollcott was 'a very stupid man'; James Agate, the critic whom I had met at my father's club, the Savage, was 'vain, pretentious, a sensualist and a drunk'. When I told him that he would be sorry to learn that Mrs Fairbank was in a home – 'I think she's gone out of her mind' – he brightened considerably: 'You do surprise me. I never thought she had a m-mind to go out of.'

Now it was his turn to break some bad news to me: 'You will be sorry to hear,' he told me with relish, 'that your godfather Tom Seyster has adopted an American marine and has changed his will. Such a p-pity, for he was going to leave the whole lot to you.' As I had never expected anything, the loss was not as painful as he hoped.

We did have one jaunt, to an auction in Nice held in a huge warehouse crammed with unclaimed furniture and bric-à-brac confiscated by the Germans during the Occupation. Dressed in a borrowed overcoat, which confirmed my suspicion that they were ashamed of my uniform, I accompanied Maugham as we wandered through the mounds of wartime detritus, like a scene from *Citizen Kane*. His taut expression tautened: 'My God!' he exclaimed at last. 'They were lucky to have such s-stuff l-l-looted!'

Has the meanness of Maugham been exaggerated over the years? Though I am fond of his memory, I fear not. He played a cat-and-mouse game with those in his power. Even with such rivals as Hemingway and Gide, Maugham was probably the richest writer in the world thanks to the manipulation of his lawyer who sold the film rights of his novels while ensuring they would revert after one or two years. This accounts for the different versions of *Rain*, *The Letter* and *Of*

Human Bondage, which gave Bette Davis her first Hollywood success. Then there were forgotten but lucrative films like *The Painted Veil* and *Christmas Holiday*, and major productions like *The Razor's Edge*, from the novel he was working on when I met him in America. It is one of the vices of the very rich that they play the game of being impoverished. Acknowledging Haxton's help in adapting *Rain* for the stage, Maugham sent a cheque for $10,000 to Bert Alanson, asking him to invest half of it in Haxton's name: 'He has been very faithful and devoted to me for many years,' he explained. 'Of course he has not been able to save anything and I should like this to be the nucleus of some provision for him in case I die.'

When you consider that *Rain* earned Maugham more than a million dollars in its various guises, five thousand is not a great amount. Syrie did better as the rejected wife: a house, Rolls Royce and £2400 a year, with £600 for their daughter Lisa. But Syrie had lawyers and Maugham lived in dread of scandal. At the end, though, he brought scandal upon himself when he tried to adopt Alan Searle as his legal heir, initiating an action against Lisa to revoke property he had given her. Searle told me that Maugham was fond of his first son-in-law Vincent Paravicini, the son of a Swiss diplomat, but disliked the second, Lord John Hope, who as Lord Glendevon died in January 1996. Lisa went to court to have the adoption declared unlawful.

Meanwhile, when I was there, he toyed with Searle sadistically: 'Oh, I do like those trousers,' he told him one morning, 'I wish I could afford a pair like that.' Searle grew to trust me and confided his fear that he might be left penniless: 'Willie tells me that he lived comfortably on £5 a week when he was a young man in London, and has made sure that I won't have less than that. He can't mean it, can he?'

Though Ted Morgan stated in his book that Maugham paid $35,000 for the portrait by Graham Sutherland, I learned a different story from Sutherland himself. As this was his first portrait he was uncertain what to ask when Maugham sent Alan Searle to bargain for it at the Voile d'Or where the Sutherlands were staying. Finally Maugham arrived in his chauffeur-driven Daimler and counted out the money punctiliously: 'Please don't think me m-mean, Graham,' he explained, 'but I've got some very expensive guests staying with me at the moment and they've all sent their c-clothes to the c-cleaners, so I can't afford to pay you more.' He handed out £200 in notes.

If Searle fancied me, the only indication was his admiration one morning after I had washed my hair. 'Isn't that better,' he demanded of Maugham who was mixing the ritual Bacardi cocktail, 'doesn't he look sweet?' Maugham shot me a look which suggested that he found me anything but sweet, but we continued to behave as if this was an ordinary visit. Possibly to stress the normality, Searle confided, as if it were a dark secret, that Maugham had known one great love affair in his life, with the woman he fictionalized as 'Rosie' in *Cakes and Ale*. When Maugham inscribed my copy in the Dorchester, he had added the words 'the author's favourite book'.

Searle had no need to worry about his future in the event of Maugham's death, though his insecurity led him to encourage Maugham to turn against his family, questioning the legitimacy of his daughter. That was a wretched episode. Neither was it pleasant to use Searle as a guinea-pig in trying out the Niehand injections in case there were side-effects. There seemed to be nothing wrong, so Maugham proceeded with the rejuvenation to which his body responded all too actively while his mind deteriorated until there was little left. He was over ninety when he died in 1965, leaving the contents of the lovely Villa to Searle, while the house was sold. The royalties, which came to more than $50,000 a year, plus a legacy of £50,000, also went to Searle. In the event Maugham's will proved impeccable, with his collection of theatrical pictures going to the National Theatre, a large donation to the Royal Literary Fund and a handsome sum to build a library at the King's School, Canterbury, which he hated as a boy.

In the end it hardly mattered to Searle, who was rich and lonely in Monte Carlo suffering from Parkinson's disease, unable to frolic to the extent he had hoped. After Maugham's death he came to visit me in North Devon and told me of the horror of the final years when Maugham's mind had gone and he could no longer recognize him. One day Searle heard a bump in the room upstairs and found Maugham lying beside the fire-grate where he had fallen, hitting his head, dislodging some mental block. Looking up, he recognized Searle again, and smiled. 'Is that you, Alan?' he asked, 'I've wondered where you've been. I wanted to thank you for everything you've done for me.' That is what Searle told me. A few moments later Maugham was dead.

At least my luggage was not worth searching when it was time for me to leave, the day before New Year's Eve. Alan Searle had told me of an incident before the war when 'a well-known peer of the realm' said goodbye to his host in the hall. As he did so, his cases were brought down and one of them fell open, a number of Maugham's valuable first editions tumbling to the floor. The peer shrugged it off indifferently – 'That's what comes of letting a servant pack your things' – as Maugham scooped them up without a word. Afterwards, if a guest was suspect, like Cyril Connolly who was found with the purloined avocados, it was like going through customs.

I said goodbye to Maugham who gazed at me with the impassivity of a lizard as he continued silently up the stairs to the sacrosanct study at the top of the house with the Gauguin door he had brought back from Tahiti. Halfway to the airport I discovered I had left my passport behind, so the taciturn chauffeur, with the impatient '*tchk*' of a man who realized he was unlikely to receive a tip, turned and drove back.

Searle hurried down the staircase waving the passport which had been found by a servant. 'Do go and see Willie,' he implored. 'I know it would mean so much, it won't take a moment.'

I raced up the stairs into the forbidden study where Maugham sat at his long desk looking so forlorn that my heart was moved. He smiled slightly when he saw me: 'Please forgive me,' he said. 'I'm so s-sorry.'

'That's all right,' I assured him, touching his arm, and ran down the staircase through the front door with the Moorish sign above, leaving the Villa Mauresque for the last time. My one anxiety was to catch my flight to London for the last of my Christmas leave.

It was on the plane that I had the chance to reflect. Mean he might have been, and mean Maugham was, but I wished I had given him a hug.

My great-grandfather, General James Negley. My father adored him:
'He made other men look like mongrel dogs.'

Above left: Christmas 1930. Aged three, in Cossack costume brought back from Russia by my parents.

Above right: Bohinsko, 1935 Throughout his travels, my father's rod was part of his luggage.

Left: My mother and pigmy during the journey across Africa in 1939 recorded in *Behind God's Back*.

FRIENDS IN ENGLAND and here, Negley Farson, Jr., 13, son of the American-born writer, and Michael Barnes, 13, pose together. Negley kept his gas mask as a souvenir; other children gave up their gas masks when they left England, used the containers as handbags. Michael finished his first year at Eton, will continue at Ashbury College, Ottawa.

Above: A 'minor ambassador', evacuated to Canada in June 1940.

Right: As a private in the US Army Corps in post-war Germany.

This blurred scene of the ruins of Munich was taken with my first Rolleiflex, bought on the black market. A few hours later I was involved in a serious car accident, and the camera was stolen while I was unconscious. The film was retrieved from the wreckage, and it was this picture that convinced me that this was what photography was all about, rather than dewdrops on blossom.

Somerset Maugham,
who befriended me
when I was evacuated.
He was extraordinarily
mean when I spent
Christmas 1947 at the
Villa Mauresque, where
I took his portrait.

Right: Photographing a
model for *Picture Post* –
a spread for the 'silly
season'.

The double exposure of Salvador Dali.

My parents at the Grey House in North Devon.

Martin Seymour Smith, Robert Graves and Robert Kee at a
bullfight in Palma, Majorca, after Graves persuaded me to buy
some worthless plates.

Below: Brendan Behan during a joyful week in Dublin in which
I followed in his untroubled wake before he was struck by fame.

Five

Seeking Out the
Facts of Life

W HEN I WAS FIFTEEN, I was so desperate to learn about sex that one evening in Pelham Place I confronted my father outside the kitchen and blurted out my feelings. He was drunk enough to give me the confidence to make such a confession, but not too drunk to understand. I failed miserably and he failed me completely, with some remark like, 'Hey, wait a minute, what's the hurry?' When my mother came in, he made a joke of it. 'Just listen to this, our little boy thinks I ought to tell him the facts of life. What do you think of that?'

The next day the subject was not referred to and I was too ashamed to ask again. Instead I bought a sex book with diagrams in Charing Cross Road, which confused me more.

There was no such thing as sex education at Abinger, but at Wellington the housemaster called a few of us together one afternoon, as if he were announcing some really bad news. He puffed away at his pipe with such furious concentration that he practically disappeared in smoke before starting a dissertation that was meaningless. Humming and hawing, spitting out incomprehensible phrases between the puffs on his pipe, he did his duty. We left his study, numbed by this glimpse into the horror of the unmentionable world awaiting us.

We found out for ourselves, instinctively. We had separate cubicles at Benson, our house, and late one afternoon I was startled to be called into one of them by a boy who was masturbating and encouraged me to join him. To make it even more exciting he was a dark-haired, athletic, sensual boy I secretly admired. This was liberation in every sense. We continued to masturbate each other and life became happier and less complicated. I grew so brazen that once I opened his trousers when he was lying beside the window in the reading-room when other boys were present, though unable to see us. Later we used the woods. After we left Wellington we met a few times in London, but he sensed I was taking the relationship too seriously. We never referred to what had happened between us except for a private smile, but now he began to mention girls and I took the hint.

Earlier, staying with my parents in a boarding-house in Woolacombe on the coast of North Devon, I had had my first wet-dream, staining the sheets abundantly with the first outburst of manhood. I was not sure what had happened, felt slightly guilty, and nervous in case I was ill, yet sensed this must be part of growing up. I made the bed carefully to conceal the crime and went down to breakfast. Meanwhile the landlady discovered the evidence, handling the 'accident' tactfully as she urged her son to show me his model boat while the sheets were changed. I realized the subterfuge and was grateful. It was after this that I asked for advice from my father. Today there would have been no need. That is one of the few good things about television, the revelation that you are not alone.

When did I realize I was homosexual? It is hardly something that occurs overnight, like measles, and I suppose it dawns on everyone differently at vastly varying ages. I felt guilty long before I knew why. Having bought a book on Oscar Wilde, I was so alarmed in case it was discovered that I hid it between the stones of the overgrown bank of the stream which ran down to the sea from our new home in Devon. I looked for that book years later, but I could never find it again.

After I moved to London to study Russian I used to spend hours listening to the oratory at Speakers' Corner, so absorbed that I was unaware of the furtive smiles, and when someone nudged me I thought it was accidental. I had no idea that Hyde Park Corner was a notorious pick-up place, even when a young Irish guardsman, with the peak of his cap pulled down over his brick-red face, followed me from speaker to speaker trying to start a conversation until he was stopped by two policemen. They asked me if I knew him and I shook my head, bewildered, and they took him away. He was not much older than me and if I had been more experienced we might have enjoyed a good relationship.

A few years later the irony came full circle when it was my turn to track down guardsmen with the perseverance of a hunter stalking big game in Africa. One night I followed a tall man, probably in his late twenties, older than myself, down street after street, crossing roads, keeping to the shadows like a couple in a story by Edgar Allan Poe. Finally he turned into a dark alley where he stopped – waiting. At this moment my nerve failed me. Not that I was afraid of the consequences, simply that I was unable to cope. I have regretted it ever since, like Mr Bernstein in *Citizen Kane* who once saw a beautiful girl crossing the street – 'and do you know, not a day's gone by that I don't think of her.'

The guardsman might have been more experienced – *he* might have been able to cope.

Why the allure of the uniform? 'He's AC and DC,' they said, 'he likes soldiers *and* sailors!' It was an attraction of opposites, the coarse guardsman's uniform the more exciting for undoing; the sailor's bell-bottoms with the flap over the crutch, and the top which was so tight it had to be pulled over the sailor's head as he struggled to get out of it, a uniform which might have been designed to provoke someone like myself. The uniforms gave the illusion of masculinity, occasionally to be fulfilled. Years later, in a Chelsea pub, I met a Scottish guardsman who was about to leave the army, and pursued him so remorselessly that we ended up living together for over a year in one of the happiest relationships I have known. That was the trouble. Unlike most of my friends, sex with strangers was not enough; I wanted to love them too.

Sometimes it worked. At this earlier, tentative stage when I was discovering myself, I met a guardsman of my age from the Midlands, about as ordinary as anyone can be, but the relationship was extraordinary for me. I had an electric gramophone and we played the current hits. When I hear them today, they evoke the atmosphere of that hideously furnished rented room above a hairdresser in Beauchamp Place, where we listened rapt to Kay Starr's 'Wheel of Fortune', Nellie Lutcher singing 'Hurry on down to my house, baby!' and Frankie Laine's 'Jezebel'. Noël Coward was right about the potency of cheap music; not only did we enjoy it but the songs gave us the feeling that we were young and alive, like the ecstasy of the Beatles years later when it felt good just to possess one of their LPs.

Like myself in the American army, the guardsman – I have forgotten his name – always wore his heavy khaki uniform, but as I was unlikely to meet anyone I knew (for I knew very few people) I risked taking him to the back door of the Palladium where we were allowed a reduced price to see the entertainers who came over from America. I remember Jack Benny for his meticulous timing, with prolonged pauses, though it came as a shock when I photographed him ten years later and found him pleasant but dull. As for sex with the guardsman, there was little more than mutual fumbling, but even that was exciting then.

Another time, stopped by two kilted soldiers in Hyde Park who wanted to find a lavatory, I led them to Beauchamp Place a mile away, for the thrill of seeing them lift their kilts, after which they left, looking puzzled. The element of danger was an integral element in the pursuit of strangers.

At a concert in the Albert Hall, where I went regularly with my grandmother, I was picked up by Desmond Stewart. As we were leaving, our eyes met and he managed to initiate a conversation, arranging a further meeting with the skill of long experience.

Is there a Mr or Miss Right? The possibility fascinated me for years and made me too selective, failing to recognize that the right person may have been there beside me. Desmond was not Mr Right: I had doubts from the start. But I turned up to see him as arranged and continued to do so, flattered that he should pay me attention, though I found his feline slyness off-putting.

Several years older than me, he had just been expelled from Oxford and wrote poetry, becoming a minor novelist and Egyptologist. He was too clever for me. Also, he was a Fascist and an admirer of Oswald Mosley, which I found distressing then. Desmond revelled in being queer, which made me uneasy, as if I was being initiated into a brotherhood which I did not fully understand. His parents and a brother lived in Ealing, nice ordinary people by contrast, who seemed relieved when I was produced as the latest 'friend'. His father was a psychiatrist in a large mental hospital, and was understanding.

I was ripe for sexual initiation, but apart from the inevitable mutual fumbling, Desmond seemed more interested in showing me how to mix a face-pack from oatmeal. We went to Brighton for the proverbial weekend while I was working for the Central Press, convinced that Guy L'Estrange could sense my guilty secret when I returned, and collaborated on a play which we actually finished, deeply profound and humourless, reeking of Ibsen. Apart from Desmond's natural deviousness, the fault lay with me. I had yet to learn what sex and drink were about, and when he took me to my first 'queer' pub, I was not ready for it. I was none too sure that I was queer, and reading constant reports in the newspapers of men arrested for homosexual offences did nothing to help me to resolve the question. I was unaware that it was my sexual innocence which was abnormal.

Desmond sent me a tiny book of Shakespeare's sonnets with his own poem on the flyleaf dedicated to 'D.N.F.: New Year's Day 1945', which meant I was eighteen years old.

> I love you more than nights and more than days.
> The greedy race of men who value gold
> I do despise as villains. And I hold
> One hour with you more valuably weighs
> The scales of life, than all the diamonds in
> The guarded storehouse of an emperor.
> Our love that lacks all selfishness and sin
> Is built on beauty; and will endure
> When every idol in which nations trust
> Has crumbled to a paltry heap of dust.

He was a lousy poet. In my naïvety, I showed this to my father, who looked alarmed.

Desmond may not have been Mr Right, but he had poor material to work with. I appeared so certain on the outside yet I was raw within. Even the American army could not change that. When I enlisted I received strange looks as I walked down Piccadilly in my GI uniform with my mother. American servicemen with English girls were familiar, but she looked old enough to be . . . my mother. Seeing some GIs whistling and shouting at two girls they were trying to pick up, regardless of the disapproval of the passers-by, I tugged at my mother to draw her attention, like a four-year-old. Presumably she assumed that one grows up on one's own accord, but even she seemed startled by such childishness. I wonder if it ever crossed her mind, or my father's, that I was in earnest when I asked for help.

At my first monthly 'short arm' inspection at Bovingdon, the reason for which I scarcely understood, I dropped my trousers and rolled back my foreskin to reveal a quantity of dried-up semen. The doctor frowned and mumbled something about the need for cleanliness after sex. He asked the man next in line if he was a friend of mine and told him to give me advice, but he was too embarrassed apart from a terse 'Oughta wash it.'

At night I listened in the dormitory as other GIs spoke about sex and being picked up by English men, and the peculiarity of British soldiers wearing kilts. They were less confused than me, but not much less. In London, when I was waiting to visit an elderly cousin in a mews flat, several men tried to pick me up, though I did not fully understand why. The closest I came to a confession was my infatuation with a stubby, snub-nosed little GI who worked in the same office at Wiesbaden, and I annoyed him so much that he smacked me in the mouth. Yet, and this puzzled me, there was another dual-national GI, a Welshman, at the base who flaunted his effeminacy openly yet was accepted because he told everyone he had been molested by an uncle when he was a boy. This won him sympathy from all except me, for I knew better, tempted to point out, 'That's *his* story!' He knew that I knew, but he was cunning. It was always a mixed blessing that I did not look what I was.

One day Lockhart and I were sent to deliver some documents to the army hospital where I passed a solitary wing with men staring at me from behind bars as if in cages. Asking who they were, I was told 'faggots' who had been found out and were awaiting trial or their army discharge. I had an uncomfortable feeling that I should join them, but my pretence was so convincing that an officer and an American civilian who were driving to Paris on a weekend furlough asked me to go with them. Visiting a brothel on our first night, I watched as the young officer fucked one of the prostitutes while the other girls caressed his back to urge him on. The girls called me 'baby' and when I refused to join in, they were tactful enough to react with a brief flutter of disappointment.

I returned to Paris at the end of my service with my $100 bonus and Henry, a GI who worked as a photographer for *Weekend*. I liked him, but I concealed my feelings. Now I wonder about him, for we went to the Carousel where men dressed as women and to a small bar where another female impersonator darted about serving drinks – a bar I looked for afterwards but could never find. Just after the war this sort of entertainment was rare enough to be bizarre.

I slept with Henry twice: the first time in Paris when the hotel cat used my bed as a lavatory and I had to share with him. When he came to Devon later that summer we tried to swim around Baggy

Point, but were cut off by the tide and sudden rising swell. As darkness fell with no sign of us, my father alerted the coastguards, who fired rockets with ropes which we tied around us, fingers stiff with cold. As we were about to be hoisted up the cliff-face, the Clovelly lifeboat charged in, throwing us further ropes, so we were caught in a tug of war until we were hauled on board the lifeboat and brought to the quay at Clovelly where the Red Lion Hotel managed to find us a room for the rest of the night.

'Do you mind sharing?'

'Not in the least,' I replied. We pressed against each other because we were freezing. Nothing happened on either occasion, and my father had to reward the lifeboat crew with the donation of a silver cup which still bears his name. 'Worst night's work I ever did,' growled one of the men, years later.

❦

Like most parents, mine found it difficult to let go, even though they were unlike most parents in other ways. A close college friend pointed out that they might have been the most worldly people in the world but were hopeless when it came to bringing up a child. He had seen the result.

Possibly they were sorry for leaving me so often, compensating with an intense possessiveness when they wanted me with them. The end of my army service was a moment when I needed to break free but they failed to understand this, asking me to spend a final leave in North Devon though I would be arriving there for good in a few weeks' time. Wisely, I had gone to Paris instead.

I felt I was starting afresh. Everything lay ahead, and the diversity of my life had turned me into a noddy-head-in-air, riding happily through life oblivious to the harsh reality around me. After a friend met Greta Garbo, he told me she was 'armour-plated by her stupidity'. Perhaps I was armoured by my naïvety.

I am touched to realize how much I had going for me then, with all the confidence that sees no failure. I was working on the first of several novels: 'I am very anxious on my return to England to have two or three months' grace in which to finish *Wretched Boy* – solely for the purpose of seeing what I am capable of.' Presumably I was disillusioned for it was never finished. *Time & Tide* published my first article while I was still at Wellington, so journalism was no problem;

I already had experience with the Central Press and *Stars & Stripes*. I intended to become a film director, writing to my mother: 'Orson Welles is filming *Macbeth*. The one man in the world who could do it better than I! I am heartbroken.' I decided to become a playwright: Harvard had abandoned their drama course, so I wrote to Yale instead to apply for their course, run by Marc Connelly.

This was more than confidence, it was arrogance. But I wrote to Yale because I was preparing to go to university under the GI Bill of Rights which would send me anywhere in the world. Soon the drama course was forgotten, and I went to Cambridge University instead, armed with letters of reference from the Dean of Westminster and Somerset Maugham – the one to take the curse off the other. I doubt if any government has ever been so generous to enlisted men after their discharge. I received a monthly living grant of $90, and $500 for tuition. This covered my basic expenses and my father contributed the rest. It was ample reward for nineteen months in the American army and I felt treacherous when my dual nationality came to an end at the age of twenty-one and I chose to be British. I am sorry I did not collect my two decorations, token though they were: the Victory Medal and the Occupation Medal. Wearing them on special occasions might have annoyed people as well as baffled them.

I learned nothing at Pembroke College. Academically it was a waste of time. I do not remember the name of my tutor, who did not inspire a single idea. As for the Senior Tutor, this elongated man was so shy that he glided silently around the walls like Count Dracula, so we seldom came into contact even in the un-dead hours of the night. Many years later he spotted an article of mine and wrote me a fan letter. It was hard to know if he had reached his dotage – he seemed in it even then – but I replied subserviently and untruthfully that I was glad to hear from him.

The only intellectual stimulus, which I needed badly, came from the philosopher Bertrand Russell, who gave occasional lectures in a high, reedy voice complaining that the Ten Commandments told you what you should *not* do, entirely the wrong approach. This was pleasingly heretical and helped to stretch the mind, unlike my tutorials which failed so dismally.

The academic shortcomings did not matter a jot. I was in my element and found Pembroke sympathetic. A number of the under-graduates had returned from the war, some as old as twenty-nine, and studied vigorously for the degrees which meant so much to their future. The degree meant little to me and I realized at once that the whole point of university was to squander every precious second to my advantage. Wasting time is one of the hardest things to do well, and where better than Oxford or Cambridge at the age of twenty-one? Hours were spent in pointless arguments at the Copper Kettle, though we rarely spoke of politics or sex, curiously indifferent to both.

I relished my new independence. Cambridge was the civilized antidote to the American army and it brought renewed friendship with Anthony West, my oldest friend since the early days of Abinger. At Butternuts on Lake Geneva I had amused myself in my attic by laying-out the dummy of a magazine which I called 'Panorama'. At Ashbury in Ottawa, Tony West and I produced a news-sheet with the same name, oozing with patriotism, sentimentality and self-importance. At Wellington we were forbidden to try anything of the sort. At Cambridge we came into our own with: *Panorama – The Cambridge Magazine*, a subtitle quickly changed to *The Young Man's Magazine* as our ideas took flight.

An outstanding printer, Tony should have run the Oxford University Press in later years, but he lacked the spur of ambition and was too nice a man to fight for a position that was rightly his. He acted as *Panorama*'s publisher and I was the editor, taking the photographs, writing editorials, short stories and features. We made a good team, one of those close friendships which are hard to explain except that we made each other laugh.

The young bloods at Cambridge were the sporting Blues, but sport was not for me and *Panorama* became my cachet instead, allowing me that vital touch of harmless conceit. From the start it was more than a university magazine, though we discovered talent lurking in the other colleges: Peter and Tony Shaffer, identical twins until you saw them together, who were asked to write on their favourite subject and chose themselves; Julian Slade, soon to become composer of *Salad Days*; and Norman St John Stevas, then the lively President of the Union, later the chairman of the Conservative Party, and finally the fatuous Lord St John of Fawsley, who wrote: 'Public life in all its forms has always fascinated me . . . at heart an individualist and even an anarchist, destined to live in an age of woolly thinking and compromise, the future offers gales and storms and of quiet havens but a few.' *Panorama* found itself when we turned our sights on Oxford: Gavin

Lambert became our film critic and Lindsay Anderson wrote on films, holding strong opinions which I was not encouraged to contradict.

Our luckiest coup was the recruitment of Kenneth Tynan as our dramatic critic; Ken was brilliant, like the strutting 'Peacock' of his middle name. At the age of only twenty-three, these vaulting years were his peak. His later criticisms may have become more profound, but he rarely surpassed his ability to convey an actor in a few words, as he managed to do in *Panorama*, even if those words were richly laced with malice. He evoked Ralph Richardson bluffing his way through a mediocre play 'as bewildered as a glass eye'; referred to 'Olivier of the accusing nostrils and short-winded, neighing valour'; said that Peter Ustinov 'does too much too well'; described Peter Brook as 'little and dapper – like something out of Kenneth Grahame, a quiet miniature thug, not pretty but glittering'; and acclaimed the young Richard Burton as 'the best of our youth . . . he is a still pool, running fathoms deep; at twenty-five he can make silence garrulous.'

In a profile of Noël Coward, Tynan dared a bravura which no one else would have attempted and few magazines would have published:

> Benign, yet flustered as a cardinal might be at some particularly dismaying tribal rite . . . Taut facially, as an appalled monolith; gracious, socially, as a royal bastard; tart vocally, as a hollowed lemon – so he appeared for us at the Café de Paris . . . Coward's fastidiousness, outrageously enough, is that of a first-rate male impersonator . . . I do not know if he has false teeth but, if pressed, I would plump for the affirmative.

Meeting him in New York later, Coward wagged a reproving finger: '*You* came out of it terribly well.'

Ken's passion for the theatre was devoid of pretentiousness – a rarity indeed. He was one of the first to spot Tommy Cooper as 'the funniest man in London' (*Panorama*, 1951) and was quick to notice the androgyny shared by so many comedians from Chaplin to Sid Field, not exactly 'camp' but dainty.

Gavin and Lindsay held a court attended by such admirers as Jill Bennett and Karel Reisz, but Ken was too dangerous and he had no time for them, preferring a more high-powered coterie of his own. I managed to straddle both camps. I was fond of Ken but knew he was a shit after I told him of my plan to write a profile of the Palladium Theatre, not just the star for once but the stage-door keeper, the usherettes, the electricians and so on. I wrote to the press officer a few days later and when I had no reply I phoned him up. 'This is very odd,' he explained after an embarrassed silence, 'but we've had someone here for the last week doing exactly what you've suggested.'

In the chill that followed, I asked, 'Are his initials KT?' They were, but when I confronted Ken he laughed it away, though he did have the grace to blush. 'If Freud hadn't lived, you could challenge me to a duel. But he has so I put it d-d-down to my subconscious!' He laughed shrilly with a wave of the arms as a shield for his stammer. It was easy to forgive him, especially as I had the satisfaction of rejecting his profile of the Palladium after it had been returned by various other magazines – perhaps it was not such a brilliant idea in the first place.

Though this made me wary, Ken was the making of *Panorama*. The magazine was useful for him, too, as a stepping-stone in his climb to fame which was determined and required courage.

In spite of Ken's stammer, Alec Guinness asked him to take the part of the Player King in his production of *Hamlet* – clever casting, though Ken's appearance suggested that he was born to play the skull. Writing of Robert Helpmann, he said he had the appalled look of someone who had just noticed an owl on his shoulder, a look that Ken shared himself, retaining the flamboyance which marked his entry to Magdalen College followed by a retinue of porters: 'Have a care with that trunk, my man. It is freighted with golden shirts.'

Despite the meticulousness of Guinness, the first night of *Hamlet* was one of those disasters which people chuckle about for years: full sunshine for the ghost; darkness for the court scene with Ken scarcely visible under a hat and plastic left ear. Curiously, he played the King as Chinese. Beverley Baxter in the *Evening Standard* wrote that he took no joy in hurting those with no defence, but Mr Ken Tynan would not get a hearing at a vicarage fête unless he was related to the vicar. Ken retaliated with a letter published on 22 May 1951, also in the *Standard*, under the heading BAXTER'S DREADFUL MAN HITS BACK, protesting that he was a good enough critic himself to know that his performance was not 'quite dreadful'. 'It is in fact only slightly less than mediocre. I do not actually exit through the scenery or wave at my friends in the audience.' Then he went for the jugular, pointing out that he was the dramatic critic of *Panorama*, a copy of which Baxter had received, which might have accounted for his grumpiness as it contained 'a gigantic pseudonymous attack on almost every prac-

tising critic' including Baxter who was denounced as 'one of the awful
people one overhears in the interval, additionally sinister because one
knows the commonplaces they utter will appear in print.' Baxter's
column was 'crammed with busybodying patter, exclamatory little
asides of prejudice, mood and fogged generalizations.' Ken concluded
that Baxter would assume that he was the author. In fact it was Gavin
Lambert, at his most waspish. Baxter replied petulantly that 'previous
to his performance (Ken Tynan as the Player King) I had never heard
of him – and after that performance I doubt whether as an actor I
shall ever hear of him again.'

He heard of him soon enough. As a fellow-Canadian, Baxter was
a close friend of Lord Beaverbrook who owned the *Standard*, but he
was sacked a few months later. Tynan got his job. Then he went too
far in warning the editor not to publish letters criticizing him, a bit
cool in the circumstances, and was sacked in his turn with Beaverbrook
complaining to his successor Milton Shulman, another Canadian, 'We
can't have a fellow who threatens to sue his own paper for libel.' Ken
had the advantage of independence, apart from his blazing talent; he
had money of his own so he did not rely on salary.

With a special rate for undergraduates, I had joined the Savile Club,
one of London's male preserves where few of the members spoke to
me for they were long established in their own careers. Ivor Brown,
the distinguished theatre critic of the *Observer*, had sent me a generous
note after *Panorama*'s first issue: 'Congratulations on your unusual and
outstanding publication. University journalism has never, I suppose,
had anything so handsomely produced.' He was friendly to me at the
Savile and if he was offended by Gavin Lambert's essay 'The Monstrous
Regiment of Critics', he did not hold it against me, though the description of himself had the cruelty of youth: 'The sergeant major who
got his stripes many years ago, and since that time has seen long and
dishonourable service.' This was libellous: happily, as an undergraduate
publication we were virtually immune. The attack continued:
'Brown's style is famous for its puns. He has brought this entertaining
pastime to a very low ebb. The kindest thing would be to assume
that he is, in fact, just tired and due for a pension, but he seems
determined to die with his boots on.'

Bored by my isolation at the end of the long communal table where
I was ignored like the dormouse at the Mad Hatter's tea-party, I
invited Ken to lunch at the Savile at a corner table, taking a few

photographs afterwards at the foot of the club's elegant staircase. The pair of us might have dropped our trousers. I was summoned to appear before the committee and told it was against the rules to take a photograph inside the club, but I sensed that their disapproval was out of proportion. Ivor Brown took me aside with some kindly advice: 'I am sorry to say this, but that, ahem, guest is not the sort you should bring here.'

I was mystified. Ken wore a splendid mauve suit with fetching lavender shoes which would not get a second glance today, but the effect on the ancient members was sensational. I was used to Ken's bizarre appearance, but they misinterpreted it as effeminate. I was so fed up that I resigned from the Savile, still puzzled by the fuss I had caused. A few years later, Ken replaced Ivor Brown on the *Observer* to become the most exciting drama critic since James Agate.

Though I remained wary, I was fond of Ken and his American wife Elaine Dundy, seeing them constantly. Sometimes they practised bull-fighting in the garden below their Bayswater flat, with Elaine as the charging bull while Ken, complete with cape, pirouetted in emulation of the matadors he adored. Foolishly, I did not pursue it when he suggested going to the fiesta in Pamplona, where I would take the photographs to illustrate his text.

One evening as we sat down to dinner in the Caprice, a message was brought to him and he paled, explaining that he had to leave because Elaine had discovered some love letters from another woman. His second wife, Kathleen, gave a different version. 'In his study he kept a small blue metal box of pornography. His wife came upon it when he was out (presumably with me). She found photographs of "schoolgirls" about to be spanked by disembodied male hands, and the stuff evidently shocked her.'

By an extraordinary coincidence, Ken took Elaine on a second honeymoon to Rome where they looked up a mutual friend who had just received my account of Ken's departure from the Caprice, which he read aloud. As this was far from the truth, the recriminations started again though I was unaware of this until Elaine revealed it later. Lindsay Anderson remarked, 'It shows how little they think of you that they forgave you.'

I remember Ken's embarrassment when I saw him in Soho with a tough young man who was known for flagellation, yet he was so blatantly heterosexual that I felt ashamed of my homosexuality. When

I told him of a song composed by Mike Mackenzie in the Colony Room called 'Strange Love', he spluttered, 'Christ, all about queers?' It was not, but it hurt me that he should be so contemptuous. Ironically, when he auditioned for the Windmill Theatre he was rejected by Vivian Van Damm: 'You're much too queer for our audience.' Ivor Brown made the same mistake.

At our last lunch, I was secure enough to ask if he had ever had a homosexual experience. 'I remember about the age of thirteen comparing our bodies with another little boy at school, but that was the closest I ever got. In a way I suppose it is a limitation in me that the whole field is unexplored territory. You cannot help being interested in it since so many of one's friends are, especially in show business where I have spent most of my life, so of course it interests me, but I have always felt like a blind man surveying the homosexual territory. I don't understand the signposts or where they may lead, because they don't lead in directions that excite me.'

Conversely, his preoccupation with sex overwhelmed him: 'Am I obsessed by sex?' he asked me. 'I have had my keenest joys from sex, anticipation and fulfilment thereof. Certainly if I had to relive five minutes of my life before dying, they would be minutes of sexual happiness.' Recalling him now, I remember the pleasure when I said something which tickled him and his face lit up and his whole body shivered with enjoyment. Yet there was a moment of bitterness: 'People think I am enjoying myself too much,' he complained. 'It was never my aim to run a National Theatre and I think I paid my debt to society by assisting Olivier for ten years, but that gets forgotten because I did one revue, *Oh! Calcutta!*, which had an erotic purpose, and used a sentence on television which included the word "fuck" – an episode which must have lasted all of ten seconds of my lifetime.'

I never saw him again after he went to America, where he died horribly and far too young from the smoking which he was unable to control and which led to emphysema. Never a natural invalid, I was told that he went out raging.

❖

Panorama was good to me too. Unaware how flattered people are by the attention of the young, I took our successes as a matter of course. The magazine paid its way from our sales and the advertisements which Tony West and I gleaned in the vacations, spending hours in the waiting-rooms of advertising agencies, emerging overjoyed when we struck lucky with Brylcreem or Cooper's Oxford Marmalade.

I was invincible. I phoned Hoagy Carmichael at the Savoy to ask if I could photograph him in his suite, which boasted a grand piano, as he rehearsed his forthcoming appearance at the Prince of Wales Theatre. He played one of his lesser-known songs, 'Memphis in June', and his team of advisers warned him that it was so slow it would kill the atmosphere. When he asked for my advice, I urged him to keep it in. As soon as he played it on the opening night the momentum died. 'Pleased with yourself?' hissed one of the entourage to me as he ran down the aisle to fabricate applause.

Noticing a distinguished-looking American in the interval of a play, I asked if I could photograph him the next day. 'Sure,' he agreed, 'why don't you come to Claridges at ten in the morning.'

'And who do I ask for, sir?'

He looked at me astounded: 'Just ask for John Huston, and that will be fine, just fine.' I turned up punctually and he treated me as if I were doing him the favour – a real gent.

I went to Paris with a college friend during the summer vacation in 1950. We had little money, but my simple bedroom with a large brass bedstead, a view over the market below, and breakfast served with bitter black coffee, warm croissants and jam, was sheer luxury. I called at the offices of *Elle* magazine in the hope of selling the photographs of a French girl at Cambridge, one of the few girls I knew there, my disinterest in her sexually adding to her disillusionment with English boys: 'L'étudiant anglais, timide, ne regarde jamais en face la gentille fille qui passe dans la rue . . .'

The editor, Hélène Lazareff, examined the shots of the girl, who was attractive, and bought them on the spot, promising to send the fee to England on publication. When she saw my expression, she paused. 'I think you would like to be paid now, yes?' and rang the accounts department. That money transformed my visit, for I spent the evening with Orson Welles and he was living on credit. I could understand why Ken Tynan adored Welles, for he had a booming relish for life and such an infectious laugh that people turned round, smiling as they listened even if they did not understand. The only man who came near him as a raconteur was my father, with the same gusto and such delight in their stories that they had to break off in the middle because they were so convulsed. Neither told jokes, the last refuge of the humourless.

The start of our meeting was discouraging – even Welles could not be on top of the world all the time.

'Look here, I've had enough,' he snapped as I entered his dressing-room at the Edouard VII Theatre, where a flashlight photographer hovered nervously. Welles was stripped to the waist, more ominous than I expected. 'It's ridiculous,' he continued. 'I can't have people coming in like this before the show. Why don't they stop them at the door?' Confronting the nervous photographer, he said, 'I'm terribly sorry, old man, but has your paper made an appointment?'

'I'm from Italy.'

'Italy?' Welles looked even more distraught. 'I can't do it, I've got to go on in a minute. Yes?' he turned to me and I apologized, explaining I had sent him a letter. He remembered it and asked me to come back after the show.

'What time does it end?' I asked. Almost in a frenzy by now, he shouted, 'I don't know, just after the show, after the show.' This was before the evening performance of his two one-act plays *The Unthinkable Lobster* and *Time Runs*. I found him afterwards, a formidable, bear-like figure in black tights and dark blue dinner-jacket with a towel wrapped around his neck, submitting to the flattery of a woman who was telling him that she was the only person she knew who liked the first play better than the second. 'That's the way it is,' said Welles in a sing-song voice and a shrug of resignation, 'some people enjoy the first play the most, others prefer the second. Nobody enjoys them both. May I say what a pleasure it has been seeing you,' and steered the woman out.

As people drifted in, Welles went behind a screen, reappearing in his underwear with a glass of champagne. Hilton Edwards, a member of the cast, asked me what I thought of the plays, and there was an awkward silence when I admitted I had not seen them, which seems inexplicably rude and stupid now. I added that I had seen his film of *Macbeth*.

'Oh, that's no use to us,' said Welles. 'The returns go to the States where the studio takes its share and my percentage is taxed.'

'Are you handling all your own finances, Mr Welles?'

He shook with silent laughter. 'Do you hear that, Hilton? What a question! Oh yes, I am! Since the backers withdrew from *Othello*, I've continued by myself, hocking and borrowing everything I can lay my hands on. I'm the first man since D. W. Griffith who had financed a film. Everything I've got is in that film.' He described how difficult it had been to film in Italy, where the sound is normally dubbed on later, so the technicians are apt to chatter while the cameras are turning. Filming one tricky scene on a hot day in a small room, some of the technicians chattered while the others warned them 'Silencio, silencio' in deafening whispers until Welles threatened to scrap the scene and dismiss them all. 'There was genuine dismay! For half an hour you could have heard a pin drop, and then came the agonized cry from the cameraman – "One cannot go on living like this!' as he sank his head in his hands and sobbed. But I'd shot just enough in that one hour of grace.' Orson laughed uproariously as if he had just been told this story by someone else. While he was aiming for realism in *Othello*, combining historical accuracy with Shakespearian intention, he said he had tried to achieve the opposite with *Macbeth*. 'As I see it, Christianity has just come to earth. It's a religious struggle – that's why I've put in the character of a priest, which makes people say I've changed the play though all his lines are Shakespearian. The trouble is that people have too fixed ideas on how to portray every academic detail.'

He seemed impervious to the bad reviews. 'I don't know if a film I've made is good or bad. I just experiment while I'm making it. I open the paper and see that *Macbeth* is the greatest film ever made; others say I've murdered Shakespeare. If I believed all the successes I've apparently had, I would be unbearably conceited. If I believed all the failures, I would have killed myself sixteen years ago.'

By now his dressing-room was filled with hangers-on and Welles broke off as Eartha Kitt, then a twenty-two-year-old blues singer he had discovered and cast as Helen of Troy, came in to say goodnight. She kissed him neatly on the brow and Hilton Edwards kissed her ceremoniously on the hand.

'Chivalry is not dead', Welles declared. He had finished scraping his beard with a razor but no soap, and was now sprinkling himself with toilet water which he handed to Hilton Edwards who passed it to me. Finally, fully dressed, he led me through the empty theatre to the rue Madeleine. 'This is the moment I like best in the whole day.' We sat down at a café, where Welles ordered a round of lager which I paid for, and as we talked about films I understood why actors were prepared to follow him to faraway locations with no certainty of a fee or even a film at the end of it. His enthusiasm was undiminished by the complications, political and financial, of making films independently. Though he wanted to work for Carol Reed, who had directed him in *The Third Man*, again – 'Who wouldn't?' – he had no wish to produce in England and he was 'scared stiff' of facing English audiences. When I suggested that he might break new ground in film-making over the next few years as he had done with *Citizen Kane*, he shied away. 'I did nothing new in *Citizen Kane*. There's nothing I've done that D. W. Griffith didn't do.' The idea seemed to shock him, and when I made the crass mistake of referring to the cinema as an 'art form' he exclaimed: 'I am guilty of every sin except talk about the *art* of the cinema. Absolve me of that!' More booming laughter.

It was thrilling for me at the age of twenty-one to discuss films with the greatest film-maker of them all. Orson Welles showed me the same courtesy as John Huston, listening enthusiastically to my ideas as if I had been de Sica, whose 'lyric' style had impressed him in *Bicycle Thieves* – 'and that's as close as I'll get to the art form!'

He wanted to make a film about sex: 'When you come to think of it there are few films actually on sex, they're usually about sexy people. This will be on obsessive love.' There have been plenty of those since then.

I mentioned my idea of a murdered man whose life was recalled by his wife, mother, children, and enemies, so differently he could be played by a different actor each time. I realize now that Welles had virtually done just that with *Citizen Kane*. He talked of another project, a film on vampires, and when I told him that Bram Stoker was my great-uncle, he fell dramatically to his knees on the Parisian sidewalk.

'My God! To think I'd meet a relative of Stoker. Let me shake your hand. I met Stoker when I came to Dublin and he told me that he had written a play about a vampire especially for Henry Irving who threw the manuscript away, calling it "Dreadful"! But do you know,' Welles's voice deepened as he leant forward, 'Stoker took his revenge. He turned the play into a novel called *Dracula*, and if you read the description of the Count you will find it *identical* to Irving!' More eruptions of laughter.

I have learnt since then that Irving came into the Lyceum Theatre one morning when Stoker and a few friends were giving a read-through of *Dracula* in a dramatized form to protect the copyright from being pirated. Irving listened, bemused, and asked an assistant what was going on. Told it was Stoker's new novel, he declaimed '*Dreadful!*' in a booming stage whisper which reverberated around the theatre, wounding Stoker deeply.

Otherwise, Orson's story had two flaws: unlike Irving, Dracula had a white moustache. More inconveniently, Stoker died three years before Welles was born.

He did not mention that *Dracula* was the first production of his Mercury Theater on Air (11 July 1938), when he played the Count in his own adaptation. I doubt if modesty prevented him from telling me this – his mind was moving so quickly he scarcely paused for breath. By now his lilting voice and explosive laughter were attracting attention. An Englishwoman wanted the 'honour of shaking hands', while two American women asked for his autograph, exclaiming, 'My, I wish I could write my name as quickly as you do!' Welles's attention was distracted as he saw an English actor heading our way – 'About as cute as an unopened pimple' – and made a dash to the lavatory inside to avoid him.

On his return I mentioned Alexander Woollcott, knowing they had been close friends. '*The Man Who Came to Dinner* was *not* entirely based on Alex,' he protested. 'That part where he's so rude to his nurse, that wasn't Alex, that was me when I had jaundice. That scene when he tries to wreck his secretary's life, that was *me*!'

By now it was one o'clock in the morning and the bill consumed most of the money from *Elle* and was worth every franc.

The next evening I photographed Welles outside the theatre, before the show. The lovely carefree mood was gone, the responsibilities of the actor-manager reasserted themselves as he stood there besieged by members of the cast with trivial questions about the evening performance, and more from those he paid to deal with such problems. He looked as targeted as Moby Dick, but submitted patiently as I photographed him.

'Thank you, young Dracula!' he boomed when the session was over, and disappeared into the theatre with hangers-on in his wake.

◆

One morning in the Christmas vacation of 1951 I called at the Cavendish Hotel in Jermyn Street to ask for Tennessee Williams, who was staying there, and was shown upstairs to his bedroom. Tennessee was in London for the rehearsals of a new play, *Summer and Smoke*, accompanied by a short, youngish man who glared as he was introduced as the secretary, which I had no reason to disbelieve. Unlike the volcanic Welles, Tennessee Williams was languorous, opaque, with a Southern sweet-potato drawl, but he received me with equal kindness and no astonishment when I explained that I wanted to publish one of his short stories in *Panorama*. It is hard to understand why he, Huston and Welles bothered with me, unless it was the short-lived flowering of the *jeunesse dorée* of which I was blissfully unaware.

Tenn, as he asked me to call him, produced two short stories typed on yellow paper with a poem, 'Orpheus Descending'. When I paid him a larger fee than usual, counting out the £10 in single pound notes, he looked out of the window, his shoulders heaving slightly with silent laughter as I realize now. Then he turned round to accept the notes with a beatific smile. 'Thank you so much. It is so well-com to be paid in cash.' He made me feel ten feet tall as I took the two stories. We went downstairs, where he introduced me to the legendary but aged Rosa Lewis, who owned the Cavendish, allegedly given her by Edward VII for 'services rendered'. Then we took a taxi to the Lyric Theatre, Hammersmith, to attend the final rehearsal where his presence sent the leading actress into a nose-dive of terror. On the drive back to Jermyn Street, Tenn asked me what I thought. I had seen *The Glass Menagerie* at the Haymarket with Helen Hayes, and *A Streetcar Named Desire* with Vivien Leigh whom I interviewed for *Panorama* in her dressing-room, watched by a beady-eyed Olivier dressed in an unbecoming teddy-bear overcoat. I had too much respect to lie to Tennessee Williams, and no tact.

'I like the play,' I assured him, 'but I think she's wrong.'

'Oh God,' he groaned, 'I wish you hadn't said that, so do I.'

When I read the short stories I was shocked. Both have become famous since, but the climate was colder then. The first concerned an old sharecropper in the Deep South who buys a mail-order bride and sends his son into town to collect her. Suffering from a seizure of anticipation, he writhes in his bed, listening to the girl and his strapping son hard at it in the room below. It seemed that every other word was 'fuck'. Shaken, I hid the yellow pages so successfully that I never found them again.

The second story, 'Two on a Party', was probably his finest, though he spoilt it a few years later when he expanded it. The story was perfect as it was, describing the friendship of an ageing 'lush' called Cora and Billy, a balding 'queen', who cruise the New York water-front together. Tennessee Williams never showed such tenderness again and I was happy to publish it in the sixth issue of *Panorama*, with a zig-zag of my black and white portraits – Tynan; Dali; Orson Welles and Tennessee Williams – on a bright yellow cover. It looked splendid.

All hell broke loose. The main attack came from a totally unexpected source: the *Bookseller*, the reputable mouthpiece of the book trade:

> To an unsympathetic reader it might very well appear to be a coolly deliberate exercise in pornography. Presumably the publishers and printers measured their responsibility before publishing such a piece in a paper specially designed for young people, and are prepared to meet any consequences of that decision. A possible charge of corrupting the young is no laughing matter.

A charge of corrupting the young? I squealed with dismay and turned to the story again to discover if something had escaped me. It seemed inoffensive, though one passage puzzled me – their pursuit of three nice Norwegian sailors. Describing Billy's good looks, Tennessee wrote that it was unfortunate that his pink skin 'showed through the silky thin yellow hair on the crown of his head where baldness, so fiercely but impotently resisted, was now becoming a fact that he couldn't disown. Of course the crown of the head doesn't show in the mirror unless you bow to your image in the glass but there is no denying that the top of a queen's head is a conspicuous area on certain occasions which are not unimportant.' What did that mean? I had no idea, though I felt it involved something I should have known about. I alerted W. H. Smith, which distributed a dozen copies of *Panorama*, and they told me not to worry. I should have exploited the minor scandal, milked the publicity for all it was worth. Instead, I was dismayed.

We had found the right mix of photographs, gossip, humour and serious articles, criticism and short stories, inspired by *Weekend* but then unknown in England. *Panorama* had gained a sufficient reputation for it to be launched as a national magazine, and we received a tentative offer from a publisher, but Tony West and I agreed to call it a day: the sixth issue of *Panorama*, Spring 1952, containing 'Two on a Party' by Tennessee Williams, was the last. All my life I have backed away at the moment of success; whether from cowardice or the dread of being caught in a rut, it amounts to choosing to fail.

Having left Cambridge with a BA, I joined the oldest advertising agency, Pritchard Wood and Partners in Savile Row, as a trainee copywriter, completing the transformation with a visit to Lock's in St James's where I bought my first and last bowler hat. I had become respectable.

Inevitably, this condition did not last. In one issue of *Panorama* I satirized a young actor, Peter Reynolds, as he might have been seen by various magazines and such photographers as Douglas Glass and Cecil Beaton. *Vogue* was an easy target – 'An alliance of comfort and good looks; the "coke" has the crisp simplicity of a London crescent'. Another dig was aimed at the dreary socialist policy of *Picture Post*, edited by Ted Castle, the husband of Barbara. I snapped Peter Reynolds sitting forlornly on a bomb-site with a caption based on a true *Picture Post* story: 'THE BACKGROUND OF DECAY WHERE YOUTH HAS TO BLOSSOM: If you are twenty-five and poor, with little more than a sandwich in the rubble, what does the future hold?' Undergraduate humour, but it hit the bullseye. I had no idea that the policy which I had lampooned was losing circulation, and nothing worries the boardroom more than that. A purge led to the sacking of Castle and a conference where the managing director waved a copy of *Panorama* to justify his action – 'The young are laughing at us!' I was summoned to his office that afternoon.

This man was accustomed to power and wielded it like a horse-whip. At first I thought he was going to sue me as he demanded to know the truth – had I taken the photographs?

I had to confess.

'And how much are you earning?' he asked, his eyes glinting at the prospect of some tough bargaining. My moment had arrived, for they were hiring and firing editors in desperation and were looking for someone young to groom as Castle's successor.

Tragically, I told the truth: less than £3 or £4 a week as a trainee copywriter. His excitement subsided like a fallen soufflé. The very fact that I had not lied to him, nor held out for an exaggerated figure, was proof of my inability to edit.

'Very well,' he sighed. 'I think we can do better than that, but not in editorial.' This was how I joined *Picture Post* as a staff photographer, rather than the boy-genius editor they were hoping for. After just a few months, I handed in my notice at Pritchard Wood, where the office gave me a surprise party and a flask encased in pigskin, and I lent my bowler hat to a friend to wear to his mother's funeral. He lost it on the journey back, but I had no need of it by then. It was while I was waiting to join the staff of *Picture Post* that I drifted into Soho.

Six

Deserting in Soho

SOHO in the 1950s was like an island overlooked by the war. Outside, the world was grey. Rationing was still enforced and currency restrictions made it difficult to travel, except for the very rich who found the necessary loopholes. The Labour Party had won a glorious victory, but that did not make life jollier. England was suffering from a post-war malaise, and to be young in some provincial town must have been very hell. None of this concerned Soho, whose genius has always been the capacity to swing with the punches while remaining independent. Though it had no physical boundaries, Soho's square mile, divided by Wardour, Dean, Frith and Greek Streets and bordered by Shaftesbury Avenue to the south and Oxford Street to the north, was self-contained.

This was where I found myself at last. I had the luck to coincide with one of Soho's most exuberant moments, with a whiff of true Bohemia, as lively as Isherwood's Berlin or the Rive Gauche in Paris and Greenwich Village in their heyday. There were no rules to be broken because there were no rules and none of the conventions regarding money, age, class or sex which curbed the rest of Britain. Outside London, the posher counties reverberated with rumours of witch-hunts and the arrest of such distinguished young men as Lord Montagu and the writer Peter Wildeblood in a series of homosexual scandals, with Rupert Croft-Cooke leaving the country to settle in angry exile in Tangier. Even in London we walked a knife-edge, with the possibility of being raided, which gave life the frisson of danger which enhanced the Blitz. News would be whispered of friends who had been caught in compromising situations in public lavatories and were now in prison. The sentence if you were caught was five years. Not only did I hide Tennessee Williams's short story about the sharecropper in case of a visit from the police, even though it was blatantly heterosexual, but I destroyed the small photograph given to me by a sailor of himself in the ring as a boxing champion in the Royal Navy. As it was his only copy, he was annoyed, unable to understand what possessed me. Yet, and this was where Soho was so extraordinary, one's sexual pursuits were taken for granted inside that square mile, and nobody gave a damn. Few places would have accepted my gaucherie so charmingly, which made me feel less of a misfit.

In the early morning when blocks of ice dribbled on the steps of shuttered restaurants, residents collected their milk from the two women who ran the Welsh dairy and local children went to St Anne's school, Soho had the atmosphere of a village. Possibly it was the markets which caught my photographer's eye in the first place and kept me there, Rupert Street market the posher, south of Brewer Street, and Berwick Street to the north, noisier and cheaper, both of them food for my second Rolleiflex.

I would sit at a wrought-iron table in the Café Torino on the corner of Old Compton and Dean Streets, a typical family venture run by Mr and Mrs Minella and their fourteen-year-old son, nice people who liked to see their customers happy. This meant that they kept their prices absurdly low, allowed credit, and did not object when I lingered interminably over a small but genuine cup of coffee, nor when I bought paté down the street and ate it there, ordering nothing more than a slice of toast. It was hard to imagine how they stayed in business except that the place was crowded from eight-thirty in the morning to seven at night by a conglomeration of dark, emotional Italians who would burst into furious arguments, which signified nothing, and order the occasional risotto.

As I waited for the pubs to open, a new experience for me which was to be repeated for the rest of my life, I was sure that something wonderful might happen. Soho exuded optimism; it was a land of anticipation sometimes realized. A man in dark glasses tried the door of the York Minster, but it opened later than the rest at 11.30, so he paused on the pavement, tilting his face to the sun, missing the girl with the chalk-white face who walked past him barefoot.

Following him inside as the pub opened, I watched as he ordered his first drink, downed it, shivered, and sighed with heartfelt relief. 'That's better.' As the York Minster, better known as The French Pub, began to fill up, I was startled to hear friends asking each other if they needed to apologize for their behaviour on the night before, and I studied the man beside me who looked as if he had been saved from a shipwreck and fitted out in the cast-offs of the rescuing crew. The zip on his paint-stained trousers was broken, alarmingly, and blood had soaked into his polo-neck sweater from the ridge of congealed gore behind one ear. On top of this he wore a British officer's 'warm', a graveyard of wine stains and cigarette burns as if he had fallen asleep in it on countless nights, and he clasped this around him, arms akimbo, like a mandarin as he swaggered up with the gait of a midget wrestler. When he noticed me watching him, he gave a smile more like a grimace, revealing a row of discoloured teeth and a tongue the colour of aubergine. I was entranced.

'Good morning, Mr Deakin,' said Gaston Berlement, the 'patron', regarding him quizzically. 'I hope you're feeling better than you look?'

The man called Deakin shook his head from side to side grimly. 'I swallowed a raw egg in a glass of milk when I got up but it was halfway down before I realized it was bad.' Gaston flinched. 'You'd better have a Fernet-Branca.' Knowing it would not be on the house, Deakin made an exaggerated hunt through his empty pockets, opening and shutting his mouth like a ventriloquist's dummy. 'I'll have to chalk it up.'

Seizing my chance to become involved, I volunteered to pay, whereupon the stranger wandered off to join his friends who were more interesting. This was my introduction to John Deakin, who George Melly was to call 'Dan's evil genius, a vicious little drunk of such inventive malice and implacable bitchiness that it's surprising he didn't choke on his own venom.' Yet for fifteen years I found his irreverence irresistible, the funniest man I had known.

When Deakin returned and discovered that I was about to join *Picture Post* as a photographer he raised a gnawed finger to his lips, exclaiming: 'Really child, you interest me strangely. You happen to be talking to the star photographer for *Vogue*.' The boast was justified, though Cecil Beaton might have disputed the title. Graduating from fashion to portraits, Deakin worked in the *Vogue* studio around the corner in Shaftesbury Avenue. It was a convenient arrangement, for he placed his subjects in front of a black velvet backcloth, previously lit, shot them full-face and profile, like prison mug-shots, and returned as quickly as he could to The French Pub.

There were two odd things about this technique: firstly that he took some of the strongest portraits of the century; next, that he must have received a handsome salary yet played the role of 'the poor boy from Liverpool' with such dedication that I suspect he believed in his poverty. He certainly convinced me.

If he was racked by the threat of insecurity, this could have been due to a childhood that was hard though probably far removed from his account of the slums of Liverpool and the leper hospital opposite. That life was followed by a whirl of sophistication once he grew up and came to London. Not once did he refer to a family. Arrested for indecency in a nightclub which was raided soon after his arrival, his defence counsel was paid for by a new 'friend'. When the prosecution asked if he thought it odd to see men dancing together, Deakin retaliated, 'How could I possibly know how people in London behave?' He was acquitted.

He was kept for a time in considerable luxury by Arthur Jeffress, an American millionaire and art collector who took him to Hollywood where he was befriended by the famous lesbian Mercedes de Acosta, and then to Italy. Jeffress rented the Palladian Villa Rotonda, or so Deakin claimed, before he bought a palazzo on a Venetian canal, complete with his own gondolier who betrayed him years later, accusing Jeffress of moral turpitude. The Chief of Police seized this opportunity, for Jeffress had made sarcastic comments about his plump wife when they were bathing at the Lido. Ordered to leave Venice in a matter of days, Jeffress killed himself in Paris in 1963 on his way back to London. Having spent much of his life in pursuit of sailors, his will left everything to a naval welfare organization with the proviso that it all went to the ratings and not a cent to Wrens or officers. He bequeathed his collection of ninety-nine pictures to the Southampton Art Gallery.

I remember seeing Jeffress at Earl's Court during the Royal Tournament, where it was the tradition to pick up members of the field gun crew, ostensibly the toughest men in the navy. As these magnificent men passed tantalizingly out of reach Jeffress murmured, 'I call this the Royal torture.'

That was after the war when Jeffress seemed a sad and lonely man. Were they happy together in the thirties? Probably. Deakin with his Mickey Mouse grin was a born jester and could have made Jeffress laugh. Deakin had intuitive taste and an excellent eye, urging Jeffress to buy paintings by Soutine, which the American was too cautious to follow. Sexually they may well have been compatible, but that was a part of Deakin I never knew or wished to know, though I had to listen to countless tales of his rampant adventures. Both a catalyst and a chameleon, Deakin joined in the charade when Arthur Jeffress enacted the role of a country gentleman with a stately home. One afternoon they joined a neighbour's house party for tea on the lawn where Deakin, to his dismay, recognized one of the guests – the young barrister who had defended him after his arrest in London. As their dachshund scampered away, the man's wife called out, 'Deakin, Deakin, come back Deakin.'

'That's an interesting name for a little dog,' said Jeffress, on the alert.

'Yes, isn't it!' she smiled, and gestured towards her husband. 'Of course he's frightfully famous now as a QC, but when he was struggling his first case was defending some fearful little person in a queer scandal and he got him off. It was the first case he won so we've called Deakin after him, for that was the pansy's name.'

At that moment her husband caught Deakin's eye and knew where he had seen him last.

The affair between Deakin and Jeffress petered out during the war when Deakin was an official war photographer in the Mediterranean, though Jeffress continued his allowance, stopping it abruptly when they met again. I was astounded by his reply when I asked Jeffress what Deakin had been like when he was younger.

'When we searched the grounds after he'd gone,' said Jeffress with a sigh, 'we found bottles everywhere, in the cupboards, in the garden, in the pool. Simply everywhere. Poor little mite.'

The empty bottles did not surprise me in the least, but 'poor little mite' baffled me. Now Deakin demanded drinks as a royal right, and on the rare occasion when he was forced to buy one himself he examined the coins – 'What is this strange currency?' – biting them to see if they were genuine.

'Really, Deakin!' someone exclaimed. 'It's so long since I've seen you with money I thought you'd pay in sovereigns.'

Yet all the time he was paid by *Vogue*, presumably rather well. Though furiously proud of his work, he seemed utterly indifferent to his job, part of the compulsive self-destruction which, as I was to discover, prompted him to destroy everyone around him.

On that first encounter we were joined in The French Pub by a distinguished man with greyish hair and glasses who might have been a judge. He gave me a nervous but friendly smile and a curt nod of the head. Deakin ignored him.

'Hum,' said the stranger, 'I see you've met this silly little man. I hope he hasn't been upsetting you.' As he spoke his face seemed to swim out of focus, humming and hawing. He waved one hand while the other clutched some books, a device he used to conceal a gammy arm. Deakin turned on him with the viciousness of a bitch on heat snapping at an attentive, jovial labrador.

'Bejesus, you bore the hell out of me,' he snarled. Then, turning to me with the pained grimace that passed for a smile, he added in a stage whisper, 'I suppose I'll have to introduce you. This is David Archer. He's rather special.' Archer shook my hand courteously, dropping his books, with a hysterical laugh as he asked my name. When I told him, I was gratified that it meant something to Deakin, who had bought the last, infamous copy of *Panorama* with the Tennessee Williams story in a newsagent's in Charing Cross Road. Obsessed by the tiniest literary fame, this brought a glint of interest from Archer. 'Ah, me!' he murmured.

David Archer was a true eccentric because he had no idea he was one. He came from a respectable family in Wiltshire – his father was an army major. His mother worried about his morning dip in the Serpentine. 'One day,' she told Deakin on the telephone, 'I fear he'll just swim and swim.' 'That's all right, Mrs Archer,' Deakin assured her brusquely. 'As it's the Serpentine he'll come out the other side.' Archer invited Deakin to the family home to meet his parents and spend the weekend. Meeting Archer on Monday, I asked how everything had gone. 'Hm,' he muttered, 'I'm rather edgy about that. Cook had gone to great trouble but the nasty little man got drunk and failed to turn up.' He gave a long sigh. 'He was the first guest I've invited down for twenty-five years.' It was Archer who borrowed my bowler hat for his mother's funeral and lost it on the way back.

Gratified by my interest, Deakin invited me to see his photographs at Archer's spacious Bayswater flat overlooking the park. By now I had no illusions about the 'art' of photography, knowing how much a photographer depends on other people – the boys in the darkroom and a lay-out editor who can transform an indifferent photo into a masterpiece. There is no denying that Deakin was lucky in having the *Vogue* studio run by Tommy Hawkyard to back him up with the immense prints which gave the harsh contrast he demanded, exposing every pore and blemish, but as he laid his prints on the floor with the wistful anxiety of a carpet-seller in a Turkish bazaar, I was stunned by their impact. Frequently, they were shots to recoil from, making Cecil Beaton's portraiture seem insipid. The cruelty was deliberate. In a rare declaration in an unpublished manuscript belonging to Bruce Bernard, Deakin wrote: 'Being fatally drawn to the human race, what I want to do is to make a revelation about it. So my sitters turn into victims. But I would like to add that it is only those with a demon, however small and of whatever kind, whose faces lend themselves to be victimized at all. And the only complaints I have had from my victims have been from the bad ones, the vainies, the meanies.'

With my usual naïvety I could not understand why Archer should pay the rent until Deakin made a casual reference to the previous night when Archer fumbled in a chest of drawers.

'What are you doing?' Deakin demanded.

'I'm looking for my favourite whip,' Archer had explained.

'Oh, for God's sake!'

'You're not supposed to shout at me,' Archer protested, 'I'm supposed to shout at you.'

By now I realized that Deakin was a marvellous photographer. Sadly, the shots I admired the most, of the down and out *clochards* in Paris, have been lost, but enough of the rest has been salvaged to place him among the greatest, confirmed by the retrospective at the National Portrait Gallery in 1996.

I also grew to respect Archer. In his dotty way, he cared so passionately about books that they destroyed him in the end. With an uncanny instinct, for he seldom read more than half a book, he recognized the potential of talent and published many of our best poets before they became famous. In 1934 he printed *18 Poems* by Dylan Thomas, who was eighteen, selling them at three shillings and sixpence; they are collectors' items today. To celebrate the event, Archer gave a party and asked Dylan Thomas the following day if he had enjoyed it.

'I hear it was very good,' said Thomas stiffly, 'but you forgot to invite me.'

'Oh, silly me,' said Archer. I doubted this story, until I knew him better.

In the thirties he ran a bookshop in Parton Street, encouraging young writers by printing their work under the imprint of the Parton Press. George Barker wandered in one day and found a character 'lost out of both Wodehouse and Proust' on top of a ladder, who asked him, 'Be an angel – hand me a hammer' which he did though the man seemed likely to bang his finger. In due course Archer published Barker's *Thirty Preliminary Poems*, 1933; David Gascoyne's *Man's Life is Meat*, 1935; and Sydney Graham's *Cage Without Grievance* in 1942. His allegiance to his poets was absolute; once he kicked a critic who gave a bad review. Even Deakin was shocked.

'David, you can't go around kicking critics!'

'Hm, one does get rather fussed. Anyhow, it was only a *tiny* kick.'

Inevitably, Deakin and Archer were ejected from the Bayswater flat, but Archer was soon in the happiest state of all, anticipating the opening of his new bookshop in Soho. Determined on this renaissance, he raised the money by borrowing against his future inheritance.

Now that it was lunchtime The French Pub filled up as if with chattering actors arriving on stage for rehearsal. Insisting that I bought him a drink, Deakin identified the characters: 'That's Henrietta and her husband Michael,' pointing at a sleepy-eyed couple, Henrietta Moraes and Michael Law, a would-be film director, who looked as if they had just returned from a party. Henrietta joined us, gave me a quick, disappointed appraisal, and pitched her voice as if she wished to be overheard, pouncing on her words in case they got away.

'Really, it is *too* bad. Tony Hubbard took us to the Caprice last night which was marvellous but he *refused* to give us the money for the taxi home so we had to walk *all* the way. I ask you. Could you believe that anyone so rich could be so *mean*!'

'He invited me upstairs last week to watch him eat his lunch,' countered Deakin.

'But that's *marvellous*! It's just *so* typical.' She was wildly beautiful, tossing her hair away from her eyes, with a laugh that was more like a private giggle – someone called her The Lady Brett of Soho, after Lady Brett Ashley in Hemingway's *The Sun Also Rises*. I was mesmerized. Deakin beckoned me aside with one of his stage whispers: 'I think, kiddo, this is going to be one of the good days.' He nodded towards a man on the far side of the bar who came over to join us, walking with the careful tread of a first-class passenger venturing out on deck in a high sea. He was laughing already, clutching his collar as he asked, 'So what are you all having to drink?' in a curious accent I grew to know as mock-cockney, apparently fashionable in London society in the thirties. This was my introduction to Francis Bacon. I had no idea who he was; he was still virtually unknown though those in the small coterie of the art world regarded him with awe.

Francis was not in the least bit awesome that day and never became so, though he could be formidable. An enchanter (he preferred the term seducer), he had the gift of instant rapport, and realizing I was with Deakin he swung round with a radiant smile and such infectious laughter that I started laughing too. If Deakin was my evil genius for the next fifteen years, Francis was the life-enhancer over the next forty.

'Well,' he announced, 'the most *extraordinary* thing happened to me! I was in the Westminster Bank yesterday and this stranger came up and asked if I knew the way to Harrods. Well, really! He could have thought of a better excuse for picking me up than *that*.' (I noticed that everyone in Soho spoke in italics.) 'As a matter of fact he was rather good-looking in a fascist sort of way, sunburnt, told me he was a colonel in the South African army, and then he asked me to lunch. He took me to the Ritz.'

'The *Ritz*!' screamed Henrietta.

'Well, it really was too amazing. At the end of the meal he said he was going back to South Africa that evening and asked if I would like to come too. He'd pay all my expenses and do you know, I said yes . . .'

'You didn't!' said Deakin.

'I thought it might be quite interesting – who knows?' Suddenly serious, he shrugged. 'Well, there you are, I shall never know, shall I? By the time the coffee arrived I'd thought better of it, after all I knew nothing about him, so I said I'd changed my mind and was sorry but I couldn't go with him after all and invented some excuse. Well, he made the most fantastic scene! He threw his glass on the floor and shouted at me. He yelled the most *filthy* things at me. Of course the waiters behaved impeccably and picked up the plates and things again, but he was really *filthy*. In the end, he went so far we were asked to leave. Wasn't that an extraordinary thing to do?'

Having told his story he lost all interest in it, though I was left open-mouthed and wide-eyed, for I had never heard anyone speak like that before. With the attentiveness reserved for strangers, he asked me, 'Shall we go to Wheeler's for something to eat?'

Wheeler's was around the corner in Old Compton Street, a minute away. That was part of the charm of Soho, that everything was so near. The moment I entered I understood why this was Francis Bacon's favourite restaurant, and it became mine until it was taken over by a conglomerate which proceeded to destroy the character which had made it unique. Fortunately, that lay years ahead. Meanwhile, Francis, Deakin and myself met in The French Pub most mornings, and laughed so uncontrollably that I noticed strangers looking at us wistfully, wishing they could share in our enjoyment, then we moved on to Wheeler's.

In the post-war austerity when the meat ration was a matter of ounces, Soho restaurants broke the rules but Wheeler's had no need to for they dealt in fish: oysters from their own beds at Colchester; dressed crab; thirty-two ways of cooking Dover sole; turbot; and lobster served with bowls of home-made mayonnaise. Apart from a few grudgingly boiled potatoes there were no vegetables apart from salad, and no puddings – 'Not even an ice?' asked my grandmother wistfully when I was able to take her there.

Curiously, the chef was Chinese and as there was no exit at the back Mr Song crossed the dining-room when he finished work while we were still celebrating. Lucian Freud always made a point of asking him how he was, relishing the reply: 'Mustn't glumble.'

Ultimately you should leave a restaurant happier than when you arrive, and food is not the only test. Atmosphere and service are equally conducive and in these Wheeler's excelled. The downstairs room and the little plush bar beyond were our favourite, we were never so happy upstairs. It was a friendly room on ground level with bare wooden tables glistening with glass and cutlery, small bowls of olives and radishes, plates of brown bread and butter, and the best linen napkins. A bar ran down the left where waiters in white aprons with the authority of ex-sergeant-majors opened the oysters behind the counter with a speed born of experience. Fish plates and prints hung on the wall behind them. The waiters became our friends. There were no waitresses.

My appreciation was instantaneous. I had seen enough to recognize that simplicity is the hardest standard to achieve, and I loved the English, almost Edwardian atmosphere created by the owner, Bernard Walsh, a portly man with a slight, endearing lisp which enhanced his ebullience. He exuded the benevolence of one of Dickens's benefactors, like Mr Brownlow in *Oliver Twist*, and he was certainly good to us. Surprisingly, in view of his present size, he had started as a 'hoofer' in vaudeville before he joined his father's fish business selling oysters in Whistable. He had opened Wheeler's in Old Compton Street in 1929 as a small retail outlet, serving a few special customers at a couple of tables which proved so popular that he rented the whole of the building for £400 a year. Fish and horses were his passions.

Francis was his favourite customer and could do no wrong. Both were Edwardian in their zest for the good things of life and their gambling. Even Francis's language was acceptable, though on one occasion an American couple at a table on the side found it unbearable and complained to the waiter. The maître d'hôtel, Peter, was ill, so Walsh was summoned instead and listened to the complaint with his usual courtesy. Then he took their bill and tore it up. If, for a split second, the American husband and wife assumed that this was a form of apology, they were disillusioned. 'There is nothing to pay,' Walsh told them with icy fury, 'but I must ask you to leave. If you return you will not be served.' With a gesture towards us, he explained, '*These are my friends.*'

We were so overwhelmed and shamed by this loyalty that even Deakin did not dare to cheer as the unfortunate Americans slunk out, mystified. Another American couple were horrified on a later occasion when they overheard Jeffrey Bernard ask Francis whom he would most like to fuck. 'I'd like to be fucked by Colonel Gaddafi.' The couple were more shocked by the politics than the sex.

Throughout that first meal I wondered who was going to pay. I knew that I could not, nor could Francis who signed the bill with his usual flourish though he left a handsome tip for the waiters. Walsh had absolute faith in Francis's future and gave him credit without a qualm. In years to come Francis paid for the oysters and champagne with fistfuls of notes and gave Walsh his promised painting, not of a race-horse as expected, but a small self-portrait which Walsh hated and sold for £17,000.

Our next port of call – and the analogy of a voyage is fair – was the Colony Room up Dean Street. The Colony Room sounds grand, but it wasn't. Better known as Muriel's, it was reached up some filthy stairs where I had to press against the wall as a man with a knife was pursued by another from the top floor which was rented by a tart. Opening the green door on the first floor, I saw a room which might have been ordinary except that its proportions somehow made it magical. The right size and space are crucial in creating a particular atmosphere in a club, and I doubt if the Colony could have worked so well if transposed somewhere else. Much of the magic was due to Muriel herself; she is why the Colony became my second home, and for long periods my first home too. Muriel Belcher was perched like an imperious eagle on her stool by the door, able to observe the antics of her members, quick to repel strangers with an outraged squawk of 'Members Only!' In those days the licence of an afternoon club was perilous – the police disapproved of such frivolity – and Muriel was taking no chances. She ran her club with the discipline of the matron of a great hospital and knew exactly who should be allowed in, though wholly tolerant of their behaviour once inside. Her special genius as a club owner lay in creating her own territory so that the Colony was not typed like the other afternoon clubs which catered exclusively to queers, gamblers, police and villains, or 'resting' actors. Reflecting her personality, which was wittily eccentric, the atmosphere that greeted me as Francis opened the door resembled that of a party in full swing. She welcomed Francis as 'daughter' and I found it extraordinarily funny and bold when she referred to men as 'she', 'Kate' or 'Clara'. Even Hitler was known as Miss Hitler, while Bernard Shaw was 'a clever little woman'. She could be cruel, but only to those she disliked. When I brought John Braine, who had scored a success with his novel *Room at the Top*, she gave a sniff of disapproval as she asked me to sign him in. Turning to a couple at the bar, she gave a disdainful toss of her head: 'She's not a pretty little lady is she?' which was overheard by Braine, as she intended. He quivered with indignation: 'I've seldom been so insulted.'

'On your way, Lottie,' she replied, opening the door, 'or I'll give you a fourpenny one.' After he left, and to my shame I did not go with him, I told her who he was and she exclaimed, 'Well, there's plenty of room at her top!' He tried to sue her for this several years later, but his solicitor advised him not to.

She could be fiercely kind as well, and immensely forgiving. Many years later I crept in one Saturday afternoon with disquieting images of 'torn faces' on the night before. The club was empty apart from Muriel, who looked solemn, her barman Ian, and a little man in a frayed bowler hat and a well-worn briefcase who was leaving.

'Know who that was?' I shook my head. 'A nice little man who came in his free time to mend the telephone you broke yesterday when I was expecting a call from one of my best-spending members and in all my years in club business I've never known such disgraceful behaviour and do you know I don't give a fuck so what are you having to drink, cunty?' She had not paused for breath, her expression remained steely, but she had forgiven me. My relief was so overwhelming that I nearly sank to my knees.

To start with I stood in awe of her, but I also recognized at once that Muriel and her members were the most fascinating people I had met. She knew how far to go in rattling the skeletons in our cupboards, and her teasing was so good-humoured that the most conventional country squire was able to giggle as she greeted him outrageously. 'Ian, look who's just come in, it's old so and so (having forgotten his name), now open your bead bag, Miss, and give mother a lovely drink'. Muriel was far from the monster she must sound. I told George Melly that the Colony was a place you could take your grandmother or father to, but probably not your mother.

'She adored *my* mother,' he protested. 'They got on famously.'

Only the truly mean and boring were unwelcome and she made short shrift of them by ordering a lavish round for all her 'lovely members', after which they fled. Where Muriel excelled and has since become legendary was her skill in attracting the most interesting painters of the day, labelled the School of London by Ron Kitaj, not that I ever saw him there. Muriel's Boys or the Colony Room Mob would have been more apt. There were many afternoons over the next few years when I found Francis Bacon, Lucian Freud, Frank Auerbach and Michael Andrews in full flow after oysters and champagne at Wheeler's. Deakin was the court jester. If there is one subject which artists detest it is art, and as Muriel knew nothing about it and cared even less, they were able to talk about the things that mattered, like sex, drink and money. Asking Francis why he loved the Colony, he replied, 'It's a place to go where you can lose your inhibitions,' which suggests that he was not so uninhibited as I assumed. When I asked why he painted Muriel so often, he told me, 'She's a very beautiful woman. It's as simple as that.' I looked at her again, with her swept-back raven hair and proud, tilted chin, and saw what he meant.

Francis had been taken to the club in 1949 by Brian Howard, one of several undergraduates who claimed to be the inspiration for Anthony Blanche in *Brideshead Revisited* by Evelyn Waugh. 'I met the old bastard across the road,' said Francis, 'and he told me "There's a new club opening" and for some reason I liked it so much that I went back the next day and Muriel came over and spoke to me. I don't know, perhaps she thought I knew a lot of rich people, which of course was untrue, but she knew I hadn't got much money and she said, 'I'll give you ten pounds a week and you can drink absolutely free here and don't think of it as a salary but just bring people in.'''

'So you were a tout,' I suggested.

'I wasn't even a tout. She said "Bring in the people you like."' It was intuitive of Muriel to sense how crucial Francis would prove to her club, for she needed customers and of course he did know rich and influential people. As for Deakin, she tolerated him, but only just. His treachery was bad enough but his meanness was worse, though he persuaded others to buy him quantities of drinks. One afternoon as Deakin bent down to stroke a magnificent white husky brought in by a country member, she turned round in mid-conversation and addressed the dog. 'Hold onto your sled, Clara, or that one will bum a free ride to Alaska.' At that moment the dog looked across and appeared to nod. 'Glad to see she's got the message,' Muriel told the rest of us.

The truce with Deakin was uneasy because he was smart enough to know that basically she disapproved of him. On that first afternoon, with Francis deep in conversation across the room, Deakin murmured 'Come on kiddo, let's go next door.'

The Caves de France was true Bohemia. If the Colony had pretensions with its fake leopard-skin stools and bamboo above the bar, the Caves (pronounced in the French way, 'cahve') was unashamedly louche. The long room was lined with gaudy pictures for sale painted by a man with a purple face and monocle, but no collar or tie, who called himself 'The Baron von Schine, artist', though he was neither. A haze of cigarette smoke and a musty smell hung in the air. If my father preferred 'hurt' people, he would have found them in abundance here. Elaine Dundy, Ken Tynan's first wife, described it in her novel *The Old Man and Me* as 'a sort of coal-hole in the heart of Soho that is open every afternoon, a dead-ended subterranean tunnel . . . an atmosphere almost solid with failure.' She failed to sense the gallantry of the afternoon people, the rejects and drifters who had known better and younger days. There were eyes which knew defeat, ravaged faces crowned with thinning, silky hair, clothes that had been worn for too long. In the camaraderie of the Caves they came alive with the shared excitement of the moment, the promise of an exhibition or the publication of a book, with plans outlined and conquests in store. There was a buzz of enjoyment which was alien to the social whirl enjoyed by the Tynans, yet just as stimulating.

Few were the failures they seemed: the shabby woman with the careworn face and old-fashioned, broad-brimmed felt hat, was Enid Bagnold, a distinguished writer and the first woman to cross the Burma Road. Another with a battered face and man's walking stick demanded: 'Give me a drink will you, deah. A double whisky, *twice*. Had an affair with your father.' This was the artist Nina Hamnett, one of the rejects from the Colony; for although Muriel was fond of her, Nina's habit of wetting herself while sitting on one of the stools with the fake leopard skin proved too traumatic. Before the war Nina had been a popular model in Paris, dancing and drinking away the nights with the best of them – 'Modigliani said I had the best tits in Europe.' Gaudier-Brzeska recreated them in his sculpture *Naked Torso*, the title of her autobiography, though one was damaged – 'I'm in the V and A with my left tit knocked off.' Now she made a gallant if anxious appearance at the Caves, a beret cocked on the side of her head, and a chuckle as she hoisted herself onto a bar stool, gasping, 'Couldn't buy me a drink, could you love?' – which I did gladly with the last remnants of my English schoolboy good manners. She liked to boast that she was the last of the Bohemians, and she had more claim to the title than most. When she lived in a bedroom above the L'Etoile restaurant in Charlotte Street, she was one of the Fitzrovians and a drinking chum of Augustus John, who had been another regular at the Caves though now too old. Nowadays her other destination was The French Pub where she sat at a corner table with the pub dog Peter Mons (short for Monsieur) Berlemont, who adored her and protected her. She did not scrounge for drinks but demanded them outright, sometimes banging a cigarette tin for contributions. David Archer was so enraged by her demands that on one occasion he lost his temper and refused to give her the pittance she was asking for. Characteristically, he returned a few minutes later with a ten-shilling note plus the consolation of a bunch of flowers which he presented with an awkward flourish.

In 1947, Nina had been taken to court by her landlady who accused her of misusing the sink. 'A woman urinating in the sink? It is not possible!' exclaimed the magistrate, much to the amusement of Soho.

He acquitted her, though Nina had to leave after she set the place on fire. Now, attending some function and trying to improve her appearance, she had taken her best grey dress to the cleaners – 'My dear, it shrivelled because of all the gin soaked into it over the years. All they gave me back was a spoonful of dust.' She was little more than that herself.

Then there were the Two Roberts, the Scottish painters Colquhoun and MacBryde, who sat smouldering at the bar blocking the way like fallen rocks obstructing a cliff path.

'Get me a whisky, will yer?' Colquhoun commanded in a thick Scottish accent, wild and windswept with a snowfall of cigarette ash on his coat, banging the counter so angrily that Secundo, the massive though gentle barman, winced.

MacBryde eyed me suspiciously, always jealous of his friend: 'Why don't you fuck off?' Too raw and poor for the Colony, the Roberts were the despair of clubs and pubs and, I assume, were barred from the French for I never saw them there. At first I was intimidated by their aggression, later I understood it. Colquhoun in particular had been a hope for British painting and when I joined him one morning on the steps of a pub as we waited for it to open, I realized he was the gentlest of men stricken by disappointment.

In the late afternoon, the Caves underwent a startling transformation. It became genteel. Secundo was the younger brother of the boxer Primo Carnera, their mother naming her sons First and Second. It took an age before I realized the club was owned by a cheerful French family who looked bemused, as if they did not belong. The boisterous spirits started to wilt around 5.30 when the Caves suffered a suburban change as three middle-aged men stepped onto the tiny platform beside the wine barrels and started to tune their instruments with the solemnity of a string quartet. They wore shiny dinner-jackets, white shirts and ready-made bow ties. One sported a jet-black toupée and the drummer had a pronounced limp. Their leader was a dignified, military-looking man with a grey moustache who attached a contraption to the upright piano, usually punished by one-fingered drunks, which transformed it miraculously into an electric organ. Then the organist, violinist and drummer launched into a sequence of old dance numbers which struck me as preposterous in such seedy surroundings until I grew accustomed to the paradox. Some of the regulars stayed or fell asleep, joined by a contingent of couples who looked ordinary by comparison but proved nearly as drunk as the afternoon men. One couple arrived every Friday and Saturday and sat on the edge of the platform swaying in a blissful stupor. He had a neat moustache like the official in an Ealing comedy, and moved his hands with serpentine gestures, raising them slowly above his head like a Javanese dancer, his eyes half-closed in concentration. She was Amazonian, with gigantic hands and feet and a flushed fat face. Sitting beside him, she danced with her torso leaning backwards until she almost fell over, when she plunged forward, swaying against the rhythm with a grimace that indicated pain, though it must have been pleasure. I never saw them speak to anyone, not even each other, and imagined they were in the throes of a passionate, illicit love affair, escaping from the tedium of their families. One Friday they failed to appear and I was so relieved to see them the next day that I even had a few words of conversation. They proved extraordinarily dull and seldom spoke because they had little to say, a wholly respectable husband and wife from the Balls Pond Road.

The owner was called Jenny, and sometimes appeared behind the bar. Her daughter Hortense was bold enough to trill light operetta with a fluttering of arched eyebrows, moues, and coy, tiny gestures. Sometimes Deakin joined her on the platform as self-appointed compere, with his own series of grimaces and sarcasms which she accepted as graciously as if they were bouquets for the diva.

'And now,' he announced, asking for a roll on the drums, 'let me present the girl' – he eyed her up and down incredulously – 'the girl you have all been waiting for. What you have done to deserve this I can not imagine.' He bowed to the few who were listening and she started singing, as he watched apparently enthralled, raising his spaniel eyes to heaven. Then, in a deafening whisper, he beckoned me. 'Come on kiddo, let's get the hell out of here.'

'Why don't you fuck off,' cried MacBryde as we left.

Once we were outside, Deakin disappeared.

Between six and eight, Soho paused for breath. Echoes came from the restaurants and clubs as if they were tuning up for the evening – the orchestra of Soho: a flash of flamenco and a click of castanets in the Casa Pepe; Mike Mackenzie transforming the gin-sodden upright in the Colony, making it worthy of Cole Porter; the thé-dansant continuing at the Caves; the beat of a steel band in a basement used by West Indians. Colin MacInnes (author of *City of Spades* and *Absolute Beginners*) took me there later and one of the members whispered to me as he went to the bar, 'We like that Colin, but oh man, he does make us feel so *black*!'

Anxious to learn more about the 'sexual gymnasium of the city', as Bacon called it, I explored the streets north of Oxford Street, more Fitzrovia than Soho, with pubs like the Black Horse and the Wheatsheaf, once filled with arguing poets but disappointingly empty at this witching hour until I reached the Fitzroy Tavern at the corner of Charlotte Street and Windmill Street, which gave a sense of *déjà vu* though anticipation kept me there. One of the ghosts was Sylvia Gough, Nina's rival though they barely spoke to each other. Sylvia had been a celebrity too, dancing in the Ziegfeld Follies in New York, the proverbial toast of London society, a model for Orpen, Sargent and Augustus John, the pub's most famous 'regular'. Nina's promiscuity was nonchalant – 'Can't see anything in it myself . . . but they seem to like it so I let them get on with it' – but Sylvia's attraction to young men was desperate. In 1936 she appeared in the Fitzroy with a black eye after she was beaten up by a twenty-one-year-old writer, Michael Bose. Another admirer took her home to protect her and when they all met a few evenings later he attacked Bose with a sculptor's hammer and killed him. 'A singularly squalid and unpleasant case,' said the judge, finding the man guilty but insane.

It was the moral of Soho that pleasure seekers paid dearly for their pleasure. Surviving on a tiny allowance, Sylvia sat there passively in the early evening, alone and apparently grateful when I spoke to her and bought her a drink. Nearly threadbare, she retained a lingering self-respect, going to the public baths each day to keep herself clean. Her skin was translucent and her body so emaciated that it revealed her skeletal bones but she remained charming and courteous and I never heard a bad word against her. Bruce Bernard, Jeffrey's brother, described her to me as 'just one of the loveliest ladies ever'.

In contrast to the *tristesse* of such ghost-like figures as Sylvia Gough, the atmosphere in the Fitzroy became rumbustious as it filled up with young men out on a spree. The walls were lined with First World War posters and the pub was popular with sailors whose strongly chiselled features were First World War too, so they enhanced each other. One of my photographs of two cheerful sailors flirting with a drunken old biddy seated at a table below a recruiting poster with the exhortation to *Follow the Drum* has a pleasingly period feel to it – such faces are unknown today.

Even now I was feeling my way, relishing the proximity of danger in such a notorious queer pub yet unable to let myself go or respond to the gauntlet of meaningful stares as I went to the gents. Writing later of one of the small queer clubs run by a gone-to-seed military man, decorated for conspicuous bravery in the last war, now black-mailed by his rent-boys, I referred to the nights of fancy-dress balls as men paused on their way to a party, some wearing wigs and fishnet stockings, or costumes of indeterminate sexuality though tight-fitting with hands sewn on to strategic points. Always photographing and scribbling, I noted that 'the wild abandon which these people enjoy on such rare evenings of outlet is rather pathetic. British law has succeeded in making homosexuality either listlessly respectable, or simply embarrassing when it asserts itself.'

How did I dare to be so patronizing? *These people!* I was one of them, even if I lacked the guts to don the wigs and fishnets, ever the observer.

After nine o'clock the Fitzroy was so crowded it was difficult to move. A bearded man in a kilt, with large hoop earrings, replied in a tiny voice when asked if he would like a drink, 'That would be very pleasant.'

It was such a jolly atmosphere that I recommended the Fitzroy to an American couple who asked me for places to go which were typically English, even though I knew that the atmosphere was wild with sailors behaving as if they were on leave in Port Said surrounded by houris, and that was the view of the Metropolitan Police when they raided it that night. Describing the Fitzroy as 'a den of vice' – rarely is such a cliché fulfilled – the police counsel stated:

> For the most part its occupants were quite obvious male homosexuals who dyed their hair and rouged their cheeks and behaved in an effeminate manner with effeminate voices. The other occupants were to a very large extent made up of servicemen – sailors, soldiers and marines. There can be very little doubt that this house was conducted in a most disorderly and disgusting fashion. These perverts were simply overrunning the place, behaving in a scandalous manner and attempting to seduce the members of the forces.

He did not add that members of the forces were also trying to seduce us. Stating that the Fitzroy was the habitual resort of prostitutes, the police pointed out that on this particular night eighty of the men present were perverts.

'Good lord,' said the landlord, Charlie Allchild, 'I didn't think it was as bad as that.'

Nor did I, wondering if the American couple had been there at the time. With typical cowardice, the brewers suspended Allchild during the hearings which he fought with such vigour that he was acquitted on all charges, at his appeal, on 12 January 1956. The brewers, aware of their profit, welcomed him back, but he had too much pride. He removed his collection of posters and left. The Fitzroy never recovered.

With the idiocy of our licensing laws the pubs north of Oxford Street shut at ten-thirty, prompting a rush south to Soho where they closed at eleven. According to a well-known story, Muriel was counting her takings one night when two rats from the Cypriot restaurant downstairs scurried through the back door of the Colony and stopped to stare at her.

'You two can fuck off,' she told them, without interrupting her counting; but as she was a kindly woman she added, 'You see, you're not members.' They left without protest.

Next door, at the Caves, I listened to Jenny trying to eject Deakin with less success.

'One more, Jenny, please one more.'

'John, we're closed, please be a good boy and go home. We're tired. We want to go to bed. Don't you want to go to bed?'

'Why should I? There's no one else in my bed. Will you come to bed with me?'

'You know I can't, now do go home.'

'I will if I can have one more drink.'

'Is that a promise, John?'

'Yes.'

'Really, I don't know, you've had quite enough.' She looked distraught and exhausted.

'I'll pay tomorrow, Jenny.'

'Oh really! You said that yesterday, what about the £2 you owe me?'

At this unkind reminder, Deakin raised his eyes heavenwards and shrugged. 'Maybe I'd better go home.'

'I don't know, John . . .' turning to me, she added, 'It's probably just as well. And he's such a good photographer.'

'Come on child,' said Deakin, staggering to his feet. 'There's somewhere else.'

The Gargoyle, across the road in Meard Street, had been wildly popular with high society – high in every sense – and the Bright Young Things in the 1930s. At one point the staff grew to forty-seven and requests for membership (including my father's) at seven guineas a time poured in to the committee. In the membership book for 1926, a year after the opening, I found the names of Fred and Adele Astaire. The Duke of Windsor was a regular visitor and so was Tallulah Bankhead. Brenda Dean Paul, one of the brightest of the Young Things though notorious for her drug addiction, was accompanied by her mother who smoked cigars seven inches long. To start with the cutlery was solid silver and the chef spent an afternoon on a single sauce. Skirts were worn above the knee and people spoke to each other in French over the al fresco dinners on the roof which lasted until dawn. Evening dress was compulsory.

Such glamour had gone with the war but there was still a certain panache. It looked marvellous: we ascended in a tiny white lift and then descended a staircase into a room designed by Matisse who bought 200-year-old mirrors from a French château, originally standing twenty-five feet high, which he cut into 20,000 small squares. There were two Matisse murals, one bought by Kenneth Clark for £600, the other sent to America. Sir Edwin Lutyens had designed the leather curtains with an African motif. The ceiling had been covered with twenty-two-carat gold leaf, and I was assured that it was still there, though I had my doubts about that. The Gargoyle had been bought by a man called John Negus, whose lugubrious appearance proved misleading; he actually liked writers and artists, however penniless, and the sight of them falling apart. Membership was now three guineas, evening clothes the pleasing exception, and people wandered about informally. Despite the evenings they had reflected, the Matisse panels remained surprisingly untarnished.

The atmosphere was that of a posh Bedlam, though the difference between the drunks and the upper-class lunatics was imperceptible. There were pockets of decorum with Lady Diana Cooper at one table, at the next the painter John Minton who was surrounded by 'matelots' in uniform. A three-piece band was led by a small man called Alec Alexander with a pencilled moustache, or so it seemed, and an equally pencilled grin as members cavorted on the stage the size of a large tablecloth, the artists Rodrigo and Eleanor Moynihan jived till the sweat poured down their faces, while a large woman spun a small man as if he were a top and an old man conducted an imaginary orchestra. An elegant couple in evening dress performed an immaculate foxtrot. Lady Diana talked on. Johnny Minton took over, gyrating wildly to his favourite number by Fats Waller – 'My Very Good Friend the Milkman Said' – until he rejoined his table and lapsed into the melancholy which further elongated his El Greco features.

Suddenly, like a wind-up gramophone running down, the gaiety ran out and waiters bustled about with bills on plates. A hubbub of complaints erupted. 'What's this?' a north-country voice demanded. 'I'm not paying any bloody ballroom fee, and we didn't have any bloody sandwiches.' Several members disputed the amount with Mr Negus personally and it was disconcerting when he cut it by half as if it was all a game of chance.

'Mr Deakin,' came an anguished voice, 'there's a matter of four shillings.'

Deakin paused on the stairs, summoning a vestige of dignity: 'You call yourself a head waiter? How dare you bother me for a measly four shillings? I'll sign for it when I come here again, *if* I come here again.' A woman screamed as he lost his balance and nearly fell backwards, but he recovered in time and tottered to the lift.

'He causes more trouble than all the members put together,' sighed the waiter to a couple at the next table. 'See the staff tonight? Recognize any of them? No, they all left because of Mr Deakin.'

I thought of my new friend with admiration: what sissies if they left because of him, and how had he succeeded in running up a bill as small as four shillings?

There was one last gasp at two in the morning, at Mrs Bill's coffee stall in the bombed waste-ground by St Anne's Church. I drank a dreadful cup of over-sweetened coffee, eyed with hostility by the unsuccessful flotsam of the night, particularly by a group of queeny young men who seemed to resent me. Perhaps I looked too fresh, too clean, too hopeful.

Still an indomitable chirrup in a doorway – 'Hullo dearie!' – and then with a sort of sigh, Soho subsided and became a village once again. I walked home.

Along the way I acquired a naval deserter – not a good idea. I am vague on dates, the more so because the deserter tended to disappear at intervals, but I am sure there were several sailors before him with whom I enjoyed a happy if fleeting relationship – ships that passed in the night. When Nina Hamnett was asked why she preferred sailors, she replied, 'Because they leave in the morning.' It was true; after their weekend leave they did not hang about, though Francis Bacon complained of casual pick-ups to the playwright Frank Norman, 'All they want is love and eggs and bacon for breakfast, and I don't eat breakfast, nor do I have bacon and eggs. I have never had any love in the whole of my life – and what's more I don't want any. All I do is cast my rod into the sewers of despair and see what I come up with this time.' But I was desperate for love and so, as Francis asserted, were the sailors. They were an amazing breed of men: uninhibited, adventurous, good-humoured, with a crazy sort of innocence which made them behave in a way which would be condemned nowadays as a form of prostitution. They were bound together by camaraderie and absolute loyalty – they even went to the lavatory in pairs like girls at a dance. They took little seriously, except for the field gun crews in the Royal Tournament which was sacred. Some of the sailors were duller than the rest, but all were honourable in my experience, and because they were tough they were kind, though easily led. They enjoyed 'a good run ashore' and delighted in pubs and clubs, though disturbed by the cost of restaurants. Above all they were fun, brought up in the naval tradition described by Winston Churchill as 'rum, sodomy and the lash'. They do not exist today.

I met one sailor who did not leave in the morning because he had been discharged. He was everything I admired and I let him go. David smelled of honey and we lingered in bed on the Saturday morning, spared the usual charade of smuggling a visitor out before the hair-dressers opened their shop below. When we surfaced at last, we went around the corner to the Bunch of Grapes in Brompton Road, which was no problem for David wore civilian clothes, and had the person-ality to be welcomed anywhere, though my neck bore the love-bite which signalled the hurly-burly of the night before. I was satiated and happy yet, when he mentioned that he was expected to join Johnny Minton at a party in the country, I encouraged him to go though he told me he had decided not to. Was it fear of responsibility which induced me to do the decent thing to my disadvantage as I gave him the fare when he was keen to stay? When I saw him in Soho a week later I tried to persuade him to go back with me, but I had lost my chance. David was one of those in need of love and he believed he had found it, but Minton soon moved on to someone else, leaving David lost and unhappy. Perhaps this was the reason why I did not ask him to stay, the curse of homosexual promiscuity, the self-deception that an even truer love was waiting around the corner. Yet David was the best; instead I landed myself with a feckless alternative who did not like sex, certainly not with me.

We met one Sunday lunchtime. Religion has much to answer for, and the English Sunday is high on the list of indictments. Sunday in London was desolate in those days, and I had no experience on how to cope. Soho was virtually closed. Though homosexuality was against the law, the heart of the British Empire was dominated by three of London's most notorious pick-up pubs: Ward's Irish House next to the London Pavilion; the White Lion next to the Criterion; and a third on the corner of Lower Regent Street whose name I have forgotten though I remember the look of it all too well. It consisted of a long, reasonably pleasant and certainly ordinary room, with a bar along one side where it did not look conspicuous if someone started a conversation with a stranger. A young man next to me looked around restlessly. He had black curly hair and an arrogant expression. I asked him if he would like a drink and he seemed pleased to talk, suggesting that we move to another pub for a last one before the wretched curfew of two o'clock.

As we stepped outside a policeman stopped us.

'Is your name Arthur Lake?'

'No,' replied my companion, so calmly that I assumed there was some mistake.

'Are you sure?' The policeman looked confused and turned to a man beside him who whispered something. 'Are you sure?' the policeman repeated foolishly.

'Of course I'm sure,' my companion laughed pleasantly. 'I should know my own name.' Turning to me, he said 'Come on' and we walked across Piccadilly Circus to Shaftesbury Avenue without looking back. After a minute we turned round and saw that no one was following. My companion grinned: 'That *is* my name but I call myself Johnson. I'm on the run.'

As we continued up Shaftesbury Avenue I felt that I was placing myself outside the law, and it could have been this element of danger that made me infatuated. More fatally, I decided that Mike Johnson/ Avery/Lake – he had so many aliases – was in need of my help, though he was more astute than myself. Beware of pity for you become pitiable. Soho was shut, apart from a basement club next to the Gargoyle called the Mandrake which was advertised as 'London's Only Bohemian Rendezvous'. I never felt entirely at ease there; the members (who included Deakin and Archer) seemed to try too hard to live up to their billing and there was the sense of failure which Elaine Dundy found in the Caves, but without the gallantry. While the owner, a large, unkempt man with swivelling eyes, looked at us suspiciously and played interminable chess, Mike and I killed the time which stretched so appallingly on Sunday afternoons, with cups of tea and coffee until the reprieve when the barmaid Ruth arrived and lifted the metal shutters which screeched with relief as she unlocked the imprisoned bar. Ruth was Soho's barmaid at the Folies-Bergère, though less glum. She appeared in a new hairstyle every week and became someone to wave to as she scooted through the streets on her Lambretta.

This was a strange romance: Johnson and I slept together that night in the single bed in my room because he had nowhere to go, but he seemed to have no interest in sex or affection, not like a sailor at all. After three days he vanished. This was the clincher. Now I became haunted by his image, the dark Spanish looks which came from his Cornish blood, the irresistible grin, the peacock vanity of the gaudy waistcoat which I bought him in the Burlington Arcade. I searched the Soho clubs, lingering in the Mandrake where I knew he was fond of Ruth. I searched with all the desperation of De Quincey in pursuit of Ann.

I assumed he had been picked up by the police.

Seven

A Lens-Eye View

I JOINED *Picture Post* in the autumn of 1951. That interview with the managing director, which had terminated with his weary suggestion that I join the staff as a photographer instead of being groomed as a potential editor, proved a blessing. Following the resignation of Tom Hopkinson after he tried to expose the ill-treatment of North Korean prisoners, editors came and went at startling speed. If trained, I would have been confined to the office in a demanding job which might have been well-paid but little fun. The staff writers were distinguished: James Cameron, until he resigned with Hopkinson; Kenneth Allsop; Robert Kee and Robert Muller — the best — but *Picture Post* was a photographers' magazine and the writers accompanied us. We were the stars. People wanted to see their photos in the magazine more than to be written about.

Picture Post exemplified the advent of photo-journalism, launched to instant success by the Hungarian refugee Stefan Lorant in 1938 and with particular relevance in the war. My boss was the picture editor, Harry Deverson, who regarded me suspiciously at first but seemed to live in a state of constant anxiety anyhow. Balding, bespectacled, he gave me a sideways smile as if he longed to be elsewhere. He perspired in his nervousness, wiping his receding forehead as he sent me out on assignments, immensely kind once he accepted me. I would have been the odd man out with my public-school accent except that the others were scarcely stereotyped. The first photographers to join Lorant were Hans Baumann and Kurt Hubschmann who came from Germany and changed their names to Felix H. Man and K. Hutton accordingly. The prima donna was Bert Hardy, hardly the leader of the pack because he worked alone with a flair for seizing the moment, finding humour in the grimmest back streets in northern towns, the closest England came to Cartier-Bresson. A swaggering personality, he accepted me readily as no competition; and he had no nonsense either about the art of photography, though immensely successful and pleased with himself. Once he used a simple Box Brownie to snap some girls on Blackpool's Golden Mile, their skirts lifted famously by the breeze, to prove that it was the man behind the camera and not the apparatus that mattered.

When I refused to use a Leica, Deverson looked pained, especially when I explained that only the Rolleiflex gave me the results I was searching for. I was too ashamed to confess that I did not have the faintest idea of how a Leica worked. Instead I found a cardboard contraption which I fitted over the Rollei's viewfinder which gave such instant clarity that I was able to focus and click away as fast as the Leica addicts as long as the film lasted, always a problem with only twelve exposures. I found a small flash which was so simple that even I could work it, and so weak that it merely enhanced the existing light without the usual staring-eyed look of horror on the victim's face. Armed with these, the Rollei became an extra limb and I was never without it. Apparently *Life* photographers worked on a ratio of at least 1000 photos taken to every one published, but we worked at 100 to one backed by a superbly professional darkroom. Of course they were black and white, as photographs should be.

Deverson let me spread my wings with odd assignments which took me to unfamiliar parts of Britain: hound trail racing in the Lake District, an opportunity to catch dogs in action; an epidemic of frogs in a Midland village; a tea party for deaf and dumb people near Cambridge, where actions certainly spoke louder than words as far as the camera was concerned. Each photographer was allowed to specialize, and as the others hated hanging about on film sets I was sent to the studios to be cosseted by press officers who were desperate for the publicity of photographs in *Picture Post*: it still had a circulation of a million, though falling fast. In that first year I covered *The Importance of Being Ernest* with Michael Redgrave, who complained that my presence on the set distracted him, though Edith Evans, who called me 'Snooper' in her swooping tones, befriended me and gave me a lift back to London in her chauffeur-driven car every evening. On the set of *Trent's Last Case*, Michael Wilding was visited by his new bride, the twenty-year-old Elizabeth Taylor, who sat on one of the canvas chairs during an endless lighting change. In a few minutes she was surrounded by silent, admiring technicians and I took her photograph, realizing she must be someone special though she appeared an ordinary, nice enough looking girl to me. I became friends with Trevor Howard, liked James Mason, and detested Claudette Colbert who insisted that I photograph one side of her face only and still had the right to veto the prints which I took to Claridges, tearing up those she disliked without addressing a word to me.

There was an uneasy moment when I was told to go to Manchester to cover *Mandy*, a touching film about a child who is deaf and dumb, directed by Alexander Mackendrick who had made his name with *Whisky Galore*. Though he was a close friend, I was closer to his wife Hilary; but it came as a stunner that same morning when I learnt that he was citing me in his divorce. I stammered some excuse to Deverson but as I dared not explain the truth he was understandably impatient. I knew that Sandy indulged in a nervous breakdown at the start of each film (a ritual accepted by Ealing Studios, less so when he moved to Hollywood), so, hoping that the talk about divorce concealed the usual attack of nerves, I decided to risk it. Sandy welcomed me warmly and lived happily with Hilary for the rest of his life, teaching film to students at an American university.

This was the second time I had been warned that I would be cited in a divorce case. Were they mad, or did I really appear as a womanizer with whom no wife was safe?

Noël Coward was the best. Having agreed to be photographed in his role of King Magnus in Shaw's *The Apple Cart*, which was due to open in Brighton, he did everything I asked without a murmur of protest, though he scarcely spoke to the journalist Robert Muller or allowed him near. I shot Coward spread-eagled on the Sussex Downs and playing a pinball machine on the pier, where no one recognized him except a violinist who played one of his numbers. Because I was the photographer I was effectively invisible and people spoke in front of me in a way they would not have dared had I been the journalist. When Coward was fussing with his hair in his dressing-room before the dress rehearsal, his dresser told him not to worry, 'It's only the behind.' Turning to me, Coward remarked crisply: 'I'll have you know that in my time my behind has been much admired and *much* sought after.' After the first night I was able to catch Graham Greene and his mistress Catherine Walston, described by Nancy Mitford as 'a Ritz version in dark mink', but even Coward cried 'enough' when I tried to follow them into the restaurant where they were having a private dinner.

Coward was less charming when John Deakin arrived to photograph him for *Vogue*. After drinks on the *Brighton Belle*, the popular express train from Victoria famous for its buffet and bar, Deakin was garrulous, insisting they had a mutual friend in West Africa, which Coward denied. Deakin was decidedly unsteady and when they took him away as the curtain was about to rise, I heard Coward admonish the press agent in a burst of ill-temper: 'Never, ever, let that nasty little man near me again, especially when I'm about to go on.' The press agent looked shaken when he joined us and told Deakin he had arranged for a box so he could see the show.

'Nuttin' doing,' said Deakin. 'I'm taking this child to see *Soldiers in Skirts* round the corner.'

'Oh,' said the press officer wistfully. 'I wish I was going too.'

❖

Few jobs could have been so rewarding – literally so when I was sent to Spain, where the cost of living was low and the rate of exchange so favourable that for the first and only time in my life I had more money than I needed. My salary from *Picture Post* was meagre, but their expenses were prodigious. I arrived in Madrid to meet the journalist George Langalan, who wrote the original short story 'The Fly', the basis for two horror films, and who had contacts in the Spanish resistance. I had not realized there was a resistance, but photographed a few shanties on the edge of the city which signified so little they were never published.

I was picked up one evening by a young man in the shadows off one of Madrid's main streets who took me to a house which served as a sort of brothel with a whore's bedroom overladen with silks and heavy satins, smelling of sweet perfume; there was a large brass bedstead covered by a voluminous counterpane and towels on a chair beside it.

My memory plays me false where dates are concerned; I cannot even be certain when I first had sex, but I believe that in my ignorance I picked up a young male tart in Piccadilly and took him back to Beauchamp Place where, concealing his surprise that I was unable to perform as he expected, he showed me the ropes. Then came the sailors, and this was more like it, including one curly-haired youth of nineteen who paid the ultimate compliment of saying that I was better than his girlfriend.

That night in Madrid must have been earlier, before the sailors, because the Spaniard wanted to have sex and I refused, still uncertain. Also it hurt. But even the usual fumbling was so elating that I went into the sunlit street in the morning hugging my guilty secret, believing that my expression proclaimed it to every passer-by – not that they gave me a glance. The Spaniard and I met several times and ate together. I dared to invite him to my hotel and took a photograph as he drank a cup of coffee which confirms his dark, uneasy looks when I study it today. A few months later he wrote to me in England asking for money or suggesting that he visit me, or both, I have forgotten, but I did not reply. I suppose it was the usual fear of finding myself in a situation beyond my control.

I found travelling easy, nor did I mind being alone – I was used to both – though always wistful for companionship. On the plane to Barcelona I sat beside another dark young Spaniard, though he looked as if he had money. To my surprise he accompanied me to my pleasant hotel in the centre of town, even to my bedroom where he watched me change – an experience which might have put him off, for nothing happened. Was he waiting for me to make the first move or had he suddenly lost interest? Later I saw him at a sidewalk café surrounded by a lively group of friends, and I waved, hoping to join them, but he ignored me.

With so much money I ordered a suit from the best tailor, a startling affair in bottle-green whipcord unlike anything worn in England, and I loved it for years until it finally wore out, having served me well. Exploring the backstreets behind the Ramblas, I saw a sensational-looking beggar, his head like that of a Greek god, the rest a scaffolding of sticks with both of his legs blown off, probably in the Civil War. He stood there in a pose of extraordinary stillness with his long crutches and the two wooden stumps, one from above the knee and the other below. Across the cobbled alley, sitting on the kerb, his companion who looked half-Chinese, one-legged with a solitary crutch lying in the gutter, accepted money. By now, I was impervious to people's sensitivity as I buried my face in my cardboard viewfinder, achieving a sort of anonymity denied by the Leica which is held conspicuously at eye level. A scene like this was grist to my mill and I clicked away – *snap!* – this was it! As the contact-sheet proved later, I caught a man in a white shirt, his outstretched arm an inch from the outstretched hand of the second beggar; figures continuing down the alley, including a tall, bald man with a sack over his shoulder, wearing shiny, knee-high boots; a solitary gas-lamp above; the alley tapering away. This remains my favourite photograph – the haughty beauty of the beggar with no legs.

I rejoined Langalan and we drove north to Cadaques, walking across the hill the next morning to Port Lligat where Salvador Dali had developed a fisherman's hut into a series of dazzling white cubes guarded by a stuffed bear in the main hallway. The land was protected by a special dispensation from General Franco in 1953 who declared the place a 'beauty spot' with no further building allowed in recognition of Dali's residence in Spain while Picasso went into exile.

The tiresomely winsome Madame Langalan tried to monopolize Dali with her girlish chit-chat, but all he wanted was to be photographed and I could do no wrong in holding a mirror to Narcissus.

I understood instantly why Dali had lived here since 1931, a year after his marriage to Gala: the light had a strange intensity reflected in so many of his paintings with the low-lying rocky perspective beyond the bay which looked surrealist. As for Gala, she said little but watched enigmatically behind her dark glasses, with a faint and rather attractive smile, different from the monster I had been led to expect. Her first husband, Paul Eluard, admired by the surrealists, claimed that she had 'a look which pierced walls'. Dali said he was impotent until he met her, though she was the type of woman who might render a man impotent and there is doubt whether their marriage was consummated. Yet it was a strong relationship and when Dali was penniless in his early years in Paris she traipsed the streets trying to sell his inventions and work, a loyalty usually forgotten. After a visit from a group of surrealists which included Magritte, Luis Buñuel and Eluard, Gala stayed behind. Dali resorted to tribal sorcery to make himself attractive, shaving his armpits to make them bleed, boiling fish glue and goat manure into a paste with oil of aspic with which he covered his body. Not surprisingly she found this loathsome, but she was lured by his fanaticism and when he threw himself at her feet she cried: 'My little boy! We shall never leave each other!'

Though their relationship remained bizarre and the end was horrible, they were happy on the day I met them as Dali clowned. At one point he rowed across the bay with a stuffed swan in the prow,

Gala and the local fisherboy he painted as the infant Christ, whom she seduced when he grew up. Later Dali beckoned me inside the house, past the white bear, while the others stayed outside watching the dark shadows cast by the rocks in the late afternoon.

'My Christ is not finished,' he enunciated in his fractured English mixed with French. 'You shall be first to see it.' We entered the cloistered studio where he placed some Bach on the American record player, drawing the curtains to avoid reflections on the canvas which was still wet. Christ was caught in the same light we had left outside. His foreshortened crucified body, in a startling feat of perspective, floated in the same evening sky over the familiar rocks. There was even the same rowboat we had used earlier, with two fishermen beside it with their nets, one derived from a drawing by Velásquez. The composition was inspired by a sixteenth-century sketch by a Carmelite friar after a vision. To adapt Stravinsky: 'The great artist does not imitate; he steals.'

Bought a year later by Glasgow Art Gallery for £8200, the highest price they had paid, the painting caused an uproar. The curators were accused of extravagance and Dali's work denounced by experts as 'crude sensationalism', even attacked by a vandal. I was deeply moved by it then, in such conditions.

'My wish,' Dali exclaimed, 'is that my Christ should be as beautiful as the God he is.' It is hard to know what to say when an artist shows his work, for praise is rarely good enough. Instead, as we walked away, I told him, 'You must be very happy.'

'I am too happy! And the best thing is not to talk about it.' He touched wood and smiled at Gala who reappeared like a shadow. As we left, Dali confessed that he was always in fear of accidents in trains, cars or boats. 'Otherwise, I do not think I will die. I am confident that before my time is up science will have found a way to prolong life. I have so much to do . . . Oh, so much to do.'

I loved Dali's joy as he showed off for us, an attractive man with whom there was an instant rapport. Conversely, I detested Robert Graves on a later assignment abroad.

This time I travelled to Majorca with the writer Robert Kee, sympathetic, highly intelligent, with a shock of raven hair and humorous eyes. Everyone seemed to like him; women found him irresistible, and he fitted into the Graves menage admirably, like a long-lost friend. This was helpful, for Graves expected adulation from those around him and received it. I was the exception. While I realized it was an honour to meet the author of *I, Claudius*, and my Rolleiflex fell in love with his appearance, I mistrusted him. It was not that Graves was rude to me, and he enjoyed posing for the photographs as helpfully as Dali, suggesting superb locations in the north of the island. However, there was one incident which puzzles me to this day. Soon after our arrival we drove into Palma for a lavish lunch on *Picture Post* before the afternoon's bullfight, and it irked me slightly that instead of letting us choose what we wanted, Graves ordered every dish in his self-appointed role as Elder, avoiding anything I fancied on the tantalizing menu. In the lull between lunch and the bullfight I explained that I wanted to buy a present for my parents and Graves was kind enough to take me to a small shop in a backstreet with the assurance that this was the place for miraculous bargains. It was crowded to the ceiling with extraordinary bric-à-brac, but before my eyes could settle Graves had decided for me, choosing a pile of whitish plates of different shapes like 'seconds' at a discount shop. I hesitated but assumed that their unevenness was proof of their antique value which Graves endorsed enthusiastically. As some were stained and chipped, I was startled to find they were hugely expensive, though Graves made a show of beating the shopkeeper down. So I bought them and returned to England burdened by this peculiar choice: far from being overjoyed my mother was aghast at the waste of money and effort, recognizing them as valueless rejects. I suspect she must have smashed them for they never reappeared. Had Graves played a joke on me? Had he punished me for not being as adoring as I should have been? Was this his revenge for my tantrum on the day before?

The day had begun blazingly. While Robert Kee stayed with Graves, I was put in a simple pension where they served me a sizzling breakfast of ham and eggs in the copper pan they were cooked in with such a delicious flavour that I have tried unsuccessfully to repeat it in England. I relished the chance to eat in the open air as the mountains around me began to smoulder, delighted to be on my own. At midday the fierce heat was alleviated for a moment after an arduous climb to swim off the rocky bay below Deyá, only to hit me again as we made the exhausting return to the top, rewarded by a lazy, al fresco lunch with Graves, his family and friends. Kee behaved impeccably, his intellect and knowledge delighting Graves and the others, but I blotted my copybook. Like many people who behave badly, I had a sense of rectitude which was out of all proportion and highly hypocritical. Graves conducted the conversation as usual, producing several sex magazines sent him from England which he quoted to the hysterical delight and laughter of everyone present, except for me. The climax was reached with the readers' letters, which asked for guidance on how best to pursue their sexual perversions. Some of these letters, probably written by the editorial staff, purported to come from middle-aged couples, and revealed a naïvety on how to have sex which equalled my own. Possibly this is why my humour deserted me.

I have laughed at such letters since in magazines like *Forum*; indeed I have written for *Men Only* myself, on topics other than sex. That I was genuinely distressed by the extracts read aloud by Graves that afternoon reveals the peculiar state I was in, for their laughter in fact was good-humoured.

One of the guests was the writer Martin Seymour-Smith who related the incident in his biography *Robert Graves, His Life and Work*:

Farson at that time seemed unhappy and awkward in our company, and could not stand up to the often outrageous Oxonian jokes which were made (though not so much by Graves) about his Cantabrian origins of which he felt, understandably, entirely innocent. On one occasion, at dinner under the stars at the Lluchalcari Hotel, after undergoing a preposterous barrage of in-jokes about the propensities of Cambridge men – the novelist Thomas Hinde and his wife, both Oxonians, were present – he banged the table and shouted impressively that he had never in his life encountered such intolerance, cruelty, lack of the ordinary decencies and so forth. He then silently munched nuts for over an hour.

Apart from the difficulty of munching nuts silently for so long, this is not as I remember it. Cantabrian jokes would hardly have upset me unless intended to do so. Seymour-Smith continued:

At the end of the meal Graves, who had been as amused as anyone else, took him aside and pointed out that the chief culprit – the man who had been making most of the jokes [Seymour Smith himself?] did not fully mean them, and that Farson should not take them seriously, or as directed at him [as they had been]. Kee said that he found this gesture moving and deeply courteous. Certainly it marks a capacity for kindness and tact in Graves which is sometimes ignored. Farson was comforted, and eventually became a popular entertainer.

The assignment ended, ironically, with Robert Kee's resignation from *Picture Post* on a matter of conscience, so the feature had to be rewritten at the last moment by Jenny Nicholson who happened to be Graves's daughter and described her father as 'this Picasso among writers'. The photographs looked splendid with Graves's striking appearance in the sensational locations in Majorca; one of them was used for the cover of a book. Years later, as 'a popular entertainer', I interviewed him for television and, for the first and only time, the camera broke down and we waited interminably for a replacement while Graves grew increasingly ill-tempered. When we started again his mind was so alert that he darted from subject to subject with such speed that the editor complained, after countless viewings, that he was unable to make sense of anything that Graves said for he never finished a sentence. The interview was never shown.

As for the photographs of Dali, there was one accidental double-exposure as he posed with two immense wooden rowlocks above his head. When it was enlarged I was sent for by the editor who demanded, 'Did you take this?' I was about to explain that the camera had jammed, when he continued, 'Bloody marvellous, a surrealistic photo of the great surrealist. How did you manage it?' 'Not easy,' I told him. He entered the portrait for a prize, and it won.

❧

At this point Johnson, the navy deserter, reappeared. Anxious to extricate him from the tentacles of Soho, I took him to Dublin; but if I had hoped that a change of scene might effect a change in him I was disillusioned. He remained unresponsive, but Dublin compensated. To start with, the city was the right size, so it was possible to walk everywhere. After a slap-up breakfast of soda bread and bacon and eggs – there was no affectionate lingering in bed with Johnson – I set out for Grafton Street to explore the city and savour its panache, with stops at the elegant wooden bars for a Guinness or its identical twin of Gaelic coffee, or just a coffee, unheard of then in a London pub.

I saw the house where my great-uncle Bram Stoker was born – 15 The Crescent, Clontarf, on 8 November 1847 – and the mansion where his brother, the surgeon Sir Thornley Stoker, held his famous parties – Ely House in Ely Place, described by Oliver St John Gogarty as 'one of the few remaining palaces of the spacious eighteenth century which exist in Dublin without having fallen into decay.' Sir Thornley collected antique furniture in lieu of fees, so the house was filled with Chippendale, Adam, silver candelabra and mantels of Sienna marble. 'A cancer, Sir Thornley, or a gallstone?' George Moore would ask when confronted by a new chair or table. He was present at the dinner party when the doors were flung open and a naked woman ran round the table crying, 'I like a little intelligent conversation!' pursued by two attendants. The guests rose politely while she was covered discreetly with some napkins and led screaming from the room. According to Gogarty, Sir Thornley sat there with his head bowed, appalled by his wife's intervention, until he broke his silence imploring the guests to keep 'this incident, mortifying as it is to me, from any rumour of scandal in this most gossipy town'. He knew his Dublin and he knew his friends. Turning to George Moore, he added, 'I conjure you most particularly, as you are the only one who causes me misgivings.' Moore rose to the occasion: 'But it was charming Sir Thornley, simply charming. Can't we have an encore?' All Dublin knew of it the next morning.

To stand outside the houses of my two great-uncles was thrill enough, though now I cannot understand why I failed to knock on the door and look inside.

Dublin was even more carefree than Soho, and there was an instant rapport with every stranger, even if they were not speaking to each other. I was cast in the role of interpreter. Like the pubs north of Oxford Street, though on a wilder scale, people gave me lifts as they drove furiously to the *bona fide* pubs in the country which stayed open longer, where the drinking was unrestrained.

Lucian Freud inspired me to go there in the first place and introduced me to his friends, including a wealthy young dilettante, John Ryan, who published an excellent literary magazine. When I was desperate to stay on for a few more days, I went to John for ideas and he suggested a 'character' called Brendan Behan who was famous in Dublin as a former IRA man who had tried to dynamite a British battleship at Cammell Laird's shipyard when a boy, and was sent to Borstal. Ryan had printed his stories and believed he showed exceptional promise. It was hardly *Picture Post* material, but I could think of no one else.

'Who?' demanded Deverson, when I phoned him. 'Never heard of him.'

'That's the point,' I persevered perversely. 'He's unknown and paints houses and writes and tried to blow up a British warship.'

'Oh.' By now Deverson was on the run, but he protected his photographers like a mother hen and I had become a protégé. By luck I had three features in the magazine that week, which was some sort of record. One was a typical frolic with three pretty girls and three photographers: Kurt Hutton, John Chillingworth and myself, beside the sea. One photo showed me stripped to the waist with the caption: 'To the girls Dan (Dare) Farson'. Looking at it today I can hardly believe I looked so choice.

Because of my three features and the wistful desperation in my voice, Deverson took pity on me. 'I suppose you want some money?' he sighed. 'All right, be lucky.' I hurried into the street elated, to buy a copy of *Picture Post* and display it to everyone in sight, though Johnson was unimpressed. I did wonder why I was looking after him, instead of someone looking after me. Of the two, I looked much *nicer*, I suppose that was the trouble.

Deverson sent just a few pounds but that allowed me to follow in the erratic wake of Brendan Behan for a further week, and I grew to love the man. Brendan swaggered through Dublin as if he owned it. More than most people, he did. He appeared to know everyone, from aged crones who shook their fists, though it was hard to tell whether this was a greeting or an imprecation, to the actors Micheál MacLiammóir and Hilton Edwards. While we waited for MacLiammóir to descend, Edwards (whom I had seen in Paris with Orson Welles) poured the three of us (I was accompanied by Johnson) massive brandies which had the advantage of steadying me for the great actor's appearance in heavy make-up under a jet-black oily toupée as he recommended the solace of masturbation. Brendan was at home in any situation, finding humour wherever he went. The hundreds of photographs I took that week have a poignancy, for they show him at his happiest before he was discovered beyond the city. A few years later, in 1956, *The Quare Fellow* was produced in London by Joan Littlewood, followed by the publication of *Borstal Boy*. Fame lay ahead like an ambush, ready to strike him down.

Meanwhile he did as he liked, responsible to no one, with enough money to buy his Guinness, dashing up a ladder to complete some house-painting to pay for the next round, but unable to afford the spirits which sank him later. Pubs were his haven, McDaid's in particular, where I photographed his pudgy fingers banging away at the ancient typewriter with his pint of the black stuff beside him. We toured the country pubs in the evening where he silenced the talk with his beautiful voice and the songs of the Irish Republican Army like 'The Old Triangle' which opened *The Quare Fellow* and gave little offence then:

> A hungry feeling came o'er me stealing
> And the mice were squealing in my prison cell,
> And that old triangle
> Went jingle jangle
> Along the banks of the Royal Canal.

As his wife Beatrice told me later, 'He genuinely enjoyed entertaining people, and he did it because he wanted to do it, not because he was a showman.' But he was a showman too, clowning as Quasimodo beside a gigantic bell at the top of a steeple, posing beside the delightful sign indicating the depth at Sandycove where he went swimming, FORTY FOOT GENTLEMEN ONLY, drawing himself up to his full height.

There was a sweet side to him, too, playing with barefoot children, visiting the markets at dawn where everyone welcomed him. Beatrice said, 'He could establish communication with people in a way that I never saw anybody else do.'

Apparently nomadic, he slept in a deserted chapel and by the end of the week was dramatically black-eyed and bruised after a fight. Unshaven, scarred, he looked magnificent, with his zest for life intact; and for once I cheated with my camera, recreating the fight outside a pub with the help of Johnson and John Ryan, though the results looked unconvincing. Brendan approved of Johnson, having fallen in love with a young British sailor himself during his time at Borstal. When he was drunk, Brendan spoke of this man with considerable emotion, for the sailor returned to the merchant navy on his release and was drowned in the war. 'You know what I'd like to do, I'd like to swim down to the bottom of the sea-bed and give old Charlie a chew.' Brendan's sexuality was uncertain: when he was asked about his homosexuality, he retaliated, 'If it came to Charlie or Eleanor

Roosevelt, I know who I'd choose.' As for approving of Johnson, it was not in his nature to disapprove. One of his spirited declarations was 'Fuck the begrudgers!' Frequently published today, and used for the covers of his books, my photographs were syndicated but never used by *Picture Post* because Brendan was not yet famous. They constitute a record of the Dublin boy before life became muddied for both of us.

I saw Brendan over the years, though never again in Dublin, an increasingly tragic figure as his props were taken away from him. Though he spent so much of his life with men, in the IRA, Borstal and pubs, he was dominated by women. Gradually they eroded him. This began with his remarkable grandmothers: Granny Furlong who was arrested at the age of seventy-seven for gun-running and served three years in an English prison, and Granny English, a tactless name in the circumstances, who owned the slum property where the Behans lived rent-free. Though not an invalid, she spent her days in bed with her balding son beside her collecting the rents from her tenants unless she was roused by the news of a funeral, taking Brendan to the wake afterwards. Once, as they staggered home, an acquaintance stopped her and pointed to the boy. 'What a shame, such a beautiful child and him deformed.'

'He's not deformed,' said Granny English indignantly, 'he's drunk.' Brendan was six years old.

After his death I made a BBC *Omnibus* documentary called *Brendan* with Richard Marquand, who went on to Hollywood where he directed several successful films, like the thriller *Jagged Edge*, and died too young. In Dublin we had surprising difficulty in tracking down Kathleen Behan, Brendan's formidable mother, though assured repeatedly that she would be back in a moment. This was the fatal Irish desire to please, for she was in England at the time. We filmed her when she returned and I asked if she had protested when Granny English indulged in her passion for funerals, setting Brendan on the road to drink.

'Oh, you daren't' she said hastily.

'Why not?'

'No. I could not.'

I was prepared to leave such a sensitive subject alone but Marquand sensed the reason for her evasion, took me aside and told me to press her harder. I did so.

'I'm sorry, I don't understand. Why not?' I persisted when we continued.

'I wouldn't like to fall out with her now, would I?'

'Even if she was turning Brendan into a drunkard when he was only a child?'

'It wouldn't have stopped her. You couldn't have stopped her.'

'Was it because she had the money and held the purse strings?'

There was a pause, and then the whispered 'Yes.'

When Brendan was sent to Borstal at Portland after his bungled attempt to blow up the battleship in Liverpool docks in 1939, he was excommunicated by his church. With one swipe, his religion was denied him. In Borstal he had the shock of discovering that the British were not so bad after all. There was a compassionate governor at the time, C. A. Joyce, who told me: 'I think he expected a reciprocal hatred and it rather knocked him back when he found that people weren't hating him.' And of course there was Charlie. Brendan's political faith was shaken, though this did not deter him from attempting to murder a policeman in 1942. He was sentenced to fourteen years in Dublin's Mountjoy Prison though released after five.

His break came in 1956 when Joan Littlewood presented *The Quare Fellow* at her Theatre Royal in Stratford East. For once this was a straightforward production of a powerful play, and it triumphed. Then came *The Hostage* in 1959. As I was to learn myself, Joan Littlewood loved her actors passionately but had little time for the written word, even Shakespeare's. She served up *The Hostage* with her usual knees-up gusto and the hurly-burly of the music hall, transforming an ungainly script into the entertainment that made it an international success.

I met Brendan in the pub opposite the theatre, where he confided that he was unhappy with the frolics on the first night. Always more intelligent than he liked to appear, he described it as a travesty of his play and looked bereft. Yet when *The Hostage* came to the West End and the show was flagging, he joined the actors on stage with a few drunken frolics of his own which delighted both the audience and the box-office. It did the play no harm either when he appeared drunk on BBC television with Malcolm Muggeridge, though he was sober when I interviewed him for ITV's *This Week*. We did it on film and the lady director was taking no chances, making certain that no alcohol was ordered during a dismal lunch at the Wig and Pen. I could tell that Brendan was suffering from a hangover, though he did his best to rise to the moment: 'Do I spend £10 a week on drink? I should think you need £10 a day in London. I'd like to drink something which doesn't give me a hangover but doesn't give profits to the capitalists. I'd like to be a rich Red,' he said defiantly, though I felt his heart was not in it. 'I like the money, but I don't fancy it otherwise – it doesn't suit me.' And this was true. When I saw him after that, his fame had claimed him, his Nero face crumpling and his body bloated, laid out on a sofa while a party cavorted around him, just able to raise a hand in the old familiar greeting: 'How's the heart?'

Rae Jeffs, the publicist for Hutchinson who published Brendan's books, resigned to help him, taking down his words from a tape-recorder. This was devotion, but fatal. No longer did those pudgy fingers need to press the keys; even his ramblings could be edited. Rae Jeffs described his deterioration: 'The last time I saw him I would not really have recognized him from the man I first met, and that was awful to watch. Brendan was a sensitive enough person to know that he was getting to the stage where he was having these imaginary conversations – I think he must have felt that his brain was going. Brendan knew he'd lost the power of conversation and also knew that his brain had these funny lapses. He was terrified of being committed.' When I asked her to explain these 'imaginary conversations', she described how he sat in the lobby of the Chelsea Hotel in New York appearing to talk to people when there was no one there: 'He was leaning forward and offering someone a cigarette, which was very disturbing.'

Waking in a New York hospital, he was terrified that it was an asylum and discharged himself. A similar incident occurred in London when he left hospital on a Sunday afternoon when the pubs had closed and stumbled, literally, into a home for alcoholics. This sounds a miracle but I believe it was disastrous: they treated him with antabuse, which makes the patient agonizingly sick if he takes a drink; the dosage is increased until he begs the doctor never to give him alcohol again. They tried that on my father, who managed to resist, realizing that this is the sort of cure that is worse than the complaint, pushing a man to the edge and over. When Rae Jeffs brought Brendan the reviews of *Brendan Behan's Island* he was unable to read them. 'It's hard to say if the cure was responsible, but some pressure had affected his eyesight.' She thought he was the saddest man in Europe: 'Awful, because you can't really help an alcoholic. Brendan would say, "One drink is too many for me and a thousand not enough." He was a weak man and people would come up and say, "Come on Brendan, have a drink . . ."'

'Was he a lonely man?'

'Very, very. I don't think anybody ever knew the complete Brendan.'

'Did he?'

'I don't think so. He needed the touch of human beings more than most of us. He was very frightened of the dark. That great remark, "I am a daylight atheist," was significant. He hated the night.'

When I met Beatrice, his wife, she told me how he rose around ten at night in order to venture out on his own in the darkness, sometimes disappearing for days. At home one Sunday evening, the wireless was playing a record of Brendan singing 'The Old Triangle', 'and he sat down and listened to it. I suppose he was well jarred, but the tears poured down his face. He said, "Is that me singing?" I said, "Yes, Brendan, it is." And the tears came out, you know, as much as to say, "This was me, and this is me . . ."'

He was barred from every pub in their respectable neighbourhood except for one at the bottom of the road where he had an understanding: 'He was allowed to go in and sit down and ring for a taxi – our phone was cut off because he used such obscenities – and he was allowed to buy a drink for anyone on condition he was never served himself. Of course he got round this by going in with three people, ordering three drinks, drinking them all himself and going out again.'

Beatrice told me that the drink was no longer a compensation. 'He kept on drinking because he felt he was dying, and the drink just kept him going. He felt that if he lay down and went to bed that was the finish of it. Which is really what happened when he went into hospital again – he was only there ten days and he died.' (On 20 March 1964.)

Others told me that he went into a splurge of alcohol for the last few months as if he was trying to kill himself, and one of his oldest friends told me why. Beatrice, who died in 1994, was stoical, but Brendan discovered that she had been unfaithful and this was the ultimate disillusionment.

Many people viewed his death as a waste which could have been avoided. Sean O'Casey said: 'He had no bitterness or venom or literary jealousy. Had he lived another ten years he would have written more and perhaps better. It was horrible to think of a man of Behan's age [he was forty-one] dying, particularly when he had so much to offer.'

Yet I wonder if he had more to give us. I suspect that Brendan would have written much the same stories and much the same play. Joan Littlewood had rejected his last play, *Richard's Cork Leg*, but she came to his funeral in Glasnevin Cemetery where his old companions in the IRA bore his coffin shoulder-high and a boy bugler sounded the Last Post. 'He squandered his life and his genius,' she declared, 'but he took the world out on a spree.'

People ask too much of others. There are artists like Matthew Smith and musicians like Delius who may not rank among the greatest but who give as much pleasure. What Brendan had to give, he gave abundantly. Rory Furlong, his half-brother, agreed: 'Just his poem to Oscar Wilde, that's enough as far as I'm concerned to make a life worth living. If you think of his generosity and kindness to the old ladies in the market early in the morning, isn't that enough to make life worthwhile?' And his poem in Gaelic which evoked the haunting beauty of the Blasket Islands.

When I asked Beatrice why she stayed with him at the end, she answered simply, 'Fighting is better than loneliness'; and when Brendan was dying and he told her that the worst thing she had done was to marry him, she thought of the best of times and their travels to Dingle, with the Blaskets opposite, on the west coast of Ireland, and replied, 'No, we had the *two* days.' Many people do not have one.

He prophesied that he would never live to see forty. 'But you see,' said Beatrice, 'he lived till he was forty-one, so he cheated death by an extra year.'

Cheated death? That is a nasty way of putting it about someone so generous, and forty-one was far too young. Still, he had the two days, and I was witness to a good one when Brendan was at his happiest and Dublin belonged to him.

◆

Johnson behaved himself in Dublin because he was happy, safe from arrest as a naval deserter, but he became a liability the moment we were back in London. He was totally dependent on me financially, which became a serious problem when I got the sack, an event for which he was indirectly responsible. Harry Deverson assigned me to one of *Picture Post*'s 'silly season' stories, photographing two girls and their donkeys on the Sussex Downs. I made two idiotic mistakes: when he asked if I could drive, I admitted I had passed my test and was lumbered with a decrepit van which shuddered to a halt at every traffic light and shuddered off again with a howl of changing gears and hoots behind us when the lights turned green. I had passed my test, but I was unable to drive. The other mistake was to bring Johnson.

I had been so rash as to take him to my parents' house in Devon when they were away in Portugal, managing to drive their car up the steep hill to the nearest pub and back without an accident. Along the way Johnson picked up two girls who proved surprisingly nice, accepting our odd relationship without question. I received a letter recently from one of them who remembered my name and commented that the young man with me was the most handsome she had ever seen.

The visit proved so successful that I stayed on to welcome my parents, failing to appreciate how exhausted they would be after a long drive exacerbated by my father's drinking. The last thing they needed was a strange guest. I recalled my father recoiling when he asked Johnson if he fished, which elicited an incident when he and some other sailors threw hand grenades into a lake and collected the dead fish afterwards. Johnson was never referred to again, erased from my parents' minds as if he had never been there, which was just as well for it would have been hard to explain him. Instead of facing the truth, they ignored it, though it is conceivable they still did not know.

The nightmare journey to the Sussex Downs had the advantage of convincing me that cars were not for me nor I for them. That was just as well, for if I had continued to drive I doubt if I would be alive. Far worse, I might have killed some blameless family.

The girls were more good-natured than the disgruntled donkeys, and, surprisingly, Johnson was at his best. All might have been saved except that one of the girls was the friend of Harry Deverson's assistant, a prim young man who would not have understood Johnson, or the reports he must have received. There was the disconcerting moment when I sunbathed on the grass and discovered curious objects among my pubic hair and, alarmingly, even on my eyebrows, my first experience with 'crabs', and all the odder due to my lack of physical contact with Johnson. I was confused and made the mistake of going to the Hulton Press doctor who prescribed a stinging white lotion. I should have known that such a visit was unlikely to remain confidential. The black marks were mounting up against me.

It was a Saturday morning when Deakin descended on Beauchamp Place in an irritatingly camp mood as he described his visit to *Picture Post* the previous afternoon in search of work. 'Needless to say they adored me,' he said of Deverson, 'and of course I had some sharp words to say about you. I told them they were crazy to employ you.'

Without a word I handed him the brief letter of dismissal I had just received in the post. Even Deakin was aghast and bought me a drink in the Bunch of Grapes around the corner in Brompton Road.

Deakin had been sacked by *Vogue* after a smart midnight party which caused his downfall. Having started too early to help with the decorations, by the time the guests arrived he was so drunk that he passed out and had to be carried off like Hamlet at the end of the play. He was ashen when he told me what happened the next morning. I tried to comfort him: 'Who are they talking about this morning? Dame Margot? Dame Edith? No, John Deakin!' But when he added that Cecil Beaton had cut him in the office lift I realized that was the end of his association with *Vogue*.

Things looked brighter when he landed a lucrative contract from an advertising agency to take the photographs for a major promotional campaign advertising cigarettes. Big money was involved and Deakin's future looked secure. He chose Johnson for one of the two models, though he did not offer him a fee, nor did it occur to Johnson that it was hardly wise for a naval deserter to have his face plastered on billboards across the country. Deakin's photos were surprisingly successful except for one flaw – Johnson was handing the girl a rival brand of cigarette. Deakin's contract was cancelled.

I was now in trouble. My salary from *Picture Post* had been modest but reliable. There was no thought of running to a tribunal and my sacking was justified, with the irony that the feature on the donkeys and the girls was spread over several pages with the text apparently written by one of the animals (which would have been funnier if the donkey had told the truth). Previously a responsibility, Johnson was now a liability.

Though Deakin adored Johnson, recognizing that he was a bad influence on me, Francis Bacon was immune to his charms, largely because Johnson took no interest in him. Their first encounter had not been a success, late at night in the Gargoyle where we had been invited by John Minton. He sat at the head of several tables put together, with art students and several sailors in uniform, one of whom looked suspiciously at the bottle placed before him.

'Champers!' cried Minton. 'Its *madly* good for you. Much better than brown or mild.'

'Rather have cider,' said the unimpressed sailor.

'Quite a place,' said the friendlier sailor next to me. Speaking in a gentle Scots accent, he was Minton's latest favourite. Johnson told the sailors he was on the run, which surprised me as this was supposed to be a secret. I wondered how they would react but they accepted it. What they found harder to understand was his deep dislike of the navy which he expressed forcibly.

'Have a glass of champagne,' Minton called out to me, as I was hoping he would. 'It's Joe's birthday and we're spending the last fifty pounds of my inheritance.' Few were so 'gay' as Minton in the old sense of that word, but soon he slumped into the inevitable melancholy.

'He's all right now,' murmured the sailor beside me, totally at ease, 'but moody. Watch out when he gets drunk.'

'I'm only liked because I'm rich,' Minton muttered accordingly. 'I can buy anyone I want.' The sailors munched their steaks contentedly. Later, Minton danced a Charleston by himself, gyrating wildly, his good humour restored.

Francis Bacon sat in angry argument in a corner with a man I had not seen before, Peter Lacy, a former Battle of Britain pilot with a slight stammer and nervous blink. Johnson went over and joined them, though plainly unwelcome. When he lurched off, I went over to apologize. Bacon's reaction was fierce: 'It's too bad that we should be bored to death by your friend and have to pay for his drinks, but now you have the nerve to come over as well, when you're not invited.' Outraged, I said I would pay for all their drinks, a gesture I could not afford and regretted immediately for it meant that we had to walk home.

When I saw Francis in Muriel's the next afternoon, he gave me a welcoming smile, poured the champagne, and exclaimed, 'If you can't be rude to your real friends, who can you be rude to?' I thought there must be an answer to that, but was glad I was forgiven.

We became so close that one morning he phoned me to say he needed money urgently and did I know of anyone who might buy one of his paintings of a Pope that same day, for £150. I was able to persuade my old college friend with whom I had shared the flat and who now worked in the City. Just married, he had moved into a petite mews cottage where the Bacon loomed at the top of the stairs, unnerving his wife who disliked it intensely. They sold it nine years later at Sotheby's for £5000, probably the first Bacon to be auctioned. At a later date, the same picture, one of many based on the Velasquez of Pope Innocent X, was resold by Christies in New York for $5,720,000.

I was overjoyed when I handed over the £150 in notes and Francis gave me a 10 per cent commission of £15, doubly welcome because it was unexpected. By now I was in such trouble financially that when I asked my father for loans he wondered if I was being blackmailed. To a degree this was true – blackmailed by my guilt over the subterfuge I had to resort to in keeping Johnson.

Poverty demeaned me. This applies to everyone but it was a new experience for me and I had not become used to it. My Rolleiflex was constantly in pawn in Oxford Street. I sold the gun my father had given me one birthday and he was furious and mystified. Worst of all, I sold the letters passed on to me by my cousin Noel Stoker in a small sack. These were written to his father, my great-uncle Bram, not in his capacity as the author of *Dracula* but as the manager of the Lyceum Theatre. Many were scrawls by Irving, others came from Conan Doyle, Hallam Tennyson, Mark Twain, and Ethel Barrymore requesting an audition, all meticulously initialled and dated by Bram Stoker. The most valuable were those from Oscar Wilde to my great-aunt Florence Balcombe with whom he had an 'understanding' before she broke it off and married Bram.

I sold the letters to a dealer in Bond Street for a few pounds to pay for our addiction to Soho and I recall the glee of the woman who bought them. Then I spent part of the money on a letter I saw in a glass case from the actor Macready. He meant nothing to me, it was worthless compared to the letters from Wilde, it must have been a gesture to alleviate the shame. The only reassurance came in the subsequent knowledge that the letters were sold to the Harvard University Library, a safe-keeping I was unable to provide.

I hated being out of work because I enjoyed working, apart from the crucial matter of salary. I joined Baron, in succession to Tony Armstrong-Jones, who ran a studio where girls hand-coloured large black and white photographs of horses which were sold for prodigious amounts to their owners. Baron himself took carefully posed portraits of society ladies trying to make them look less like the horses. He was good at that, though not a great photographer as he was the first to admit, praising my photographs of Francis Bacon and Lucian Freud. He was one of the founders of the Thursday Club which met upstairs in Wheeler's and that could be disconcerting when he trooped down and saw me sitting there. He was frequently accompanied by the Duke of Edinburgh to whom he introduced the variety star Pat Kirkwood.

One evening he invited me to his flat for drinks with a few friends which coincided with my return visit to the Royal Naval Reserve on a boat anchored off the Thames Embankment. Intoxicated by my friendship with sailors, and the uniform, I had volunteered, welcomed at first though they rejected me now with no explanation. I was convinced that my name had figured in a police file as someone who picked up sailors and was therefore unfit to be one, so I arrived at Baron's in a state of shock, scarcely able to utter, which he might have mistaken for deliberate bad manners, and wearing a sports jacket which was right for the RNVR though wrong for the party. More bad marks, but it was a fuss over a borrowed camera which I had pawned that caused my dismissal.

I worked as a freelance for *Harper's Bazaar*, accompanying Ken Tynan to the Edinburgh Festival to photograph Richard Burton trying to strangle Claire Bloom as Ophelia. *Harper's* became a lifeline. Jane Stockwood, the kindly features editor, invited me to a posh restaurant in Curzon Street with coronets above the banquettes to mark where royalty had sat. She barely flinched when I removed my dark glasses to study the menu, revealing two black eyes, though Elaine Dundy stared with horror. Normally I would have relished the pretentious atmosphere and lavish food, but I spent the meal wondering if it was possible to focus a camera properly with only one eye, for the other was closing rapidly. Jane Stockwood chatted merrily as if my glasses were a mere affectation, and my photographs of Elaine were published, in sharp focus after all.

Fighting with Johnson had become routine. The black eyes were caused when we fought on a bomb-site the night before near the house where Jeffrey Bernard was staying, with bricks and stones all too readily at hand. I never win but have the pride of cowardice which urges me on at the moment when it is time to call retreat.

There have been at least five times in my life when I have been lucky not to have been killed. If I lose my hair, my head will resemble the craters of the moon.

When I was nearly slaughtered, Johnson staggered off. Without the strength or spirit to make it home, I stayed the night on Jeffrey's spare bed, shaking from sobs 'of despair as if I had a fever. Jeff and I were bonded by youth, Soho and poverty, once travelling together to a primitive cottage in North Wales overlooking Lake Bala, with water from a freezing well. We must have been desperate to make such a journey, especially as our love lives were so different.

However, it was vital to get away from Soho. For some reason, possibly an echo of the happy week in Dublin with Brendan, I believed that everything would be better if we went abroad. Recklessly, I obtained a false passport for Johnson, remembering the name and address of a young farmer I had photographed who was most unlikely to apply for a passport himself. It proved easy to trace his birth certificate at Somerset House and acquire a copy. Then I got the application form from the Passport Office and persuaded two teachers at the Royal College of Art to sign it as guarantors of respectability, which they did without a murmur. Their names could have been traced, but nothing went wrong. Next I persuaded *Picture Post*'s rival, *Illustrated*, to send me to Venice to cover the filming of *Romeo and Juliet* with Laurence Harvey and a nineteen-year-old discovery from Chesterfield called Susan Shentall. Finally, we called on John Minton early in the morning to borrow some money. In those days I expect it was no more than £50, but Johnny was reluctant, knowing there was no likelihood that he would see the money again. I wish I had repaid it.

We set out by train for Lake Como as our first destination where Charles Crichton was filming an Ealing comedy called *The Love Lottery* which promised well but proved dire. It starred David Niven and Peggy Cummins, who was polite but cold when Johnson tried to seduce her. The press officer, Vivienne Knight, met Deakin on her return. 'Who on earth,' she asked him, 'was that extraordinary young man with Dan, called Alwyn?'

As Alwyn was the name on the passport, Deakin was mystified until she described him. 'Oh! That's *Johnson!*'

We continued to Venice where even the approach by train is spine-tingling as the skyline comes in view. 'Look,' I cried emotionally,

Venice!' but Johnson was stuck in the corner with a comic book and did not look up. For the first time I felt a chill of dislike.

Romeo and Juliet was an easy film to cover though Laurence Harvey had turned against his co-star, reducing her to tears by his cruelty, probably in the knowledge that the film would prove a disaster. The Italian director, Renato Castellani, rehearsed her remorselessly, acting out her part in the balcony scene gesture by gesture and she did her best to copy every move. Her film career was over before it had begun and everyone knew it, especially Susan Shentall.

The film's press officer did his utmost to look after me. We stayed in a hotel called the Fenice, with a splendid restaurant below where they served tagliatelli with fresh green peas and butter, and he invited me to the casino at the Lido. This was my first experience and I placed my chip on my lucky number 22 and walked away. When I returned, people touched me for luck; 22 had not only come up but had done so twice. As the original stake remained on the number, a pile of chips awaited me. This good fortune transformed our visit, or would have done except for Johnson and the Queen. We were in Venice on Coronation Day and the British were invited to the British Consul's to celebrate the enthronement of Queen Elizabeth II. Johnson said he wanted to get drunk instead, so I went to the party with Dame Flora Robson, who was playing the nurse in *Romeo and Juliet*, and so brimful with emotion that she wore dark glasses which failed to conceal the tears that rolled down her cheeks on this damp and dismal afternoon.

The hotel manager was waiting when I returned and asked me into his office. He looked so grave as he told me there had been an accident that, for a split second, I thought that Johnson had been killed, until he explained that Mr Alwyn had been unable to find the room key and had smashed down the door. Though badly splintered with a drooping lock, it was not as bad as I expected when he led me to view the damage upstairs. 'It is most unfortunate,' he sighed, 'that the police were called.'

'The police?'

'Your friend was drinking in the bar down the street and,' the manager made a sweeping gesture, 'he destroyed it. You will understand why I must ask you to leave.'

I walked down the street, dodging into doorways to escape the rain which fell accusingly. The bar was not destroyed, just badly damaged like the door. With devastating aim, Johnson had hurled a tumbler which struck a key bottle at the base of a pyramidal display, bringing the whole lot down. The broken glass and sticky rivulets still oozing onto the pavement made it look worse, but it was bad enough when the hysterical owner counted up the cost. He did not know where Johnson had gone to. I settled up from my winnings at the casino and the rest went towards the door, evidently all the manager was worried about, for he allowed me to stay on. This left me with no money until I borrowed a small amount from the press officer.

Johnson was surprisingly sober when he reappeared and we discussed what we should do.

'Let's sell the camera and go to North Africa,' he suggested. For a moment it made sense, simply to disappear. Then I realized it was time to pick up the pieces of my life again. I could help him no more. Instead, with the money I had borrowed, I took the vaporetto across the water to the Lido on the following afternoon. The glamour of the casino had gone as I joined the few other gamblers who looked like mourners at their own funeral. I lost the money in less than five minutes.

Returning to England, Johnson continued his unlikely affair with the wife of a distinguished poet, before he left that menage to move in with a woman referred to by Deakin as the p.l.w. – 'plucky little woman'. She was a widow with a small boy and a dog called Snappy, and she worked gallantly to keep them all going. I hoped he was happier with her than he had been with me; not that I cared any more. I was satiated with Soho.

Eight

Around the World with
a Dishcloth

INCURABLY ROMANTIC, I thought of the merchant navy in terms
of a novelette – red evenings on a rusty tramp ship limping down
the coast of South America. I had set my heart on South America.

Someone told me that the Norwegian merchant navy would take
anyone, so I phoned their embassy. 'No, you don't need experience,'
the man confirmed, 'but you've got to be under sixteen. Are you
under sixteen?' Quietly, I put down the phone.

The main shipping line for South America had its office in Liverpool, so I went to the imposing City headquarters of the Royal Mail
which acted as an agent. The official was sympathetic: it was the old
Catch 22 – without experience I could not join the union, without
the union ticket I stood no chance of gaining such experience. As an
afterthought, he asked what I had been doing.

'But that's perfect,' he exclaimed. 'Why don't you come as ship's
photographer? We can arrange that and you won't have to go through
the Pool.'

But that was cheating. I did not hesitate: 'I'm giving up photography,' I explained. 'That's what I'm trying to get away from.'

He shook his head impatiently and said I had come to the wrong
place anyhow: the office where the men signed on was down at the
docks, a weary journey with hours of changing buses, asking people
the way, finally walking down miles of cobblestones past lines of ships.

'Not a chance,' said the man when I reached the office. 'No one
will take you without experience.' He flashed the falsest smile.

One of the surprises of life when you are young is that if you want
something badly enough you can get it. By now I wanted this job
badly and the next day I tried to join the seamen's union at the

Shipping Federation. The official at the desk eyed me up and down as if he were contemplating revenge, a young boy perched in the corner gazed at me with dismal eyes. After their scrutiny, I stated my position.

'How old are you?' asked the snooty official, and when I said I was twenty-eight he released a sigh with the weariness of a High Court judge unable to give as long a sentence as he would like. If I cared to return to the docks I might get taken on as a nightwatchman or a fireman-coal-heaver (it sounded like), though he did not think this probable.

The Pool resembled a stage-set: strange figures lounged in a large room, black men in black leather jackets and white tee-shirts, others lining up before iron grilles, a snow-storm of notices on the walls. With the proverbial kindness of seamen, someone told me of a large company which needed men urgently at that moment. I phoned at once but there were no more vacancies; I was applying at the start of summer when everyone wanted to get away, I should try again before Christmas when seamen wished to stay ashore with their families.

Help came unexpectedly from Francis Bacon. One of his patrons was Sir Colin Anderson, director of the Orient Line, who told his secretary to get me an appointment with the company's catering superintendent. By now I was resigned to joining as a steward rather than a deckhand as I had hoped. I cheated, after all.

I took the train to Tilbury. The catering chief was a large man in a hurry, who caught me off guard by offering me a short trip as a letter-bureau attendant. I had neither the nerve nor the spirit to refuse and was handed the necessary forms to take to the doctor. It was over in seconds. I had joined the merchant navy, but there was no elation in being assigned to the purser's office as a floating postman. The doctor was out for lunch, so I crossed to the bustling pub that lay in the centre of a ramp between the lines of ships.

Three extraordinary figures advanced towards me, painted, mincing, with bouffant hairstyles, chattering like monkeys though they paused to ogle and whisper as I passed by. They were the more grotesque because each was over six feet tall, so they seemed to teeter on stilts as they fluttered by. Macbeth was less surprised by the witches than I by this apparition.

A liner had docked and inside the pub a group of stewards were having a farewell drink. Brazen in my innocence, I asked for their advice, which they gave readily; and it became plain that the 'cushy' job I had been offered meant that I was neither crew nor passenger. This was what I feared. They added that it would not even count as experience in the eyes of the union; at the end I would be no closer to my South American run on the rusty cargo boat.

I hurried back and caught the superintendent as he was leaving his office. By now he realized I had no influence and was not too pleased to see me. 'Very well,' he said abruptly when I asked to join as an ordinary steward, 'but there are no vacancies for steward. Only thing left is utility steward.' He waited impatiently for my reply and I agreed at once.

On the train back to London I shared a carriage with two Australian deckhands who had paid off the *Orcades*, the ship I was to sail on in a week's time. 'It's pretty rough,' they said. 'Couldn't believe it first night out, all these birds sitting around the pig (the Pig and Whistle was the crew's bar), except they weren't girls, just stewards dressed up, women's blouses, make-up, earrings, all that sort of thing, camping their heads off.' They gave a warning. 'Never speak to them. Once you do they never leave you alone.' The uglier Australian added: 'They stopped bothering me when I threatened to thump them if they came near me. You do the same.'

I gave a serious nod. This was more promising than they realized.

'And what,' I asked, 'is a utility steward?'

'The lowest of the low,' they replied grimly. 'You can't get lower.' That too was encouraging.

Returning three days later I was passed by the doctor, though unable to pass water until I had had a cup of tea in a nearby caff. Accepted by the union, I paid my three guineas membership, received my book and cards, and emerged as a seaman at last. It was a hectic week, with articles to finish for the *Evening Standard*, in a sudden demand for my work which would have been welcome before.

I noticed that several of my Soho friends seemed annoyed.

'You won't enjoy it,' warned Deakin nastily.

'Why are you doing it?' asked someone else, and I could think of no answer except 'to escape' – which I kept to myself.

My mother thought it 'a pity'; my father went further, as fathers do. 'Don't you think it's time you got somewhere in life?'

Only Francis and Lucian understood. Sensing my excitement, Lucian invited me to a party and it was a full hour before I realized it was being given in my honour. I felt so inadequate that I scarcely thanked him for the trouble he had gone to, a case of sinking to the occasion which I regretted afterwards.

The *Orcades* lay by the quayside like a stranded whale when I reported a couple of days before we sailed, held to the quayside by Lilliputian strings which proved to be massive ropes close to. She weighed nearly 30,000 tons, a great dead object, though the life around her was chaotic as food and stores poured into the holes in her side and cranes lowered cargo into the depths below. A constant stream of tiny figures scurried up and down the gangways.

The crew totalled the staggering figure of 634: waiters, bedroom stewards, deckhands, engine room, clerical staff, and the U-gang at the bottom, to which I was assigned. For some reason I thought my rank was second steward, which brought me some odd glances as I asked my way through the labyrinth of steel corridors and stairs carrying my kitbag with the uniform of white steward's jacket and blue trousers which I had bought in the store that morning. In fact my chit ordered me to report *to* the second steward, the most powerful man on the ship as far as I would be concerned, after the chief. He proved a compact man with piggy eyes and a look of cunning that was not deceptive. Not much older than myself, he called me 'laddie' from the outset. He gave me a quick glance and studied my papers while I waited.

'Yes?' he demanded as I handed him my chit.

'Could you tell me what cabin I'll be in, sir?'

He leaned forward. 'Look here, laddie, don't bother me about your cabin. I'll think about that later, if I have time. Now I'm going to lunch. You don't want to make me late for my lunch, do you?' He waited.

'No, sir,' I assured him.

'That's right, laddie.'

'Where should I leave my kit?' His slight though sinister smile faded as he looked at the bag beside me and my typewriter which looked decidedly out of place. 'Not here. Don't let me catch you leaving it here.' He left for lunch.

His own steward, a Scots boy who could not have been older than sixteen, had been watching us: 'Don't mind him,' he mumbled. 'It takes him an hour to shave.'

'Why's that?'

'Because he has so many faces!' He grinned hugely and led me to the crew quarters, climbing down numerous companionways until we entered the hot iron jungle that was now my home. The floor was littered with the detritus of the previous voyage, pipes hung overhead, everywhere. Then he left too and it took me ages before I found the gangway off the ship. It was days before I knew what deck I was on, months before I knew my way around.

I returned to the dockside pub for a drink and a sandwich, where I talked to another member of the crew who urged me not to accept the job of utility steward if I could possibly help it.

'Try anything else. Go for engineer's steward. You can easily fake a reference, sneak into a posh hotel in London and get a sheet of their notepaper. They never check.'

But by now I had accepted my fate in the U-gang and was not going to jeopardize it. I was so elated that I hardly noticed the squalor of the cabin finally assigned to me. Since then I have been startled to hear attacks on conditions on board ships which I would have found luxurious. There were eight of us in the small space, and every inch was precious. The best of the bunks were taken, so I put my bag on a lower bunk in the centre, glad that it was not an upper though I missed the refuge of a corner. A man was already unpacking and an Irishman joined us, then a strange, owlish man who was bald and slobbered through blubbery lips as he asked where I came from.

'London?' he echoed as if I had mentioned Zanzibar. 'Why, I'm from London myself.' For a moment I thought he was going to add, 'What a small world'.

Then there was Squeezy, a cockney boy with a broken tooth which gave him a disarmingly crooked smile. He spoke or rather swallowed his words with a thick East End accent as if his mouth was full of chestnuts, and did not know what on earth to make of me.

Squeezy and I were ordered to scrub a corridor, which sounded simple enough. Nowhere could we find a bucket, and those who had one refused to lend it. We returned to the second steward.

'Look here,' he said, pointing at his watch, 'you've already been an hour on this job, for fuck's sake get a move on.'

'Carn't,' said Squeezy with a scowl. 'Carn't get a bucket, can we?'

'I don't care about that,' said the second angrily. 'Get that work done, I've more when that's finished.' But Squeezy was unmoved, having lost all fear after several trips at sea. As soon as we were out of earshot he suggested we had some tea and I followed after him clutching a mop I had found in a cupboard – I was not letting go of that. The galley was a spacious room where no one seemed to be doing anything and Squeezy started a filthy conversation with a greasy-looking man, who wore a white cap on the back of his head and wielded a cleaver. He was the butcher, and his lascivious smile revealed his taste for the younger stewards, which was mental rather than physical, with a streak of sadism.

Squeezy had lost heart as far as buckets were concerned but I was anxious to get the job finished and returned to the bucket-locker where I spoke to the steward in charge with my finest Cambridge accent and a tone not used to disobedience: 'Please, I must ask you urgently to let me have two buckets, at once.'

The man handed them over immediately as a special favour on condition that I return them within the hour, which inspired Squeezy to find another mop and fill the buckets with a caustic mixture far removed from soap and water. None of this struck me as odd, for I had no idea what to expect, and scrubbing can be as soothing as gardening though it was disheartening when people walked past and over me leaving a trail of black prints where I had cleaned the deck. There was also the suspicion that the second had invented the job for the hell of it. I needed to make a last dash to London and explained this to the assistant second steward, a pleasant young man with fair hair who looked startled when I explained that *Picture Post* had commissioned me to photograph Dean Martin and Jerry Lewis at the Palladium.

'What's this?' exclaimed the second in disbelief when he was told. 'Want to go to London? So do I, laddie. I'd like to be able to leave my job just like that and go and say goodbye to my family, but I've work to do.' I stood there in a hangdog pose, subservient and silent.

'You need him, Mr Forster?' he asked the assistant second. The young man hesitated – for the sake of playing the game, I thought. 'No, I can keep Squeezy on the job. I guess I can spare him.'

'Report tomorrow six in the morning and mind you're there,' said the second. Ignoring a Dickensian scowl from Squeezy, I hurried to the dock gates and was promptly arrested. The evidence looked damning, for I was carrying my typewriter and a borrowed camera. By chance I had travelled as far as Gibraltar on the Orient Line (though not on the *Orcades*) when I went to Morocco for *Picture Post* and my passenger's label was still on my bag. And, by an unlucky coincidence, a Rolleiflex had been reported stolen. My explanation, that I was due to photograph the stars rehearsing at the Palladium and to finish an article on Big Ben for the *Evening Standard*, sounded so unconvincing that I was starting to doubt it myself when the policeman let me go.

The next morning I was appalled by my first sight of the 'plate-house' beyond the kitchens. I was sent there after a muster at 6.30 when the entire ship's company filed past the captain and the directors of the Orient Line. Our names were checked off a list with unsmiling stares – a moment of apprehension like the first day at school, feeling uncomfortable in my starched white jacket and blue trousers, the only time I wore them. After that it was jeans and tee-shirt, though this was overdressed in the jungle heat of the plate-house in action. The din was hideous as waiters raced by, throwing down dirty plates which we seized, scraping off the scraps with our fingers into the garbage bins. Then the plates were hurled into an ancient dish-washing machine where rubber wheels revolved crazily in murky water. We piled them into wooden racks which were lowered into boiling water before they were dried and stacked. After this we carried the blistering pyramids to various parts of the galley where more plates were needed. 'Silver' dishes were a separate torture, their heat even more agonizing. It was all a parody of hell, our half-naked figures glimpsed through bursts of steam and eyes half-blinded by sweat – all it needed was a crack of the whip to confirm the impression of a Roman galley where the men were flogged. In truth, the operation was run efficiently on a conveyor-belt system and the worst part was the monotony, though at the end of that first lunch my hands were shrivelled like the skin of an embryo in a bottle.

The *Orcades* was moving. Suddenly the sensation hit me. As soon as the last plate was stacked I raced on deck and leant over the rails, breathing in the air as we made our slow progress out of port, tiny figures waving goodbye, the shore receding slowly then more quickly when we reached the mouth of the river, busy with ships large and small, tankers and pleasure boats, Norwegian, French and Dutch.

As the great liner towering above them tore away from the land and thrust into the open sea, I felt an overwhelming relief. No telephone to answer, no letters in pursuit. Everything lay ahead. This was common-place to most of the crew but it breathed adventure for me.

'My God,' I told myself. 'For once you've done the right thing!' It was one of the happiest moments of my life.

◆

Luck was with me all the way. Later that afternoon the assistant second told me I was being transferred to the fruit locker: 'Cushy job. Bags of overtime.'

Overtime was the last thing I wanted; undertime would have been preferable. My hours in the fruit locker were 6.30 to 10.00, 12.30 to 3.00 and 5.00 to 10.00 – an eleven-hour day, seven days a week. But I was escaping from the drudgery of the plate-house and the overtime did prove a welcome addition to my monthly paypacket of £26.10s.10d. Now I would receive an extra 3s.6d. an hour for any work over ten hours. Most of the crew depended on overtime; the ship revolved on graft, and the fruit became my bargaining power.

The first evening was chaos. An angry surge of waiters, known as 'wingers', with their trays protested in front of the locker shouting for pineapple and melon like a demonstration. I was supposed to cut off the tops of the pineapples and barrel out the flesh with an empty tin, cut this in slices and put them back together with the plume of green leaves on top. This was simple enough except that pineapples come in different shapes and sizes – nothing to worry about at a small dinner-party, but overwhelming with several hundred pineapples to cut up and serve in a matter of minutes.

To my surprise, the second steward came to my assistance and instead of abusing my clumsiness he stripped off his braided jacket and waded in, subduing the wingers into sullen silence. First-night panic was nothing new to him.

Over the next few days the haze of impressions began to clarify. The plate-house seemed less of an inferno when I was sent there to help out, the smells from the galley hardly noticeable. Since childhood I have been fastidious about food, feeling nausea at the very appearance of a fried egg floating in a sea of rancid grease as in most canteens. On a liner, however, everything has to be kept clean and ventilated, hosed down and inspected every day, more hygienic than the kitchen in any restaurant.

Down below there was little feeling of being on a ship. There was practically no sway which I was glad of when I emptied the refuse from the fruit through the gaping hatchway on the side. Once I staggered perilously with a pile of crates as I slipped on some rotten garbage. 'The slightest heave and I'd have been overboard!' I exclaimed to the second who was observing me impassively. 'Would they stop and pick me up if I went over?'

'Hardly worth it, laddie. You'd be sucked straight into the propellers.'

The pressure of work and the lack of time to do it in were daunting at first. Having relished fruit I began to loathe the sight of it. Crates of oranges, apples and grapefruit had to be lugged up from the stores, hundreds of melons sliced, gallons of juice poured, and this was just for breakfast. Mangoes were hateful with their big stones in the middle, mostly unripe and dirty the moment they were cut, until we reached Fiji where we brought them on board fresh and I realized how perfect they can be. Even worse were the pineapples, whose acid juice burnt into the cuts on my fingers which were becoming raw. I heard worrying rumours about my predecessor who refused to continue, preferring to swelter in the depths of the laundry-room. I was told he suffered from such a bad case of scabs from the pineapples on the last cruise that his entire face had to be covered with blue ointment. I looked at myself anxiously each morning but I looked much the same, even healthier.

Gradually I developed the cunning which had failed me in the outside world. I became part of the barter and the thousand rackets on board. This was my perquisite as King of the Fruit Locker, far more advantageous than any overtime. With no time to sit down in the crew's mess I indulged in the accepted though forbidden practice of eating the passengers' food. In return for generous portions of fruit and juice to favourite waiters who hoped for handsome tips from their 'bloods', I had my choice from the first class menu which they brought me before the meal in appreciation of special service and unlimited fruit.

As the waiter raced by he would rest his tray for a moment to collect the fruit while a plate of crayfish would vanish under the counter below. I dined on paté and steak and baked alaska; the only thing missing was the wine. From the stores below I even had caviare. If the chief or second steward passed at the crucial moment, the waiter simply asked for his order and carried on with mine into the passengers' saloon. I became adept at holding food motionless in my mouth until the danger passed. Then I crouched on the floor and seized a mouthful.

For the next few months I seldom sat down to a meal but ate with my fingers: my digestion survived, if not my table manners.

Graft was the incentive from the chief steward to the smallest laundry boy. Many an engineer or deckhand in odd corners of that gargantuan ship was handed the evening's menu, with every course served by a steward who knew he would be 'seen all right' at the end of the voyage. Always a glutton, I was so delighted by the arrangement that the waiters took pleasure in recommending the best and rarest dish of the day. Conversely, they hated their 'bloods', though they lived in expectation of generous 'dropsy'. The bloods were the enemy, especially the Americans and Australians who ate staggering amounts. One of the Greek waiters from Claridges complained to me: 'This man he eats like an 'orse. He starts with melon, then homlette before the main course – oh my God!' I hated the woman who insisted on bottled ginger with every meal though it was not on the menu, which meant a special dash to the stores below. I resisted at first but the passengers won with a simple complaint to the second steward.

The passengers fascinated me because I glimpsed them so seldom and usually when I was scrubbing the main stairs, so I knew them largely by their shoes. I pestered the wingers for gossip, but the only scrap came from the head waiter known as Mary Queen of Scots who told me of a colonel and his lady wife at one of his tables on the first evening.

'I say, waiter,' complained the colonel's wife, referring to some notice from the purser. 'There's no card in our cabin.'

'Noël Coward!' exclaimed the colonel, horrified. 'What the devil is he doing there?'

As nerves started to fray with constant argument with the impatient waiters, the second sitting would suddenly be over and the tension forgotten as I hurried on deck for an afternoon of 'bronzing', two blissful hours of relaxation. As we crossed the Atlantic to Trinidad the days became hotter, but there was always a breeze. We had the forward deck, to my mind the best on the ship as I gazed over the side at the flying fish that skimmed the spray in a burst of fleeting colours, or the porpoises which seemed to jump for joy out of the water. At such moments I was sure there was no life so worthwhile.

After several days I realized that I was reasonably popular, liked for myself alone, which had seldom happened before. That was the joy of such an existence, that there is no point in being anything but what you are for no one will be impressed. In this respect it is wrong to compare a liner to a floating hotel where the staff can escape and indulge in a private life of their own, for on the *Orcades* there was no privacy and no escape except inside the pages of a book. We were dependent on each other, but like school and the army such self-containment was impermanent, ending the moment we saw the coast of England on our return, never the same friendship once on land.

There were eight of us in my cabin. Squeezy had mellowed: 'Fought you was educated, didn't I?' he said with a crooked leer. 'But it's all right now I know you're not.' A teddy boy arrived in full regalia just before we sailed. He had a swagger and dark looks and seldom spoke. Instead he sat on his bunk hour after hour playing with a pocket knife. He had a double in the next cabin and they stuck together closely, lost without their velvet collars and slim-jim ties. 'Owly', the Londoner, had been replaced by Mad Paddy. Probably every ship has its Mad Paddy and at times I fantasized that he had been signed on in order to boost the morale of the crew by making them feel superior, for it seemed incredible that any doctor could have passed him. I wondered also if he had the laugh on us, for he used his goofiness to his advantage: when ordered to go somewhere he lost his way; when he was on stores he threw a crate so violently that the man next in line refused to work beside him. Finally the second gave up and Paddy loped about doing less than anyone on board.

He was the only person I have known whose eyes looked as if they needed dusting. Tall and stooping, his movements were as unco-ordinated as a puppet's, his endless arms dangling despondently near his knees. I suspected he had TB; his skin was a sickly white as if someone had lifted a rock and he had crawled out. He was twenty-two and did not know where he came from in Ireland.

Paddy's fame spread throughout the ship. To start with he was dressed differently from anyone else. Instead of the usual blue-jeans and white tee-shirt, he wore a pair of shapeless grey flannel bags, a grey singlet intended to be white, and an indescribably filthy tweed jacket. His rare appearances on deck, when he stood blinking in the light and muttering to himself, or making long strides as he stared fixedly down, could hardly have gone unnoticed. Paddy had been thrown out of his last cabin because they could stand his dirtiness no longer, and as we were the lowest of the low he could descend no further. He never washed, or shaved the few vagrant hairs which met in the failure of a moustache, he had long dank hair and never wore socks. He had the bunk above me and as we reached the tropics the smell became unbearable; we threatened to throw him overboard. Finally we hounded him into the shower-room where he stood miserably under the water in his gum-boots, his worm-like body so pathetic we did not have the heart to go further and gave up. In his revolting way, Paddy was a survivor.

Then there was Den, a good-looking Londoner with a false tooth which he sucked in and out interminably. He looked pleasant enough, but had such a violent temper that he was unknowable. At the slightest provocation he started a fight. Bitterness constantly creased his brow as he recalled his prison sentence for robbery with violence, but as he told me more I felt he was lucky not to have been charged with manslaughter.

Bert was a hypochondriac, always convinced he was going to catch cold. As soon as it was dark and the air was blowing pleasantly through the ventilators, making the hot night bearable, Bert turned them off. Sure enough, he finally caught pneumonia and much to our relief was sent to the sick-bay. Bert was replaced by Marilyn: his real name was Alfred, but he hated being called Fred. Marilyn looked all the paler for dark, plucked eyebrows, the black mascara and the scarlet gown worn on special occasions, the only sign of the 'drag' deplored by the Australians in the train. Disappointingly, the present captain forbade it unless it was worn for a show. Marilyn was small and slim and not so young as he pretended. He was rarely in our cabin; unusually he had a regular lover and neither bothered to conceal it. Moreover, the 'husband' was one of the handsomest young waiters on the ship, dark curly hair, blue eyes, full lips, a pleasant open face – the conventional good looks that any girl would be proud to be seen with. Beside him, Marilyn looked sallow. When I asked about their sex-life I was assured that nothing really happened. However, another man in the 'husband's' cabin complained to me bitterly of the moans and groans which interrupted his sleep and which could have explained why Marilyn looked so worn out.

And then there was Saint Cecilia, real name Cecil, who joined us after the first two weeks after being demoted down the ship, starting as a wine steward, ending up with us. Ordinarily, I would have fled from Saint Cecilia. Large, perspiring, bald, he had the unpleasant habit of dribbling. Saliva ran weakly from his mouth in a distasteful trickle and one was apt to be sprayed when he spoke because he did so with the force of an erupting volcano, especially when he laughed. His vitality was endearing. At first I thought he took drugs, he was so perpetually 'high', but I saw no proof of this. Saint Cecilia had been an actor, and had not a good word left for that profession: 'My dear, it's absolutely finished,' he spluttered, 'no future there!' He disowned the stage, yet indulged in a stream of gossip referring to the stars by their first names. As I made the mistake of mentioning that I had met Edith Evans I was the natural target for his verbal spray: 'Dear Celia Johnson, my namesake, now there is a lovely actress! What wicked things the press are saying about poor John. I always say Noël is a real professional.' On board ship, people could indulge their fantasies and others would believe them, so it was sad to discover that Saint Cecilia's role in the various productions – 'Drury Lane in '52; with Larry at the Globe last year' – was that of scene-shifter. He confessed that his only performance on stage was that of a hump-backed footman in a northern pantomime.

Cecil's background sounded impressive – servants, titled parents and an Eton education. I doubted the latter and questioned him cruelly about the House he was in, and had he been a member of Pop, until he was careful to avoid the subject. That was unkind of me. Disconcertingly, many of his more outrageous claims turned out to be true, the final subterfuge of the liar.

At first I was so tired at the end of the day that I fell into my bunk and a deep, sound, sleep. Soon I looked forward to the 'Pig' in the evening. When the last sitting was over, I cleaned and locked up, hurried to the cabin to change out of my dripping tee-shirt and joined the line, mug in hand, for the weak beer which was the only drink we could buy from the Pig and Whistle. Even then, there was seldom time left for more than a couple of pints. Afterwards we would sit on deck or go down to the rec-room which sported an old piano and familiar prints of Renoir and Van Gogh. There were distractions like wrestling bouts and a film show once a week on deck if the weather was fine.

Though there were hundreds of crew they never seemed so many because the various sections preferred to keep to themselves. Broadly there were two main groups – straight and bent – plus apparent in-betweens like myself. The *Orcades*, indeed any liner of that size, was a queer's paradise with no need to dissemble. For most it was a non-stop cabaret, a preposterous projection of their fantasies, preening, posturing, with their own language and codes – 'bona', 'polari' – I was never entirely sure what they meant or how to spell them. Occasionally there were outbursts of jealousy and bitchiness revealing real and sadder selves. But the queers were indomitable, as essential to the running of a ship as the propellers. After a hard day's work which should have left them exhausted, they danced and sang long after everyone else crumpled. 'Gay' was indeed the word, with a party every night and a bottle of spirits in the cabin. Often a gramophone was rigged up on deck and the stewards danced with each other, and sometimes with normal waiters who enjoyed the exhibitionism and proved amazingly proficient. I remember one who twirled two stewards simultaneously with clockwork precision, for this was the era of rock 'n' roll. At times the passengers, hearing the music, would pause and look from the deck above on the crew enjoying themselves, then move on, puzzled, while the deckhands and engineers shouted ribald encouragement. The shipping line was wise: far from causing trouble, the feminine element was a necessary distraction in this unnatural society where men wrestled and the bedroom stewards liked to pretend they were girls, performing a show for the crew.

On some ships there were 'marriages', with a full ceremony and the 'bride' in white. On the previous voyage when the *Orcades* docked at Sydney a clergyman came on board to hold a full-scale service complete with bridesmaids. The couple left for a pretence honeymoon covered in confetti and cheered by the guests. Unwisely, a journalist and photographer had been invited to cover the event and the subsequent scandal when the pictures were published shook the directors of the Orient Line into issuing the ban on all 'drag' except for concerts. This was a disappointment, though I wonder how far I would have dared to go if circumstances had been different.

On the *Orcades* the queers exaggerated the illusion of femininity, realizing, as Hollywood did, that if you label any product cleverly enough the label is believed in spite of the reality. A sex-symbol is halfway to becoming one if called so.

Georgina took advantage of this phenomenon, closing the crew concert with a striptease. He claimed he had starred at the famous Carousel in Paris and produced a programme to prove it, explaining that his picture was not included because he was in a different show when the photos were taken. I doubt if he set foot there, but he knew the tricks, though he was built like a heavyweight wrestler, and gave a professional performance which transfixed the crew. Distracting their eyes with his G-string, he finally unhooked his sequinned bra revealing two tennis balls, which he bounced on the stage as he hurried off in the semi-darkness.

'Cor! I couldn't half go that,' exclaimed Squeezy, who would have hit any man who dared to suggest he might have 'gone with a queer'.

Georgina perpetuated the fantasy with his claim that he had auditioned as a female impersonator in a cabaret at Honolulu and though he failed had lived happily for several months with a sergeant in the American Marines, so he said.

I saw Georgina years later staring bleakly into a shop window full of delicate and tiny lingerie. He was barely recognizable, the features bloated like those of a punch-drunk boxer. When he shuffled away I did not call after him, pleased, though ashamed, that not a twinge of jealousy remained.

<hr />

We sailed into the tropics and I appreciated my kingdom of the fruit locker with its own porthole, ice-chest and supplies of cool fruit juice. Every day after the breakfast sitting, I revelled in a cold shower, repeating it as often as possible, but even so and despite taking salt tablets I had the common rash of prickly heat. Never have I welcomed sleep so gratefully nor slept so well.

When we arrived at San Francisco a cold mist was clinging to the top of the Golden Gate, lifting in time to reveal the other span of the delicate Oakland Bridge shimmering across the bay, and the island of Alcatraz as grim as its reputation. The sun broke through and I saw the city in front of us, sloping up the hill as clean as if it had just been washed. This is one of the greatest landfalls in the world, with the docks at the foot of the hill instead of the usual, deadly ride away from the centre of town. I hung over the rail absorbed as the *Orcades* slackened speed and docked interminably in the centre of the waterfront.

Mail arrived containing a cheque from American *Harper's Bazaar* forwarded from England as payment for a photograph – no more than £6 or £7, half of which had to be saved for Vancouver, but it was made out in dollars and I was rich. Few cities were as generous as San Francisco, before it became famous as the centre for hippies and subsequently as the gay capital. It had an innocence, then, and the main street was curiously deserted as I walked up the hill with Teddy in his velvet collar and his hair carefully enticed into a D.A.

'They look at us as if we're from Mars,' he complained.

'Can't imagine why,' I said.

Talk of the world being one's oyster! Everything was right that night. As darkness fell and the lights came up we chanced on the opening of a new club called Jazz City where Jack Teagarden was playing mournfully on his trombone, but even this was half-full and the most enthusiastic customer was Teagarden's sister. As we left a girl came up and started talking above the music. I said 'No', assuming she was a hostess, but her cry of 'Isn't this a small world' with an English accent made me look again and recognize Booey, a girl I had known and liked in Soho when I killed time with Johnson. She was crossing the States with another girl selling magazine subscriptions. They were leaving town that evening in a beat-up car. Seeing me count my money, she gave us two dollars before she left with mutual vows to celebrate Christmas together in London, never fulfilled.

We moved on to Chinatown, as sedate as a side-street in Purley, scattered with souvenir shops, and for a moment the night began to sag. In the Barbary Coast we parted company; Teddy wanted to go to a striptease while I, with some built-in radar, stumbled on a smoky, crowded bar called the Black Carnation, a cellar of a place unlike the usual long bar on ground level, with people dancing though scarcely a woman in sight.

Before I left England I had bought some clothes from 'Vince', whose real name was Bill Green, the inspiration for Carnaby Street. I have no clothes sense but for once I was dressed for the occasion – or rather the Black Carnation – in thin, tight jeans and a canvas-type jacket. I was absorbed into the atmosphere at once and the discovery that I was off a ship gave me instant popularity. It felt terrific to be stared and smiled at like a character out of Genet or Tennessee Williams.

When the Black Carnation closed I was driven to a warehouse which sold illicit drink in the loft above, and danced to an old piano lit by candlelight on crates. At four we continued to the top of a tower in the old part of San Francisco which had survived the earthquake. More greenhouse than penthouse, it was an extraordinary apartment with a glass roof which was so high that I looked up not merely at shrubs but at trees, the foliage so thick it had to be brushed apart as we walked through as if in a jungle. When a butler brought trays of glasses, I should not have been surprised to see him hacking his way with a machete.

One of the young men who had invited me disappeared, and in due course the butler asked me to follow him, pointing to an ordinary room where an old man lay in bed. He beckoned me to him with a desiccated smile reminiscent of Maugham's.

'How kind of you to come and see me. You're new aren't you, your first visit?' He spoke with such exquisite politeness that the next question jarred. 'And you're in the "merch"?' I nodded stupidly.

'I won't waste your time,' he continued more abruptly. 'I'm sure you want to enjoy yourself, but do me a favour dear. Take off your pants will you?' I gaped.

'Nothing more.'

Reassured, I started to undo my tight jeans.

'No,' he waved a hand impatiently. 'Don't drop them. Take them off.'

Too confused to argue I undid my baseball boots and took off my jeans. '*Ah*!' said the man appreciatively. Luckily I was wearing a pair of very brief Vince briefs and stood there hands on my hips like an erotic drawing in a physique magazine, without the peaked studded cap or motor-bike. Suddenly he thrust out a finger which he ran quickly inside the briefs.

Then he sank back, and as I put my trousers on again the butler reappeared as if by a secret signal and shut the door behind us on a faint 'Goodbye.'

'Goodbye,' I called back.

The butler handed me an envelope and pointed the way back to the party. I opened it behind an orange tree and stuffed the ten dollars into my pocket.

I left soon afterwards. My companion drove me to his home, a small, pleasant apartment in a large block. In spite of the drink I had remained sober, partly with the shock of it all. I studied him as he fried me a large hamburger, realizing how ravenous I had become. He was a couple of years older than myself, clean-cut, good-looking, with a slight but constant frown. We slept for an hour. He said he supposed I was the ship's tart and I did not deny it, wishing desperately that it were true. He drove me back to the *Orcades* in the early light.

I saw a couple of stewards looking down with admiration at my arrival in the open sports car. We said goodbye formally at the bottom of the gangway without any pretence that we would meet again, and smiled.

Then I ran up the gangway laughing out loud. The reality had surpassed the fantasy.

◆

On to Vancouver – red earth and forests and snow peaks above the clouds with the air crisp and scented with pine. The town had that dismaying Canadian gentility though it looked Wild West from outside. In one bar giants staggered in from the outback with fistfuls of wages, but were made to sit down at small separate tables while a Palm Court orchestra played sedately in the background, occasionally interrupted as a lumberjack staggered to his feet to smash a chair over another man's head.

Into the Pacific, with skies which were vaster than ever before. The *Orcades* had taken on more passengers for the run to Sydney, Americans hungry for fruit, so my locker was besieged by wingers swooping and shouting their orders like Red Indians on the warpath. The pressure grew so overwhelming that I was given an assistant called Walter. Though a bellboy, he had the ageless face of Stan Laurel and told me of his home town, in which he had a macabre pride.

'You know the sawn-off shotgun murder case?' he asked.

'Yes.'

'And you remember the photo in the Sunday paper of the policeman who found the body?'

'Yes.'

'Well he lives at the end of our street.'

Or: 'You remember the woman who sold her babies?' I found it saved time to say yes, and he continued: 'She lives in the next house but one . . . from a mate of mine.'

I interrupted to ask if he had enjoyed his time in Frisco. 'We went for a drive and stopped at that cliff where all those people were killed. I had a smashing time, me.'

In the afternoons we tanned and talked. I made a particular friend of a winger called Sam. I only saw him on deck for he refused to go to the Pig or the rec-room: 'It's my gesture against the ship,' he explained.

'A pretty silly gesture,' I pointed out. 'I don't suppose anyone minds if you come to the Pig or not.'

He slapped a brown leg in irritation: 'Don't you *see*? I'm trying to make my life as unpleasant as possible. Every time I get home I swear it's for good but after a couple of weeks I'm broke and I sign on again. I've given up smoking now. I want to hate the life so much that *nothing* will bring me back after this trip.'

Sam was a romantic, embittered yet idealistic, yearning for higher things, desperate to learn, to read, to talk. He had wide eyes and dark curls falling over a nut-brown skin, and a jutting jaw. Everyone accepted that he was a loner, neither popular nor unpopular.

'On my first trip,' he told me with disgust, 'I'd have walked off if I'd been able to find my way. These queers in the cabin with wigs on, mirror smeared with lipstick, talking of their 'usbands and how they'd scrub their cabins for 'em and dhobi their things – made me sick. Never left me alone. "You'll go with us," they said. "I'll spit in your eye first," I told them. "You will" – but I never did.' I listened sympathetically.

Sam confided in me because he spoke to no one else. He was thrown out of school when he was thirteen: 'I knew nuffin'. Fuck all. Didn't know the arts existed. I went to work in a wood factory – chips floating down, tears in my eyes and bread and jam in my pocket. Then the remand home. Spent a week painting a picture of some apples and they hung it on the wall. Happiest week I ever spent! Then a labourer over in Ireland, dancing every night, drinking, doing bad, but a strange thing happened – I began to know principles. Hurried back to my own bed every night, thought of nothing but work. Then came home, left for Butlin's and there I met this cute little barmaid, but I walked out on her, just left, ta ta! Hold on Sam! Been a dog all my life, must do better, so I joined the merch and it was a right disillusionment – all those dresses and wigs in the cabin – and when I complained and was transferred the next cabin was even worse – they'd come in with their guts bursting with beer, and make wind and shit all over the place. I'd turn on the blower so I wouldn't have to smell them, but I couldn't sleep.'

Idealistically, I joined in as we made our plans for the future, spurred on by Sam's determination to stay ashore. I remembered them when I received a letter a year later headed 'Pacific Ocean, Homeward Bound'; still a prisoner of the sea.

Daniel – how are you? I often wonder what happened to those
wonderful plans we made which came to nothing whose to blame
because they didn't, guess they were just the dreams of a couple of
seamen – plans are very stupid aren't they Dan but what can we do
without them . . . Only time I've placed you other than being part of
this life was while (and only when I was well in it did I realize so)
reading the Brothers Karamasov, Daniel you were Alyosha.

If only I were, I thought, reading it recently, if only I were.

As we neared Australia the talking-point was the 'dropsy from the
bloods', the tips expected from the passengers; without the hope of
lavish tips there was little point in signing on. The wingers schemed
for this moment: if a passenger asked for an order they made it sound
so difficult that when they reappeared successful it seemed a triumph.
The one exception was Sam. On principle he treated his bloods so
badly that there was no question of them offering him a tip and if
they did, or so he vowed, he would stay in the plate-house unable to
receive it. Ironically, his passengers adored him and I heard they had
even prepared a little speech. Instead they filled an envelope with
pound notes which made him depressed, or so he pretended.

It was close to riot in the first but especially the tourist class saloon
the night before we docked. The Greek waiters abused certain passengers and even fought them. With my wretched streak of priggishness
I was shocked. When I learnt of the passengers' meanness I was more
shocked. After a voyage of two months one passenger handed a tip
of ten shillings to his waiter who called over one of the bellboys and
gave it to him. When another waiter was offered five shillings, he
gave it back: 'Obviously you need this more than I do.'

'Perhaps so,' snapped the passenger who had seen the waiter, one of
the sharply dressed 'cowboys', sitting at the next table in the Honolulu
nightclub where he had taken his wife.

One woman left three 2½d stamps under a plate, but she was
forgiven with characteristic sentimentality because she was old and
reminded the waiter of his mother. Others gave as little as 2s.6d. and
some sneaked off without paying at all. That night I saw one Greek
reduced to angry tears while another had to be held back forcibly by
the chief steward to prevent him attacking the Australian who ate

'like an 'orse' and left no tip while insisting on a second portion of ice-cream. Other wingers came through the swing doors with radiant smiles as they counted tips up to forty pounds.

All was quiet when I went on deck as we glided into Sydney Harbour at five in the morning.

'What a cute château,' said an American woman above me.

'My, my,' cried another, 'that Captain Cook must have been real captivated.'

I was less captivated, too rigid in my expectations, for though this is one of the finest natural harbours in the world, jigsawed with small bays and inlets, in those days it was marred by a conflicting mass of buildings which clashed along the shore. Even Bondi Beach looked small and uninviting. Perhaps it was the dreary weather, the lack of money, or because Pyrmont where we docked was such a desolate district. Yet the Montgomery waited at the dock gates and there was little need to go further; all the good times were there. Monty's was one of the world's great dockland pubs, a happy confusion of people, and it was here on my second night that I made friends with a group of young Australian dockers who drove three of us to a ramshackle wooden house in Paddington which they kept as a hideaway for all-night parties, flirting and drinking, having sex across the railway lines when they took us back – or trying to, for we were interrupted by a patrol car to my lasting regret. They were as nice and innocent as we were, but the last party on a night of torrential rain proved different, with new faces, arguments and dissatisfaction. My Vince jacket, which had done me proud, was lost and my despondency grew when two queers who had gatecrashed the party dragged two of the dockers back on board to their cabin. I was pleased the next morning when they discovered that their rings and jewellery had gone, appearing with long, glum faces.

They were not alone. Many of the crew had been beaten up on shore, returning with cuts and bruises. Saint Cecilia had been arrested, or so it was rumoured, for he had disappeared after the first night when he was seen on another ship, visiting the cabins as if he was taking an inventory of a neighbour's house, gossiping as he criticized. He was picked up the next night climbing over the wall of a public lavatory. The Australian police must have shuddered as they took him in, his heavy make-up clashing with his baldness, for he was dropped at the gangway after a brief appearance in court where he was charged a nominal fine. He had two black eyes. 'Wee! I told that judge. "You want immigrants do you? Then you must be mad. This place is a *bloody* disgrace."' He seemed shaken all the same.

There was violence on board, too. Two wingers who had made a trip on the *Orcades* three years earlier had nursed a grudge against the head-waiter, Mary Queen of Scots. By chance their new ship docked in Sydney at the same time as us. They burst into the first class saloon before the sitting and sent a bellboy to fetch Mary Queen of Scots, a martinet who looked like Himmler. While the other wingers watched, too terrified or too pleased to interfere, they messed him about, ruffling his hair, tearing his collar, before they smashed in his face and tied him with a rope to one of the pipes. As they walked out they picked up any silver cutlery they could lay their hands on and threw it out of the porthole, continuing calmly to the Pig to exchange a beer with a couple of mates before they left a minute before the police arrived. When Mary Queen of Scots emerged from his cabin a week later, he still wore dark glasses.

Then there was Marilyn's 'husband's' brother Jack, who happened to be on the same ship and was told about his brother's affair by a jealous steward in Monty's. Drunk and disturbed, Jack came on board to look for his brother and found him in his cabin with Marilyn on his knee, straight from a party and wearing the scarlet gown. Marilyn described the scene to me as the two brothers fought each other without a word until they no longer had the heart to do so. 'See you ashore tomorrow at Monty's,' said Jack tearfully. Jim, who had taken most of the punishment, nodded. 'That's right', he said, but the moment his brother had gone he turned on Marilyn, threw him across the cabin so his head smacked into the wall, and ripped the scarlet gown to shreds. Marilyn slept in his own bunk next to mine from that night on, while the brothers met the next day as if nothing had happened.

'I hate this place,' said Marilyn with sudden intensity as we looked at the quayside before we sailed. 'There's always trouble.'

We stared glumly at the crowds below who had come to say good-bye, a moment of departure which never failed to move me. The cheerful band that seemed so inappropriate, considering the grief; the boys scrambling for cigarettes and even money thrown by the passengers; the streamers that stretched to the quayside with coloured, forced gaiety; the awkwardness as friends waited interminably for the ship to

I met Colin Wilson on the weekend when *The Outsider* made him famous, and we became inseparable for the next few months.

Below: Cliff Richard, who improves with age.

Above: Drifting into Soho. The York Minster, better known as The French Pub, was my first port of call and became my second home. The balding Gaston Berlemont behind the bar.

John Deakin. I found his wit and irreverence irresistible.

Above: On board the *Orcades*; Squeezy leering behind me in the Pig and Whistle.

Below: The nudists in *Out of Step,* which emptied the pubs and leapt into the top ten ratings.

Caitlin Thomas gave me my first taste of notoriety when I had to fade her off the air. Photograph by John Deakin.

Below: Playing myself in the film *The Angry Silence* with Michael Craig.

The beggar in Barcelona.

Far left: Noël Coward, whom I photographed for *Picture Post*. He did everything I asked, including being snapped on Brighton Pier, where no one recognised him.

Left: Barbara Cartland in *Success Story*. When I asked if she suffered from doubt, she demanded, 'What sort of doubt?' 'Self-doubt.' '*Never!*'

Below left: Trevor Howard, a man of exceptional charm which was wholly natural.

Below: Richard Burton during the Edinburgh Festival where he appeared as Hamlet.

Miss Carrie James, the old lady of Tasmania and the most remarkable interview I had, with her total recall of the convict days and the flagellator visiting Hobart from Port Arthur.

Below: Boy at Barnstaple Fair.

leave, and the moment of sudden panic as it moved away, with a girl crying out passionately, 'I love you, I love you!' as if she had never been sure of it before, while an old woman shook with the sorrow of knowing that this would be the last farewell. People waved and waved long after they could be seen. Shaken, I went below.

My undoing came at Auckland in a pub filled with men drinking against the clock as the infamous 'five o'clock swill' began: the pubs closed at six. The *Orcades* was about to sail. Plastic pipes poured beer into schooners like some alcoholic garage and a number of wingers sent over drinks as my 'dropsy' for all the service I had given them, refusing to accept a drink in return. Never have rounds whirled by so rapidly. I downed a dozen glasses of whisky, never my favourite drink, as they were thrust so generously before me. Suddenly they took effect. While some of the crew collapsed in a cab, I burst into the main street and ran down the hill to the ship hooting impatiently at the bottom. Other members of the crew ran past me as I stumbled legless, and to make it more surreal I was joined by the tallest man in the world and a midget, inseparable friends who were among our passengers, part of a travelling circus. We were followed by a gaping crowd of New Zealanders who had never seen such oddity before. As we reached the gangway I passed out.

When I came to in my bunk with a splitting headache Saint Cecilia was standing over me, which did not make me feel better. 'You're for it,' he chuckled. 'You're for it. Got you at last, they have. Better look out.' He told me that while I was unconscious the second entered the cabin and gave a sinister smile: 'I'm going to squeeze that dishcloth dry,' he muttered.

'But what did he mean?' he asked. I knew. I had posted an article to the *Evening Standard* about joining the merchant navy which was published under the heading 'Around the World with a Dishcloth'. Obviously this had come to the notice of the second, possibly the captain. Several of us were assembled on the bridge with hangovers, dressed in our uniform with the tight-necked white jacket.

'Farson, inside!' I was marched forward. The captain sat in the middle of the line of officers, a Union Jack behind him. When it was my turn he lost all control of himself.

'Around the world with a sweat-rag. I suppose you think that's funny, but we don't like people who write what we do on board.' I stood mute, though his venom startled me. 'You're here to do a job,' his voice grew shriller, 'not to write for the cheap London press.' I nearly giggled, thinking how hurt the *Evening Standard* would have been by this description. The captain was noted for his phobia about seamen dodging National Service, but he could hardly accuse me of that as he shuffled my papers in front of him. Then, in a splutter worthy of Saint Cecilia, he cried, 'You've come to sea to dodge something. What is it? I know . . .' he leaned forward with an alarming glare. 'You've come to sea to dodge taking photographs.' It was harder not to laugh this time but I managed to keep a straight face because his wild accusation had a grain of truth. Disappointed, he sat back and concluded: 'Ten shillings each charge, half a day's forfeiture and if you're up on the bridge again, a bad discharge.' I was dismissed. Afterwards I was told that he believed I had got drunk on purpose in order to get copy from my appearance on the bridge, which explained his excessive rage. I did write it up on my return, but the kindly *Standard* thought it showed me in too bad a light and cut it.

Suddenly we were homeward bound. Colombo, Bombay, Aden, the Suez Canal, Marseilles and up the English Channel, where the chill penetrated our bones and it was 'Channel Night' when Marilyn was beaten up by a guilt-ridden stoker and Saint Cecilia tried to kill himself, dramatically though ineffectively. Tilbury, and the stranded ship lay unfamiliar and inert. No romance of the high seas lingered. Most of us passed easily through customs, though one officer rummaging through Marilyn's cases was surprised by the quantity of feminine underwear. 'Bought for my girlfriend,' Marilyn explained unconvincingly. Saint Cecilia, who was next in line, fully recovered, hissed, 'Yes, all *used*.'

I had sailed round the world, almost 50,000 miles, and crossed the equator four times. I had conformed to the customs of the merchant navy with the foible of an identity bracelet above the tattoo on my hand, procured in Honolulu. My clothes and hair were different, but the change was greater than that: I looked young again, more self-reliant, and had lost the taint of Soho. When I returned to North Devon, Billy Henderson at the end of the lane stared at me astonished: 'I wouldn't have known you! You're different.'

Nine

Negley and Eve

MY PARENTS had settled at the Grey House during the war, having fallen in love with it when we were holidaying at Woolacombe in 1942, after my return to England from Canada. As well as the house there was a piece of land, with the stream where I had buried Oscar Wilde. Negley had bought the property with the proceeds of his book *Going Fishing*.

Eve had stuck by him all those years, travelling the world with him in greater or lesser discomfort and somehow coping with his relentless alcoholism. What she could not cope with, and what broke her, was his infidelity, especially with Sybil Vincent. This *femme fatale* loomed through my childhood and adolescence, with the added complication that the parents of my best friend at prep school, Anthony West, were Sybil Vincent's closest friends as well. There could be embarrassing confrontations if my father arrived for Parents' Day with my mother, for he knew the Wests far too well.

My grandmother, in a burst of indiscretion, assured me that Sybil Vincent, who had red hair and green eyes, had driven three men to suicide. My curiosity was tinged with awe, and she went up in my estimation. It seemed admirable that my father should be entangled with someone so dangerous.

What drove my father away? The easy explanation was sex, or the lack of it. He described this with astonishing transparency in his novel *The Story of a Lake*, based on the years he and Eve spent in British Columbia. Like many people who behave badly, he was an idealist and suffered remorse, so it is hard to understand why he made no effort to disguise his characters. In *The Story of a Lake* he confessed to the affair with the painful candour of a diary. My mother became 'Christina', named after the wife of a close friend; his Russian mistress Sura became 'Luba', and Sybil Vincent was 'Flick' – 'unbelievably the one woman he had been looking for – the perfect combination of brains and beauty'. As a form of expiation, he inscribed the novel to my mother as 'our book', yet she must have been humiliated by his frankness:

> One side of their married life, the side that most people assert is the all-in-all of it, had been as absent as if there had been no such thing. Within a month of his marriage night he was appalled by the tragedy he had let himself in for. For, even then, he had no idea of deserting Christina. It was just how could he reconcile things. A man like himself! And then Christina had taught him other things. He had found a beauty with her in life that had no connection whatever with the marriage-bed. In spite of it; in spite of the daily little annoyances and the inescapable tautness from living day to day with someone with whom you rarely sleep. A monk, he often thought, had far the easiest time. Christina and he clashed; and they did not have the safety valve of physical relief. They did not kiss and make up. They either talked or laughed themselves out of it. His way was to laugh, laugh at himself. They could talk, because mentally, he and Chris had become hand in glove. He had never known anyone capable of inspiring such devotion and faithfulness. Therefore he had been straight.
>
> In short, he had lived a life – ten years of it – of constant tribute to Christina. And he had never dared tell her about it. If she had known how often he had got up and walked to the window and simply bitten at his fingers at night, then she would have suffered unbearably because she would have known she had not satisfied him, and even the companionship they did have would have been spoiled.

She would have known it when she read *The Story of a Lake* and, I am sure, suffered unbearably from such a public humiliation. Significantly, Eleanor Roosevelt, who concealed her husband's unfaithfulness, wrote highly of it as one of her favourite novels.

In my mother's inadequacy, my father found an alibi for his other problem: 'When the physical urge became too strong at times he had deliberately deadened it with drink.' Unlike my mother, Sybil Vincent was able to match him glass for glass: 'If she was going to glory in her waywardness, he could be dissolute too. In this hard way, with bits in their teeth, they raced against each other. He could drink desperately, wholeheartedly now. It amused him to make Flick drink.

It was rare now when they had their moments of peace together: it was neck and neck to whatever calamity lay ahead of them.'

He was thrown into jail in Panama, but suffered a worse ignominy when asked to leave his favourite hotel in Pamplona because of their drunkenness. The climax was reached in the book when Luba came to Christina to beg for her support against Flick, a real event which my mother found hard to bear: 'She came over to mother's this afternoon . . . she said such beastly, beastly things.

'"You don't know what a ridiculous position you've placed me in," said Christina. "That one of your mistresses should come to me and complain about another."'

It is tempting to think that my father wrote this with humour, but it would not have seemed funny to anyone at the time. Years later, and I cannot imagine how such a subject came up, my mother startled me with the remark that my father had not been that sensational in bed himself, with the further implication that he had always been half in love with the memory of Jo-Jo, the boyhood friend with whom he had sailed the Chesapeake Bay. A photograph of them on the yacht hung in his bedroom.

As for my own sexuality, I am sure he knew. One afternoon, rather drunkenly and with immense goodwill, he queried a friendship of mine with the assurance that it did not really matter, provided I achieved something in life. On that and other occasions, he referred to John Gielgud as a prime example. Conversely, in one of my mother's diaries written during a winter's journey to Portugal, she described a young Englishman who was staying in the same hotel and was kind enough to help my drunken father to his bedroom, referring to him as 'a fearful pansy'. I cringed when I read this after her death. Did she not realize that I was 'a fearful pansy' too?

Throughout my childhood she did her best to conceal the threat of Sybil Vincent, which alarmed me more than the scraps I was able to overhear. A child can cope with difficult truth more easily than subterfuge. When we went to stay with a friend who was devoted to my mother, she embraced us tearfully as if we had just been saved from a shipwreck. 'Oh, you poor darling,' she cried, hugging me on my arrival. 'Oh, that poor Yeva,' as she turned to clasp my mother. Instinctively, I was frightened by such an excess of emotion which I did not fully understand.

One night I woke in a small room which had been a dressing-room, adjoining my mother's, and heard loud whispers. Tiptoeing to the connecting door, which was slightly ajar, I heard my mother's voice racked by sobbing. The words meant little but the grief must have unnerved me for I moved forward and was instantly engulfed.

'Oh, the poor, poor darling,' moaned my mother's friend.

'What is to become of us?' sobbed my mother, and I joined in the tears with little understanding.

Unable to choose between the two women, my father divided his life disastrously. When he was with my mother he suffered the agony of frustration; when he was with Sybil, he was tormented by remorse. If he had been more cynical he might have enjoyed himself more, but he was too 'decent', to use one of his favourite words, for his own peace of mind. At Christmas 1936 he wrote reassuringly to my mother from a clinic in Hamburg where he was being treated for alcoholism; but as I have remarked before, there is no deceiver like the self-deceiver:

> Perhaps the finest Christmas present I have given you this Xmas or any other for that matter – is a letter I wrote to Sybil yesterday – a short one ending 'I shall be leaving here about the time this reaches you. There is no need for you to write so forget it.'

That this was harsh to Sybil did not occur to him. He confirmed to my mother that 1937 would be their lucky year: 'and I will make it or bust and I am *not* going to bust. So watch out for London reactions; I have an idea she will be a bit poisonous on that end. I have done this because I think it would ruin your life otherwise – and you have been too good a brick to be treated like that.' For once there is some deviousness: casting himself as the martyr while my mother has the lesser role of 'brick'.

The following year I wrote to my grandmother from Sweden:

> I am going to tell you the exact truth. Pops *drunk a lot* of beer and acribite on the boat. He got thoroughly Ga-Ga and said he was going off to China for ever and leave us some money. Well anyhow we didn't listen to him and got him to bed in a Hotel. We were coming back to England if Pops was still bad in the morning. He came to me in bed that morning perfectly all right and said don't believe that China stuff. When I get drinking I say foolish things. Well he's perfectly all right now and we had a lovely day today.

I was ten. When the going was good, we could hardly have been happier, possibly because the shadow of his alcoholism made us appreciate the good times all the more.

Then, just as we were starting to believe in some miraculous conversion, my father would disappear and resume his drinking. The pace was too great and he started to crack up. 'Darling Moley' (they called each other Mole and Toad) he wrote from yet another clinic, 'You are making the most awful mistake . . . Sybil was not with me in Denmark [it amazes me that he was still able to travel so extensively]. I did not see her until here in Hamburg. She stayed over here a few days to see me.'

By April 1938 he was sane enough to know that his mind was in peril. Coupled with guilt towards my mother was the added guilt about his work:

Anyone who has ever fought against drink will know what I mean when I say that I loathed seeing the daylight come into my room. A thing I never do unless I am desperate, I slept with the blinds down. I never knew what time it was when I woke up; I never wanted to wake up. I wanted to be out of this world: sleep was the only way I could escape. My bed-clothes were like sheets thrown into a laundry basket; in the paroxysms of my nightmares I had twisted them all over the bed. My clothes lay wherever I had flung them before falling into bed. I woke up fully dressed without even having had the decency to take my shoes off. My suit-cases were a revolting mess: books, clothes, suits all piled in confusion. My typewriter, untouched, was a constant reproach to me.

I have taken that same road: the detritus of the morning after, the accusation of the scattered clothes, the struggle to find a cool place on the pillow, the meaningless equation which racks the brain, the angry images of the night before.

There is the danger in quoting him that I will fail to convey the indescribable joy of the man and might introduce a note of self-pity, an emotion that was completely alien to him. It was not self-pity but self-disgust. He never knew how he arrived in Munich in his desperate bid to seek help from the remarkable Dr Bumke, allegedly flown to Russia in case he could save the dying Lenin, and Hitler's doctor too.

My father woke fully dressed in a hotel bedroom, his bags stacked by a table, one of them containing a bottle of Martell. 'Anyone who has suffered the misery of heavy drinking will know the feeling of *Power* that gave me.' After the cognac had settled his nerves, he rumpled his bed to make it look slept in, forced himself to eat three soft-boiled eggs, and soaked himself in the hottest bath he could stand. Dressing in a fresh suit of clothes, he went downstairs and asked the manager to put him through to Bumke's sanitorium. When the man put down the telephone, he spoke with genuine sympathy: 'The Herr Professor is in Venice. They do not know when he will return.'

In the days while he waited for Bumke's return, my father believed he came close to the delirium tremens he had escaped so far. When, finally, he entered Bumke's study in the state hospital, he knew he had reached it 'only just in time'.

I saw a slender little man, grey with an air of great learning. He had none of the affectations of the near great, but got down to business at once. I think he saw in my face that I knew I had come into good hands. I believed in Dr Bumke from the first time I saw him. He made me undress completely. He directed me to stand facing a window and pulled up a chair and sat behind me. There had been a premature spring in Bavaria, or an exceptionally late fall of snow; and I shall never forget my feelings, my forlornness, as I stood there, staring at that fresh growing life, so beautiful and gay under its clean snow, and thought of the dirty mess I had made of my own life.

Almost simultaneously, he received a letter from Sybil asking him to join her in Vienna, an appeal he could not resist. On the excuse of needing money, he asked for his passport from Bumke who nodded, but left the room locking the door behind him. When he returned he spoke slowly: 'Mr Farson — your mind is in grave peril. You must believe me. I do not want you to ask me for permission to leave here. If you go to Vienna, why, Mr Farson . . . No, you must not go. No, Mr Farson. You are in a condition now where I can help you. Please do stay here.'

My father looked through the barred window on to a courtyard where the mental patients were walking, about five hundred altogether, and started to undo his tie: 'Very well Dr Bumke, I will stay.'

The next day he wrote to my mother:

When I wanted to get out of here yesterday, he was ready to get the

American consul to give him a permit to restrain me – he is that kind of professor. In fact, except that I am being attended by German nuns, I might as well be`in jail.

He thinks my mind is imperilled if I drink now.

This whole business of torn-decisions that I have gone through these last two years [since the triumph of the *Transgressor*] is the history of a disordered mind. And as I can never remove from my soul my deep love and remorse for the sorrow I have brought you – I want to have my mind clear to see things in focus. In my opinion it is worth any amount of torture or loneliness for me if I can reach that point of a clear-thinking mind *about myself*.

My mother suspected that Bumke used hypnosis, and my father's fury at this suggestion seemed to confirm it, but I believe it was simpler, that he tapped the strength that my father still possessed and enabled him to find himself again.

'You have had an unusually wide experience of life,' Bumke told him. 'Why don't you give yourself the benefit of it? Be kinder to yourself.'

Bumke gave him injections, too, from a syringe an inch wide and four inches long, filled with a liquid which looked like port. Pushing in that needle was no fun for him, nor for the doctor who leaned on it and groaned. But one day when he was sitting on a wicker chair in the corridor, he fell asleep and when he woke he felt a sense of ease that was almost ineffable – 'as if all the tensions inside me had suddenly been let down – and while I was enjoying this drowsy languor of a peace I had not known for years I was aware that Bumke himself was standing there looking down on me.' And he was smiling.

There was one last hiccup: putting through a reassuring phone call to my mother, the confused operator repeated Sybil's number to her by mistake – the one he had been asked to ring afterwards.

Totally in command, my father went straight to the Sailing Club at Chichester Harbour to work on *The Story of a Lake*. This time he did not have to choose between the two women. 'I told Eve that I was going to keep away from the family for some time – I did not know for how long; but one day we should be together again. She understood.' He was on his own.

With his enthusiasm recharged, he set out for South Africa and after several months he sent for my mother to join him at Dar es

Salaam. As they had sailed across Europe, now they drove across Africa, and it was only after fifteen months, when he was weakened by malaria and overdoses of M&B for gangrene which had infected his old leg wound, that he started to drink again. By then it seems likely that Bumke's treatment was wearing off, for the venom flowed in a torrent of accumulated bitterness. Things were said and things happened that were too vile to be more than hinted at afterwards. After his death, my mother asked me if I minded if she destroyed his more painful letters, and I felt I had to agree though they might have explained his actions, if, indeed, there was any explanation apart from the pent-up bile.

Heartbroken, my mother returned to England on a German boat from the Cameroons shortly before the outbreak of war. My father went into a hospital at Accra which promptly collapsed in an earthquake which he reported with his professional skill intact. I remember my mother's misery on her return; I have seen few people so destroyed, her face puffy and her eyes red from weeping. She was wearing a coat made from one of the leopards he had shot in the earlier, happier part of their journey. It was too tight and, as they say, it would have looked nicer on the leopard. I wince whenever I see such a coat today, even the usual fake. His cruelty must have been refined to cause such utter desolation; an excess of decency can be as dangerous as the lack of it. Yet characteristically forgetting the hideous climax, he dedicated *Behind God's Back*: 'To my Wife – my sole companion on the drive from coast to coast across Africa; she was better than any man.'

One evening in London, during my protracted adolescence, my father startled me:

'Do you know how long it is since I last poked your mother?'

I shook my head in my confusion, and he continued: 'Well just you listen to me, the last time was . . .' I did some rapid arithmetic, wondering if he was about to reveal that I was illegitimate, but this was drunken talk and he continued interminably, 'And you know what that does to a man?' I had no idea and shook my head again. 'Well just you listen, and you might learn something.'

A few mornings later he asked me to accompany him as he left the house in Pelham Place. His hair was combed back blackly with water, his skin was dry from alcohol and he was short of breath. His limp was noticeable in town and we walked slowly down Pelham Crescent while my grandmother watched us anxiously from the drawing-room window, wearing her hat as always. At the end of the graceful curve of the crescent we crossed the road to the Admiral Keppel, where the barman, who had just unlocked the door, gave my father a beady glare as he ordered his first restorative drink of the day. I sensed there had been trouble, but my father was too formidable to rebuke. To the barman's obvious relief, my father did not settle down; we moved on to a house in a quiet street near the King's Road.

The door was opened by a greying, middle-aged woman with a fag in her mouth who looked tired and none too pleased to see us. Obviously we were not expected. She led us into an airless, silent room and I sat on the edge of a chintz sofa in a conflict of guilt over such a betrayal of my mother, and yet exhilaration at meeting Sybil Vincent at last.

What had happened to the flaming red hair, now lack-lustre? And the green eyes, now red-rimmed? The only wickedness came from an empty glass which smelled of whisky, and the cigarette drooping from the corner of her mouth.

I felt a sharp sense of disappointment, almost indignation, at having been misled. She and my father looked so vulnerable. After a few minutes I made an excuse and left. Outside, my step was stronger than before. I had come of age. My father was fallible.

When he was sixty, my father embarked on yet another cure as if in expiation for his drinking. This time he went to a clinic, or 'loony bin' as my mother called it, in Copenhagen. A girl I shall call Miss Svenson took a cardiogram of his heart and apparently lost hers in the process. When she took him to lunch with her father, an eminent Nobel Prize winner, my father told him that his Nordic myths were a lot of boring nonsense, which may have been true but did not endear him.

As the ultimate confessional, my mother bared her feelings in the diary that I discovered after her death. It started with her surprise when my father returned from Denmark in the middle of January and she collected him from the airport where he was drunk but in the best of moods, anxious to settle near his pile of luggage and tell her all about Miss Svenson, who had never been mentioned in his letters. My mother realized that he was infatuated. 'I never touched her,' he assured my mother. 'That girl is as straight as a string. She is a virgin.

I told her if I had met her forty years earlier – but there is too much difference between us.'

On her side, Miss Svenson pursued him with letters and he cabled her to fly over. After a week's silence, she replied that this was impossible because her father would not allow it, whereupon my mother made a foolish mistake. Obviously relieved, she sent a warm letter to say how sorry they *both* were and how she must come at a nicer time of year. With this sanction came the instant reply: 'Fetch me Waterloo 12.25 on 21st.'

I found them in the afternoon, sitting on the sofa in the drawing-room of Pelham Place with Miss Svenson having tea with my grandmother. She was boyish and not at all smart. Her most striking feature was her eyes, large and blue with long black lashes, though her hair, which needed cutting, was yellow. Not blonde but yellow. Her worst feature was a mouth filled with prominent teeth which prevented her from being pretty. Either she had the innocence of a schoolgirl or an inner sophistication; it was hard to tell for she remained mute as if dazed from her journey.

'I think she's rather sweet,' said my grandmother generously after they had gone downstairs to rest. A few minutes later they reappeared and my father announced they were off to the sherry bar around the corner, though I warned him it was shut. Sure enough, it was, so they continued to the Savoy, returning an hour later with Miss Svenson looking more dazed than before.

'You must be very tired,' said my grandmother sympathetically.

This time she spoke. 'Very tired, very sick.'

My father rang for another taxi to take us to the Ecu de France in Jermyn Street. Over dinner I wondered if Miss Svenson was regretting her arrival as my father became increasingly maudlin.

'Isn't she the sweetest? Isn't that a sweet face?' I had to agree every time, though more interested in the excellent food in a restaurant where my father was still welcome and made to feel important. Later I rang my mother to reassure her. 'I don't know what to make of her,' I admitted, 'but I think she's miserable.'

Surprisingly, they caught the train to Devon next morning and my mother met them at the station. She confided in her diary:

Friday 22nd: A bull-doggy little schoolgirl in an ugly grey school coat and no hat. Very abrupt. Quite monosyllabic but chiefly silent. Sits hunched up with a very round back staring into space and never volunteering a remark and seldom even answering when one is made to her.

Considering they had spent the whole journey in the dining car, N wonderfully little tight. Just enough to keep on '*Isn't* it a sweet fripette? Did I say a word too much?' She seemed used to it. I laughed and said 'I quite agree with you but I'm not going to discuss her and embarrass her.' No comment from Miss S.

23rd/24th: She is *the* most baffling girl I have ever met anywhere. She *can* speak very good English but never does. She has brought no clothes whatever except one rather soiled pair of blue slacks and a very dirty eiderdown sleeping bag in which she sleeps inside the other bed clothes and shuffles along to N's room and even down to breakfast.

Hour after hour she sits or lies in N's room — never uttering. At last he came out and said, 'I must say she gets on my nerves!' Sunday he took her for a drive along the lovely Lynton coast. It was sunny and blue but she made no comment on anything. I have no idea if she is in love with Negley but should doubt her capable of it.

The clink of the morning tea is the signal for her to lope along in the sleeping bag and slump onto his bed. When I am in bed at night and the passage light is out — her door opens and along she hops and shuffles again — shuts his door and flops on to the foot of his bed where she stays for one or two hours — he declares never speaking. I can only say it is the most extraordinary infatuation I have ever known and can only be explained by his never having seen her really sober in Denmark — when he was I mean!

It is an infatuation no longer. This morning he and I agreed that the poor girl is mental. Quite sub-normal.

January 27th: Not nearly so good yesterday. In fact a horrid day with he and her in firm alliance, and I feeling like someone on a desert island who had not been introduced to the two at the other end. If I speak, neither of them answers.

Their neighbours, Eve and Malcolm Elwin, relieved the tension by inviting them all to lunch. The other Eve thought my mother was wrong to have stayed there and should have walked out, saying she would not have stayed for a single hour. She did not believe Miss Svenson was a bad or scheming girl, just that it was an impossible situation.

'I have never prayed so hard or so often in my life,' my mother wrote in her diary, which was odd as I had never known her pray before.

It doesn't seem to help much, but perhaps without it I should have been much worse. It is horribly cowardly and self-pitying to keep thinking of suicide but when I look out to sea I can't help thinking how easy it would be to rush into those clean icy waves and finish it all. This agony of love for Negley that gets no response, and always makes me say and do the wrong thing and is tearing me to pieces. Far better really, just to leave him – but I can't face being without him while we both live.

January 28th: Why should it infuriate me when N tells me to give her sewing things so she can mend his coat! Of course it is obvious why.

After dinner N and I talk about old days in Russia and tho' she doesn't utter the atmosphere is a little calmer. They go up to my room early to get the water-bottles boiled – and then the trips to his room begin. She stays until 12.30 this time and I didn't get to sleep until after 2.

We lunch again with the Elwins. Kind Eve says it will make this ghastly a trois a bit shorter and Malcolm is touchingly kind and friendly. Bitterly cold and I keep taking up kettles to the poor hens whose water is a solid block.

Miss S is exclusively clothed in all N's clothes, having none of her own, even a dressing gown.

January 30th: We woke to find snow and heavy frost and the postman reported roads impossible without chains – so no chance of our going to see her off. Luckily I had booked Clarke last night to come and fetch her – which N seemed delighted about. He seemed terrified something would stop her going. How queer it all is.

Well, she's gone and I think things are almost worse than ever! N hasn't said a word all day and I think is very wretched and 'taut'. I have really tried my damndest as I feel wretchedly sorry for him – if I am gentle, natural and cheerful I hope and think it will pass.

It was my duty to look after Miss Svenson on her return to London. My father telephoned her while we were having dinner, then in desperation I took her to Soho. At our first meeting I thought she was either shrewd or naïve. Now I was positive. Far from being intimidated by the Colony, she adapted and flirted easily. No longer was she silent.

'A clever little number, that one,' said Muriel.

In The French Pub she met her match in Deakin, who flattered her outrageously while she looked arch. 'What charm!' he exclaimed, eyeing her up and down. 'And so chic, a real little Danish pastry.' She blushed prettily while he raised his eyebrows behind her back.

Meanwhile in Devon, my mother made a disastrous attempt to break the atmosphere of doom. Dressing up in an eiderdown, she clumped along the corridor to my father's bedroom as if in a sleeping-bag. The joke misfired, for my father rushed out thinking she had fallen and was furious. This was nothing compared to his fury with me when he received a brief letter from Miss Svenson informing him that I had not seen her off at the airport as instructed. As I was working, it would have been difficult but I had not admitted this to my father, who rushed off a letter saying that I was second-rate, could never be depended on, only made contact when I wanted something, and then made no return. His words were blistering and true, though no one thought it odd that I should have been told to chaperone Miss Svenson in the first place, nor that my grandmother (my mother's mother) should have been asked to house her.

As so often it was my grandmother who acted as peacemaker, pointing out in a gentle letter that I had gone to considerable trouble in showing Miss Svenson around. A generous letter followed from my father.

Did he have an affair with Miss Svenson? I should have thought so if I had not met her. Probably it was a yearning for one more new horizon. My mother wrote in her diary: 'My life seems to close in and get narrower and more useless each year.' If she could write that it is possible to imagine my father's desolation after Miss Svenson went home.

Ten

The Idol of Millions

I WAS REASSURED, though slightly hurt to find that I fitted back in Soho as if my spell with the merchant navy had never happened. Conversations were resumed – 'Dan, we were just saying . . .' – and few people asked about my travels. With a new objectivity, I realized this was the nature of Soho and felt relieved; it was like not having to bother to unpack. Deakin was still feuding with Archer: 'This silly little man just invites trouble,' Archer explained as if I had never met Deakin before. 'I do believe he likes it.'

'Shut up,' Deakin replied, 'I've had enough of your boredom. Buy me a pink gin.'

'Must I?' Archer gave a dramatic sigh.

'Yes, you must if you want to hear what happened to me last night.' This was typical blackmail, tantalizing us with tales of disaster to be unfolded when he had a glass in his hands.

'Obviously you're dying to tell me,' said Archer, reluctantly paying for the drink while offering me one with his usual courtesy. 'What did happen?'

'Tony tried to murder me last night.'

Archer gave a raucous laugh. 'Oh, is that all! You mean the nice Spanish waiter chap.'

'That's what he says he is,' Deakin frowned. 'The man's a lunatic. He should be locked up. This is where he tried to strangle me.' He pulled down the stained sweater and pointed to a red mark on his neck.

'Oh, don't be ridiculous, Deakin,' cried a well-dressed woman beside us. 'It's a drink flush.' Deakin looked hurt, if not by the Spanish waiter.

'A fat lot of sympathy. He was hanging around all evening and I simply refused to speak to him, that's all. He stood there with that idiotic smile until I turned on him.' Deakin re-enacted the scene with unnecessary realism and volume, staring at me as he did so. I nodded and smiled sympathetically in case anyone thought the words were directed at me personally.

'"If you wonder why I'm speaking to you, I'll tell you. Frankly you bore the bejesus out of me. Go away." Then at two o'clock I heard the doorbell and looked out of the window in Berwick Street and saw who it was. "Oh, poor Tony, he's probably got nowhere to sleep"' – Archer gave a drawn-out sigh of disbelief – 'so I threw down the key. He charged up the stairs, seized a saucepan of coffee from the kitchen, threw it all over me and started to strangle me. He is terribly strong you know,' he added, with a note of admiration. 'At first I tried to resist, but I was too weak. Well, you know how drunk I was in the Mandrake, so I pretended to cry.'

'My oh my,' said Archer.

'Well, I had to. Then he said he wanted a drink. I told him there was a club round the corner which stayed open all night and I managed to get him outside. Thank heavens there was a policeman. "Constable," I said, "I'm making no charges, but kindly remove this man. I don't want him here."'

'What happened then?' I asked, startled by the entire episode.

'Then? Oh, he went away.'

Archer had seldom been happier, having opened his bookshop in Romilly Street with the sign: DAVID ARCHER BOOKSELLER PARTON PRESS. This was the fulfilment of his dreams, with a coffee bar run by Henrietta who served dangerous watercress sandwiches, and an exhibition area in the basement appropriated by Deakin for his photographs. The bookshop was doomed because Archer loved his books so dearly that he hated to part with them. Once I heard him tell a potential customer to try Better Books in Charing Cross Road. 'But you have a copy on the shelf.' I reminded him as the disconsolate man wandered off.

'Well, yes, but it's the only one.'

Deakin was shameless in taking advantage of Archer's good nature without actually helping himself from the till, though he might have done so when no one was looking. One morning I was talking to David when Deakin arrived carrying a crumpled suit.

'What are you doing with that?'

Deakin seized his chance without a second's hesitation and rounded on him. 'What do you think? I'm desperate. I'm pawning it, I have to pay my rent, don't I?'

'Dear me,' said Archer, 'I thought I'd paid that several days ago. Ah well . . .' he gave him two pound notes, a considerable sum. Outside, Deakin gave his Mickey Mouse grin. 'I'll pop these in the cleaners, which is where I was going, and I'll see you in the French.'

Archer's generosity may have been foolhardy, but he was a truly kind man and gave selflessly. He was so considerate that when he gave someone a ten-shilling note he would slip it into an empty matchbox to spare the man's embarrassment as he handed it over. Sometimes the recipient, hearing no rustle of matches inside, threw the box away.

When I asked what the well-designed bookshop had cost, he shied away. 'Hmm, I'm rather edgy about finance. About three thousand pounds'; but he brightened when I asked how it differed from the Parton bookshop in the thirties. 'Dear me, that was just a hole in the corner thing. This time we're going to specialize in poetry and criticism. And I'm going to publish, too.'

That was the glorious aspect of Archer, that he seemed a mad dilettante but he put his flair of spotting new talent into practice. This time it was a book of poems by the young Indian Dom Moraes, dedicated to Henrietta who became his wife. *A Beginning*, probably the last Parton publication, won the Hawthendorn Prize, though Henrietta dismissed her husband later as 'that twenty-four-hour poet'.

'All David really wanted,' she told me, 'was a sort of salon, that's why he wanted a coffee bar. Strangers used to come off the street, rather attracted by this sort of bookshop, and he'd say, "Hey, don't ask me about that, there's a very good shop up the road called Foyle's, go there." I used to shout and scream at him, "Don't be so idiotic. Of course we can sell them those books," but he wasn't interested in commerce.'

'Strangers used to come off the street' – that was exactly what Archer was hoping for and in this sense the bookshop was successful. One of the strangers was Colin Wilson and it is apt that one of the most rewarding friendships of my life began in Archer's one Saturday afternoon in 1956.

'I suppose you two should meet each other,' Archer said awkwardly, waving his good arm while the other clutched the usual stack of books not for sale. Since he failed to introduce us, we introduced ourselves, laughing, and I was able to hand Colin a copy of the evening paper which contained the first review of *The Outsider*. There are few things more calculated to lift the spirits than glowing praise for your first book, and I was the bringer of good news. We took to each other at once, vowing to meet again on the Monday. By then he was famous after the acclaim from our two leading critics, Cyril Connolly in the *Sunday Times* and Philip Toynbee in the *Observer*. During the next few months I witnessed the onslaught of fame which descended on the self-styled genius whose humorous, student's face, owlish spectacles and polo-neck jumper became as familiar to the public as a pop star or football hero. With time on my hands I spent hours in his squalid bedsit in Notting Hill Gate, gagging from the reek of sausages cooked in month-old grease over a Primus ring, washed down with the wine he could now afford in plenty. A shaky table was littered with unwashed plates and broken chocolate biscuits. An Einstein quotation was scribbled on the wall next to a pin-up of Nietzsche and various loony-looking girls wandered in and out enigmatically. This was a boy-scout Bohemia which had passed me by so far, and I listened cross-legged and happy as Colin talked brilliantly on subjects I half-understood.

'What is an Outsider?' I asked him.

'We're technically too rich. We've moved too far from life. The Outsider is the frustrated creator in conflict with a civilization that has become too complex.'

'What advice do you give to the post-war generation?'

'Discipline, you must have self-discipline.'

On other days we bicycled for miles around the East End looking for the sites of Jack the Ripper's murders, an obsession I began to share.

I was between jobs once again. On my return from sea I wrote for the *Evening Standard* so frequently that I had my own place at the features desk with such established Fleet Street figures as the critic Milton Shulman and Alan Brien. I never worked with Ken Allsop on *Picture Post* but saw him regularly now. For some reason we avoided El Vino's where most of the journalists gathered – perhaps that is why we avoided it – meeting instead in the Cock Tavern. Robert Muller, the journalist who accompanied me to Brighton to interview Noël Coward, hurried in one day with the dramatic news that he was being sued for libel by the busty starlet Sabrina. 'Who will take the word of a harlot against that of a serious writer?' The astonished pause which followed was broken by Alan Brien. 'I recognize the harlot,' he pondered, 'but who is the serious writer?'

The *Standard* asked me to write a series on London's publishers, promoted by posters proclaiming A CRISIS IN THE BOOK TRADE. There is *always* a crisis in the book trade, and few activities please publishers more than writing indignant letters to the editor with the chance of seeing their own names in print instead of their authors'. Even so, the volume of the complaints was alarming. The final straw was a letter from David Archer, whose bookshop I had featured out of kindness. Not content with that in his craving for publicity, he wrote to the editor pointing out that I was inaccurate in stating that he could take the credit for Dylan Thomas's first poems, in fact there had been a collaborator, and so on in Archer's long-winded but impressive way. He meant well, but the charge of inaccuracy rankled and I was told off for carelessness.

But the incident did me no harm. I was woken early one morning by the editor Charles Wintour with the news that Lord Beaverbrook wanted to see me at Arlington House at two-thirty. This was a proverbial move in the Fleet Street game of snakes and ladders, a summons from the Beaver, who took a keen interest in his staff, especially a young journalist who might be groomed for great things in the Express Group. Some became editors.

I was punctual for once, shown into the lavish penthouse next to the Ritz, overlooking Green Park. There were three jars of honey on a table with labels reading 'Lord Beaverbrook', and I was about to sneak a look at some papers beside them when Beaverbrook entered the hall, showing out his luncheon guest, a large man who puffed complacently at a large cigar. Then he turned to me.

'Thank you so much for coming here,' said the Beaver in a thick Canadian accent. I murmured that it was a great pleasure. He was tanned, tiny and older than I expected, but surprisingly sexy. His eyes were weak but demanding. 'And how long have you been on the staff of the *Express*?'

My heart sank. I explained that I was a freelance for the *Standard*.

'Yes, yes, quite so, that's what I meant,' he said irritably, and asked if I was married. In as deep a voice as I could muster, I said I was not and felt that my face was covered in rouge and smeared lipstick.

'Do you write every day?' I assured him that I did.

'Do you work hard?'

To my dismay I heard myself reply, 'Yes, but not as hard as you do.' He did not seem displeased by such insufferable archness.

'Do you intend making journalism your career?'

'I certainly intend making writing my career,' I replied pretentiously.

He asked more questions and I mentioned the articles I had written – 'Around the World with a Dishcloth' on the merchant navy, and the controversial series on the book trade. Then he asked how much the *Standard* was paying me. I told him.

'For each article or the whole series?'

'For each article,' I replied, startled that he should be so out of touch with his staff's salaries. Then he mentioned my father: 'Gifted man, doesn't work hard enough.' I remembered the hours of struggle in the greyness of the early morning, the countless sheets of paper crumpled into balls in the waste paper basket, as he tried to break the block which was holding him back from his new book. I thought of the thousands of articles, the *Transgressor*, the books published, and flushed in his defence, replying that he was one of the hardest-working men I knew.

'Is it hot outside?' asked the Beaver, who could hardly be described as a good listener. I said it was, but when his valet brought him a light overcoat and the Beaver led the way to his roof garden, he found it so cold that he demanded a second overcoat, sinking into a deck-chair like a peevish gnome with his two coats, a rug and a peaked cap. As he seemed about to doze off, I seized my chance, telling him what a relief it was to work for such a professional paper. Today I wince at such transparent sycophancy, but he beamed, he chuckled, rapport established at the last moment.

'No, not every paper is professional, Mr Farson.' Then he caught sight of the tattoo of the shark on my hand (though Francis insisted it was a sardine), and stared at it intently for nearly a minute.

'Thank you for coming to see me,' he concluded. 'I've liked what I've seen. What I've seen is good. I shall speak to the editor about you.' Calling for his valet, he told him 'Look after Mr Farson, James, I want you to look after him.' For a moment I thought I might be given a signed photograph or one of the jars of honey, but I was shown the door. Perhaps he did speak to the editor. Two days later Charles Wintour asked if I would mind vacating my place at the features desk, and did so with such politeness that it took some hours before I realized that I had been given the sack.

To this day I do not know how I offended Lord Beaverbrook. Was it because I dared to answer back regarding my father? Surely that would have been too petty? Because I was unmarried? That had not prevented his championship of Tom Driberg, securing a newspaper blackout when Driberg was charged with seducing two coalminers he took home with him. Because of my tattoo? My odious sycophancy? Perhaps the Beaver was simply unimpressed and did not like what he saw, though he told me otherwise.

A few weeks later I was passing a dismal Saturday evening in The French Pub, reflecting that I should rejoin the merchant navy, when Peter Hunt, the genial producer of ITV's *This Week*, mentioned that he was looking for interviewers and wondered if I was interested.

'Fine,' I replied sharply, dismissing this as Saturday night chatter. 'I'll call at your office first thing Monday morning.'

'Hold on,' he said, as I expected. 'I'll keep in touch.'

I had appeared on television once before, in a series call *Seconds Out* with the Fleet Street editor Frank Owen whose assistant Anna Phillips sent me a telegram: CAN YOU DO CONSCRIPTION PROGRAMME WITH FRANK ON MONDAY FIFTH STOP DOCKER CANCELLED. This was baffling. I knew nothing about conscription, and if one docker had cancelled why not find another? Anna Phillips phoned to explain that it was Sir Bernard Docker who had dropped out, but I could still think of few people with whom I had less in common.

She asked if I was in favour of conscription. 'All for it!' I replied with a show of enthusiasm, sensing that was what she wanted me to say. She sighed with relief: 'We were hoping you'd say that.'

The programmes went out 'live' at 10.25 in the evening, but such phrases meant little to me, having scarcely seen a television set before. On Monday we lunched at a restaurant near the House of Commons where Jeremy Thorpe, who acted as chairman, vied with Owen with his impersonations of such fellow Liberals as Lloyd George and Lady Violet Bonham Carter. Anna Phillips gave me a beaming smile, delighted that everything was going so well, but I became increasingly anxious. Holding on to Owen's sleeve as he hurried off to another appointment, I asked, 'What am I going to say?'

'Anything that comes into your head!' he boomed, breaking free.

'*Nothing* is coming into my head,' I called after him.

The truth of this was borne out in the evening when I was not only lost for words, I was lost for a word. The moment the rehearsal began I was speechless. Trickles of sweat began to flow down Owen's ashen face as he realized he had made a disastrous mistake. When the alleged rehearsal was cut short, I asked the producer if they could get someone else.

'Impossible. We're on in less than an hour.'

Frank Owen looked aghast, Anna Phillips incredulous. Jeremy Thorpe looked amused and suggested we move to his chambers in the Temple nearby and try again there. I have forgotten who gave me the purple hearts or where we bought the bottle of gin, but these were poured down my throat like petrol through a funnel as Owen gave me the questions and I tried to learn the answers by heart. Returning to the studios in a daze of apprehension I was fully aware of the humiliation ahead and can still remember the make-up girl painting out my tattoo: 'Goodness, how cold your hand is, just like a dead man's.'

With this encouragement, I sat down. A count of three . . . two . . . one, a wave of a hand, the purple hearts and the gin collided inside me with a bang and I was off. I talked uncontrollably while Owen and Thorpe stared at me dumbfounded, for they were speechless now, unable to get a word in. Afterwards we went on to a club where I spent the night in a state of euphoria in a talking marathon which lasted for eighteen hours. Peter Hunt, who had seen my performance, remarked that I seemed to have 'plenty to say'

Having lost my place at the *Standard*, I applied for a job as an ITV newscaster. When Ludovic Kennedy's autobiography was accompanied by a TV documentary, they found the clips of those auditions and I was surprised to see myself among the final ten, along with him and Robin Day. I failed, but as Geoffrey Cox, the head of ITN, told me later, I was lucky; by then I had series of my own. But the idea of interviewing for *This Week* was tantalizing.

Meanwhile I sold a series to the *Daily Mail* on the young lions soon to be embraced as the angry young men. 'In the theatre,' I wrote, 'this post-war type is exemplified by John Osborne's angry young man Jimmy Porter.' I did not invent the phrase 'angry young man' – that credit is due to the publicist of the Royal Court Theatre which staged *Look Back in Anger* – but I brought the various examples together. In his book *Success Stories*, Harry Ritchie quoted me as saying that 'literature's Post-War Generation had suddenly emerged', adding, 'It was a classic example of a journalist being in the right place at the right time,' this was July 1956. 'Farson had already developed a friendship with Colin Wilson after happening to meet him the day *The Outsider* was first acclaimed, and had just written his feature on [Kingsley] Amis for the *Evening Standard*' ('The Crisis in the Book Trade').

I asked John Osborne why *Look Back in Anger* caused such controversy.

'It's about real people and audiences aren't used to seeing that. It's so fashionable to be indifferent to human beings nowadays. I hate the smart people at cocktail parties who do nothing and stand there destroying things.'

Tynan had helped to lift a flagging box office with his declaration in the *Observer*, 'I doubt if I could love anyone who did not wish to see *Look Back in Anger*'; though it was not until extracts were shown on the powerful new medium of television that the play really took off. I invited Colin to see it with me and heard him fuming in the darkness: 'If I was in the same room as that insufferable Jimmy Porter I'd give him a jolly good kick in the pants. I'm sick of mixed-up kids.' I invited Osborne to a wild party in Colin's room at Chepstow Villas where the word 'genius' was passed around like Kleenex and Mary Ure, who played Alison, burst into tears when Colin dismissed the play. She proclaimed loudly that Osborne, whom she married the following year, was the greatest playwright since Sheridan.

Over a surprisingly gloomy lunch in a Leicester Square pub opposite the statue of Sir Henry Irving – 'Old Nonsense' as Kingsley Amis called him – I introduced Kingsley to Colin and mentioned that *Look Back in Anger* had been described as 'an Amis sort of play'.

'I'm astonished,' said Amis. 'I don't like glum chums. Amis likes laughing. I'm sick of all these people who claim to be more mixed-up than the next man.' He downed his beer contentedly. 'Amis is very keen on human qualities. Amis likes love and affection.'

The Saturday before 'The Post-War Generation' started in the *Mail*, Ken Allsop drove Colin and myself down to my parents' house in perfect English summer weather, racing along the empty roads in a red open car especially adapted for Ken who had lost a leg in an accident.

The weekend was memorable for the delight of my father, who forged an instant rapport with Ken and Colin, relishing their conversation like a dog released from a kennel. Ken was reluctant to go swimming from the beach below, which my father understood instantly, exposing the hole in his own leg which still needed daily dressing. With my father supporting him, Ken hopped into the surf and told me later that this had been a psychological breakthrough. Ken was one of the most charming men I have known, always stimulating company, and the Grey House rang with laughter as my father told his stories, true experiences but never 'jokes', with such enthusiasm that at times he laughed so much himself that he had to get up and leave the room, speechless with exuberance. It was wonderfully infectious and though I knew the stories well his zest made them fresh every time.

The compatibility with Colin was steeped in literature and in their insatiable curiosity, though their experiences were far apart.

The mutual sympathy lasted until my father's death. Colin and his girlfriend Joy Stewart escaped to the Grey House after a dinner party when her father burst in with a horse-whip and the immortal cry: 'Wilson, the game is up! You're a homosexual with six mistresses.' Concerned for his daughter's welfare with a man separated from his wife and child, John Stewart had discovered a journal which he misinterpreted as Colin's private diary; in fact it contained jottings for a novel on a sexual psychopath, duly published as *Ritual in the Dark*. While Colin rolled on the floor with hysterical laughter, a fellow guest, the infamous Gerald Hamilton who was the original Mr Norris for Isherwood's novel *Mr Norris Changes Trains*, crept out and phoned the *Express*, receiving a small fee. The weeping father explained: 'I went with a horse-whip to drag her home. Neither her mother nor I could reason with her and I wanted to teach Colin a lesson. She thinks he's a genius.'

Colin and Joy fled to North Devon pursued by reporters, who were thwarted by my mother: she denied all knowledge while Colin and Joy were walking on the sands below. Eventually the *Express* caught up with them with a front-page splash – 'Tousle-haired Colin Wilson, twenty-five-year-old author of *The Outsider*, moved into a new hideout last night with his girlfriend Joy Stewart. Soon after dawn they waved goodbye to author Negley Farson and wife Eve, at whose home they stayed the last two nights. And their second "flight" in three days was on.'

Colin was unworldly. When my father asked if he had any drink in his bedroom during a subsequent visit, Colin produced a bottle of brandy, though he knew of my father's alcoholism. 'My God,' said

my mother scathingly, 'you may be a genius but you are a bloody
fool!' Even so, he did not deserve the onslaught which descended and
in which I played a shameful part. He believed that he could use
publicity to his advantage, unaware that it was using him. Daphne du
Maurier warned him not to expect a good review for the next ten
years, and Victor Gollancz, who published Colin and my father, urged
him not to publish a word for the next three. Privately Gollancz wrote
to my father, 'I'm desperately worried about Colin. Ever since the first
big success, I've been trying – with a really tremendous expenditure of
time and energy – to save him from a disastrous future: but he has
defeated me.'

During that first halcyon weekend I recorded Colin interminably on
my new Vortexion recorder, in the twin-bedded annexe which we
shared. As usual he made outrageous claims which look conceited in
print.

'You think of yourself as a genius?' I asked.

'Oh, of course. I mean, one makes that assumption in any case. It
may prove untrue but I've got to work on that assumption.'

'But I don't think most people assume they are geniuses.'

'This is why the age produced so much lousy writing. This is
the very thing I'm in revolt against, an age that doesn't make that
assumption.'

And so on. I edited these remarks for a feature in a new literary magazine, *Books and Art*, which was part of the Beaverbrook Press. All my
favourable comment was cut out – only the damaging quotes remained,
under the inevitable heading COLIN WILSON EXPLAINS MY GENIUS.
My father sent me a follow-up in the *Times Literary Supplement*:

Mr Wilson was made to speak, as he has done before, of his genius,
and there was elicited from him the statement: 'I believe the age
makes the men in it. Florence was ready when Savonarola came along,
Germany was ready when Hitler came along . . .' The interviewer
[myself], not unnaturally, attempted to trap Mr Wilson into saying
that England was ready now that Colin Wilson had come along. Mr
Wilson repudiated the suggestion that he was to be a leader of this
kind, but nevertheless concluded by saying that the whole burden of
the age lay upon his shoulders and that he might be the only man to
bring things back to consciousness in the age.

It is not pretty.

The writer added the qualification: 'Yet we may doubt whether it is journalism of this kind which has done Mr Wilson most harm. The overpraise came in the first place from highly sophisticated people who might have been expected to have known better.'

Colin wrote to me: 'Am in a daze of misery about that terrible article of yours in *Books and Art*. Can't you see how much such a thing damages me, especially just before a new book is published?'

The forecast of the *TLS* was borne out with a vengeance on the publication of *Religion and the Rebel*, dedicated to my father and myself, which was savaged by the critics who had lavished praise on *The Outsiders*: 'Unhappy sequel' wrote Toynbee; 'A deplorable piece of work' wrote Raymond Mortimer, deputizing for Connolly in the *Sunday Times*; 'Egghead scrambled' chortled *Time* when it crossed the Atlantic. The glee was unabashed. 'This is not the ambush that Ken Allsop predicted,' wrote my father in a letter, 'it's a massacre.'

After this literary lynching, Colin left for Cornwall where he has lived ever since, bringing up his family devotedly, never failing to help his friends by writing introductions to their books, the most generous of hosts and the best of friends. 'I have often thought,' he wrote to me, 'that perhaps you actually did me a favour by writing the piece in *Books and Art* which seemed at the time such a disaster. In a way no "serious" writer is cut out for success – at least, the kind of success he can easily get nowadays.'

His output has been prodigious and he is a cult figure abroad, but the English literary establishment has not forgiven his early triumph. When he is eighty they will rediscover him and heap him with belated honours as if they had supported him throughout. Meanwhile, I can only be glad that he has forgiven me and remains a friend.

Inadvertently, Colin Wilson was responsible for my own change of direction. Seeing my series on the post-war generation in the *Daily Mail*, with an article on Colin titled I MEET A GENIUS WITH INDIGESTION, Peter Hunt remembered our conversation in The French Pub and suggested I script a filmed item for *This Week* and do the interviewing myself. Then I was asked to film Cecil Beaton, followed by a live interview in the studio. I was launched on a new career.

I had the luck to join ITV at the beginning. We made our frontiers as we went along, astonished to discover how far we could go, encouraged by the public's insatiable appetite for documentaries, allowed a freedom of speech unthinkable today.

I was told to stick rigidly to a prepared script but I noticed that interviewers who did so moved on to the next question regardless of the previous answer, as if they had not listened to the reply. Though accused at first of 'laziness' I aimed for spontaneity, sensing that the pause as you saw the person think was equally important as the answer, and sometimes more revealing.

I was lucky because I had few rivals and that gave me time to prove myself. The wife of the managing director of Associated-Rediffusion liked my haircut. He was an eccentric ex-naval officer, Captain Brownrigg, who approved of my accent. In the lift at TV House one day he barked in his naval way: 'Farson, who's this woman Maria Callas? They're all going mad because she's failed to turn up. I asked 'em, anything sunk, anyone drowned? If not, calm down.' An admirable naval philosophy. He once asked Laurence Olivier what he did, confused the Australian premier Robert Menzies with the prime minister of Canada, and dismissed one of the technicians when he learnt that the man was homosexual.

'But sir,' he was told, 'there are lots of homosexuals in A-R.'

'That's all very well among the artistic personnel,' he replied curtly, 'but cannot be tolerated in the engine room.'

Running the company like a ship from the upper deck, removed from all the internal intrigue, worked surprisingly well. Finally, he was nobody's fool.

At first I worked exclusively for *This Week*, which was made up of very short items. Rebecca West took part in a brief programme on Harold Macmillan, because he was her publisher, and I had to tell her we had one minute fifty seconds on air. She accepted this as a matter of course because everything was so new. When I interviewed Macmillan, he told me, as if it was a revelation, 'I am all in favour of the young.'

Interviewing two adventurers who had attempted to cross the Atlantic in cockleshells, I pointed out the cost of their rescue and suggested that exhibitionism was their motive. 'Mr Farson pulls no punches,' wrote Milton Shulman in the *Standard* the next day, which was invaluable in strengthening my position, especially as he praised

This Week as a refreshing change from the ' "but on the other hand" technique. It has opinions and is not afraid to express them pungently.'

Simultaneously I became the 'authority' on a quiz show called *Two for the Money* with Bernard Braden. As the 'expert' I sat behind a table with a telephone allegedly leading directly to the offices of the Encyclopedia Britannica. I sympathized with my predecessor, Derek Bond, who had played the lead in the film of *Nicholas Nickleby*. 'Name as many words as you can ending in the letters TH as in *width*,' said Braden.

'Breadth,' said one of the contestants hesitantly.

'*Heighth*,' said the other, and this was the 'expert's' downfall, for instead of declaring that the word was *height* and stopping the game, he let them go on.

'Fourth!' cried the first contestant, suddenly inspired.

'Fifth!' cried the other, catching on.

'Sixth' – 'Seventh' – faster and faster – £20 – £40 – £80 – 'tenth' – 'eleventh' – £320 – £640 . . . When the time was up they were thousands of pounds richer and the producer was in a state of collapse, though he managed to descend from the control room to the set below where he sacked the actor on the spot. Which is how I got his job.

Watching *Two for the Money* by chance, Caryl Doncaster, the formidable Head of Features at Associated-Rediffusion, summoned me to her office and demanded to know why I was appearing in such rubbish without her permission. Amazed to learn that I was a freelance, she gave me a weekly salary with the hope that I would not take part in such a programme again.

The constant variety of *This Week* suited me, ranging from a politician one week; music hall the next; John Osborne astringent about the 'debs'; to a comic item I scripted on American tourists. I interviewed the Archbishop of Canterbury, slumped in self-satisfaction, though the charm of Gary Cooper was irresistible.

The desiccated, deadpan charm of Paul Getty appealed to me too. 'Why are millionaires so mean?' I asked.

'I wouldn't say they were mean, they simply have a healthy respect for money.'

'Do you respect money, Mr Getty?' I sounded like Kane talking to Mr Bernstein.

'I've noticed that people who don't respect money seldom have any.'

'Mr Getty, what would you like for Christmas?' This was before he bought Sutton Place and he was living at the Ritz.

'A tree,' he replied wanly, his face as expressionless as Buster Keaton's. 'And I'd like some presents hanging from the tree.'

He admitted that begging letters were destroyed unopened, which meant that many genuine letters were lost unless they were sent to a coded address, and that he doubted if any of his wives had loved him except for his money. Finally, I asked why someone so busy had been prepared to see me.

'Because you have to make your living just as I do.'

Inadvertently it was John Deakin who established me when he asked, 'Why don't you interview Caitlin Thomas?'

I should have been warned, especially as I had met her twice before, the first time in The French Pub at midday when Dylan sat on the banquette, hungover and apprehensive of the lecture tour he was embarking on in America, which was to prove fatal. Noticing the magazine I was holding with a new story by Raymond Chandler he asked if he could have it to relieve the tedium of the flight and took it gratefully.

The second meeting with Caitlin was more dramatic. She had been told that Dylan was dying in New York and was waiting to fly out to join him. Deakin was with her in the Caves de France adopting a teasingly intimate tone as he assured her that he knew what she was going through, as if no one else in the world could. This was unwise for as he demanded a drink from Secundo she came up behind him with a silver-topped walking stick which she raised her head – a warning cry from Secundo, Deakin dodged – and the stick crashed down with such violence that it left a dent in the wooden bar. Deakin's skull might have shattered.

When I suggested the interview to Peter Hunt he agreed. Deakin escorted her to the studios, and it was obvious they had been drinking in the Caves throughout the afternoon. Deakin denied this indignantly. 'She's only playing you up,' he whispered as Caitlin refused to discuss what we would say. After the rehearsal, when she scarcely uttered, he leered 'Fasten your seat-belt, kiddo, it's going to be a bumpy night.' I moved away in case people realized I knew him better than I pretended.

I was summoned to see Peter Hunt, who led me aside with the director: 'Do you think we dare take the risk?' Remember, *This Week* went out live.

For once I had the sense to be circumspect: 'That is entirely up to you. I take no responsibility, but if you wish to go ahead I am happy to ask the questions.' I suggested a code if anything went wrong. 'I'll say "I'm afraid my questions are upsetting you, Mrs Thomas" – and you can cue into the next interview.' Word was passed along the line to the other networks that there could be trouble.

A few seconds before we started, Caitlin decided that she wished to stand instead of sit, which threw the sound and lighting men into a state of panic as they tried to adjust. Four . . . three . . . two . . . the wave of the hand, the music from Sibelius, the terrifying lift-off. The interview started stickily when I referred to Dylan's poverty compared to the recognition since his death. For some reason I mentioned that he never had a chequebook, which seemed to irritate her, though there was probably a good explanation. Then I moved to a new book by John Malcolm Brinnin which had caused much controversy, describing her arrival in New York as her husband lay unconscious in an oxygen tent after an 'insult to the brain' from too much alcohol. I did not mention that she had tried to light a cigarette, nor that she had bitten an orderly as she was removed, or seized a crucifix from the wall, smashing it on a statue of the Virgin Mary in the hospital chapel until she was restrained in a straitjacket. I avoided all this while admitting that many of her friends had been distressed by the book. Caitlin twisted with annoyance. 'Oh, the bloody man was in love with my husband,' she snarled with a toss of her golden hair.

'I'm afraid my questions are upsetting you, Mrs Thomas.'

The camera moved smartly to the next interview, but the sound man was so enthralled that he forgot the cue. Caitlin's voice was superimposed on the face of the foreign secretary, or some politician, and we heard her professing: 'I'm not upset, what do you mean upset, I want to go on.'

By the time the programme finished the telephones were ringing and with Fleet Street around the corner Caitlin and Deakin were decanted from the hospitality room where they were helping themselves to drink, and hurried out of TV House into a waiting taxi which took them back to the Caves. The press arrived in pursuit a minute too late.

This was my first experience of notoriety. The incident was reported on every front page next morning and my name was prominent throughout. The story could be taken in two ways: tactless interviewer upsets grief-stricken widow, or the widow was drunk.

Deakin telephoned, absurdly business-like. 'By the by, you know that photograph I took during the rehearsal? I sold it to the *Sunday Graphic*, sight unseen. It's rather super.'

'Oh, Deakin,' I moaned, 'you can't. They told you it isn't allowed to take photographs in the studio. Haven't you done enough harm?'

'Tough shit,' he said. 'I have to make my living. See you at the Caves, I've got to take the prints to the *Graphic*. *Andiamo!*'

'Use the best one of me,' I pleaded before he rung off. When I entered the Caves that afternoon I found myself the centre of controversy. Caitlin was an exceptional woman and her friends were understandably upset. Deakin was holding court, recounting his role in the drama, and excluded me as if I had been responsible for the débâcle. The writer Constantine FitzGibbon, a friend of Dylan's, came up to me and poured an entire pint of beer over my head. I went home, damply.

At least Caitlin did not blame me, as I discovered when I read the Sunday papers. Every report made careful mention of drink – she had not been given enough, or she was given too much – 'she said, with a glass in her hand'. She wondered if she would receive her fee. Opening the *Sunday Graphic*, I found myself across the centre spread in two of Deakin's photographs under the headline THE CAMERA THAT DIDN'T CUT THE WIDOW. I thought I looked sympathetic.

On the Monday morning, my worried secretary handed me several letters: 'The ham-fisted domineering approach of the interrogator is distasteful. We have seen this person in action before and have wondered why his "victims" have not struck him.'

I turned to the next letter: 'I for one will switch off very promptly whenever he appears for fear of what he will do next.'

I smiled. 'Obviously they're a hoax.'

'I don't think so,' she said anxiously. 'I think they're genuine. There've been lots of complaints from viewers who phoned in.'

I met Deakin at lunchtime and told him of the letters. 'You see what you've done?' I said savagely.

'Don't be ridiculous, buy me a large pink gin. It means you've arrived.'

And this was true. I discovered I was a celebrity. Returning to

Television House people stopped me to shake my hand for my handling of 'a tricky situation' and boys around the entrance asked for my autograph. My euphoria evaporated when I was told to report to the Controller of Programmes, John McMillan, but he greeted me with a smile, or as much of a smile as he could ever muster: 'I thought you'd like to know,' he said, 'that we want you to join the staff at an increased salary.'

I would have regretted putting the merchant navy behind me except for the excitement of this new experience and my luck with the programmes I was given. My first series was *Members' Mail*, about the problems facing MPs in their constituencies, which sounds deadly dull but embraced such subjects as teddy boys, a miner dying from pneumoconiosis, the thieving of cats and wrongful arrest. One programme dealt with the old age pension, a measly two pounds in those days. After speaking to several pensioners who replied with proud anger and not a vestige of self-pity, I heard of two sisters who shared a small room with a cat as their companion. They were flustered by my arrival and alarmed at the thought of being filmed, indulging in a long-established double-act.

'If I say yes I won't get a wink of sleep,' said one.

'Don't mind her, she's deaf,' said the other. 'She doesn't know what she's saying.'

One of the sisters was applying for more National Assistance, as Social Security was then called. She was not eligible, yet it was obvious that a few shillings would make a difference.

'What do you need the money for?' I asked.

'Well, you know,' she hesitated. 'The living . . . and all that.'

'It isn't as if we live extravagantly,' said the other unnecessarily. 'We don't have many luxuries.' I looked around the shabby-genteel room, ashamed to realize that the indifferent lunch I had just finished in a pub would have been a treat to them.

Suddenly the idea of being filmed became an adventure. 'Should we wear make-up?' they asked.

'Oh yes, and your very best clothes.'

The make-up boxes were produced and there was a moment of horror when they opened an old trunk which revealed the body of a small dead animal. This was a fox fur, a well-worn reminder of better days. The interview started with confusion.

'How old are you?' I asked directly.

'Thirty-six,' came the heartbreaking reply. No one looked less like thirty-six.

'Oh no you're not,' said the other sister with a despairing glance at the camera, 'you're sixty-eight.'

'Sixty-eight? Oh, yes, so I am.' She laughed.

Poignantly, they remembered the past.

'My husband, you see,' explained the sister who was lucid, clutching the fox fur round her throat, 'was a lieutenant in the First World War.' Her voice conveyed a lifetime in a sentence.

'And what do you miss most about the past?' I asked, gently. She thought about this, answering slowly:

'Father . . . having a home . . . freedom . . . and everything was so much cheaper then, if you know what I mean.' The camera crew were mesmerized, totally silent. When I asked the other sister what she would do with the extra money, she leant forward confidentially.

'I can't tell you here,' she whispered, 'but I need some new under-clothes so badly.'

This was it! She had forgotten the camera – '*I can't tell you here.*' From that moment this was my aim in television, to establish such a rapport that all the paraphernalia of lights and cables – the bulk of the camera alone was formidable then – became invisible. Not an inter-view but a private conversation. Such moments made everything worth while and I became aware of the extraordinary phrasing and speech rhythms of people who might have been considered ordinary. This approach was a novelty then. Writing in the *Guardian* about the two sisters, Bernard Levin quoted the remark about the husband who was a lieutenant in the First World War: 'Fifty thousand speeches and forty tons of White Papers could not have brought home with greater poignancy the situation in which such people find themselves today.'

A series was in preparation called *People in Trouble*, dealing with the problems of meths-drinkers, midgets, illiterates, spinsters, discharged prisoners and people who were disfigured. Nicknamed 'Cripples Cav-alcade' in TV House it had the reputation of the 'kiss of death' before it had even started, and the presenter, an excellent man called Michael Ingrams, withdrew, partly because he had fallen out with the Head of Features. I was chosen instead and contrary to expectations, the series became an immediate hit with the public. There are many such programmes today, but nothing like *People in Trouble* had been seen before. Some of the items were filmed, like the opening programme on the meths drinkers in Whitechapel's Itchy Park, but most were directed by Rollo Gamble against a stark grey cyclorama. Our researcher had the knack of finding people who were prepared to speak honestly, confiding secrets to the camera they would not have told their neighbours. All I had to do was talk to them as straightforwardly as possible, and listen. But it was becoming too easy as I learnt the tricks and lies of the television medium, lowering my voice, leaning forward to stare into the other person's eyes with a deep well of sympathy in my own. Filming an hour-long programme on adoption, one woman was reduced to tears, and when she recovered there was no time for me to shoot my reverses or 'noddys', which are inserted later in the editing room and bind the film together. I was good at these, realizing they should not be too pat but should reflect the natural hesitation of ordinary speech. In this case we filmed the reverses several days later, when the tension had gone, and the words were so intimate that I collapsed with laughter every time. Finally, by thinking of income tax, I pulled myself together and asked my questions again with suitable sympathy. When the programme was shown, the *Daily Mail* critic wrote that no one watching my expression could doubt my sincerity. 'So much for truth,' commented the cameraman.

The series was extended from thirteen to twenty-six programmes and could have continued. I found to my alarm that I was being cast in the role of do-gooder – 'Scenes which should stir the conscience of Britain,' wrote one reviewer – and when I saw my picture in a woman's magazine with the heading 'A Candle in the Darkness' I thought of my own feet of clay. When I was arrested for being drunk and disorderly, it was widely reported in the press and I was rebuked, because I had become 'a father figure to the nation'.

Rollo Gamble, the best director I worked with and a true friend, began to have the same doubts. One morning he was flippant as we prepared for the 'op'.

'Good morning, nurse,' he said to Nikola Sterne, our researcher. 'Next patient, please.'

'Yes,' she said, 'I'll wheel her in.'

'Are you ready, doctor?'

'Ready,' I replied, pulling on an invisible pair of rubber gloves. We looked at each other and realized we felt the same about the vaulting success of the series which had 'o'erleapt itself'. This cynicism was our release and much to the annoyance of the A-R management, we decided to move on.

As an antidote, *Out of Step* was a light-hearted look at such minorities as vegans, people who believed in flying saucers, witches on the Isle of Man, and A. S. Neill at his do-as-you-like school Summerhill. The programmes were pre-recorded and went out late. One evening I strolled down to the King's Road in Chelsea to find that the pubs were surprisingly empty.

'Where is everyone?' I asked a barman.

'At home, watching Dan Farson with the nudists.'

I had forgotten; nor had it occurred to me that a glimpse of naked men and women would be so irresistible, though the viewers must have been disappointed by the discreet long-shots as naked couples played tennis in Spielplatz Camp. 'The first appearance on TV of naked women,' wrote one newspaper. 'Some historian of the future might care to have the date – Wed. Oct 2nd, 10-30 P.M. 1957.' Only one person phoned the switchboard to complain, a mother whose teenage son walked into the room unexpectedly and came face to face with life in the raw. This was the first time I leapt into the Top Ten ratings and the first time I was impersonated by Benny Hill, complete with special wig though our hairstyles were almost identical.

To be impersonated was the ultimate compliment. A friend in A-R phoned me one Saturday to warn me to stay in and watch another Benny Hill programme: 'They haven't told you in case you object, but you ought to watch it. I'm not supposed to tell you.'

This time Benny Hill had filmed an entire item based on the interview with Barbara Cartland in my series *Success Story*. He played myself, Barbara Cartland, her mother Polly, her daughter Raine and their butler. The Cartland interview had been transmitted out of sync, but as the opening sequence showed Cartland opening fêtes, cutting ribbons and accepting bouquets while her voice trilled 'I'm in love' on a recording, the technicians failed to notice that anything was wrong and went out of the control room for an illicit smoke. When the interviews started, Barbara Cartland was speaking with my voice and I with hers and the chaos continued for several agonizing minutes until an executive ran down and pulled the plug. When it was shown correctly a few weeks later, Bernard Levin said he preferred the first version. He had spotted me doing my research, pressed between Barbara Cartland and Denise Robbins, another romantic novelist, over lunch at the White Tower. They were dressed up for the occasion with large frothy hats and he compared me to the filling between two meringues.

'Do you ever suffer from doubt?' I asked Barbara Cartland in *Success Story*.

'Doubt?' she demanded. 'What sort of doubt?'

'Self-doubt.'

'Self-doubt? NEVER!' with the ringing tones of Lady Bracknell.

'What would you have thought if Raine had been born an ugly girl?'

'Ugly?' she gave a sort of laugh. 'IMPOSSIBLE!'

We followed *Out of Step* with *Keeping in Step*, intended to show that the majorities could be just as odd as the eccentrics: the Stock Exchange, the English wedding, Winchester College, Harrods and the Guards. Though not so popular as *Out of Step*, this was closer to the affectionate satire I was hoping for.

The Stately Home opened with a peaceful panning shot of the grounds and lake at Kedleston Hall, shattered as Lord Scarsdale shot at some passing birds. Holding his smoking gun, he told me, 'I'm head of the RSPCA and I've killed a lot of things but I don't think I've ever been cruel to things.' I understood what he meant.

The film finished with the meet of a foxhunt complete with stirrup cup in courtyard and horsey ladies with top hats. As they trotted away I crossed the great hall strewn with the skins of tigers shot by Lord Curzon in India. 'If the fox really enjoys being hunted, as I've just been told,' I addressed the camera, 'then the fox must be even dottier than those who hunt him.' This produced an angry letter to the chairman of A-R saying that Mr Farson was no gentleman.

Rollo Gamble was a joy to work with, his name suiting him perfectly for he was round, bearded and twinkling, able to adapt to any situation. Producing one programme a week, which would be unthinkable today, meant that we had no backlog so we could not afford a failure. With an absurd filming ratio of two to one we struggled for realism, before the fancier name of *cinéma vérité*, with cumbersome equipment that would seem neolithic now. My nerves screamed as opportunities were missed during the interminable setting-up with A-R's film department insisting on such technical perfection that every shot was lit as if for Anna Neagle. I protested that if they had filmed the Crucifixion, they would have scrapped it for the slightest shake of the camera.

Each time, even with our limited ratio, we had enough material for half an hour, but at least our ration of 12½ minutes left the viewers eager for more. And every time Rollo directed with a panache worthy of Cecil B. de Mille.

Imperceptibly, I was being developed as a 'TV personality', one of the 'telephoneys' as Gilbert Harding called us with characteristic bitterness. We were an unlikely group of contemporary idols, but the power of television made us so: my colleague Michael Ingrams; General Sir Brian Horrocks; the great Richard Dimbleby with whom I was caricatured in *Punch* with Peter Haigh, each of us holding microphones; Michael Westmore, who chaired *This Week* before Ludovic Kennedy; John Freeman with his incomparable *Face to Face*; and Kenneth Clark, largely BBC men. I found my share of TV fame increasingly spurious, as if, like Alice, I had fallen into a tunnel and emerged in another world. It was so unreal. A mother wrote to me: 'You're my son's favourite. As soon as he knows you're coming on he shaves and puts on a clean shirt to watch you.'

In Petticoat Lane comments volleyed as if I were invisible and deaf:

'Smaller, ain't he?'

'Putting on some weight.'

'Not half.'

'Course it's him. What a dear old face.'

'She always watches him,' pointing to a baby in a pram. 'Wouldn't miss him for the world.'

'Waved to him last night, I did.'

A taxi-driver told me, 'You're the dead spit of that Daniel Farsons.' Adding 'No offence meant, of course.'

'Looks like Dan Farson,' said a couple in a pub, discussing me in detail, 'but he's not like that at all!' Today there is no mystery left, but it seemed miraculous then, as if my shadow had sprung to life. Always forgetful, I found myself greeting strangers warmly and cutting friends.

I was photographed, caricatured and interviewed: 'Daniel seems the nicest and newest style of young man' (*Woman*); 'Groom bait? No, Daniel Farson admits he's one of the roving kind' (*Picturegoer*) – that was always tricky, with the implication of girlfriends in the background. 'He sleeps in the nude, likes casual clothes, and *never wears a hat or gloves*' (*Reveille*).

The telephone began to ring, and letters followed: 'Am I forgiven?

You should come round sometime. I shall be only too glad to entertain you, and if I'm not here there's always members of the DFFC (work that out for yourself) who will oblige. Don't forget that if you ever get lonely. But then I don't suppose you do . . . Do you know who's in the picture frame with you? A wonderful person named John – my son. He's only five so there's no competition. I've just said good-night to your picture, only I wish you were looking right at me.' I went ex-directory.

A woman wrote to *TV Times* wanting to know more about me because I was 'the handsomest man on television'. Addled she may have been, but I cannot deny that I was pleasantly amused. Fortunately, Deakin was around to bring me down to earth, introducing me as 'the idol of millions, without a friend in the world.'

I was nominated for the award of 'TV Personality of the Year', but failed to win because of my indifference, which alienated even my supporters, and my failure to socialize with my colleagues, preferring to rush back to my haunts in Soho. This was not as conceited as it sounds. I did not use the bar at TV House because it did not occur to me that the people I had worked with all day would want me hanging around afterwards. I learnt it would have been elementary politeness, but that came too late.

The TV critics voted me 'best television interviewer', with Robin Day second and Fyfe Robertson third, but the poll was published in a trade magazine so few people saw it and I did not receive an award. I have to accept that I am not an award-winning person.

Meanwhile the carousel continued. I avoided fêtes as far as possible, knowing how disastrous I am at public speaking, though no one believes this until I open my mouth. Stepping on to the stage of the Lyceum before an audience of several thousand, sandwiched between a crooner who went down on his knees and a Scottish comedian, I pointed out that my great-uncle, Bram Stoker, had managed the Lyceum for Sir Henry Irving. The names meant nothing and created a sudden, uneasy silence until I stumbled off and the comedy resumed.

One hot summer evening I found myself speeding through the outskirts of London in a black limousine with sleek upholstery and a glass partition to protect me from the driver. The car stopped at a suburban cinema, and several large men in shiny dinner-jackets led me into the foyer where I met the beauty queens. To my relief one of them *was* a beauty, dark-haired, dark-eyed, cynical and sympathetic.

When the film stopped I was taken onto the stage and as the lights went up couples edged apart in the wide open spaces and stared at me reproachfully. They had even less idea what was happening than I did.

I opened my speech cleverly with the comment of Orson Welles after he fought his way through a snowstorm to address an equally sparse audience in a village hall in Wisconsin. 'What a pity it is,' he said, looking at the rows of empty seats, 'that there are so few of you and so many of me.' All that was required were half a dozen words but I made a speech which made less and less sense as the audience sat there stunned, not with amazement, just stunned. There was a brief quiver of interest as the girls paraded before me, and of course it was not the beauty who won. Instead I was asked to crown a healthy, ample girl with a farmer's complexion. The local photographer moved me into position. As I raised the crown to the flash of the camera and polite clapping from the committee, I overheard one of the organizers mutter to another: 'It's so often the case. They're such a disappointment in the flesh.'

❖

Filming on a lightship in the Bristol Channel in 1960 for my series *Farson's Guide to the British*, we watched my hour-long programme on teenagers, *Living for Kicks*, on the ship's flickering set. Reception was poor, as if the programme had been filmed in a snowstorm. The reception from the two crews – TV and Trinity House – was worse. This was disappointing, but I forgot about it as an emergency call came through for the lightship and we were dropped hurriedly at the nearest port, which was Milford Haven. The camera crew wanted to stay there overnight, but when I learnt that an express train came through at midnight I decided to catch it. As I raced onto the empty platform, the station master emerged and ran after me calling, 'Mr Farson? You're wanted on the telephone.'

This was surreal. How did anyone know where I was? How did he know who I was?

'They've been ringing all evening,' he added alarmingly. I discovered later that newspapers had bombarded the press office of Associated-Rediffusion, who put them through to Trinity House, who told them to contact the hotel, where they were told I was catching the train. 'But what did they want?' I gasped as I ran beside him.

'Something to do with the police I . . .' At this moment the express roared in and there was no time to go to the phone. I paid for a sleeping berth but my brain pulsated to the rhythm of the train – Living for Kicks, Living for Kicks, to do with the police, to do with the police . . . I drifted off wondering what I had done.

It was six in the morning when we drew in at Paddington and I bought the early papers from a news stall. All was explained by the front page of the *Sketch* which was filled by the banner headline SEXPRESSO KIDS IN TV PROBE:

Plain-clothes police moved among teenagers in coffee bars last night after a TV programme shocked a town.

The police were sent in by the Chief Constable of Brighton, who was ordered to make a report after ITV's *Living for Kicks*.

In that programme couples necked in the background as Daniel Farson talked to teenagers in the Whisky Go-Go, a Brighton coffee bar. A youngster said no teenage boy would marry a virgin and that teenagers have no time for religion. Another said he regularly got thrown out of cinemas and added 'older people are scared to go into a cinema if we are there.'

As angry parents and teachers flooded ITV with protests last night . . .

For the next few weeks, *Living for Kicks* was a *cause célèbre*. Opinions were virtually undivided: I received more than a thousand letters, only six in my favour. One of those was from Denis Mitchell, the pioneer of BBC documentaries: 'I hope you won't mind my writing to say how very much I enjoyed and admired your teenage film. I thought it quite first-class. Many congratulations'; and from Leslie Grade, the brother of Lew and the father of Michael: 'May I just drop you this note to congratulate you on one of the best television shows I have ever seen. I thought it was beautifully done and tremendously interesting and exciting.'

In other quarters the programme was condemned as degrading. 'People all over the country are horrified by what they saw,' protested Alderman Gerald Fitzgerald. 'Sex was openly discussed by a boy of fourteen. It is time these coffee bars were closed down.' The Brighton Watch Committee had a field day, demanding the police report: 'The programme was pornographic and designed to show up the beastliness and worst side of people. A skilful interviewer took advantage of youngsters. It was a lousy lie to put this over as a sample of the young people of Britain.'

I had intended nothing of the sort; to attempt a 'typical' portrayal would have been a waste of time. Rollo and I had presented a cross-section and any 'beastliness' was in the eyes of the Watch Committee. Perhaps I was naïve in seeing nothing wrong with the teenagers I spoke to in the Whisky Go-Go and failing to anticipate the furore caused by a teenage poet, Royston Ellis, who said he believed in sex before marriage. In those days, mentioning sex was only marginally better than saying 'fuck'. I was dismayed that a programme which told the truth was traduced as an attack on all teenagers. Newspapers were deluged with angry letters; I appeared on a Sunday religious programme to defend myself; Hells Angels from the East End invaded Brighton on their motorbikes to beat up the gentle girls and boys who used the Whisky Go-Go. The scandal got out of hand.

A week later the town's Chief Constable released his report SEXPRESSO KIDS SHOW WAS 'STAGED'; quickly interpreted in the press as 'FAKED', with copies sent to the two Brighton MPs, the head of the Independent Television Authority and various vigilantes. Considering our cumbersome equipment and the limitation of the four-minute film magazines, Rollo and I had come remarkably close to the vaunted *cinéma vérité*. We were only suspect in filming two boys in a pub who were under age, but as this was out of licensing hours it was hardly heinous, certainly not 'faked', and no one noticed it anyhow.

Irked by the slur of 'fake', I saw Captain Brownrigg to explain that I was considering legal action. Brownrigg proved remarkably perceptive in advising me not to do anything of the sort, reminding me that the viewers were unaware of the back-room process of making a programme: the technicians and lighting men, the need for a sound level, the fee of a guinea paid to the teenagers who took part. (Royston Ellis was paid our top whack of fifteen guineas. It seems charmingly old-fashioned that we paid in guineas.) But any payment could suggest that they were bribed or used as 'actors', which was one of the charges. Then there was the crucial editing, which could, indeed, alter the balance of everything said. To the uninitiated, this could sound 'rigged'. His point was valid and I did not pursue the matter.

I was making so many programmes at the time – another on lorry drivers was shown that same evening – that it took me several days before I realized that *Living for Kicks* had made me a 'TV celebrity'.

The newspapers may have attacked the programme, but they were generous to me personally: 'Dan Farson becomes Poor Man's Dimbleby' (Richard in those days, not David or Jonathan); 'Suddenly all is Farson'; 'The teenagers did it,' exclaimed *Picturegoer*. 'It took one programme to do for Dan Farson what months of steady interviewing had failed to do – make him a BIG TV personality . . . the frankness that Dan evoked from the youngsters he interviewed suddenly made him a national celebrity. Learned Sunday papers now print profiles of him, less learned Sunday papers solicit his views on teenage sex life. Currently the talk around the TV studios is: "After this Dan can command the biggest salary any TV star ever had."'

That last sentence alarmed me. I certainly was not getting the sort of money everyone seemed to assume. John Redway, a leading agent, secured me an exclusive salary of £3,300 for 1958, and much of that went on sex, food and drink. I seemed perpetually hard up. This state of affairs led to my first painful brush with the press when a journalist called Olga Franklin came to interview me for the *Daily Mail*. Oozing charm, she disarmed me as the phone rang incessantly with queries regarding the 'faked' police report and an invitation to some dinner where I was expected to receive an award. Trying to appear modest, I laughed the accolade away, said I doubted if I could attend as I did not have a dinner-jacket and wondered if I could afford to buy one. Unwittingly I was feeding her a different story from the sympathetic profile she had in mind. In the event, she did not write her story. She gave it to someone else.

Travelling by bus to Television House the next morning, I noticed people smirking at me and two girls sniggering, and put this down to the usual recognition until I turned to the back page of the *Daily Mail*. HOW SAD, HOW SAD TO BE DAN FARSON ran the headline across Tanfield's gossip column. It could hardly have been more humiliating, seeing my silly quips exposed in the merciless self-pity of print. My father was furious – 'The sort of damn fool thing he would say,' he complained to my mother – and people in TV House avoided my eyes. An outright attack would have been preferable to the description of my 'dingy flat', my 'sad blue eyes' and how I was dreading a dance 'because my shoes hurt and I can't afford any more'. My tongue-in-cheek complaint about *not* having the highest television salary in the world was reported in such a bleat that a clergyman invited me to spend a few days with his family in Hove because I sounded 'in need of a rest'.

The kind of fame I had inadvertently achieved seemed quite unreal. When I was arrested for being drunk and disorderly the street outside the magistrate's court was crowded with photographers trying to snap me as I escaped by taxi, like a scene out of *La Dolce Vita*. And of course it made the newspapers. What my parents made of it I am not too sure for they refused to have a television set – or 'the television' as they called it – in the house, so the strange world I inhabited must have been even stranger to them. Disconcertingly, my mother stuck the bad press cuttings as well as the good in her scrapbook marked 'Daniel Farson II' (the first was devoted to myself as a child), possibly as a gesture of reproach. Luckily one of them, with the heading POLICE BLEW UP AT DAN'S BOMB, was written by an exceptionally decent journalist, Ron Evans, later to become a loyal friend as the managing director of Harlech Television, who made the incident humorous. I had been stopped by a policeman late at night who demanded to know what was in my carrier bag. In fact it was filled with groceries, so why was I given a ride in a Black Maria? ' "Actually, old boy, I suppose it was because I told them it contained a bomb . . ." said Farson smoothly. "I stayed at the station for ten minutes and then drove home. No hard feelings on my part . . . I'd been filming in Soho on a programme about Bohemia. You may say that I caught the atmosphere." ' Thanks to Ron Evans I got off lightly, for the episode was not particularly funny.

Living for Kicks is still shown occasionally on Channel 4 and at the National Film Theatre on London's South Bank. It is one of the programmes I am proud of because it broke new ground as a documentary, Ironically, the impression today is one of vanished innocence, the teenagers wistfully eager, immaculately turned out, with the boys in dark suits and teddy-boy haircuts and the girls with beehive hairstyles. They belonged to a less tarnished age. Only the adults who snooped and complained come across as mean-minded.

◆

I realize now that my drinking had become more of a problem than I admitted. If there is no deceiver like the self-deceiver, there is no self-deceiver so obtuse as the drunk. One of those tiresome women who try to take over one's life persuaded me to see the latest wonder-doctor in Harley Street whose patients included numerous celebrities. He took tests and I phoned him from Tottenham Court Road tube station – I can remember the actual booth – on my way to Television House to appear on *This Week*.

'I'm afraid it's very bad news,' he told me.

'What's wrong?'

'I can't tell you on the phone, you'll have to come in.'

'That's impossible, please tell me now.' He did so reluctantly, for this was hardly playing the game. 'Well,' he hesitated, 'if you continue drinking I don't give you more than a few weeks.'

'To live?' I exclaimed incredulously, 'you mean no alcohol whatsoever?'

'Perhaps a light ale once a week. Otherwise, nothing. What will you do?'

'Change doctors.'

You could say that we lost touch after that. Possibly his warning was wise though, as it turned out, incorrect. It would have been more helpful if he had recommended a few days at a health farm like Champneys where I retreated on a couple of occasions when I was able to escape from the pressure of work and emerged feeling restored, fit, looking years younger to Deakin's unconcealed annoyance. The greater danger was not just my zest for drink but my inability to cope with its effect. I have always been a lousy drunk, wild, euphoric and abusive after that beautiful preamble, and the terrifying thing is that I have not improved in forty years. If anything it has got worse with age.

There were two alarming incidents which should have alerted me. Rollo and I had been filming in the East End and somehow ended up in a large drinking club off Leicester Square where I had not been before. The place seemed full of villains, two of whom were harassing a woman so unpleasantly that I went to her defence. It was none of my business and I should have learnt that whenever I fight I fail to carry it through and end up the loser. I was beaten up and my black eyes looked so nasty that the people I interviewed the next day recoiled in horror in spite of my dark glasses. The subject was witchcraft, which was suitably macabre, but I was unable to film my 'reverses' to camera for several weeks.

The other incident occurred in yet another drinking club in Soho. I was not on the friendliest terms with the owner, who presented me with a bill that was so absurd that I said I would call the following afternoon and settle it then. At this he reduced the bill by half, confirming my suspicions, but I insisted that I would call back. He agreed, reluctantly, shaking my hand in the street outside, which struck me as odd. Two young men had been watching us throughout and now they approached me asking for money; I suspect that the handshake was a signal for them to move in. One was a Scot, compact and unsmiling, the other an ungainly Cockney, and they followed me up Gerrard Street, which was lined with Chinese shops and restaurants. Guessing that they intended to rob me, I made the mistake of going into a door which was not a restaurant but proved to be the home of a startled Chinese family who had no wish to be involved as they saw the two men moving in on me. Then I made my second mistake: instead of handing my money over I fought back. Realizing within seconds that I was about to be beaten up, I made as much noise as I could, hollering to attract attention, and the Cockney did run off. The Scot kicked me violently in the throat and neck as I fell to the floor and ran down the stairs as a Eurasian-looking woman started to scream for the police. 'He's dying, oh he's dying, oh do something, someone.' She held my head in her arms and I fear that her clothes must have been ruined with my blood.

As we waited I felt strangely peaceful; later I heard the bell of the ambulance, but I only dimly remember the drive to the Middlesex Hospital, where I was taken straight to emergency. A cut, apparently from a razor, had sliced past my ear and it was miraculous that when the stitches were finally removed the scar was scarcely visible between my earlobe and sideboard. Far worse was the kicking in my throat which left me speechless for the next week and has weakened my voice ever since. The whole affair was so pointless that I kept it private, though I might have recognized that Scot if it came to identification.

Such incidents did not happen lightly. There might be years between them, but they came too often, a shameful catalogue of self-inflicted woe as if I were a murderee inviting violence. Combined with downing an average of two to three bottles of spirits a day at my worst, it was a slow form of suicide.

I did have one regret – that I did not get drunk more often with my father. Once we drank together at a restaurant in Brompton Road, over a long and liquid lunch returning to Pelham Place happy to have come so close to each other through the mutual sympathy of drink, which encourages friendship to go that little bit further. As my father stumbled off to bed to sleep it off, my mother looked at me sorrowfully: 'I should have thought after all you've been through with him, you'd have known better than that.'

Eleven

A Stranger in a Strange Land

M Y BEST ASSIGNMENT was Australia.

There was an innocence then, an appealing lack of certainty. What strange people they were: so tough on the outside, so wistful within; so generous, yet intolerant of the unconventional; straightforward, yet suspicious of authority; so brash, yet genteel with pictures of ladies in crinolines on the doors of the 'ladies', and a 'gents' called *Adam's Boudoir*. So anxious to be liked, though the last to admit it.

Since then they have grown up, like television, and the innocence has faded. I loved it then.

My return in 1961 was a striking contrast to my first visit on the *Orcades* a few years earlier. This time I was a novelty, a television 'celebrity'. Alan Whicker and Cliff Michelmore had not been seen on Australian television, and even Richard Dimbleby was barely familiar, but my programmes had been shown regularly. Associated-Rediffusion had sent me to film a series of thirteen stories, eventually transmitted as *Farson in Australia*. We had a local camera crew, even an accountant, an English expatriate with the delightful name of Bob Wealthy. I flew out with a scriptwriter, David Kentish, and the director Rollo Gamble, without whose good humour the journey would have been exhausting.

Rollo described our belated arrival in Sydney:

It was frightfully hot, we were sweating copiously . . . I remember David's shirt, a sort of poison-bottle green with great black patches of his sweat. My own state was hardly more attractive and Dan, I think, had gone into some mystic trance induced by heat and boredom. We longed for a taste of the famed Australian beer at Sydney airport, with a shower and a shave to freshen us for the 2,500 miles to Perth, but this was not to be. Three dishevelled 200-pounders were seized by a pack of journalists, their bags thrown at the customs man who was hardly given time to make his chalk-mark, and ushered upstairs to a private room with a trestle table loaded with drink. Thank God, in a way, but no wash and shave. Thank God they were only interested in Dan who, already at the point of exhaustion, was interviewed, photographed, and filmed until he was almost fit for the undertaker.

'How do you like Australia?' I was asked immediately. As all I had seen was the tarmac it was hard to find the right answer, though I sensed the need for reassurance.

'Are you here to shock us?'

'No. We simply wish to record some impressions,' adding, with a feeble smile, that we might give a couple of tiny shocks as we went along. This was headlined the next morning FARSON HERE TO SHOCK US, which is what they wanted to hear. I settled for unqualified approval and it was only at the end of my journey that I volunteered, 'There's not enough *wrong* with you,' which baffled them.

◆

The approach to Kalgoorlie could not be described as pretty, through identical miles of disheartening scrub known as mongrel-mulga, yet the land had a certain grandeur. The town was scarred by the Golden Mile of derelict mines and dominated by a slag-heap like a miniature Ayers Rock. Parched and pitted now with deep cracks like running sores, and dusty thistles the only vegetation, the residents spoke of it proudly as 'the richest square mile on earth'. It spelled romance at the start of the century in the gold-rush days. These began when Paddy Hannan rode out from Coolgardie twenty miles away with his two partners and while they searched for a wandering pack-horse and fresh water, Hannan struck gold on 15 June 1893. In the next few days they sifted 100 ounces of the stuff and sent Hannan back to Coolgardie to file his claim with the warden to thwart their rival prospectors. At first the 'new place' was known as Hannan's, changed by deed poll in 1895 to Kalgoorlie, from the aboriginal Kalgurli.

When I arrived in 1961 Hannan's statue with his water-bottle adorned the single main street, and Hannan's Modern Lounge nearby boasted the slogan 'Say Hannan's. Like Gold, sets the Standard'.

I loved the look of the place, the wooden hotels with their covered arcades to shut out the sun, the elegant cast-iron balustrades above, and high, broad windows to encourage every breath of air.

Prostitutes moved into Hay Street during the gold rush and, incredibly, were still there. Judging by glimpses through the wooden bars they might have been the same women. I assumed they were kept behind bars by law, but an old-timer, a spruce, sardonic man with a head as oval as an egg, assured me it was to protect them from trouble-makers. They did not require a licence and the police left them alone.

In 1903 the goldfields water scheme piped water all the way from Perth. Until then it had been so scarce that it cost as much as beer, two shillings for a gallon of brackish liquid taken from the ground, steamed and condensed, which is why the flash landlord of the United Service Hotel in Coolgardie used to bathe in champagne. Mrs McCall, in her nineties, told me that she scrubbed Paddy Hannan's back in her grandmother's house in Perth when he returned from the goldfields. 'He hadn't had a bath for months and he stank.'

The old-timer had seen them turn on the water: 'Why, I reckon that was the best day we've ever seen,' he chuckled. 'Everybody went to the bars and got drunk. They also got shot.' He chuckled again.

You can picture their excitement: the temperature was 103 on the day the water reached the town, and it rose to 114 degrees over the next few days. When I went there Kalgoorlie had an Olympic swimming-pool holding half a million gallons of water, costing £3 million to build, which is less overwhelming when you realize that the strike yielded £500 million. Paddy Hannan ended up broke, existing on £150 a year donated by the state.

'Drink and two-up and dice,' said the old-timer in a broken chair outside his dilapidated shack. 'Everybody was friendly, they wouldn't see a person wanting a feed or nothing, yet I think gold is one of the most foolish occupations in the world. Here we are digging it out of the ground and sending it across the world to Fort Knox where they bury it again. A sort of madness, and all that glitters 'tis not gold. Take the Bardock murder: one man at the bottom of the shaft fifty feet down, sent up a bucket of shiny ore. Now the fellow at the top was obsessed with the idea of making millions, so he started dropping rocks on his mate in the shaft to keep it all himself. Thought he'd killed him, but he hadn't. Bardock, crushed and fly-blown, crawled to the surface and accused his murderer before he died. Anyway, it wasn't gold at all.'

In spite of the inevitable heartache, men were still obsessed by the prospect. In Coolgardie, nearly a ghost town with a few crumbling façades and a dwindling population of hundreds compared to the peak of twenty thousand, I escaped from the blinding sun and the persistent attention of an aged Aboriginal with white hair, wearing a tattered jacket with a safety pin instead of buttons, into the cooler refuge of a hotel, the fancy word for pub. There were two left: the Railway, now the most inappropriate of names, and the Denver City, which sounded equally bizarre. It was in the Denver that I met the two romantic Otters.

Asking for a schooner of beer, my English accent ricocheted in the cavernous silence. The older Otter beckoned me over and shook my hand, explaining that he had served in the Royal Navy until 1924. His son was a typical Australian by comparison, in a white vest over nut-brown skin, uttering a few laconic remarks like 'My word!' and 'That's for sure!'

They were lone prospectors and the father's motive had a beautiful logic; a lighthouse keeper, he was so sick of the sea that he tried to get as far away as possible when he went on leave. The goldfields provided the answer.

I climbed into their splendid 1928 Rugby among the picks and shovels and we set out into the bush where they were working a disused mine with three shafts, renamed the Three Jolly Britons. For ten shillings they had staked their claim to twelve acres and by now they were eighty feet down. As the day grew even hotter, they worked with slow satisfaction. The lean and wiry son crushed the stone – 'It's a poor man who can't crush eight tons a day,' he confided in a sudden gush of words – while his father washed it, peering at the pan through a magnifying glass. He showed me a few grains of glistening yellow and reckoned that by the end of their holiday they would have collected twelve ounces, worth £200, enough to cover their expenses. The incentive was the hope of a strike.

'If I struck some rich dirt,' said the son with another burst of loquacity, 'we could make as much as £75,000 and then I wouldn't be working no more and I'd take the family to see the Old Country which Pa has told me of.' They said it was a mug's game as I left them, blissful with their dreams.

When I stumbled on a story about a cattle station in north Queensland, Rollo shared my enthusiasm and we made a reconnaissance trip in a tiny Cessna, returning by road through the rich Atherton Plateau and countryside so stupendous it would have been hard not to feel exhilarated. The journey from Cairns took a mere nine hours, though it took the first settlers with their cattle several years. One of the earliest pioneers was a man called James Atkinson, who left the coastal town of Bowen in 1861 and settled in Wairuna. Now his descendants flourished on the homestead, 'not a big affair' the sons assured me, just the size of Denmark. Even in 1961, the nearest shop was seventy-six miles away.

Here was the essence of all that was decent in Australia – space, simplicity, a love of nature and a zest for life. The patriarch of the clan was Ken Atkinson, who told me that his grandfather had travelled with everything he possessed and 500 cattle and sheep. Rich herd-owners by now, with 8000 head of cattle, life at Wairuna remained tough. Cattle were their passion: at night the Atkinsons talked of little else and I have never eaten so much steak, starting at breakfast.

This was the peak of a boom and every six weeks 700 bullocks were rounded up and dipped. I watched them being gelded with red-hot tongs, a traumatic sight though the animals did not appear to suffer as much as I expected. Castrated at fourteen months, the stags, as the young bulls had become, lost interest and kept clear of the rest.

Every fortnight the two Atkinson sons, Bob and John, rode round their territory to check their fences. The danger came when they separated the animals for the trek south to market.

'It can be frightening, 500 cattle all going one way, rushing towards you,' said Bob. 'If they hit a fence, possibly the first fifteen are crushed to death before the fence is pushed down and the rest are away. When they're unruly, we use dart tranquillizers. It's like the animal's dead for four minutes, a total paralysis.

'Wild horses, we shoot 'em. They're fantastic fighters; once they bite they never let go and they're so darned clever they go for the knee. When young colts grow up and start taking an interest in the mares, the stallions hunt 'em or kill 'em, though they leave the fillies alone.'

The last of the wild Aborigines had worked here. 'He was a different tribe from the ones that were already here,' Ken told me. 'I had to go away for a few days and I left him with another boy who was also from a different tribe and I was careful to send the other boys in another direction. But while I was away they came in and knocked this fellow on the head and ate him.'

'Ate him?' I echoed.

'Part of him, anyway.'

'Did he die?'

'Oh yes, he died. He didn't die immediately but he had a great chunk of beef taken out of his back. It was a tribal thing, they thought it would make them strong and brave. To my knowledge, that was the last case of cannibalism in Queensland.'

In several weeks' time a priest was arriving to christen two little Aboriginal girls, Queenie and Joycey, and the baby boy, Shane James Atkinson, for every Atkinson is christened James after the first pioneer. This would be the christening of the fifth generation, a big occasion with a bush wedding nearby and the picnic races at Mount Garnet. As I have frequently discovered, men who are truly tough can afford sentimentality too. As I was leaving, one of the Atkinson sons slipped a piece of paper into my hand with evident bashfulness. Reading it later, I was amazed to discover that this silent man wrote poetry, and though it is raw and untutored it is so heartfelt that it evokes that splendid scene and brings it tumbling back:

> No dearer place could I desire than this
> To watch at sunset fire,
> The tired stock horses, one by one
> First rolling in the cool white sand
> Remove the mark of girth and band
> And then feed out towards the sinking sun.
> No sweeter music could I seek
> Than horse bells ringing down the creek.
>
> No velvet lawns of some older land
> Can hold me like that trampled sand;
> No garden wealth can thrill me through
> As these burnt broken wattles do
> For there upon those Australian plains
> They all but hold my heart in chains.

Kalgoorlie echoed the past; in Cooma I saw the future. This was the heart of the immense Snowy Mountains hydro-electric scheme, with Cooma as a boom town. Twenty thousand men – Greeks, Poles, Yugoslavs, Czechs, Hungarians and Germans – had been brought in to divert the course of rivers, making them flow west instead of east, in order to irrigate the land. Eight colossal dams, ten power stations, and a hundred miles of tunnel cut through mountains, creating new lakes and drowning townships in the process. It was eerie to look down from a boat and see the steeple of a church below the water.

The scheme cost £375 million and the men came here to make their fortunes, earning as much as £100 a day. I met an Italian who owned six trucks worth £12,000 each and claimed he made £800 a day. With little to spend their money on, they came down from the camps in the mountains to drink and gamble their wages away in the Wild West atmosphere of Cooma, which was little more than one street lined with banks and bars.

These were the New Australians, and they had stories to tell. Hearing me offer them our pittance of a couple of pounds for an interview, a friendly barmaid took me aside. 'Don't insult them by offering money,' she said. 'It's so little and they don't need it 'cos they're stinking rich. The only way you'll get them to talk is to drink with them, match 'em drink for drink.'

I have taken part in some drinking marathons but few so tough or so rewarding. One of the many pleasures of alcohol is the rapport that comes before the euphoria and finally the rot. Then it is possible to achieve an intimacy with strangers which could well be denied to their friends and families. Suspicion was quickly overcome as they realized that I, too, was a stranger in a strange land, and once I had their confidence I had it absolutely.

I was hurled into a party to celebrate the arrival of a huge Greek. At first it was odd to sit in a room for half an hour and not hear a word of English spoken, but drink overcame language barriers as six bottles of whisky were stuck in ice-buckets and emptied in an hour by the five of us, though whisky is never my favourite poison. A Spaniard passed out on the floor; the Greek danced on the table and tore off his shirt; as we lurched past midnight I found myself in another bar talking earnestly to an attractive, tough young Australian and rested my hand on his knee to emphasize some point. WOW! as they say in the comic strips. The man leapt up with a scream of 'Poofter!', prepared to hit me until a group of Greeks pulled me away and bustled me out of the place and back to my hotel. They warned me of something but I could not understand.

I woke suddenly in the motel with images of the night before, and groaned. Already a surfeit of swimming and constant flights on different planes, had left me slightly deaf (I needed an operation after I returned to England), so I felt doubly dreadful. Meanwhile Rollo, who was not feeling too good himself, had been summoned to the reception desk to witness an angry scene. The young Australian from the bar had come to arrest me. He was the assistant chief of police.

Sensing the situation instantly, Rollo rose to the occasion in his full glory and asked the man to join him for coffee. When he was told that I was about to be arrested, he clapped his hands with pleasure. 'But that's *marvellous!*' he exclaimed. As the Australian glared at him suspiciously, Rollo confided, 'Frankly, and this is between the two of us, this is just the shot in the arm we've been needing. As you may know, Dan is hardly known over here but a huge name in England, and this will cause a sensation there – and in Sydney with the ABC. I can just picture the wonderful publicity for Dan. We need it desperately.'

I was told this by the sound man afterwards. Rollo then asked: 'By the way, what *is* the charge? Something serious, I hope?'

'Well,' the policeman mumbled, disconcerted by now. 'He put his hand on my knee and I'm going to charge him with assault.'

Always an actor *manqué*, Rollo gave one of the finest performances of his life. 'Your *knee?*' he exclaimed incredulously. 'But this is the loveliest thing I've ever heard. We must get a photograph of the two of you together. "My word," as you people say, I can see the front-page picture now and the headline – ENGLISH TELLY STAR PUTS HAND ON POLICEMAN'S KNEE.' Sounding and looking a bit like Sydney Greenstreet, he added, 'My word, I admire your courage, sir, indeed I do.'

Apparently the assistant chief of police left abruptly, muttering dark threats that he would beat me up if he saw me again. He tried to do so over the next few days, making several half-hearted lunges in my direction, but each time he was restrained by a cordon of Greeks and Poles who hated the man and befriended me.

They poured out their hearts. Wally the German told me of the card games which could last for days at Cabramurra, the highest settlement in Australia. Sometimes as a diversion they played with photographs sent by mail-order brides who wanted to come from Europe, the most attractive receiving the highest points. Until then I thought the tales of proxy brides were far-fetched until I realized that the men out-numbered the women by a hundred to one and learnt that the Black Maria paid a weekly visit to the railway station to intercept the prostitutes from Sydney and send them back.

Wally described Christmas as the hardest, loneliest day in the year. 'Have seen real tough chaps cry at Christmas like little dogs.'

Ivan the Czech had gone to Sydney to collect his mail-order bride to discover she had married a Pole on the way over. This happened so often that it was suggested that migrant ships should be segregated, limited to one sex only. As Ivan stood disconsolately on the quayside, a woman raced up and threw her arms around him: 'Marry me, for pity's sake marry me. I've just seen my husband and can't stand him.' Ivan smiled nostalgically. 'We stayed together for a weekend. Not bad. No good for wife.'

Though they preferred women from their own countries, I tracked down a Bulgarian in Sydney who was waiting for a Yugoslav bride whom he had never seen though he had sent her the fare. Milete could hardly speak English but his smile was beatific in anticipation. He may not have been scared, but I became increasingly nervous for him as we waited interminably for the Italian ship *Flamina* to dock at dawn, with Milete standing beside me in his Sunday suit, holding her photograph for identification.

They met at last and embraced awkwardly. She was not as glamorous as her photograph. My heart sank further as I realized that neither spoke a word of the other's language. She clutched a bouquet of artificial flowers which seemed absurdly inappropriate. However, in her other hand she held a bottle of Yugoslavian slivovitz which she presented to Milete on the quayside as her dowry. This was a good omen and I was in tears as Milete said goodbye to me and left to introduce his wife to her new home in a new country.

❧

Tasmania has always been underrated by the Australians and is virtually unknown to the British, though Anthony Trollope wrote that 'everything in Tasmania is more English than is England herself.' This must be the silliest statement he ever made. Everything is different: the light so vivid it spotlights the emerald hills in the distance and bounces off the white weatherboard churches. The population is less than half a million, so the place is virtually empty and free from din. The names may be familiar – Launceston, Sheffield, New Norfolk, even Gretna Green – but they are belied by the immensity of their setting, by the forests of gigantic gum-trees and the limitless spaces without a habitation in sight.

In the early days Tasmania was one of the vilest spots on earth. When the island was known as Van Diemen's Land, 15,546 convicts were transported there in less than five years compared to 1605 to New South Wales. Altogether, more than 50,000 male and 10,000 female convicts were subjected to conditions as bad as those on Devil's Island, with the irony that the worst cruelty was the most refined. In the model prison at Port Arthur, the solitary cells had heavy doors to keep out the light, and the warders wore carpet slippers to ensure silence. When the convicts were allowed out to attend Sunday service in church, they wore calico masks with slits for their eyes. Not surprisingly, a lunatic asylum was built nearby for those who survived. Yet, and here was a further irony, when I saw it first, before it became the tourist attraction that it is today, Port Arthur was one of the loveliest settings on the island, with trees and fields, sloping down to the sea. At the end of filming I made the heartfelt comment, 'If I never believed in ghosts before, I believe in them now.' Our cruelty to the convicts, transported for petty offences in the name of colonization, is one of the nastiest moments of our history. Simultaneously we exterminated the native population, which had survived for tens of thousands of years.

Tasmania was so tranquil in 1961 that it was hard to find good stories. If the Australians paused in the middle of sentences, the Tasmanians did so in between words. In Hobart I asked a taxi-driver as I had often done before, to take me to the one place where I should not go. He drove me to the docks, pointing to a pub at the far end. 'Ma Dwyer's,' he announced. 'And no cab'll take you closer than this.' It sounded promising, and sure enough Ma Dwyer's proved the toughest pub in town, a haunt of foreign sailors with a brothel upstairs run by Ma, who had the proverbial heart of gold though she seemed in a constant rage and kept out of prison because the cleverest lawyer in town was on her payroll. Over the next few days her customers grew visibly more battered due to the nightly drunken brawls. There was no hope of filming a story there, everyone was too far gone.

We made one programme on the scallop fishermen further down the coast, where I stayed with a friendly family who fed me fried scallops for breakfast, scallops mornay for lunch, and curried scallops for supper. When I sailed out with the boats, I ate scallops fresh from the sea with the coral like a red sauce, even better than oysters. It was an attractive subject visually, but short on words, and I searched desperately for a second story on my return to Hobart.

A freelance journalist told me of a remarkable woman, Miss Carrie James, who was ninety-four and recalled the early days when Hobart was a convict town. She was kept alive by the responsibility of looking after a retarded nephew in his sixties who was in danger of being committed to an asylum unless she vouched for him.

Jack Millar and I called at her sloping house in Upper Bathurst Street, constructed from the timbers of HMS *Anson* which had sailed on her last voyage from Portsmouth in 1843 with 500 male convicts. Either Miss James did not hear us or was refusing to open the door and after two more abortive attempts I gave up. It was too risky to rely on her for a programme, and Rollo was eager to fly to Melbourne and cover a football match set up for us by David Kentish.

During a last subdued dinner at the pleasant Wrest Point Hotel, Millar arrived in a state of excitement – 'She'll see you!' When I returned an hour later I described my extraordinary encounter without any calculated guile, for I assumed it was too late to film her. Rollo groaned at this lost opportunity. Then Bob Wealthy murmured that it might be possible to change our tickets . . . That was all the encouragement Rollo needed, though he insisted on seeing Miss James for himself. 'Of course we must do it,' he announced after five minutes, leaving her to rest. 'There's no doubt about it.'

The next morning I had considerable doubts. The football story had been cancelled, to the bitter disappointment of the crew, who were bored with Hobart. The alternative of an interview with an old crone on the verge of dementia was not so appealing, and I did not have the courage to warn them that she might refuse to open the door. This private dread was confirmed as we knocked repeatedly, hearing strange scufflings inside, but as we turned away, myself abject, the crew furious, the door opened and Carrie James welcomed us inside.

As scrawny as a shag, she had eyes that were neither pale nor watery but beady in their intensity as her mind returned to the convict past, remembering the females who had been set free, standing behind their garden gates, arms akimbo as they smoked their clay pipes and spat at the few passing settlers. 'They hated the migrants. They hated everyone – hate in their hearts.'

Her own parents were migrants, but she was born in Hobart. Her mother's family had sailed to the island which adopted 'the more euphonious name of Tasmania' in 1853, and her father was so much in love that he followed. This sounded romantic until she told me of her loveless childhood. 'Always a cane on top of the Bible. Father read the Bible and mother held the cane. Mother was cruel – "If you can't break their spirits," she said, "break their backs." But you break the spirit of a child and you ruin it for life. Sad old days and I shouldn't have lived among it . . .' she broke off dramatically, and cried out in anguish, slicing the air with her skeletal arm, 'Oh, don't they ruin a life, never a cuddle, never a kiss.'

It is probably a mistaken twist of memory, but I have the impression of a rocking chair, unless she leant backwards and forwards so often that it seemed so, as she swung between total recall and confused senility. This was one of her best days as she took us back in time.

She remembered two convicts with special affection. 'There was Charles, tall man, he got subservient, you know, but mother wouldn't have that. His spirit was broken, he left a comfortable home and loving mother, you see. He said: "I wish I'd never been born." How could they be happy? I never saw a happy one. Homesick and broken spirited. Charley was going along in London, only a boy of nineteen, when an old man with a barrow full of stuff said, "Give us a lift, lad," and of course he did – one of the softy sort – and the man ran away and the police found the boy with the barrow which was stolen.'

Her mind wandered off. 'I think they all wished they were dead, but, you know, life is *sweet*.'

Dick Stanton's crime was high spirits. He told his story to Miss James's father who wrote down the notes which inspired my subsequent novel *Swansdowne*, based on the convicts transported to Van Diemen's Land. The account started with a flourish: 'Richard Stanton – of Her Majesty's Navy, at your service.' After reading *Robinson Crusoe* at the age of eleven, he had 'an uncontrollable desire to follow a seafaring life' and enlisted in the Royal Navy at Portsmouth. He was fiercely patriotic, but ironically Queen Victoria proved his downfall.

After service of twenty months an event happened that altogether altered the course of my life's career. Her Majesty, Queen Victoria, who had been Queen of Great Britain for some seven years, paid an official visit to the Fleet. The exciting news spread through our ship that the young Queen was to come aboard on the morrow. I very much question whether any other event could have imposed more strenuous duty upon us all: standing gear had to be overhauled, the decks, always as white as holy-stone could make them, had to have an extra scouring, and the brasswork of which there was a warship's profusion, came in for exceptional burnishing.

As the royal vessel approached, some halyards came loose and he leapt to catch them.

In my descent I canonaded against a midshipman, a mere boy much my junior. He rolled down from the poop to the main deck, a distance of about three feet. He got up absolutely unhurt but in a frenzy accused me of deliberately assaulting him, and no expostulation on my part was of any avail.

Miss James told me she often wondered if Stanton had collided with the boy on purpose. The incident might have passed with a reprimand, but he had marred the special occasion. He ended his account with the touching comment: 'I was put under guard and so I missed the great delight I had anticipated of manning the yards to welcome Her Majesty.'

Miss James shook her head sadly. 'Of course they needed men in those days,' which explained his sentence of two years' transportation to Van Diemen's Land. That meant life. Torn from his grief-stricken family who knew they would never see him again, he sailed in the convict barque *Argyle*.

On one bright day the look-out reported, 'Sail ahoy to starboard!' and away in the distance were five ships of the line homeward bound from the Cape. To my experienced eye, how stately they were and I felt the hot tears coursing down my cheeks and I thought of the homeland I had been wrenched from. The chief officer saw my emotion and asked what offence I had committed. I said, 'None at all.' 'Ah,' he said, 'you all say that.'

When Stanton was assigned to a major in Van Diemen's Land he was given two large baskets of ladies' underclothing to wash and iron on his first day. 'I looked in astonishment, I remarked I would not disgrace the flag I sailed under, and danced "Jack's the lad with a hornpipe" on them.' This impertinence cost him twenty-five lashes, for Miss James explained that once a convict was assigned as a servant his master could have him flogged as he pleased. Beating was part of life in the penal settlement of Port Arthur where Stanton was sent for further punishment and subsequent flogging from Sam Burroughs, the flagellator.

Rocking in her chair, Miss James spat out the words, 'We *hated* him. Quiet, the whole street was quiet when Burroughs came to Hobart, we all got on our doorsteps and watched the man go by with our little eyes . . . when Dick returned he would only show his back to our boys, the convicts didn't like the girls to look, but I thought "I'll see that back," and one day I crept up and I did. Oh, *shocking!*' Her hand sketched the cuts across his back: 'Like a piece of leather, scored, great weals, cross to cross.'

As Carrie James peopled the past with her memories, I imagined Hobart eighty years earlier, as a town where settlers, clergy and army officers were the exception, and convicts, or freed men and women, the norm.

'There was Mrs Rusk, you know, with one eye. She was a lady, you could tell – educated. Why she was sent out I don't know. And poor Mrs Buff, a lawyer's wife.'

'Why poor Mrs Buff?' This question produced a flow of unexpected images.

'Mrs Buff?' she gave me a look of surprise as if she had never heard of her. 'Never knew. She was a very quiet woman. Lived on potatoes. She was burnt to death. She was starving, there was no pension those days, and the worms crept about her arms like this –' she gave a graphic gesture, brushing them off. 'And she used to cut off wisps of her hair and eat them because she was told that would kill the worms. She used to come here and mother gave her food and was very kind to her, and put her in a rocking chair. She used to do a bit of washing around the place, but I bet she wasn't fit to do washing.'

'How did the burning take place?'

'Her clothes caught alight. She ran out of this awful little room at the back of the public house – you should have seen the flames – if they'd only made her lie down, but they were bashing her with bags . . . she didn't live long.'

This was the backdrop to Carrie's childhood: a boy of seventeen being marched down Macquarie Street to be hanged; screams at night; waterfront bars where seamen came in from the whaling fleets. Yet Carrie's humour was undiminished and she burst into cackling laughter when I asked if she regretted not having a family of her own.

'I had opportunities but I couldn't click, somehow. No sex-appeal! My sister, oh, she had heaps of boys. I had a boy for a day or two but he got sick of me. I was never meant to get married. I'm waiting for my spiritual mate.'

'Do you think love is the most important thing in life?'

'Yes, love is all, more than religion, love *is* all, love is all. I'm ninety-four and I know. It's not what man possesseth, no, it's the heart; keep the heart with all diligence, for out of it are the issues of life.'

Instead of being alarmed by our invasion of her sloping timber house, with all our paraphernalia and lights, the experience seemed to revive her. As the crew lugged their equipment into the street, each of them took me aside to say how right Rollo and I had been to stay on.

When we said goodbye at her front door, she told me, 'Your visit today made this the happiest afternoon of my life.' I gave her a kiss and she waved to me merrily as I skipped down the hill to the nearest pub, a quiet little room where I intended to get gloriously drunk on my own, knowing that I had just completed the most remarkable interview of my television career.

Twelve

Soho Lives

ON THE WAY HOME from Australia, I stopped off in Rome, where I had arranged to meet John Deakin.

He was at his best, plainly thankful to see me; and I was greedy for his wit after Australia, where it had been in short supply. Having saved most of my salary while on location, money was no problem for once, and a necessary luxury with Deakin in tow.

Knowing and loving Rome, he took pleasure in showing it off, taking me to the usual haunts like the Fontana di Trevi and his favourite catacombs replete with skulls.

I booked into one of the nicest hotels bang in the centre, and met a young, dark-haired Italian who was probably on the game but seemed to enjoy my company without making demands. He accepted Deakin as a Hermione Gingold-type chaperone, though I had long outgrown the role of Gigi in which he and Francis had cast me years before.

Deakin's relief at seeing me was that of escape. He had taken the train from Genoa where he was staying with a dress designer who was trying to give him work and reform him. 'He's like Hitler,' Deakin complained bitterly. 'His wife's an absolute pig and his Alsatian dog is in love with me.' Reading between the lines, I had some sympathy for the unfortunate Gianni Baldini. Evidently there had been a fashion show which ended disastrously when Deakin got drunk and lost several trunks.

'By the way, I'm married.'

'You're not!' the news had the desired effect.

'I have two strapping stepsons in Australia. I should have asked you to look them up.' Having dropped this bombshell, Deakin affected to lose all interest, demanding drinks and cigarettes, playing with my impatience. I was a gullible victim on such occasions; Deakin was just as anxious to tell his news as I was to hear it, but he made me suffer until he was ready.

'Oh, go on,' I surrendered, 'order anything you want, but do go on. Who is she? Why isn't she here?' Deakin explained.

A few months earlier, when he was stranded in Rome with little money and without his Rolleiflex, which had been stolen by a pick-up, he was drinking in his favourite bar one morning when an Italian asked if he wanted to get married.

'Is this a proposal?' replied Deakin, but humour was wasted on the Italian. He said that if Deakin was single, as he believed, he had a friend who wanted a husband. She was fifty-six years old.

'Broke I may be,' said Deakin frostily, 'but even I have my limits.'

'On the condition,' continued the Italian, 'that the man do not claim his marital rights.'

'Are you kiddin'?' said Deakin, with a lift of his eyebrows.

'She do not wish sleep with you, or see you again.'

Deakin lowered his glass. 'Really, child? You interest me strangely. Pray tell me more.'

He learned that the woman was not Italian but stateless, having left Hungary after the abortive uprising in 1956. Such refugees needed passports. She had escaped with her jewels and was prepared to pay five hundred dollars to the man who would marry her.

'All expenses paid?' asked Deakin, for the lady lived in Milan.

'Oh yes, my friend is a generous woman.' Deakin agreed, but he confessed to doubts as he waited for her in the foyer of the grand hotel. 'I expected this old bag to come down the stairs dressed in black bombazine. I must be mad, I thought, and then I heard this voice behind me – "Mr John Deakin?" – and turned round to see this really elegant woman.'

'This is for you,' said Anna in the taxi, handing him an envelope. 'I think it is better when the husband pays.'

'You are so understanding,' said Deakin admiringly. The future Mrs Deakin had reserved a table in the best restaurant in Milan, where she explained her vulnerability and the dread of the knock on the door at any time of the day or night.

'You can have no idea what it means to be stateless. Only the other day the police burst into my apartment in the early hours demanding to see my papers. It is so shaming. With a passport I shall be secure.'

'Have you been married before?'

'Twice.' Apart from the stepsons in Australia, Deakin had a step-daughter in Brazil.

'I thought you would be different,' she admitted at one stage.

'In what way?' asked Deakin archly.

'Oh, I don't know, perhaps . . .' she looked embarrassed, 'somebody "more on the make" as they say, more the gigolo.'

Deakin was not sure if he should be pleased or hurt, and she rested her hand on his for just a moment. 'But I know now that *you* are not like that.'

The next morning started badly with a visit to the British consul, who had known Deakin in England and greeted him warmly with considerable surprise.

'I say, this is good news. I never thought of you as the marrying kind, still . . . Now,' arranging the various forms in front of him, 'how long have you known the good lady?'

'Since yesterday,' said Deakin, deciding it was safest to tell the truth. When the consul learned that she was stateless and fifty-six, he realized that Deakin was still not the marrying kind and concluded the proceedings with chilly formality. Deakin was thankful to relax at the wedding feast after the ceremony.

'All the Hungarian colony were there,' he related, 'to celebrate her good fortune. She showed them her shiny new British passport as if it were the rarest diamond in the world. The wine and food really flowed. They were all terribly nice, marvellous to me, and thanked me so much I was quite embarrassed. The lawyer took me aside – I suspect they were having an affair – and handed me the envelope with the five hundred dollars. At the end of the meal, when she heard I was leaving to catch my train, she insisted that I flew to Rome in time to arrive "for the cocktails". The lawyer arranged the ticket and they saw me off to the airport.' Deakin shook his head from side to side as if in excruciating pain as he remembered this. 'When I said goodbye to her, she whispered "I am not sure that you are not the nicest husband I have ever had, Mr Deakin."'

'No!'

'Of course,' he replied sharply. 'And do you know, I had been thinking of those five hundred smackers for the last week and now I felt I couldn't go through with it. I took out the envelope to give it back . . .'

'You didn't!'

'Of course not. Are you mad? But it crossed my mind.'

So Deakin returned to Rome in his crumpled pale-blue suit with the Chianti stains and the little TWA bag with his spare shirt and razor and the envelope. Joining a group 'in time for the cocktails', he told them what had happened and how he would buy a new camera the next day. When he finished, Peter Ustinov announced that there was only one thing left to do: 'We must put a notice in the Births column of *The Times* – "TO JOHN AND ANNA DEAKIN, A ROLLEI-FLEX WAS BORN".'

A few years later in London when he needed money desperately, he sent a telegram to Anna who cabled it back instantly. He never troubled her again.

For the next two days, Deakin and I and my Italian friend ate and drank, but talked and laughed so much that it kept us sober. Near midnight we found a club where an Italian male singer entertained us with such sweepingly romantic songs that Deakin was constantly in tears. The stay was perfect, without a cross word. Deakin looked at his most woebegone when I climbed into the bus to take me to the airport, though he brightened when I reached through the window and handed him the wad of Italian banknotes that remained.

Deakin returned to Genoa where he quarrelled so irrevocably with Baldini that he moved in with a woman he called the Princess, peppering his letters with references to 'the princess and I'. Soon he took sides with her mother-in-law against her, and after the Princess had a nervous breakdown, he returned to Deakin Towers in 'Berwick Strasse' in Soho.

❖

Soho remained constant. This was still the best place to get pissed in because no one really minded, probably because they were too far gone to notice. While people came and went, little that really mattered seemed to change, except that Archer had fallen. The beautiful book-shop was doomed. The warning signals had included the alarming sight of Archer jumping up and down on the petty-cash box trying to extract some money. When he was forced to close, the shop was sold, the debts were paid off and there was nothing left.

For a time he worked in a rival bookshop whose owner told me she was in awe of him as the publisher of Dylan Thomas. 'Please employ me,' he asked her. 'You don't have to pay me a lot of money.'

At first he was happy for his friends came to see him – John Davenport, John Minton, and Colquhoun and MacBryde, who could be troublesome. 'They'd all go off to lunch and then he would ask me to cash a cheque and of course it would promptly bounce and the bank would be rather noisy about it, so I suggested that perhaps I should pay him every day. He thought that was very agreeable, and after a while he left.'

He surfaced, surprisingly, in the lampshade department in Selfridges. I called to see him there, failing to realize how tactless this was for I had no intention of buying a lamp. The staff took no interest when he tried to organize a cultural group where people could 'get together and make a go of it', and his old-fashioned courtesy disconcerted the customers. Paul Potts remembered a fussy suburban woman who ordered Archer about. 'Very lower middle class. And when it came to one o'clock he just bowed to her and said, "Excuse me, madam, it's time for my luncheon now so you'll have to excuse me." He didn't say lunch, he said luncheon.'

When Deakin visited him in a basement off the Edgware Road, he found him in bed where he now spent most of his time, surrounded by piles of old newspapers and empty milk bottles. The electricity had been cut off, so he read by the light from dozens of candles. 'The effect was rather striking,' Deakin reported, 'like Versailles.'

Archer ended up in Rowton House, a hostel for the down-and-out in the East End. I saw him once more in the Colony, paler, almost translucent; older, but still erect. His eyes gleamed with pleasure as he watched me having a fierce though brief argument with Francis Bacon, and I was glad that I did not feel pity for him as he smiled across the room. This façade was more of an effort than I realized. A few days later, after dinner and drinks with some young friends who had not deserted him, he wrote a few thank-you letters to people who had been kind, and killed himself with an overdose of aspirin.

The inquest stated that Mr David Alderly Archer, aged sixty-four, had come down in the world. 'He was alone, but he had a few friends.' That was true, but not that he took his life because the balance of his mind was disturbed. It was razor sharp.

Merilyn Thorold, a friend and benefactor to Paul Potts as well as Archer, was presented with the casket of ashes and a final note from Archer enclosing the last of his money to go to an unnamed boyfriend she never traced. 'It was about £1.50. I didn't know what to do with it. It was almost sad, seeing the casket go at Castle Eaton where he was buried beside his parents. One had got extraordinarily attached to it. Every time I looked at the casket I thought of David and it made me smile.'

A mention in the parish magazine came to the attention of the governor of the school which had been endowed by Archer's grandfather. Now the school was being closed down and the substantial endowment was no longer needed.

'I am so sorry to read of Mr Archer's death,' the governor wrote to Merilyn. 'We had been trying to contact him for some time wondering if he could make some use of this considerable sum of money himself.'

❧

Conversely, Francis Bacon had torn away from the earth like a rising sun and was soaring into the sky.

One of Francis's strengths was the ability to bide his time. When I researched his biography I discovered that he had worked secretly for several years, leading up to the images which leapt on an astonished world when he decided he was ready to release them. Along the way, as these images became more concentrated, the preparatory work was destroyed. That was a further strength: knowing when to stop and when to scrap. Another was a touch of ruthlessness. Though he would have denied it with ridicule, he knew perfectly well that he was both different and better than the rest. The rules did not apply. He had to be single-minded and had no time for the niceties of life. That is the price of genius. Altogether, he was the strongest man I have known because he was devoid of guilt. But he could be one of the kindest.

I cannot remember my parents ever taking me to an art gallery and during my two years at Cambridge I did not set foot in the Fitzwilliam Museum, though it was up the road from Pembroke College, a hundred yards away. So Francis was my introduction to art, and as I knew nothing about it I was unable to irritate him with opinions of my own; I had no opinions and listened to what he told me. This was a period when his paintings had an energetic grandeur which overwhelmed me then, and still of greater appeal to me than the more clinical though no less daring techniques he evolved later. These were the years following the sensation caused by the triptych of the *Three Figures at the Base of a Crucifixion*, followed by those mysterious *Figures*

I and *II* in an unnamed landscape, hinting at assassination. The grin became a scream of pain in the *Head I 1948* and a howl from *Head VI*, based on the Velasquez portrait of Pope Innocent X, which was used as the poster for the first Tate retrospective in 1962.

During these early years, Francis was handled at the small Hanover Gallery by a loyal and patient dealer, Erica Brausen, who was one of the first to recognize the importance of his work. I remember her as a neurotic, suspicious, possessive lesbian, but Francis was a constant problem with his gambling debts and she kept him going. His private views, the catalogues just a few sheets of paper with some black and white reproductions, were scenes of reverence and revelry, with the Soho crowd poncing and pouncing on the free plonk, Francis looking on with a smile of detachment and Deakin, finger to lips, behaving like Diaghilev as he pronounced, 'No, this really *is* rather good!' as if anyone had said anything different. On one occasion a picture was still wet and unprotected by the usual heavy glass. Henrietta Moraes was pressed against it in the crush, walking away with part of the image on her back. That exhibition included four studies for portraits of Van Gogh painted during the previous two years. The first, which had been bought by Robert and Lisa Sainsbury, was based on *The Painter on the Road to Tarascon 1888*, which they lent to the show. It was due to Erica Brausen that they admired Bacon's work long before it was fashionable and bought everything through her, becoming his most important patrons, an admiration that turned to affection.

One evening, hating to be on his own, Francis took me to the Sainsburys' elegant home in Westminster where I was shown such wonders as the bronze of the *Petite danseuse de quatorze ans* sculpted by Degas in 1878. As we continued up the stairs I turned brightly to their son, David Sainsbury, trying to think of the right thing to say as I recognized a Bacon portrait: 'I say, that's an awfully good likeness of your father.'

'Yes,' agreed David Sainsbury stiffly. 'Except it's my mother.'

A year after the 'Van Gogh' exhibition at the Hanover, on 27 August 1958, I interviewed Francis on television. He was led to this unwillingly, assuring me that he had no interest in appearing unless we paid off his accumulated bill at Wheeler's. Rollo and I had been asked to do a favour for the managing director by filming a close friend, an artist called Cowan Dobson of whom we had not heard. This was the only time that such a request had been made so we agreed and set off to Dobson's home in Chelsea. We were appalled. A genial cove, he painted abysmal society portraits and referred to his wife, correctly though proudly, as 'the most painted woman in London'. My memory may exaggerate, but I am sure he wore a bow tie, smock, and floppy velvet beret. We needed Bacon as the antidote, and hurried off to our appointment at Wheeler's with Bernard Walsh who asked his accountant for Francis Bacon's bill. Our top fee was around £15 and the bill was closer to £1500, astounding for those days. We sat there stunned as Walsh regarded us unhappily. Then he had an idea. 'I say,' he exclaimed with his usual enthusiasm, 'If you agree to film in Wheeler's – which was exactly what we hoped to do – 'then I could charge the bill against publicity.' We agreed enthusiastically and Francis was hoist by his own petard.

Our film The Art Game was one of many destroyed by A-R when they lost their franchise; a pity, for it was the first time Francis spoke about his work before the celebrated interviews with David Sylvester published in 1975. I had no idea of its importance at the time, which saved me from being reverential.

'Do you paint for money?' I asked.

'No, I paint entirely to amuse myself.'

'Then why do you exhibit?'

'Because afterwards I need the money to go on.'

'Do you mean to say that if you had enough money of your own you would not exhibit?'

'No, certainly not. There's no pleasure in exhibiting at all. The only pleasure is to work for yourself and hope that sometime you'll do something that you really want.'

I found this hard to believe at the time, and he contradicted it later when he said: 'Art matters a great deal, because all the greatest aspirations of the human race have been left in art. We would know nothing about the civilizations of the past if it had not been for the traces they've left through art.'

I suggested that many people felt hoaxed when they went to art galleries and found work so remote from anything they knew.

'Well, most people are hoaxed all their lives, so I don't see why they should go to an exhibition of paintings and expect to have a moment of revelation.'

'Surely that's one of the things that art is supposed to do – to reveal things to people?'

'It might reveal to people *after* they have knowledge, but why would it suddenly occur to someone who is completely unlearned and knows nothing about it? Why should he expect suddenly to know what is going on? Because, actually, modern art is a very simple thing. It's not more complex than art has been in the past.'

'Surely in the past,' I persisted, 'the ordinary person could recognize the subject and could bring standards by which he could tell whether they were good or bad? But how can he possibly tell what is good or bad among all the stuff that's done today?'

'Well, he couldn't actually tell what was good or bad – superficially, he could tell if the painting was *like* somebody if it was a portrait, or if it was a bowl of fruit or something. On that level he could think about the representation, and now the representation has been cut to a great extent and he does feel himself a bit hoaxed by the whole thing.'

If that was true then, it is more so today with the emphasis on video, conceptual and installation art. At the time, I was referring to the fashionable 'Action' painters, who also featured in our film.

'The means don't matter,' Francis explained patiently. 'It's only the end that matters. It doesn't really matter if you bicycle all over your picture, or what you do to it. You see, if you take the late Rembrandt paintings – he was perhaps the greatest, in a sense, action painter. Because if you take the very late Rembrandt self-portraits you'll find, if you look carefully at them, that there's no mouth, there's no nose, no eye socket, but the thing is he made a very great image . . .' This is equally true of Bacon's *Head VI 1949*. 'The only difference with action painting,' he continued, 'is really, unfortunately, and unlike the Rembrandts, it's a form of decorative art. He tried to make a head or portrait of somebody, whereas action painters are nearly always trying to make a decorative pattern.'

'Is that good?'

'No, that's a very bad thing. But action painting is only a very recent thing and probably a passing thing. The only interesting thing is that if you splash a spot of paint down on the canvas, it is more interesting – because it has more vitality – than the inanities of academic art.'

Asked if a bad painter could paint a good picture, Francis revealed his own approach. 'It's unlikely; after all, painting is not cricket. The rules are there to be broken if you can break them to your advantage, and it's quite possible that you will find that the greatest luck goes to the greatest painters because they're the people with the sensibility to make use of the luck which is given them from time to time.'

I referred to his notorious tone of contempt when he said he 'sloshed' the paint on canvas.

'I often say anything, you know, to pass the time.'

'It isn't as simple as that?'

'It isn't simple at all. But sometimes, naturally, every painter hopes that the paints are going to work for him and that he will be given all the things he was trying to do. That one day there'll be a coagulation when everything will come together, and for a moment he will have fulfilled what he wants to do.'

Francis, the most fluent of painters, admitted that it was almost impossible to talk about art: 'I think Pavlova was right when somebody asked her what she meant when she was dancing the dying swan and she said: "Well, if I could tell you, I wouldn't dance it." One hopes the greatest art is a kind of valve in which very many hidden things of human feeling and destiny are trapped – something that can't be definitely and directly said.'

I asked why his work was described by some people as sensational.

'What do you mean by the word "sensational"?'

'They're shocked by it. They find it evil, horrifying, unpleasant . . .'

'I think it is that sometimes I have used subject matter which people think is sensational because one of the things I have wanted to do was to record the human cry, and that in itself is something sensational. And if I could really do it – and it's one of the most difficult things to do in art, and I wouldn't say I've ever been able to do it, or perhaps anybody has yet been able to do it – it would of course be sensational.'

'When you say "the human cry", what do you mean?'

'The whole coagulation of pain, despair . . .'

'What about the reverse side of life, Francis? Happiness and love. Why paint only despair and pain?'

'*Well*,' he drew the word out as usual. 'Happiness and love is a wonderful thing to paint also – I always hope I will be able to do that too. After all, it's only the reverse side of the shadow, isn't it? It's only due to your own nervous system that you can paint at all. And you know – this is perhaps an aside, but there was a very interesting thing that Valéry said about modern art, and it's very true. He said that modern artists want *the grin without the cat*, and by that he meant that

they want the sensation of life without the boredom of conveyance.
One of the things that is very interesting is that in the last fifty years
people – all the movements – have been abstract . . . so the thing is,
how can I draw one more veil away from life and present what is
called the loving sensation more nearly on the nervous system and
more violently.'

'And you're the Salome of the modern art world,' I suggested,
'taking off the veils.'

With one of his huge, expanding smiles, verging on self-mockery,
he replied, 'I am sad to say I would hardly say that. But of course it
would be a very nice thing to be.'

'Have another glass of champagne,' I said, seizing the rare opportunity to play the host.

'Thank you very much, Dan.'

By this time we were merry for each film magazine ran out after
four minutes, taking an interminable time to reload, during which we
consumed oysters and drank champagne liberally. When the filming,
which lasted all afternoon, was edited down to fifteen minutes, our
cheerfulness appeared to increase with startling speed, though the
intensity of the moment kept us sober.

Fortunately the transcript survived and I have treasured it ever since,
for this was Bacon's declaration of his philosophy, culminating with
the quote from the symbolist poet Paul Valéry which I had heard so
often in the Colony: '. . . the grin without the cat'.

When *The Art Game* was transmitted, I watched it at Rollo Gamble's
flat with his wife, my mother and father on one of their rare visits
together to London, and the American writer John Gunther and his
wife. Perhaps my father was on the wagon, for I remember him as
remarkably sober, but my parents and the Gunthers were puzzled by
Bacon's assertion that 'Art is not cricket.' As for Cowan Dobson, who
appeared briefly in a programme he believed would be devoted to
himself, he was so enraged that he wrote a letter of complaint to the
managing director accusing me and Rollo of insulting him by including
him with such a despicable creature as Francis Bacon. The controller
of programmes sent us a pained note. No one appreciated that the
film was historic. We were not asked to do such favours again.

A few weeks later (17 October 1958) Francis called at the Hanover
Gallery 'in some trepidation'. Knowing that Erica Brausen was on
holiday, he told her colleague Michael Greenwood that he was in

such a mess financially that he was planning to join the more established Marlborough Gallery. Greenwood suspected, correctly, that the contract had been signed the day before, for Bacon flourished a cheque to clear his account, adding that he had needed an additional £5000 to cover his gambling debts.

'He felt that you would never be able to take over such a liability,' Greenwood wrote to Erica, 'and therefore had not spoken to you about it. He knows that you will be distressed, as he is himself, but he says that his position was desperate and that he had no alternative. I'm terribly sorry about Francis after all you have done for him all these years.'

This is where the touch of ruthlessness comes in. It was justified; it is the inevitable fate of the smaller gallery to be replaced when the artist becomes commercially desirable. It was true that Erica Brausen had been his champion, feeding him faithfully with small cheques, protecting his interests, even taking the risk of displaying *The Two Figures in the Grass 1954*, known affectionately as 'The Two Buggers', though she put it upstairs in case anyone complained to the police. But she was inadequate to Bacon's special needs as I realized when I discovered a letter sent to her by Alfred Barr the year before: 'You are very kind indeed to send me the colour photos of the recent Bacons – but tantalizing, too, since you do not say if all are sold or, if not, what prices. I like best the least expressionist, the Munch-like one with van Gogh standing still. If unsold, how much is it? How big are they? And are these really the only records? Can't you let us have some black and white photos for our files? You really ought to document thoroughly the work of England's most interesting painter! Who else will?'

'England's most interesting painter!' This was a shrewd appraisal at such an early date, coming from the Director of the Museum of Modern Art in New York who had bought Bacon's *Painting 1946* from Erica, his first work sold to a museum, for which she had paid him £350 in £5 notes.

Perhaps Francis should have broken the news of his departure to her himself, though I am sure he dreaded the recriminations. He knew it was time to move on, and, as breaks go, it was reasonably clean.

The moment Francis joined the Marlborough, now protected by Valerie Beston who guarded his interests jealously up to and after his death, he was on a different level. Though he exhibited with the Marlborough in 1960, it was the retrospective at the Tate two years later which established him. Francis took me to see the exhibition after the hanging, on the evening before the private view. The rooms were empty apart from a few attendants, who seemed as awestruck as myself. Why Francis bothered to ask me to join him is hard to understand, except that I was neither reporter nor art critic, just a harmless appendage. For once Francis seemed nervous and for once I kept quiet as we walked around the gallery, an amazing moment as I witnessed the fruition of his early talent: those mysterious Figures in Landscapes hinting at disaster; the portraits of Van Gogh which few other artists would have attempted; the screaming, twisted, half-formed Heads; the *Two Figures in the Grass*; the *Three Studies for the Base of a Crucifixion*, unlike anything seen before; and the first of the Popes howling behind their glass. In later years Francis became more skilful technically, but few pictures equalled the roaring splendour of these years.

Never contemptuous of professional advice, always well-behaved when it came to his advancement, Francis had devoted himself to the exhibition without argument or the self-indulgence of a tantrum, cancelling an urgent flight to Tangier where his friend Peter Lacy was seriously ill.

As we left the Tate, I sensed that he knew he had achieved something extraordinary. I was speechless and had the tact to remain so.

Early the next morning I received a phone call from a snooty secretary who worked for *This Week*. She asked if I could go to Paris.

'Yes,' I replied.

'But we need you there this afternoon,' she protested.

'Fine.' I realized I was the last resort.

'Well,' she admitted, 'someone has let us down and Jeremy Isaacs wonders if you'll interview James Baldwin.'

'Delighted!'

Grudgingly, she told me what flight to take and where to meet the director. It meant that I would miss the private view at the Tate, but I felt that my personal viewing was unique and I could do without the public. Baldwin proved an interesting man to interview, and Jeremy Isaacs sent me a telegram of congratulations afterwards, though he never asked me to work for him again.

The next morning I wallowed in the Parisian luxury of strong French coffee in Paris in springtime, on the sidewalk outside the Deux

Magots, and devoured the English papers with the reviews of the Bacon retrospective. Few artists have received such recognition in their lifetime; for years there had been rumblings of his impending triumph, now everyone knew that a painter of unparalleled excitement had arrived, the rarest thing in art – a true original.

Returning to London that afternoon, I entered the Colony eager with anticipation. For once I was sober and the scene which greeted me was so violent that I recoiled. Not only were they drunk, but hysterical too. My God, I thought, is it always like this, and I never noticed? Many were in tears, including Elinor Bellingham-Smith, a painter married to Rodrigo Moynihan. As she was usually in tears this was no surprise, and I assumed that the others were crying with the excitement of Bacon's triumph.

'Have you heard the news?' she asked sobbingly.

'Yes,' I beamed, 'isn't it wonderful!' She slapped me hard across the face, which did surprise me. At that moment Francis saw me in the mêlée, beckoned, and led me to the lavatory at the back where he told me that he had opened a score of congratulatory telegrams that morning, the last informing him of the death of Peter Lacy in Tangier the night before. The fates had given and they had taken away.

Everyone in the Colony knew that Francis had been in love with Lacy, though they were unaware how difficult Lacy could be, which encouraged Francis to love him all the more. Behind the gentle, blinking façade of the wartime hero, black sheep of a respectable family and remittance man, lurked a dissatisfied homosexual with a sadistic streak which appealed to Bacon's desire to be dominated and whipped. Ultimately it was the masochist who emerged the stronger and their relationship was scarred by emotional scenes which had less to do with sex than with jealousy. When I researched my biography of Francis in Tangier in 1991, David Herbert remembered their tempestuous visits: 'Peter Lacy? Oh yes, I knew him well. Played the piano in Dean's. I don't think he had any money at all. He was awfully sweet but I remember him getting very drunk. Darling Francis was having his first show and Lacy was so blind drunk that they had a fearful row and Lacy slashed thirty of his canvases. Can you imagine?' Herbert looked aghast. 'Yet Francis told me, "You know I rather enjoyed it." I believe the pictures were intended for his first Marlborough show in New York.'

Peter Pollock and Paul Danquah took the story further. Francis had lodged with them in Battersea and they witnessed his raids on Tangier, where they live today.

'Surely Lacy was good for Francis?' I asked with my old naïvety.

'Terrible,' said Peter.

'A horror,' said Paul. 'Francis had a need for that kind of affair. Francis was desperately in love with him. It was obsessional.'

'Peter Lacy was flinging pictures out of the window wherever they went,' said Peter drily. 'He had an uncontrollable rage. Trails of canvases were flung from their hotels.'

'He was strikingly handsome,' Paul conceded.

'I always saw him as a romantic figure,' I ventured.

'*Any* fighter pilot was romantic,' said Peter sardonically.

'He had a funny arrogance,' Paul added, trying to be kinder, 'about everything and everybody. But when you heard him play the piano the way Sinatra sings, you'd think, "No, he couldn't have done anything so nasty."'

Paul concluded with a recollection: 'One of the saddest times in Battersea, when the relationship between Francis and Peter was very strong and they were exchanging letters, was when he received a card which wasn't as warm as it should have been. I remember him holding up the card, and he looked so sad that I realized he was very much in love with Lacy.'

With Lacy's death the Tangerine days were over for Francis, the *raison d'être* had gone.

❧

When I researched my biography, I thought it fair to check on Francis's claim that when she visited the Tate Gallery Mrs Thatcher asked who was our greatest painter. When told Francis Bacon, she recoiled – 'Not that horrible man who paints those dreadful pictures!' which pleased him. At the annual summer party in the back garden of the *Spectator*'s offices in Doughty Street in 1993, the crush was so formidable that I heard cries of 'The Baroness – the Baroness is coming,' and turned round to find myself pressed against her, eye to eye. Unable to move away, I thanked her for replying to my letter.

'Who are you?' she demanded imperiously, though not discourteously. When I explained, she reiterated: 'I have *absolutely* no recollection whatsoever of ever saying such a remark. I am a *great* admirer of his work, but as with any artist there will always be some works which are preferable to others.'

I caught sight of the *Spectator* editors – Alexander Chancellor, Charles Moore and Dominic Lawson, plus Enoch Powell, higher up, looking furious, and shrugged to indicate that far from monopolizing her, I was unable to break free.

'I asked them to show me modern art,' she continued, 'and I couldn't see anything in it at all. The next time I began to understand.' Suddenly she jabbed a finger in my chest: '*See, see, see,*' she told me, '*learn, learn, learn.*' At that moment the crush shifted and the editors advanced like a human chain in the surf to rescue her. I believed her denial; more likely, the other remark was what Francis wanted to hear, hating her as he did.

Thirteen

On the Bend of
the River

WHEN I MOVED into Limehouse I did something right. If one
can have a love affair with a place – and I know one can –
this was mine for the next few years.

My yearning to live beside water had taken me to the posher reaches
of Battersea with its cluster of houseboats, but I knew I would tire of
the cheek-by-jowl bonhomie. I thought of renting a room in the
house where Wren is supposed to have stayed across the river from
St Paul's, but I would have been answerable to a jolly but formidable
family of strangers. All along, I was drawn to the murkier and mysterious stretches of the East End and the London docks. Taking a pleasure
boat to Greenwich, I made notes of houses which looked habitable;
but these were few and when I returned on foot during long summer
evenings they proved to be derelict or occupied by the river police.
With no concept of mortgages, it did not occur to me to renovate
one of the abandoned houses in Shadwell. I enjoyed my explorations:
black shadows from the looming warehouses cutting the streets, which
were deserted apart from the West Indians along Cable Street, supposedly the 'wickedest street in London', who greeted me charmingly
from chairs they had placed on the pavement to catch the last warmth
of the sun.

The riverside was an unexpected maze of alleys wandering in no
sensible direction until they halted at the water's edge where ferries
took passengers across to the other side, to pubs like the Town of
Ramsgate at Wapping Old Stairs where Judge Jeffries was caught while
he waited for the ship to take him away from justice.

The Thames was still gloriously alive then, a working river with
barges and freighters, lined by wharves and cranes. Here was the

romance I was looking for, yet, with London's disdain for the Thames, few people wanted to live beside it.

Then I heard of a small house that was being converted above a barge repair yard in Limehouse. I kept my plans quiet as I tracked down the owner's son, a smart young man called Ken Fisher, trying to persuade him with a lavish lunch at Wheeler's, using my secretary (who resembled Marilyn Monroe) as further bait. He protested that the place was unsuitable, with the implication that I belonged to Mayfair rather than the depths of the East End. Then I met his mother, Mrs Woodward Fisher, 'Dolly' (Dorothea), also known as 'The Tug-boat Annie of the Thames', who controlled a fleet of 200 barges by radio from her large and genteel home in Blackheath. With her bark of a voice, often mistaken for a man's, she roused her workmen from their tea breaks if they lingered a moment too long. Dressing and looking like George Arliss, with well-cut suits and a monocle, she dominated her son and her husband William, who as a young man had won the Doggett's Coat and Badge in the annual rowing race of six strong watermen. I never lost my fear of this outspoken octogenarian, but behind her gruff exterior lurked a sympathy for anyone who loved the river. Laughing at my anxiety, she mentioned a figure for the rent and became my new landlady.

Why did I love 92 Narrow Street so much? Simply, I had found the place I was looking for. Associated-Rediffusion advanced part of my salary so I could furnish it and I was so enthusiastic and proud at having a home of my own that I could not wait for the beds to arrive and slept on a mattress on the floor.

When I stood on my balcony I thought I possessed one of the most exhilarating views in the world, and on good evenings I was right – as light richocheted against the water around a barge being rowed upriver with the tide by a man standing out in silhouette as he used a pole to steer by. At night the cargo boats hooted as they waited to enter Regent's Canal Dock; a friend found the noise disturbing, but it made me think of elephants approaching a water-hole, trumpeting with pleasure. I did not hear the din, nor notice the stink at low tide or the grime from the coal-wharf nearby, but I saw the two wild duck making their nest in the pilings, and a flight of swans beating downriver in single file.

At high tide it would have been possible to dive into the water from my balcony, though you were advised to have your stomach pumped out if you fell in accidentally. Upriver I could make out the famous frontage of the Prospect of Whitby and Tower Bridge above the skyline. On the òther side I looked four miles towards Greenwich, just obscured from view. Opposite was a desolate stretch known as Cuckold's Point.

The one drawback was the barge repair yard below, where they worked with an excruciating scream of electric drills as they scraped the rustier hulls of Mrs Fisher's fleet. This was nerve-racking in the daytime with the fumes lifting the new Caucasian carpet from my scrubbed wooden floor, yet I doubt if this stretch had ever been peaceful. I found an engraving by Whistler made in 1854, with barges clustered below a nearby yard, and I assume there was an equal amount of hammering then. The scene was reassuringly the same. When the dead body of a woman was washed up on the gravel shore directly below, this was in keeping with the days when Rogue Riderhood rowed his boat at Limehouse in search of floating corpses he could rob in the opening of *Our Mutual Friend*: 'It's a curious thing,' wrote Dickens, 'but the river sweeps in here and the tide settles the bodies among the piles and craft. Rogue knew that.' The river police, three men in a boat on eight-hour shifts, picked up a large number of bodies, both dead and alive, every year, and one told me that if a boatman fished up a corpse on the south side he received 7s 6d but only 6s on the north side. Invariably they were taken to the south.

Dickens was alleged to have stayed at number 92, according to Mr Fisher, and though such claims are legion there is no doubt that he knew the stretch intimately. The Bunch of Grapes at the end of the street before the entrance to the Regent's Canal Dock boasted a Dickens Room, on the basis that this was the original Six Jolly Fellow-ship Porters in *Our Mutual Friend*. To my delight and the disenchant-ment of the surly landlord, I discovered an early print at Trinity House which showed a pub called the Two Brewers, a few yards to the other side of me though now a brick wall, which fitted Dickens's description more exactly than the bow-fronted Bunch of Grapes – 'a tavern of dropsical appearance ... with a crazy wooden verandah impending over the water; indeed the whole house inclusive of the complaining flag-staff on the roof, impended over the water, but seemed to have got into the condition of a faint-hearted diver who had paused so long on the brink that he will never go in at all.' Dickens wrote of his explorations, finding 'vessels that seemed to have got afloat –

among bowsprits staring into windows and windows staring into ships.' I found the same, with the constant parade of river traffic: tugs hauling strings of barges; dirty freighters with trees tied to the masts on Christmas Day; cargo ships with romantic names – *Velasquez*, or *The Cyprian Shore*; coasters from France with lines hung with the family washing like bunting, and a mongrel dog scampering along the deck; a passenger ship from Poland with passengers staring uncertainly as they passed; a naval frigate with ratings standing to attention, even a submarine; a man on water skis. Best of all were the peaceful evenings with the barges rowed up the shimmering river. All the flotsam and jetsam of the waterfront. Others failed to see the charm, clasping their ears as the barges thundered in the wake of a passing ship – 'How can you sleep?' – and they complained that it was 'hell to get to. Few of your friends will bother.' Exactly.

I explored Limehouse on foot. With copious research from the archives at Trinity House, I learned that Narrow Street used to be Fore Street, and before that Limehouse Street, probably named after the lime kilns, as Ratcliff Highway was due to red cliffs that once lined the shore, though that was harder to believe. They were villages when Frobisher left Ratcliff to sail in his search for the passage to China, and Raleigh left Limehouse on his third voyage to Guyana.

Gustave Doré's engravings of London included a sensational *Night Scene* of the docks along the Highway when London was one of the busiest ports in the world, with men fighting outside one of the 'dens' known as Paddy's Goose – presumably an Irishman ran a pub called the Swan – where the tables and chairs were screwed to the floor to prevent them being used as weapons. A forest of masts rose in the murky background. Even now, the streets echoed the local activities and the trade from the Orient: Gin Alley, Cinnamon Street and Ropemakers Fields, with the great thoroughfare of East India Dock Road leading into London. The old Eastern Hotel, at the junction of West India Dock Road and Commercial Road opposite Hawksmoor's church of St Anne, was now a pub. I liked going there to watch the woman with one eye and dyed scarlet hair screaming 'I ain't got nobody' to the accompaniment of a banjo and a silver trumpet.

Conrad used the Eastern Hotel as the base for one of his sea captains in *Chance*, referring to the turmoil outside:

. . . the inhabitants of that end of town where life goes on unadorned by grace or splendour; they passed us in their shabby garments, with sallow faces, haggard, anxious or weary, or simply without expression, in an unsmiling sombre stream not made up of lives but of mere unconsidered existencies whose joys, struggles, thoughts, sorrows and their very hopes were miserable, glamourless, and of no account in the world.

I saw such a man 'without expression' in Brick Lane, what they used to call 'a shabby genteel' with stained bowler hat and frayed collar in a last attempt to keep up appearances, belied by the hollow, despairing eyes which had abandoned hope and which haunted me for days.

Yet, for once, and it takes nerve to suggest this, Conrad was wrong. It was the genius of the East End masses that they rose above the conditions they lived in. Perhaps Conrad understood the East better than the East End, for he failed to appreciate that the people had to defy them or go under, and they did so with the gaiety of Cockney wit and the gusto and glamour of music hall. This became a new passion as I learned how Marie Lloyd, who was born in Hoxton, staggered on stage in her role as a drunken old woman, clutching her cock linnet in its simple wooden cage, and confided to the audience, instead of the cheerful trill adopted today, that she had to move away:

> 'Cos the rent we couldn't pay,
> The moving van came round just after dark;
> There was me and my old man
> Shoving things inside the van,
> Which we'd often done before, let me remark . . .

Booze and bailiffs and moonlight flits – the audience roared – they *knew*! And when Marie appeared later in her directoire dress – 'quite a fashion plate' – it heartened them that one of their own could look so glamorous. There was always the wistful hope that they might have a bit of luck themselves. Here was their strength: that they were able to laugh at adversity and having laughed, accept it more readily. 'Unadorned by grace?' The grace of life in the East End was miraculous.

This spirit just survived when I moved in, the people so tough they could afford to be chivalrous. At first they suspected me of slumming until they realized that my affection for the place was genuine, and then I was accepted. Soon the pleasure boats were pointing me out as they passed, and on Sundays I could tell the exact time – nine o'clock – as the bigger steamer, the Empress or Countess of Something, approached on its way to Southend, crowded with trippers, the loud-speaker booming out as she passed: 'And this is Limehouse, notorious for its haunts of vice and opium dens and now the home of TV personality Daniel Farson.' Sometimes I looked out and waved and a hundred arms waved back. If I had a stranger in bed beside me, or someone had crashed out on the sofa after a Saturday night party, they looked bemused, as if they were hearing things.

Cecil Beaton, my neighbour in Pelham Place, was exchanged for Chalky, a punch-drunk old boxer who lived on an upper floor above the yard. The house on the other side was derelict and I paid a nominal rent to keep it so.

The process of making a new home was deeply satisfying. I found a junk shop in Cable Street run by an African with tribal scars on his cheeks and bought a huge mirror, which ran from the ceiling to the floor to extend the view of my small sitting-room. Also, for a few shillings, the damaged earthenware figure of a cloth-capped newsboy whose 'Extra Special' placard advertised: CLAYMORE The Favourite Scotch EVERYWHERE. I have it still and continue to gain pleasure from it, delighted to see a postcard in the Victoria and Albert Museum of a similar figure, dated 1910.

The floorboards were sanded, I laid black and white vinyl tiles in the room leading to the balcony, and I indulged myself in the one extravagance of a patterned block of Italian marble from a smart antique shop in Pimlico, which fitted into a brass base to provide a table.

The river stank so much in the old days that the parlour looked over the street while the lavatory was relegated to the back, probably emptying straight into the water. Fortunately Mrs Fisher had reversed this arrangement. Unfortunately she had removed one Victorian black iron fireplace, but another survived in my bedroom with a double curve of unusual elegance, and I tried to redeem the modern fireplace with an expensive wooden frame. There were two large bedrooms upstairs, with mine overlooking the river, and a useful attic with a smaller bedroom to which I retreated sometimes for it was quieter, with a welcome sense of isolation.

My pictures ranged from two large ship scenes painted by members of the crew, which I bought for thirty shillings each from a shop near Holborn, to a large black and white portrait by Frank Auerbach which faced my bed. Studying it each morning I wondered if it looked like Christ or Abraham Lincoln, though it was described as *Head of E.O.W.*, who turned out to be a woman. Other paintings included a portrait of John Deakin which I bought from Lucian Freud, a drawing of Somerset Maugham given me by Graham Sutherland, and the head of a surgeon, with a light strapped to his forehead, retrieved from Francis Bacon before he could destroy it. On my grandmother's death, I inherited a sketch of a tiger by Gaudier-Brzeska which I had always loved, the perfect simplicity of just a line or two.

At the back I planted bay trees in tubs, and plants and creepers in barrels and window-boxes. When the weather was fine, I ate my meals there and typed away when I was not in Television House.

I arrived in time to witness the last gasp of Chinatown, with the Chinese lettering starting to crack and peel on the shuttered shop-fronts, little more than façades. A courteous Chinaman with skin like faded parchment showed me the Chun-Yee club in Pennyfields where the members played mah jong, and I drank in the Commercial on the corner of West India Dock Road where I heard more Chinese spoken than English and did not feel welcome. I ate in the Old Friends in Mandarin Street before it was replaced by the smarter New Friends nearby, and the Friendly House run by Mr Lo-Cheong and Mrs Farmer and their lovely, smiling Eurasian daughters. Otherwise I had to depend on memories of the pukka-poo gambling cards, like an early form of football pools, and the labyrinth of small houses connected by passages so that when a man ran from the police into a house at one end, he emerged in another street altogether. I learned also of the Chinese funerals, lavish affairs with good food placed on top of the grave.

'Why waste good grub like that?' asked a Cockney. 'You think 'e'll get up and eat it?'

'Why you put flowers?' replied the Chinaman impassively. 'You think 'e come up and smell 'em?' Sadly, the opium dens were features of the past, or I should have tried one.

With such material, it seemed natural to open my new TV series *Farson's Guide to the British* with *The London River*. This included such characters as the rat-catcher who threw the rats into a bag when they escaped from the drains at high tide. He told me, 'There was this one rat, see, which was crippled, so I was going to set him free when he goes and bites me in the finger. "Orl right," says I, "that's your bloomin lot."' He snapped his mouth to show how he had bitten off the rat's head, evidently a party trick.

'Aren't you afraid of getting poisoned?' I asked.

'Lor no,' he replied with scorn, 'the rat wot bites me will get poisoned hisself.' But when I saw him biting a rat later, it was either so tough or his teeth were so weak that he had to gum it to death as he pulled it in half.

❖

When I moved into Limehouse the East End was a separate country, as if I had crossed a frontier post at the Tower before heading down the Highway. West Enders rarely set foot there except on business or a pub crawl, and East Enders, with their different looks and accents, felt ill at ease if they ventured 'up West'. This was nothing compared to their total isolation before Jack the Ripper threw a spotlight on 'the people of the abyss' in the autumn of 1888. Until then they were not only out of sight but out of mind, as if such wretchedness did not and should not exist. Because of the Ripper, Queen Victoria herself demanded changes such as better lighting in the dark alleys, and the young Bernard Shaw sounded off in the *Star*: 'If the habits of Duchesses only admitted of their being decoyed into Whitechapel backyards, a single experiment in slaughterhouse anatomy on an aristocratic victim might fetch in a round half million and save the necessity of sacrificing four women of the people.'

As a gesture of goodwill, the American actor Richard Mansfield cancelled his production of *Doctor Jekyll and Mr Hyde* at the Lyceum after a final benefit performance for the homeless. 'Experience has taught this clever young actor that there is no taste in London just now for horrors on the stage,' declared the *Daily Telegraph* approvingly. 'There is quite sufficient to make us shudder out of doors.'

A wave of public sympathy spread towards the 'unfortunates' in the East End when it was learned that starvation was commonplace and that 55 per cent of children died before the age of five. If prostitution was rife, the conditions made it so, and the girls provided easy prey for the murderer as they wandered the streets in the hope of raising fourpence for a wretched night's lodging. After the third murder, of

Annie Chapman, the *Daily Telegraph* wrote: 'She has forced innumerable people who never gave a serious thought before to the subject to realize how it is and where it is that our vast floating population, the waifs and strays of our thoroughfares, live and sleep at night and what sort of accommodation our rich and enlightened capital provides for them.' The Port of London was exposed as no better than Port Said.

Colin Wilson had been my first guide round the Ripper's haunts; now, living more or less on the spot, I planned to follow up *The London River* with a programme about the murders. Seventy years after those terrible events, I was surprised by the response when I went on television and asked for information – the first time this had been tried. It was unlikely that the hundreds of letters would include an eyewitness account, but I came close. One delightful old lady had been in service as a young girl and was sent by her mistress for sixpence-worth of fish for the master's supper. Running down the street, Annie charged straight into Jack. 'And there he was,' she told me gleefully, 'with his big black bag with all those knives ready to cut me up. And he had a little black moustache. My son, he do make me laugh, says "It was Charlie Chaplin, Mum!" I forgot about the fish and was scolded by the mistress, but I wouldn't go out again, and didn't on my own, for ever such a long time in case I saw him again.'

The encounter was a high spot in her life and I did not have the heart to tell her that her dates were wrong – it occurred *after* the murders.

In meeting her and the others I learned more about the East End itself. I tracked down Annie to a pristine house in a new town on the outskirts in a suburb of grim gentility and spoke to her in a spotless room where a speck of dust would not have dared to rest. When we were alone she confided how much she hated it and missed the slums where she grew up and that special close companionship she had known. She looked as out of place as a stuffed animal under a glass dome.

Another reply came from a charming old man who had not confused his dates. A boy at the time, he had been given his first job and was perched on the back of a horse and cart driven through Hanbury Street when he heard the cry of 'Murder!' Being a lad, as he explained, curiosity got the better of him; he jumped off the cart, losing his job in consequence. 'There she was,' he told me in his gentle way. 'All her entrails steamin' 'ot. And I'll never forget it because she had red-and-white stockings on.'

Even with the Ripper, there was light relief – there had to be. Acting as decoys, various reluctant policemen were dressed as prostitutes. One of them stopped an ambitious journalist, also in drag, asking him: 'You're a man, aren't you? Are you one of us?'

'I don't know what you mean,' said the journalist indignantly, 'but I'm not a copper.'

An East Ender wrote to me describing his father's embarrassment when he was made to dress up, insisting on keeping his black moustache under his veil.

A particular stroke of luck brought me a valued new friend. I was staying with Rose McLaren at her home in North Wales when she asked me what I was working on and I mentioned Jack the Ripper.

'That's extraordinary,' she said. 'We're going to see mother-in-law this afternoon. Her father had something to do with it.'

Christabel, the Dowager Lady Aberconway (the mother of Rose's late husband, John McLaren), was the daughter of Sir Melville Macnaghten who joined Scotland Yard as Assistant Chief Constable in 1889, the year after the murders, when the file was still open and it was largely his job to close it. In 1903 he became the head of the CID.

Lady Aberconway remembered accompanying her father to the Yard when she was a child. Left alone in his office she rummaged through his desk, uncovering the photos of the Ripper's victims, which were hidden away. There was consternation when Sir Melville came back and found her looking at them. Though alarmed by his reaction, they meant nothing to her – 'To me, the mutilated bodies looked just like broken dolls.'

Despite the difference in our ages, Christabel Aberconway became a close friend, one of the most delightful women I have met. She had been the mistress of Samuel Courtauld, the rayon millionaire, and lived in a beautiful house in North Audley Street which he had given her, a pavilion for a royal mistress, when Grosvenor Square was open country. There was a courtyard at the back, shaded by an old fig tree, with a fountain, but I was shocked on my first visit to find the elegant rooms hung with reproductions of such famous pictures as Picasso's *Boy with a Dove*, and the Impressionists which Courtauld so admired – a woodland scene by Cézanne, a railway station by Monet, rippling water and a boat by Renoir, a Corot. Then it dawned on me that they were the originals, all now in the National Gallery, exchanged for death duties.

Thanks to Lady Aberconway's gift of her father's private notes on the case, which revealed that Montague John Druitt was the main police suspect I began to play detective in earnest. The result was a theory concerning the murderer's identity which I laid out in my book *Jack the Ripper*, published in 1972. Several authors have taken my evidence further, others continue to propose different solutions. Our obsession with the Ripper is insatiable.

It was easy to make friends in the East End. Someone took me to the opening of the Kentucky Club in the Mile End Road. Across the seething mob which filled the tiny steaming room, on a makeshift stage the size of a plank, I was startled to see Billy Daniels in his toupée belting out 'That Old Black Magic'. I was equally impressed to be introduced to the mayor of Hackney and the local clergyman; their names were on the committee of the Kentucky which was run by two 'civic businessmen' who asked me in the over-amplified uproar if they could add my name as well. Flattered, and anxious to confirm that I was now an honorary East Ender, I nodded my agreement.

A few days later a police inspector called at Narrow Street. He seemed to have difficulty in coming to the point – that it was not a good idea to have my name on the Kentucky Club notepaper as a member of the committee.

'Why on earth not?'

He looked at me with incredulity. I pointed out that my name would be alongside that of the mayor and the clergyman. Only now do I see what a tricky position he was in, unable to credit that my ignorance was genuine. He could hardly trust in my discretion, though if he had come clean he might have gained my confidence. All he could say was that the two businessmen, Ronald and Reginald Kray, were known to the police and it would be unwise for me to be associated with them in an official capacity.

A vague memory came back of being taken several years earlier to a snooker hall called the Double R, where I was introduced to the owners who asked me to help them on television with their campaign to release from Dartmoor a man called Frank Mitchell, the axeman, who had, they claimed, been wrongfully committed. When I said this was impossible they looked displeased and the atmosphere became so hostile that I left. It occurred to me now that the two Rs might have been Ronnie and Reggie.

Faced with my stupidity, the inspector advised me to think again and departed. Judging by the clicks I heard afterwards, I have the strong suspicion that my phone was tapped, and there was no doubt that the Limehouse police became less friendly. On my next visit to the Kentucky I told the Krays of the visit and said I thought it best if my name was not on their letterhead after all. They were unamused, wanting to know what the inspector had said, finding it hard to believe that he had told me nothing. They accepted my decision and did not refer to the subject again, accepting my naïvety more readily than the policeman had.

Before my wild behaviour became too much for them I used the Kentucky regularly, especially at Sunday lunchtime, until I discovered the entertainment featured in so many of the pubs. One lunchtime a man offended Reggie Kray by flirting with his girlfriend. I noticed several people leaving hurriedly when Reggie asked him outside into a back area the size of a tablecloth where they fought ferociously, though they did so with bare fists, Gentleman Jim stuff, and shook hands afterwards. How decent the East End was, I thought.

Why did I tolerate the Krays? There is a glamour surrounding boxers and gangsters and I was not alone in finding it attractive. The film actor Stanley Baker used the Thomas à Becket in the Old Kent Road where I interviewed Henry Cooper and his twin brother in the boxing gymnasium upstairs. I was friendly with the East End boxers Sammy McCarthy and baby-faced Terry Spinks, and filmed an entire programme on George Walker and his brother Billy, the 'blond bombshell'. I went to boxing matches and revelled in the roar of the crowd, the tarnished celebrities like George Raft introduced from the ring, the dimming of the lights and the fanfare of trumpets as the would-be champions ducked and weaved as they made their entrance. For me, the fights were secondary.

I made friends with the Barry Brothers who ran the Regency Club and brought such friends as Lady Rose McLaren, continuing to their parties afterwards.

Just as the Krays wanted to be a part of show business, numerous stars were drawn to them, like Danny La Rue and Barbara Windsor, and if there was an element of danger, that made them the more enticing until the full horror sank in. Living in the East End, it is understandable that I was hoodwinked by the aura that surrounded them. To many, they were local heroes.

While Francis Bacon was attracted to 'men in suits' like the Krays, whom he knew from Esmeralda's Barn, their gambling club in Knightsbridge, Ronnie fancied pretty boys: 'Little angel faces, less evil than girls.' I overheard his latest angel extolling the virtues of the Krays to Francis who listened, bemused.

'They're good to their mother.'

'Yus?'

'If one of the Firm goes inside, they send flowers to the family.'

'Yus.'

'At Christmas they send more than 300 cards to their mates who are banged up and if a member of the Firm goes inside, the Colonel [a nickname for Ronnie] sees their families are all right, flowers to their wives, and presents for the kids . . .'

'Oh, yus!'

Finally Francis could stand the litany of virtue no longer and interrupted. 'It fair touches the heart.'

'Oh it does, doesn't it!' exclaimed the boy gratefully.

The Krays viewed my drunken raids with some alarm. 'Do watch your language, Dan,' Ronnie would plead with me, 'there's ladies present.' This gentility delighted me. When I worked for Joan Littlewood on her film *Sparrows Can't Sing*, I introduced her to the Krays and she took to them at once. 'My lovely couple of clowns,' she called them, to their surprise, but she missed the humour of the Kentucky with the crimson flock wallpaper, the white leather banquettes, the men immaculately suited and the women dressed like fashion models, and an atmosphere of strict decorum apart from my own louche self. Instead, Joan installed a juke-box and filmed a girl in a slit skirt dancing sexily beside it. The Krays relished the publicity but could not understand why Joan did not film the Kentucky as it was.

I began to feel their welcome towards me was cooler; perhaps my usefulness had run out. Also, I took risks. When I mentioned I had taken Deakin to the Kentucky, Frank Norman gasped, 'Christ, you like to live dangerously. The way you two behave you're fucking lucky that his tongue and your eyes weren't cut out. Blind and deaf, you'd be the saddest couple in London.'

I remained woefully unaware of the true nature of the Krays' empire, thinking of them as stalwarts of the East End. If they indulged in 'protection', that was the nature of the place. When number 92, easy to break into from the waterfront, was burgled yet again I confided in the Krays rather than the police, and they suggested a minder called Ted Smith.

Ted moved into the attic bedroom. He proved an odd one, with a certain charm when he was not morose, fitting in easily with my friends. The trouble was his dog, Fritz, a Dobermann whose head had been bashed about with a brick by one of the Krays' entourage. Understandably he attacked everyone in sight apart from Ted.

'Had a good day, Fritz did,' he declared proudly after a walk in one of the East End parks. 'Met this 'orrible terrier, yap, yap, would have torn him to bits till I called him off. Blood everywhere, bloody woman screamin', should have heard her.'

My God, I thought, I need a minder to protect me from the minder. This was truer than I realized. Years later, in the summer of 1995, my housekeeper Rose told me she had found a revolver under Ted's pillow and had taken it home to her husband in case I was in danger. Well-meant but risky, as someone pointed out. Ted might have assumed that I had taken the gun, and thought he was in danger himself. Surprisingly, he never mentioned it. Rose's husband Bob insisted that Fritz was locked up when she came to 92 Narrow Street or he would forbid her to go there. Finally, Fritz had to go and Ted with him, paid off to travel to South America. I met him a year or two later wearing a chauffeur's superb green uniform as he waited outside a shop off Oxford Street and we greeted each other like two respectable old friends.

The one creature Fritz tolerated, apart from Ted, was my labrador mongrel, with whom he was so infatuated that he followed her every-where, drooping when she refused to play. If Fritz was fearsome, she was fearless. I was annoyed when the interfering woman next door, who was in no danger whatever, complained to Mrs Fisher about the 'beast'. Discovering that she was not referring to myself but to a wild animal, Dolly Fisher came to 92 Narrow Street to investigate. I was out but Ted opened the door. Fortunately Rose was there, so Fritz had been locked up and with considerable presence of mind Ted produced my puppy Littlewood, who played her part by smothering Mrs Fisher with kisses.

'Can't think what she's on about,' said Ted innocently.

'Nor can I,' snorted Dolly Fisher, depositing the cheerful puppy on the floor. 'I'll phone that woman and tell her she's mad!'

With my distorted sense of humour I was amused by such situations, which were not really funny at all, like the time an artist arrived with money in his hand to buy back a portrait he had sold me, having received a better offer. When Ted opened the door it must have been a nasty shock for the artist, for it was one of Ted's jobs to collect the Krays' gambling debts; I assume that the painter had patronized Esmeralda's Barn. Equally startled to see him, Ted respected the East End code of hospitality while I tried to hear their muttered words and promises, after which Ted emerged with his sly smile and the artist left looking pale. He must have known that I had no idea he and Ted had met before, and he behaved impeccably afterwards.

It was not until Ronnie Kray's death in 1995 that I knew I had been playing with fire. Under the sardonic heading NICE MAN RONNIE, AND GOOD TO HIS MUM, the *Independent* ran a photograph of the Krays shaking hands after their 'release from a menaces charge in 1965'. In between, smiling awkwardly, was 'their friend and drinking partner Edward "Mad Teddy" Smith'. All wore immaculate dark suits, white shirts and matching handkerchiefs in their breast pockets. I had heard vaguely of someone called Mad Ted, but had no idea that this was *my* Ted Smith. As for the Krays, they may have had an ulterior motive for suggesting Ted as a minder, but I doubt it. Perhaps they believed they were doing both of us a good turn, his presence as their friend acting as a deterrent to others.

In 1962 the world premiere of *Sparrows Can't Sing* was held at the Mile End cinema. The proceeds were going to a Docklands settlement charity and Princess Margaret would be there, the summit of the Krays' ambition.

I went to the club that evening half-expecting an invitation, though I had seen the film at a preview. It was obvious that the Krays wanted no part of me; nothing should spoil their big night. They were surrounded by the Firm dressed up like gorillas, should those gentler creatures ever wear dinner-jackets and black ties, in the tradition of the gangster movies starring James Cagney and Edward G. Robinson. They had bought up the entire circle in the cinema so their seats would surround the Princess, giving them the final seal of respectability. After this, the police would think again. Someone at the Palace had the sense to take notice of a discreet warning from the local police. Princess Margaret went down with 'diplomatic' flu and the Krays looked decidedly unhappy as they crossed the road, leaving me alone in the Kentucky. Princess Margaret was represented by Antony Armstrong-Jones, now Lord Snowdon, who handled the situation skilfully, but this was not the photo-opportunity the Krays had been hoping for.

Idolized in the East End they came to the notice of the West End gradually. Their control of Esmeralda's Barn seemed legitimate and they were doing good business, making £1000 a week in 1960. It was four years later that they came to public awareness, with the claim that a well-known peer had conducted a homosexual affair with a gangster. Rumours were rife about an alleged photograph and various unfortunate peers were suspected until the *Sunday Mirror* made the mistake of publishing the photograph, which identified the peer as Lord Boothby, seated smilingly between the twins. It is possible that Ronnie catered to Lord Boothby's penchant for young boys, but the libel was so gross that when Boothby was phoned the news as he was sitting down to Sunday lunch in the south of France, he came back dancing: 'Now they've identified me I can sue. This is what I've been waiting for.' And sue he did, represented by Arnold Goodman as his solicitor, and Gerald Gardiner QC, a future Lord Chancellor. He won £40,000 in damages and emerged glowing with virtue. For the first time I realized the Krays were dangerous.

The American Mafia took them seriously, they advised artists like Billy Daniels to cultivate them. The Krays told Francis Wyndham, 'George Raft – there's a nice man – he's immaculate. And he still dances a lovely tango.' Sophie Tucker was 'a very nice woman, knew such people as Al Capone. She said he was a nice fellow, "Al Capone, a greater gentleman you couldn't hope to meet."'

When Judy Garland came to England, I was invited to a party she gave at the Boltons through a mutual friend, Burt Shevelove who wrote *A Funny Thing Happened on the Way to the Forum*. I was talking to the solicitor David Jacobs and Danny La Rue who gasped as he saw the Krays: 'My God, look who's just come in.' After the Boothby scandal they were recognized and a hush followed their entrance as Ronnie looked around the guests for someone he knew. Now increasingly schizophrenic, he was accompanied by a bodyguard, not to protect him but to stop him attacking anyone who unwittingly caused offence. To my dismay, Ronnie came straight towards me, eyes opaque with hostility, and said in a chilling voice, 'Hullo, Dan, long time since I've seen you. Last time you slagged me something rotten.'

'Did I?' I squeaked, unsure if an apology would make it worse. 'Well, you know how silly I am in my cups.' The minder hovered in the grim silence which was broken, to my utmost relief, by one of the sweet grey-haired ladies supplied by Harrods, the caterers, who entered with the deafening cry, 'Mr Reginald Kray? Is there a Mr Reginald Kray? He's wanted on the phone.' She could hardly have caused greater alarm if she had announced, 'Mr Al Capone, there's a Mr Dillinger on the line.'

Ronnie Kray moved on and that was the last I saw of him, though when I began my biography of Francis Bacon I thought I should contact him for my research. The prospect of visiting Broadmoor daunted me. I felt I would be tainted if I went there, though the actor George Sewell, who was braver, told me of his visit to discuss a film. 'All he did was complain about the people he was locked up with. "They're mad," he kept on saying. "This place is a nut-house!"'

I wrote to Ronnie instead, receiving a reply from Broadmoor Hospital on 12 May 1992.

Dear Daniel, Thank you for your letter, I hope you are well. Yes Daniel they were good times in the East End in the few years past, Daniel, Frances Bacon was good Freind of mine it was my privilege to be his Freind, and I am proud that he had me as one of his Freinds. It was Stanley Baker that inturded me to Frances. I always found Frances a kind and nice man. I only know good about Frances there is not much more I can say about my Freindship with him. I hope that your Book goes well and I wish you all the Happyness for the future. May God Bless You, from Your Freind Ronald Kray.

Plainly he had written this himself. The reply from Reggie Kray, who was supposed to be saner, from HM Prison at Colchester, was virtually unintelligible: 'I never met Francis Bacon . . . Have you read my Books,' ending with a similar 'God Bless, Reg Kray.'

I have to admit that the Krays treated me impeccably throughout. When I ran my pub on the Isle of Dogs, Ronnie told me, 'You know we wouldn't come to the pub without an invite, Dan.' I gave a vague smile and did not extend it. He was polite as always, his black eyes expressionless.

Arthur Mullard said it all when we appeared together on *This is*

Your Life for Queenie Watts. We sat in the last cubicle before the plywood doors, with Eamonn Andrews on stage.

'You knew the Krays, didn't you?' asked Mullard.

'Yes,' I nodded, trying to remember my few lines. Then I made the fatuous remark: 'I rather liked them. After all, they only killed their own kind.'

'Yuss,' he looked at me stonily, ''uman beings.'

Fourteen

A Huge Old Lion

DURING THE WAR my father recorded the Blitz in his book *Bomber's Moon*, and covered the Russian front for the *Daily Mail* from as near as he was allowed, a hundred miles away. His last vestige of faith in Communism ended when he was taken off a train with his companion, an Australian journalist called Mac, halfway to Murmansk as they tried to leave Russia.

'I have experienced various degrees of fright in my life,' he wrote, 'but this was something I had never known before and have never known since. It made our battering on the [North Sea] convoy, which was continuous from the afternoon after we left Murmansk until we got air-cover off the coast of Iceland, a mere joke by comparison. This was terror.'

What frightened him was the sight of a train on the opposite platform, crammed with political prisoners. Between the sliding doors in the centre of each of the forty cars were objects which resembled the tails of large fish, until he saw that each contraption was a long V-trough of two boards nailed together for a latrine. The only light came from two high, eighteen-inch windows:

> There were faces at these windows. Some of them opened their mouths and poked fingers in them. This was the way they begged for food. From one or two of these ghastly squares with a sub-human face, a little canvas bag tied on a piece of string was hopefully lowered. No one came near them. No one looked at them. All day the faces remained at the windows: eyes that looked at passing life with a misery beyond description.

My father had fallen out with Communist officialdom, and thought he might end the same way: 'Better people than I had been put away.' The station commandant had been in constant telephonic contact with the authorities in Moscow, alarmed by the presence of two hostile and probably drunken foreign journalists. When he was told to let them board the next train to Murmansk, they needed no encouragement.

It is hardly surprising that on his return to England my father was thankful for a chance to recover. By now he had bought the house by the sea in North Devon, made of rough grey stone impervious to storms. One of only six houses at the southern end of Woolacombe Bay, it was built above the dunes with miles of sand below and a nearby line of rock. At high tide I could race from my bedroom, down the rickety wooden steps, and plunge into the surf in less than sixty seconds. Hoping that the sun and salt water would help to heal his leg, my father could hardly have chosen better than the Grey House. As he told me, 'This is the perfect place for journey's end.'

He bought it with the proceeds of *Going Fishing*, probably his most popular book, which survives in dribs and drabs of new editions. It was voted recently by a fishing magazine as the best fishing book ever written, yet it has a readability which can be savoured by someone who has never held a rod or cast a fly. The title was a close-run thing, as the publisher came up with ever fancier ideas until my mother exclaimed in exasperation, 'Why not call it "With Rod and Gun Down the Alimentary Canal"?'

My father added, 'Or simply, "Going Fishing".'

When he bought the Grey House he said that if he ever saw a stretch of sand and sea which was a surf-caster's dream, this was it. Hardy's, the famous sporting shop in St James's, made him a greenheart rod. A friend in the American Embassy, for this was still wartime, obtained a Von Hofe reel from New York, and he bombarded his American publishers with requests for further tackle from Abercrombie & Fitch, with such baffling names as cutty-hunk line and bloc-tin squids. He spent a fortune in this way and for once he overreached himself. All for nothing.

'For two desperate years,' he wrote, conceding defeat, 'night and day, every turn of the tide, I fished the sea right in front of our house. No fish. I can't describe my dismay. And I am absolutely certain that if I had been able to do my bit of surf-casting, I should never have begun to wade in those oceans of alcohol that I then began to take on board. To stick it out, and not just pull up anchor and try to live somewhere else, was one of the hardest bits of moral discipline I have made myself face.'

Yet the fish were lurking there all the time. When Anthony Pearson, the author of *Successful Shore Fishing*, took my friend Peter Bradshaw to fish on a high tide beside those rocks, they came back half an hour later with several gleaming silver bass. Incredibly, my father had used the wrong bait. There was no need for all those expensive gadgets which were so alien to his nature – all he needed was the common lugworm dug from the mud-flats in the nearby estuary. He could have paid someone to bring him buckets. It would have cost far less than those bloc-tin squids.

It was a tragic mistake, for without such incentive he was bound to be bored. This explained his excitement when guests arrived, though he was equally glad to see them go; and why he went on his 'benders', though these were now fewer. No longer did my mother fight so hard, offering to phone him a taxi at once when he thought of going to the nearest pub, which rather killed the fun of it. 'Now hold on,' he would protest, 'Just a minute.' Not that she had grown to accept his drinking: it distressed her still, with the aftermath of recrimination and interminable finger-wagging, but she understood his boredom and the need for distraction, collecting him from the pub at closing time after the landlord phoned her for help in getting rid of him. While he slumped in the car she attempted to pick his pockets, throwing half-bottles of whisky into the hedgerows, providing a treasure hunt for surprised hikers in years to come. When I was there, I would creep into his bedroom while he slept and slip my hand under the pillows to see if any bottle had been smuggled in, as it usually had. I am amazed that he never complained.

Now, it was not the alcohol that worried her as much as the nicotine that was killing him. I interviewed him three times on television and noticed that his breathing was becoming increasingly difficult. An oxygen cylinder was placed beside his bed to help him through the spasms of phlegm that threatened to choke him, and my mother was cast in the killjoy role of warder, rationing his cigarettes one by one. She had no chance of winning. With my father's persuasiveness, people offered them though his coughing should have warned them not to. Friends who would not force sugar on a diabetic do not hesitate when it comes to drink or tobacco: 'Just the one won't hurt you.'

The danger of the benders was no longer the drink but the reckless smoking they involved. Yet, almost as if he needed to continue his cures to justify the transgression of his drinking, like a man of honour who courts disaster, he went to the Digby Clinic near Exeter where the doctor told him, 'The one thing that will ever make you stop drinking is your own common sense. If this doesn't make you stop, nothing will.' From my own experience I know that doctor was correct, like the Swiss professor who told him to keep his conflicts.

It is one of the penalties of the alcoholic that he is thought of as perpetually drunk. Who remembers Brendan Behan silent or Dylan Thomas sober? Yet both could be abstemious. An official of Alcoholics Anonymous told me in a television interview that he lamented the tragic waste of talent of W. C. Fields and Sid Field, and there seemed no point in explaining that drink was part of W.C.'s personality, while Sid had the discipline to go on stage night after night. Why do people drink? My father believed that their daily lives are not interesting enough to hold them steady. 'Plain boredom, emptiness, the absence of things one can fervently believe in: these, I think, are responsible for more of today's alcoholics than all the phantoms of our past. It is the *present* that makes us crack up.'

There is no single explanation, for every man's case is different; though it may end up the same in the desperate search, not for oblivion, but obliteration.

My case is different from that of my father: he hated alcohol, I love it until it gets the better of me. In 1992, when we met by chance on the train to London where he was going to address a conference on alcoholism, my doctor told me, 'You are not an alcoholic, just a drunk.' That was a relief, though I have my doubts.

That train to London: my father knew it well. This was his escape when North Devon became stultifying and he felt that he was letting the years slip away. 'I had made much too big a break, too quickly; and into the wrong setting.' Yet again, there is no deceiver like the self-deceiver, and he knew it: 'The danger, of course, was that I went in over my head every time I stepped out of this mood. The train to London meant the luxury of sitting in the dining-car, of watching the clouds pass by over the rolling West Country, and of gin after gin after gin . . . I won't say that I regret those gin-inspired reveries, but by the time the train reached Waterloo I had already lost the game. No theatre, no movies, not even friends . . . Dressing eagerly in my room on these mornings to be driven to the station, I exulted as I shaved: "Now for some real life! What a joke." '

Once he booked straight into the Savoy, rang for room-service and stayed there until he mustered the will-power to return to Devon. Another time he took me on a tour of the few haunts that would welcome him, for he had sent his resignation to the Savage Club once too often and it was accepted after members complained. His old friend Mario of the Ivy, now the maître d'hotel at the Caprice, asked him to save embarrassment by not returning, and I cursed the insolent barman in an empty bar at the Café Royal, where I had been taken as a child, who did not conceal his indifference as my father asked about friends who were famous long before the barman's time. Sometimes I would help him back to Waterloo Station with the obligatory stop at Heppel's in Knightsbridge for the 'pick-me-up' to help him on his way.

As always, my mother provided the home to come back to, always waiting, always welcoming, where he was able to recover. Far from a backwater, my father found that he was able to observe the world's vicissitudes with a greater clarity from the sidelines, dictating regular articles for the *Daily Mail* over the phone. His enthusiasm never faltered. I remember him at the breakfast table in his polka-dot dressing-gown with sheets of paper in front of him as my mother served relays of fresh coffee. Tousled with the sleep of youth as I came down the stairs, I was met by a barrage of questions demanding total attention, for he had been awake since dawn.

The newspapers arrived with the post around ten o'clock, later if Garrick the postman stopped for tea at every house. When my father found the wait unbearable, he drove to Croyde, striding into the general store in his pyjamas and dressing-gown, opening the paper on the spot to read his article with smiles of appreciation. It might have been the first time he had seen his name in print, he was so excited, and it had nothing to do with conceit.

Guests were a lifeline to the outside world, a mixed bag collected on his travels: Claud Cockburn, the witty editor of *The Week*, the political forerunner of *Private Eye*, which published the stories my father and Stefan Litauer dared not break in their own papers unless Cockburn leaked them first. Like many ugly men, Cockburn had a beautiful wife, Patricia, whose left-wing views irritated my mother so much that she exclaimed, 'What a pity they didn't christen you Plebia!', a comment which received a frozen silence and a furious glare from my father. Kingsley Martin, the editor of the *New Statesman*, arrived with Dorothy Woodman who spent the nights close to the wall in her sleeping bag. Gerald Reece was the taciturn ex-Governor of British Somaliland where he was an absolute ruler, unable to adapt to England. David Waruhiu, whose father was the first African chieftain to be murdered by Mau Mau, had perfect manners but looked bemused by my father's constant affectionate references to my mother as 'that nigger'.

My mother's most regular guest was the ornithologist David Bannerman, whom I found embracing her when I burst into the drawing-room in Pelham Place. Leaping apart, they looked dismayed. I should have been delighted that he was fond of her, yet I was shocked. When his wife died, Bannerman married J. B. Priestley's widow Jacquetta Hawkes.

Having worked in the Ministry of Information in the war, my mother had plenty of interesting friends of her own, including a popular novelist and broadcaster of the time, E. Arnot Robertson, whose outspokenness was part of her appeal, though lost on my father. When she insisted on making a soufflé with dried egg, despite my mother's assurance that our hens laid perfectly good fresh eggs in their coop above, she took so long that my father opened the oven door to see what was happening whereupon the soufflé sank to the consistency of a wet pancake.

'Oh, you stupid man,' cried Arnot. 'Really, Negley, you're such a bloody fool!'

My mother and I exchanged glances, for people did not talk to my father like that. Sure enough, he left immediately for the pub.

I had no qualms in inviting my own friends, though I was astonished when John Knight, with whom I shared the flat in Beauchamp Place until his marriage, had told me: 'Your parents may be the most worldly people but they're totally unfit to have children.' As John was the kindest and most straightforward of my college friends, this made me look at them with new interest, feeling less of a failure.

One of my guests was a disaster. It seems inconceivable that I could have been so rash as to invite John Deakin, though it was more a case of Deakin inviting himself in a tragic letter from London implying that a few days in the country would save his sanity.

After we had met several trains, Deakin finally arrived. The phrase 'fell out of the train' is used lightly, but Deakin did so literally. As he picked himself up, he introduced himself to my mother: 'My God, Mrs Farson, if I'd known it was going to take so long I'd never have come.' I could tell his visit was a mistake by mother's strained politeness.

Deakin looked awful in the Devon light of day. There was tea outside when we got home, with two lesbian lady neighbours who looked at him with some alarm. My father recognized another alcoholic and tensed.

Far from being witty as I hoped, Deakin indulged in nervous gossip. He followed me into the kitchen: 'I'm dying for a drink.' My mother was preparing the tea and apologized for the lack of drink in the house apart from a bottle of sherry which she used for trifles, disguised as vinegar. Deakin assured her that sherry would be 'delicious' and it was poured into a delicate gold-and-white Rockingham teacup with a slice of lemon floating on the top to make it convincing. With one twitch of the nostril, my father sniffed that out and rang for the taxi within the minute. While he launched himself on a three-day bender, Deakin decided he had arrived for a rest cure. After draining the sherry he refused alcohol even when my father pressed it on him after reeling back from the pubs with bottles. As my father disappeared again, or coughed and groaned in his bedroom, Deakin sat outside in a deckchair as if he were on board ship, huddled in blankets, his face to the sun as he turned a shade of puce. Far from being outrageous company, he was no company at all. After he left, my father declared, 'I never want to see that man in this house again.' 'Hear, hear!' cried my mother.

Yet, on a subsequent visit to London, my father met him in the French Pub. Unfortunately I was not there, but Deakin told me he had his Rolleiflex and thought 'That's an interesting face,' until they recognized each other and spent the evening in Soho together.

'That Deakin!' my father exclaimed the next morning, lying in bed in Pelham Place. 'He's got something. Godammit — I *like* the man!'

My mother looked pained and asked me to appeal to Deakin not to use the photograph he had taken. 'If Negley was asleep, it would be so hurtful.'

Deakin was outraged. 'As if I would! Anyhow, where could I sell it?'

Despite all the vicissitudes, people enjoyed coming to the Grey

House, where my father was at his best. After a visit with his wife Moira Shearer in 1957, Ludovic Kennedy wrote in his weekly column:

Tobacco and gammy leg may have restricted his activities, but nothing had diminished the alertness and curiosity of his mind. He sat in the sun like some huge old lion, the wind gently ruffling his mane . . . There was something of Winston Churchill about him, something of Ernest Hemingway, something of Lionel Barrymore. He is sixty-eight and age has not wearied him nor alcohol condemned. My God, I thought, what a tough old boy you are.

'Poor Dan,' murmured George Melly when he read this. 'Churchill, Hemingway and Barrymore – what a lot to live up to!'

❖

'DAN FARSON'S FATHER DIES' ran the headline in the London *Evening News*. The next day the *Daily Mail* asked 'What is fame?' in their gossip column. The irony had not been lost on me, increasing my contempt for the spurious notoriety gained by appearing on television. The *Mail* scarcely referred to my father's writing, though they had published his dispatches from Africa in the late thirties and sent him to Russia in the war, but they ran a news item confirming that a television interview I had filmed with my father would still go ahead.

My father had lived as full a life as any man can hope for. He died in seconds in his armchair, his cat on his lap, his dog at his feet, my mother opposite, in December 1960. Earlier in the day he had tied labels on their luggage for yet another journey, this time to Portugal. I could not grieve for him; instead I felt an elation. My mother's grief was absolute.

After a late night I had been woken by the persistence of the telephone and her distraught voice: 'Oh, Danny, where have you been? Didn't you get my telegram? I tried to phone you all last night. He was sitting there . . . Oh, Danny, what is to become of me?' Now the responsibility was mine alone and I was incapable of bearing it. How she must have longed for a loving daughter or a dutiful son, with a horde of doting grandchildren. That was the problem: I was different. On a visit to London to see my grandmother, she confided in her diary: 'Dan picks me up at 7.30 and we go to Lady Rose's lovely Georgian house in Smith Street. Am enchanted with her.

Charming. How I wish she would marry Dan, but tho' they kiss in a sisterly fashion I can see no sign of it.'

Equally, when Rose asked her children if they would like me as a new Daddy, they replied contemptuously and correctly, 'Are you mad?'

My father was buried in Georgeham churchyard near the stream that flows down from the hill, with the simple inscription: NEGLEY FARSON – WRITER – BORN PLAINFIELD NEW JERSEY. My great-uncle Reginald Bruce had travelled down to comfort my mother as best he could and the three of us set out for the funeral together, my mother so awash with tears that she crashed the car into a hedge on the way. Reg was shaken and I felt inadequate during the service which was attended by a large congregation of friends, especially when I read the entry in her diary: 'Dan is so kind. He held my arm in such a firm grip and I felt what a man he was.'

It was impossible to tell her the truth. At times I wonder if the confessional of a diary is intended to be read by the subject afterwards.

My mother and I agreed, as the *Mail* reported, that the three interviews I had made with my father should be transmitted together in a new series called *Farson's Choice*, and we watched them in London three days later at the home of Jeanne and Rollo Gamble. The last shot showed my father sitting on the low wall outside the Grey House, pointing to the immensity of the Atlantic and the black folds of Baggy Point. This was when he described it as 'the perfect place for journey's end'. At the end, instead of the usual titles and music, there was just the gentle fall of the surf, with pictures of the waves breaking over the rocks. 'Oh, Danny,' said my mother, 'he was a *great* man.'

Was I heartless? Cruelly, in my failure to understand that happy memories are no substitute for life. Why could she not accept that they had led a miraculous life in spite of the drink and his infidelities, which were now of no account? They had travelled the world and at the end they had been together. Was it impossible to be thankful for what she had been blessed with, with no reason to reproach herself for anything? A few women can adapt to the role of the gallant widow, but that was not for her. I pointed out how hideous it would have been if he had died a week or so later on their way to Portugal, with no one there to help her, which she conceded, grudgingly. Also, and far worse, if he had recovered to continue as an invalid, speechless and inert – he, of all men. Would she have preferred that? I believe she would, just to have him there.

Unless I am using it as an alibi, my reserve, alien to my nature, was largely due to my unmentionable homosexuality and the guilt it involved. She told me she would like to kill herself except for the bad publicity for me. This put me in an impossible position: should I say, 'Oh, please don't' or 'There's no need to worry about the publicity, I can cope with that'? I urged her not to.

She told someone else: 'You know there is only one thing I dread, that I shall continue to live for a long time.'

Resenting her grief, I sought the advice of Bernard Walsh at Wheeler's, who gave it with his usual perspicacity, pointing out that at her age there was nothing to hope for. I could only hope that the cliché would prove correct as it usually does, that time is a great healer.

A year later I was stuck with a different programme, on lonely old people at Christmas. The director was unsympathetic, and the camera crew in a vile temper after carrying their equipment up flights of stone stairs to the top of a tenement. My researcher had promised 'a really remarkable character', but she proved an odiously self-satisfied woman who had known better days and was now full of self-pity. I was struggling to make her appear gallant in adversity when an electrician came up as the camera was reloaded to say I was wanted on the phone. The director snapped: 'Take a message,' but the man returned to say it was an emergency. 'Very well,' sighed the director, 'make it quick; we have your reverses to do and I want to get away.'

I picked up the receiver; the man at the other end was hard to understand, probably German. 'Your mother is lunching with Lady Goldsmid,' he shrilled. As Nancy Goldsmith was her closest friend this was reasonable, but I was confused when he continued: 'She fell and we are taking her in ambulance, but before that you must identify the body.' *Identify the body*? Surely her husband or her two sons could do that, or my mother, unless she was too upset.

'I don't understand,' I said. The man sighed and used an appalling phrase: 'Officialdom demands that you identify the body.' I experienced a split-second of doubt until the phone was snatched away and Lady d'Avigdor Goldsmid told me that my mother had been lunching with her and had fallen from the top of the stairs, and was dead. 'I am so sorry you should have heard of it in such a way.'

I put the phone down and took the director aside, telling him what had happened. He insisted I continue with my reverses, which I did calmly, before continuing to Lady Goldsmid's house where I was given my mother's handbag with the few possessions inside, which seemed pitifully meagre. The odious doctor who had phoned me sent me a bill. This was the start of the obscene trappings of accidental death. It would seem a natural act of humanity to spare a relative the ordeal of identifying the body, but the law demands it. With the happy memory of my father when he was alive, I was determined not to see my mother's body, and this became an obsession. At the last moment I learned of a loophole which allowed the executor to identify the body, but by then it was too late. At midday on a Saturday morning in vivid sunlight, I arrived at the mortuary in Hammersmith where an official told me the well-worn lie – 'She looks so peaceful' – as a shelf was pulled out as in a supermarket, and a cover lifted as if to reveal some joint of pork. Behind the glass, her hair on end like Struwwelpeter's, her cheeks waxen, lay the corpse. I nodded and ran into the street dense with weekend shoppers, catching sight of my anxious friend John Knight, the executor, who had received last-minute permission to identify my mother. I shook my head and blindly stumbled on. Perhaps I am over-sensitive. I had a close friend who made up his mother's face as she lay in the coffin, but I am haunted by that waxen image, for this is how I remember her.

That was not the end of it. The following week there came the formal inquest, with statements including the eye-witness testimony from Lady d'Avigdor Goldsmid regarding my mother's fall. Her statement was read by the coroner in such detail, in a voice so redolent with suspicion, that I turned to her and heard myself saying, 'It's all right, I don't believe you did it.' Her husband, a stiff-backed MP of considerable influence, shot me a look of cold fury, and refused to speak to me afterwards, not that I was keen to linger.

At last the body was collected by Harrods and I accompanied it on the evening train to Devon, by this point slightly delirious. I was sharing 92 Narrow Street with a Scot called Tony, the guardsman I had seen in a Chelsea pub. I was determined to know him, and when he was discharged from the Scots Guards I persuaded him to move into Narrow Street, where he settled surprisingly well. We shared a bed but our relationship was platonic, which is probably why it survived. His Glaswegian accent was so thick that many of my friends found him unintelligible, but he had the gift of making them welcome as if their arrival enhanced the day. When he heard I was travelling to the funeral alone, he insisted on coming with me, taking time off from his job as foreman on a building site. I accepted gratefully, though he was hardly the natural companion for a family funeral in a Devon village. I was less pleased when Deakin announced that he would like to come too. 'I need the rest.'

'I'm not going down for a holiday,' I snapped.

'You're not, but I am. Don't be so selfish,' he replied, putting me in the wrong. 'Anyhow,' and he shot a disapproving glance at Tony, 'you'll need adult company in the restaurant car.' By the time we left Paddington and entered the restaurant car, we were in a party mood. We should have changed trains at Taunton, but when Jeremy Thorpe and his mother saw us they offered us a lift in their car which was waiting at the station for they were travelling to the funeral too. It was halfway across Exmoor that, in an attempt to be entertaining, Deakin gave his appraisal of my family: 'That drunken old father of yours and that boring mother who never liked *me* . . .' Mrs Thorpe stopped the car with an anguished screech: 'How dare you talk of dear Eve and Negley like that? Get out! All of you,' which we did, sheepishly. We were miles from the nearest village on a black December night and I took Jeremy aside to whisper my anxiety that I might not reach Georgeham in time for the funeral the next morning. Deakin was told to apologize, and kept quiet as we drove in deadly silence through the night.

At ten the next morning, Deakin wandered into my room brandishing a glass: 'Look what I've found – the remains of an old bottle of Cinzano and some sherry. Do you think they'll make an interesting cocktail?'

'For God's sake, Deakin, if you want a drink, have one. I've got a funeral to go to.'

'Shall I go along, too, though I'm not dressed for the part?' he volunteered.

'No,' I told him emphatically. I did not have the heart to refuse Tony, who was wearing his best suit in the latest style. I knew it would look bizarre in the Devon churchyard and pictured the stony stares and hard eyes of the numerous tradesmen and neighbours who adored my mother, and I was correct.

I did not care. I was immune to everything after I went to Charlie Brown's Limehouse pub on the evening after my mother's death.

'See the old girl's snuffed it!' an old man called out.

'What?'

'Dead, ain't she. Just heard it on the ITN News – "Dan Farson's mother dies in a fall."'

Such was my ill-gotten fame.

Fifteen

The Waterman's Arms

'I SUPPOSE you'll be giving up your job?' asked my great-uncle Reg in Pelham Place. I looked at him in amazement: 'What do you mean?'

'Well, you can afford to now.'

It was a stupid remark, but Reg was not particularly bright, though good-natured. I believe he was a repressed homosexual at a time when many men had male friendships they valued but did not fully understand. He had a close friend called Horace, referred to constantly with admiration, also an unfortunate French wife he picked up on holiday for the sake of convention, taught to be 'a lady' by his sisters, an education she did nothing to deserve, and a wretched adopted daughter. He owned a farm which lost money at a time when this was considered an impossibility. It was there that I heard Neville Chamberlain announce the outbreak of war on the wireless while Uncle Reg looked suitably grave. On later visits with my grandmother she made veiled though meaningful observations when Reg and his wife disappeared into the bathroom every afternoon in the vain attempt to make love.

By the time Reg spoke to me with his fatal assurance about my future the farm had gone, the wife had left, the money had dwindled, and he lived in Brighton near Horace. No one was less suited to give advice; yet, incredibly, he had also been a solicitor (in what capacity I cannot imagine), and as he was the alleged 'man of the family' I respected his judgement. He proved to be but one of several unfortunate advisers, including my parents' kind but ineffective accountant and a succession of stupid bank managers.

Reg's words threw my life off balance in a sentence. With no head for business, I needed restraint; instead he gave me the excuse to spend, expiating my sense of guilt at having money in such circumstances. In any case, I was in no position to give up my job had I wanted to. Solicitor or not, Reg had forgotten all about death duties, which descended with particular vengeance after the deaths of my grandmother, father and mother so close together. They seemed so formidable that my bank manager advised me to sell Pelham Place. A fatuous snob with a revolting moustache, he had invited me to dinner after I left Cambridge under the illusion that I might be a 'catch' for his hideous daughter. He began to have doubts when I moved into Beauchamp Place, vulnerably close to the Westminster Bank over which he tyrannized in Brompton Road; from there he could send a runner to demand my presence. Momentarily confused, he brandished a number of cheques he was about to bounce: 'Muriel Belcher, Muriel Belcher,' he cried indignantly. 'Who is this woman you're living with?' When the truth dawned, he must have found it hard to forgive me, and his advice might have been an oblique form of revenge. Otherwise, it is hard to understand how he could have contemplated the outright sale of such a valuable property. Brought up to respect authority, it did not occur to me that the man was an incompetent; I trusted his judgement, which shows how badly mine was impaired.

Francis Bacon, who had the only intelligent bank manager I have heard of, warned me that I would be making a serious mistake if I sold, but did not explain why.

Knowing that my mother had tried to sell the beautiful Nash house to Cecil Beaton, who lived next door, and thought of adding it to his own, was a further inducement. Beaton was considering a figure of £12,000, so I thought I was doing well to accept £13,000 for the property, which is now worth a million. Anxious to put all this behind me, I arranged for its sale, with the contents, too quickly. My only excuse was my infatuation with my new home in Limehouse.

With the delusion of wealth, I thought I should invest some of the money. First I thought of a cheerful betting shop decorated with my sporting prints – that could not lose money, could it? When I realized that my prospective manager knew less about the business than I did, I abandoned the idea with relief.

I bought a car and employed a driver, Alan, a gentle giant from the East End who became a loyal companion, one of my few wise decisions.

I bought a turbo-jet speedboat from Dowty in Cheltenham and

moored it in Limehouse Cut on the other side of the barge-yard.

Like Charlie Kane with his newspaper, I thought it might be fun to run a pub. Crazy though this idea was, it seemed a logical outcome of my new interest in popular music. Virtually unknown to the West End, the music pubs of the East End resounded with local talent – the taxi-driver who sang Al Jolson numbers in the Rising Sun, where Welsh George was the compere specializing in Jewish numbers like 'My Yiddisher Momma', and Tex, a hunchback in a stetson who sang country and western, overshadowed by his horse. At the Deuragon, the waspish Ray Martine made mincemeat of his hecklers; at the Ironbridge, Canning Town, Queenie Watts belted the blues. There was jazz across the water at Bermondsey.

This was entertainment I could appreciate. My grandmother's close friend Dame Myra Hess put me off the classics when she sent me to a grand lady pianist who may have looked reptilian but was unable to teach me scales. I have returned to the classics in recent years, but by the time I joined television my taste had settled for the potency of cheap popular music. I interviewed Cliff Richard, very nice and very dull, and met Tommy Steele when I filmed the Two Is coffee bar in Soho. An ambitious messenger boy called Terry Nelhams asked me to act as his manager and I included him in the last of my series *Farson's Guide to the British* as an example of a pop star making his first appearance as he sang 'Brother Heartache and Sister Tears' in a nightclub. Afterwards the manager, Harry Meadows, took me aside to tell me it was wrong to encourage a boy with so little talent.

In *Dan Farson Meets* I introduced a range of musicians in the massive studio at Wembley, including The Shadows, Dudley Moore, Joe Brown, who was the friendliest and least pretentious of them all, and little Terry Nelhams who had changed his name to Adam Faith and found himself a manager, pretending he did not know me as he kept to himself, studying the City pages in the *Evening Standard*.

Beat City took me to Liverpool when it was throbbing with the new sound which shook the smoke-filled Cavern. This was the first film directed by Charlie Squires, who had edited most of my programmes with his flair for putting pictures to music. He proved a weak director, which was unfortunate as I had decided, with untypical goodwill, to let him do it his way and not to interfere. As they say, no good deed should ever go unpunished. We saw Brian Epstein, who offered us the Beatles on two conditions: the first was a big fee, which could have been agreed on; the second was the inclusion of a young girl singer he was trying to promote called Cilla White, later Cilla Black. To my dismay Charlie proved difficult, anxious to exert his new authority. He was a sweet man, but his personality, that of a huge, Bunterish Cockney, did not appeal to Epstein. This is where I should have stepped in, taking Charlie aside to insist that we seize this heaven-sent opportunity to film the Beatles who were poised for success. Instead, Charlie chose Gerry and the Pacemakers, endlessly crossing the Mersey, in the belief that they would endure longer. Talking to Paul McCartney and Ringo Starr in the Blue Angel in the evening, I realized what I had missed. Perhaps that is why I attempted to become a manager myself, signing up a group called Rory Storm and the Hurricanes, almost as popular in the Cavern as the Beatles. It worried me slightly that Rory Storm had a stammer, though this vanished the moment he sang. We realized as soon as I returned to London that my aspirations to emulate Epstein were wasting Rory's time.

This was the background to my hour-long programme on pub entertainment in the East End, *Time Gentlemen Please!*, which made the point that music hall was back where it began a hundred years earlier when taverns had adjacent rooms for entertainment, literally 'music halls'. In both cases there was the need for the artist to subdue the din and win his audience in seconds by the force of his personality. In the old days the musicians were screened by wire netting to protect them from the trotter bones thrown by the East Enders. One singer was heckled so viciously that a man in the gallery shouted down, 'Give the poor old cow a chance, will yer!' She looked up gratefully: 'Thank God there's *one* gentleman in the house.'

Now the music pubs had microphones, but the entertainers still needed to rise above the roar of conversation and the clash of crates and shouts for orders. If they were exceptional they gained attention, but there was nothing genteel in their reception.

There was such pleasure in seeing them perform live that I thought, illogically, that it would be justice to make a programme on entertainers so far removed from American showbiz. My colleagues were not keen on 'a bunch of amateurs', though the cameraman shrugged: 'I suppose if one is a welder, we could cut away to a shot of him welding.' Cringing from such an idea, I persuaded Rollo Gamble to visit the East End to see for himself.

'They're marvellous!' he enthused at the end of the evening.

'Exactly. That's what I've been trying to tell you for weeks.'

With Rollo in full sail as the Cecil B. De Mille of the telly, flattering the performers by treating them as 'stars', we went ahead with our local talent, unlike anything shown on television before: Tommy Pudding wearing a stained hat, with a face like suet, singing 'Put a Bit of Treacle on Your Pudding Mary Anne' with a Max Miller leer; Sulky Gowers, a bald man with a stick – I think he had an artificial leg – and dressed in the style of Al Capone, who gave a heartfelt rendering of 'Buddy Can You Spare a Dime'.

Along the way I found the Newcastle Arms. Deakin was right to scorn my speedboat as a status symbol but he had no inkling of the pleasure I gained as I sped down the Thames on summer nights to Greenwich or as far as Gravesend. I manoeuvred into inlets and canals, and because the boat was a turbo-jet with a no propellers, shallow water made no difference. Several times I moored at a slipway on the Isle of Dogs and walked to the large pub, the Newcastle Arms, at the top. There seemed to be something wrong. Invariably it was empty, sometimes I had to knock to be allowed in, and one evening the landlord fetched our drinks from the pub next door. I asked what on earth was going on. Nothing was going on; in the jargon of the trade the pub was 'on the floor', with the brewers refusing further credit. The landlord wanted to leave with his family as quickly as possible, but he was trapped, for no one was interested in taking over 'the pub with no beer' as it was known locally. They would have to be mad. As I looked around me I wondered.

I liked pubs; I relished the riverside; my home was around the corner. The pub was on two levels and I visualized how it would look if I knocked down the adjoining wall and looked down into the saloon as if it was a sort of music hall. I was preparing for the filming of *Time Gentlemen Please!* and could feature the pub, giving it valuable publicity. So I contacted the broker, who put me in touch with a sceptical district manager, who referred me with some doubt to his fearsome head office, where I persuaded them with my enthusiasm: 'You don't imagine I would contemplate such a venture if I thought I might lose money?' Once they realized that I was serious, they welcomed me like a godsend, for their figures proved that the pub was doomed. In becoming the new tenant, I paid a going-in price, a deposit and rent. I would pay the brewers for all the beer and spirits

I ordered and would keep the profit that was left after my overheads. I went ahead with the arrogance of ignorance.

With no head for business or for drink, I was proof that a fool and his money are soon parted. Brewers, like banks, are feudal tyrants in their autocracy, and have one purpose only – to make money. Ind Coope and the incredulous landlord of the Newcastle Arms could hardly believe their luck. At no point did anyone advise me that the bargaining power was mine. If I had insisted on buying the Newcastle Arms as a free house, though tied to them for beer and spirits, they might have agreed, for they had little alternative. Because I had seen the pub from the river, I had a false perspective. If I had found it by land I might have had doubts, for it was situated at the far end of the Isle of Dogs, with no passing trade, not even close to the West India or East India Docks. The four regulars seldom drank more than a pint of bitter each. I was taking over a derelict pub from scratch. The challenge of bringing it back to life appealed to my vanity.

I started to explore the Isle, not really an island though connected by bridges to the docks. I should have been warned by the long, deserted streets and the air of desolation that once accounted for the disparaging phrase 'going to the dogs'. Samuel Pepys had described it as 'a chill place, the morning cool, the wind fresh to our great discontent', a forlorn aspect for sailors returning home, greeted by the bleak marshland, its shoreline dotted with prisoners hanging from gibbets engulfed by every tide. In palatial contrast on the other side of the Thames stood Greenwich; Charles II kept his spaniels on the Isle of Dogs to distance himself from their barking, a possible derivation of the name.

The history was recent. As late as 1800 the Chapel House was the only habitation on the marshes. By 1900 the atmosphere had improved so drastically that Walter Besant called it 'a place where one might deliberately choose to be born', but by 1961 it had lapsed into the previous lethargy, forgotten by the rest of London.

There were large empty spaces as I crossed bridges and walked past high walls dwarfed by even higher ships, through backstreets with the evocative names of women: Sophia Street, Maria Street; or the Indies: Havannah Street, Cuba Street; or ships: Barque Street and Schooner Street. Blackwall was named after the massive walls which kept out the tide, and Millwall after one of the mills that stood there. One point nagged me – the name of the Newcastle Arms, which seemed ridiculous. I decided to rename it after the tiny riverside pub which was now my home in Limehouse, having discovered a print in the Port of London Authority archives of the exterior and another of the main room, now my sitting-room, where a few people huddled for the warmth of the fire and beer at a penny a pint. The brewers saw my point and after a pile of paperwork the name was changed to The Waterman's Arms.

On 5 November 1962 I appeared at the Brewster Sessions with my manager, a close friend just out of the navy. There was a nasty moment when the police referred to my conviction for being drunk, though they added that they had no objection to the licence being granted. Then they produced my manager's 'record of larceny', the theft of a beer-mug in a Portsmouth pub when he was in the navy. Everyone laughed and we became the new licensees. In far-off Kalgoorlie, which I had described as 'the most god-forsaken spot on earth', the *Commerce-Industrial and Mining Review* made the astringent observation: 'It is interesting that Mr Farson has reached his level in a Cockney pub.'

When the changeover morning arrived I found the various brokers with little piles of money in front of them. The broken-down furniture was valued and the existing stock counted, usually a formidable item but just a few empties in this case. I paid my cheque to the brewers, just over £1000, the largest I had ever signed. 'A good investment,' smiled the accountant as I pulled my first pint as publican, though I would seldom be behind the bar. In the evening I returned to brace myself against the onslaught as the doors opened. Nothing happened. After ten minutes one of the locals peered in, and retreated. Returning a few minutes later with his wife, he pointed dramatically through the wall: 'The *Great Eastern* was launched around that corner. *And it sank!*' Grateful for their custom, I poured them a Guinness on the house. Then another aged couple came in and did so every night for the next few years. These were our regulars. A stranger wandered in and out. The silence was desperate as the staff waited for something to happen. Rather than meet their eyes I wandered into the kitchen and ate a pancake roll under the impassive scrutiny of the Chinese waiters; at least I could not tell what they were thinking. Learning at the last moment that people would expect a drink on the house, I had gone to the absurd extravagance of being original by hiring Chinese waiters from the Lotus House to hand round bits of food.

Suddenly, at eight o'clock, as would happen so often, the doors

clanged apart and a torrent of people poured inside. Queenie Watts
seized the microphone, the pianist played, the smiling Chinese waiters
entered with their trays held high, and I discovered the rare capacity
of the East Enders to enjoy themselves. However, at closing time I
found one of the barmen having trouble with a tough-looking man
as I emerged from the lavatory with some *Keep Britain White* posters
I had removed from the walls. Remembering the times Gaston Berlement had asked me to leave The French Pub, I tried the same tactic.
'Now, now,' I said unctuously, 'you know I can't serve you after
hours and the law's outside. Tell you what, come back in the morning
and have a glass of champagne with me.' I held out my hand which
he shook warmly before he staggered out.

'There,' I told the barman. 'I don't know why you look so nervous.'
'Don't you, Dan? He's one of the Richardsons.' Amazingly, we
never had trouble in the Waterman's Arms except when some guards
officers stole the microphone.

After the excitement of the opening came shrouded weeks of dust-
sheets. Trying to arrange some makeshift entertainment, I was helped
by a friend in Tin Pan Alley who sent me a xylophonist and an aged
dyspeptic pianist with the expression of a dismayed bulldog, and others
who were plainly friends on the skids, desperately in need of work
while resenting the idea of appearing in a pub.

To be fair to the brewers, they agreed with my ideas and paid for
the structural alterations, which were formidable. They appointed a
brilliant architect, Roderick Gradidge, who worked for Ind Coope as
a freelance and who by luck was in total sympathy with my plans for
transforming the saloon into a pub music-hall while the upper public
bar would reflect the riverside.

My interest in music hall was inspired when I filmed the end of
the Metropolitan Music Hall in the Edgware Road for *This Week* on
one of the many farewell evenings after it received a closure notice
to make way for a main road. After it was demolished, they discovered
that the planners had made a slip of the pen, a slip of a hundred yards,
otherwise the Met might be with us today.

I hired the Met one afternoon to record an LP called *Music Hall*
while some of the veterans were still around, a gallant band of survivors
though past their prime – G. H. Eliott, the 'Chocolate-Coloured
Coon', who sang of 'Palpitating Niggers'; Hetty King the male impersonator – 'All the Nice Girls Like a Sailor!' – introducing them myself

with such embarrassments as, 'Now we have Albert Whelan who is still going strong at eighty-five having thankfully recovered from the recent operation in which he lost his leg. He is still whistling his famous signature tune.'

Above all I warmed to Ida Barr, who retained her vitality and performed the love song she had brought back from a tour of America, 'You Great Big Beautiful Doll'. That it should have been sung by a man to a woman made no difference. She gave me a photo of herself in sepia, radiant at the age of sixteen when she weighed thirteen and a half stone – 'They liked a lot of woman in those days' – with a shamrock on her bust. We blew it up to life-size, placing it beside the lavish gilt stage Roddy and I had commissioned, along with music-hall posters, my collection of song-sheet covers, and the plaster figures I seized as they demolished the Met.

Don Ross, the husband of Gertie Gitana ('Nellie Dean') gave me a big red poster billing Marie Lloyd, and I bid for the Ospovat pastel of Harry Tate and a huge coloured portrait of Dan Leno at the auction of Collins in Islington, yet another music hall destroyed.

Our chandeliers were bright enough, but when the lights came on for the filming of *Time Gentlemen Please!* the effect was so magnificent that even my cynical friends were impressed. Ida Barr sang 'Everybody's Doing It', another number she had brought from America, and the big surprise was Kim Cordell, the buxom singer I found in the Rising Sun, who was now our compere. As I looked down from the arches of the public bar onto the salon packed with East Enders enjoying the entertainment, I knew I had pulled it off. The former landlord of the Newcastle had returned for the occasion and shook his head in disbelief when he caught my eye.

When *Time Gentlemen Please!* was transmitted a few weeks later, thieves broke into Narrow Street, probably assuming that I was in the studio. This was why I needed Ted Smith as a minder. Disconsolate the next morning, 6 December 1962, I opened the papers in case the programme was mentioned. I gasped.

'Let us see US more often,' wrote Dennis Potter in the *Daily Herald*, 'the best pub crawl the sober little screen has ever witnessed.'

'CHEERS FARSON!' *Daily Mirror*.

'CHEERS, I SAY FOR THIS BOUNCING FUN AT THE BAR. The wheel has come full-circle, for music hall was born in the bar and moved out into the theatre. Now it is dead and its roisterous, bawdy, irresistible spirit has gone back to whence it came . . .' *Daily Mail*.

Prophetically, in the *Sunday Times*, Maurice Wiggin wrote: 'In this new venture he is mining a rich vein of ore; if it doesn't give out he may well find himself setting a fashion.'

◆

The euphoria lasted for a year. *Time Gentlemen Please!* was entered by Associated-Rediffusion for the Montreux Festival, but they followed it up with a travesty of a studio version, *Stars & Garters*, which defeated the point of showing the entertainers in their real surroundings. Extras sipped weak tea posing as beer, fights and 'spontaneous' sing-songs were staged. It was well done because Rollo was asked to direct it and brought in Ray Martine and Kim Cordell as the presenters. He asked me if I minded and I said I did not, but our friendship was never the same afterwards. It irked me that the studio series dashed my hopes of going north to film the vigorous local talent in pubs and working men's clubs.

Stars & Garters was reasonably popular with the viewers, but the critics spotted the difference and pounced: 'ISSUE MUST BE FACED – FAKE OR REALITY? The show is, of course, the love child of an excellent documentary about public entertainers in the East End, but with the almighty difference that it is just a fake – fake setting, fake customers, fake drink, fake conviviality.' Another wrote: 'I wish Mr Farson would be returned to us, and repeat his enormously enjoyable explorations.' But *Stars & Garters* put paid to that.

As if in compensation, I brought the East Enders to the West End in a show called *Nights at the Comedy* produced by William Donaldson, who was hoping to repeat his success with *Beyond the Fringe*. The two of us went to see Bernard Delfont to ask him to back it, and I explained my concept of a new, boisterous music hall rather than the twee reconstruction with a chairman and a hammer. He asked who I had in mind, and looked doubtful when I mentioned Mrs Shufflewick: 'No, that's wrong. He sends music hall up.'

Now the one artist I was certain of was 'Shuff'. I had seen him at the last night of the Met and asked him to appear at the Waterman's, which he did regularly with great success. 'Broad-minded to the point of obscenity', Mrs Shufflewick began by fingering a dreadful piece of fur. 'You like this? It was given me by a hundred sailors with a pound each, so I wasn't done was I? I can't remember myself, the gin and tonic has fogged the brain I'm happy to say.' He continued to recount the disasters of the night before which ended on a 29 bus – 'and all these people looked at me, as if they'd never seen a naked woman on top of a bus before'.

I stood my ground. 'To my mind Mrs Shufflewick *is* music hall.' Willie Donaldson winced, but Delfont pressed his intercom and spoke to his assistant Billy Marsh: 'What does Mrs Shufflewick mean to you?'

'If it's anything to do with music hall there's no one better, but . . .'

'Thanks,' said Delfont. Turning to me, he smiled. 'All right then, go on. I'll back it.' Outside the office, Willie and I whooped with joy, but Delfont later withdrew.

The first meeting of the cast took place in a room at the YMCA which smelt of wet carpet, cabbage and cat pee, on a depressing morning in December. The artistes had little in common and took an instinctive dislike to each other. Sulky Gowers arrived like an old-time gangster, very smart; the Red Indians drooped from the cold and looked moth-eaten in the light of day; Jimmy Tarbuck was suspicious; and the eminent actor Nicol Williamson, our unlikely compere, arrived in a frayed jacket and docker's boots, his shoulders hunched in such misery that Tarbuck took me aside and demanded to know what such a person was doing there. Then Nicol pulled out and I replaced him with a camp, portly, middle-aged comic I had seen in Manchester, Jacky Carlton.

The opening on the first night must have been one of the simplest ever, as Kim Cordell came on stage singing 'If you were the only boy in the world and I was the only girl'. She was followed by Mrs Shufflewick, who muttered 'funny looking fellah' as he passed her, and started his monologue. In the *Sunday Times*, Harold Hobson wrote that 'he times his lines as skilfully as Mussolini did his trains'. Rex Jamieson was the funniest female impersonator I have ever seen, except that impersonation did not come into it, for he *was* Mrs Shufflewick. On subsequent nights when we stood at the back of the stalls with drinks from the bar he was formidable, caustic and brave. As Rex Jamieson he was meek. When he wore a straw-coloured toupée like a new thatched roof, on special occasions, he would have looked pathetic except for his clown's face, similar to Dan Leno's. An alcoholic, he was supplied with crates of Guinness by a friend from the street below which he hoisted to the window of his dressing-room. We went to absurd lengths to keep him sober for the first night. It was Queenie Watts who descended the gilded staircase so much the worse for drink to steady her nerves that I closed my eyes as she started to sing, but even that was true to music hall.

A few evenings later I arrived at the Comedy Theatre to coincide with Shufflewick leaving it, carried out on a stretcher after collapsing from a surfeit of gin and purple hearts. I wish I had seen his entrance at the Charing Cross Hospital and could only imagine the faces of the nurses as he was wheeled in wearing his dress and the extra heavy make-up for the stage, but without his wig. Trouper personified, he returned in time to close the show.

That opening took me by surprise, as if I had thought it would never happen. I was entranced by the glamour of show business, amazed to find myself part of it with the pile of good-luck telegrams waiting in the box-office. This was the last time the great variety comedian Jimmy James appeared on stage, flanked by his stooge Eli who held out a matchbox which contained two lions – 'I thought I heard a rustling' – and helped him out when he forgot his lines.

It was Jimmy Tarbuck's West End debut and a come-back for Ida Barr, resplendent in black velvet, who delighted the audience when she waved aside the microphone: 'I don't need *that*.'

But the director, Eleanor Fazan, and I had tried too hard. Apart from the Red Indians, we had fire-eaters, a man called Bob who banged his head with a tray as he sang 'Mule Train', a noisy teenage pop-group, Karl King and the Vendettas, who now appeared regularly at the Waterman's, and a yard-of-ale contest in the interval. It is one of the hardest lessons to know when to stop, and I had not learned it. Nor did we end with a bang, though we had kept a space at the end for 'Astonishing Guest Artist'. Joe Brown had volunteered to appear out of friendship, singing such favourites as 'Knocked 'em in the Old Kent Road', but Willie Donaldson had his doubts and chose the Alberts instead, a 'comic' group of middle-aged men with beards, top hats and large musical instruments who 'died the death of a dog', as Hetty King would have said. Yet, in the grip of first-night hysteria, I forgave them and toured the dressing-rooms with reassurance and congratulations, finding Ida Barr overwhelmed by the flowers and visitors. At the party afterwards, a woman who was not connected with the show said, 'You really *are* on top of the world, aren't you?' She was stunned that anyone could be so naïve.

The reviews were kind, with the *Daily Mirror* calling it 'an evening of nostalgia, cheerful vulgarity, raucous singing ... a wild wild evening. The only clean crack all evening was made by an Indian with a whip.' Another critic was more accurate when he wrote, 'Farson tries without really succeeding.'

Meanwhile the Waterman's became one of *the* places to go. The visitors' book swelled with the names of celebrities. An East Ender told Claudette Colbert that she looked like Claudette Colbert – 'Yes, I'm often told that!' – while Groucho Marx was disgruntled because no one recognized him. Clint Eastwood was absorbed as if invisible. Joan Littlewood brought Jacques Tati, who asked me to appear in his next film – but I expect he said this to everyone. Francis Bacon brought William Burroughs. Bernard Delfont arrived in his Rolls-Royce but did not stay long; Frankie Howerd viewed the pub as a possible setting for his next LP, and fled, but it was used for an LP called *The Entertainers*, and Kim Cordell made another of her own.

A nice elderly queen, who wanted to call himself Simon Sailor until his friends persuaded him to change the name to Simon Fleet, brought Lady Diana Cooper, who stood in the crowd near the stage and refused to sit down. Sycophantically, I told her how many people were saying how beautiful she looked: 'I much prefer pretty,' she replied, and she was right. Lady Aberconway, her rival, waved graciously to the populace below from a chair placed in the public bar beside the arches. 'It's nice to see her sitting,' said Lady Diana tartly when I pointed her out. 'She's spent most of her life on her back.'

I gave extravagant parties with food from the New Friends. Brian Epstein came to one of them, but he and his friends treated me as a waiter. He came back to see Karl King and the Vendettas, whom I was promoting in the ridiculous hope that he might see them as potential Beatles. Unfortunately Karl was ill that night, the usual musicians booked elsewhere, and my contact in Tin Pan Alley promised a worthy replacement who proved to be the dyspeptic pianist with the bulldog face. Epstein left at the first chord, and Julian Slade inscribed the visitors' book, 'Shoot the pianist.'

We became part of Swinging London: *POW!* exclaimed the *Sunday Mirror* with a centre-page spread of photographs, '*So this is what really goes on in our great FUSED capital.*' Hoist by my publicity, I had made it trendy to go East, having blazed the trail with *Time Gentlemen Please!* West Enders dressed down for the occasion, with headscarves and jeans. The atmosphere began to change and when Kim Cordell complained that a group of dockers had come in straight from work in dirty overalls and were surrounding the stage, I turned on her afterwards: 'This is a dockland pub. We should pay them to dress like that.'

Usually taken to nightclubs, Americans enjoyed the different atmosphere. Annie Ross brought Tony Bennett and Sarah Vaughan, and I gave a party for Judy Garland on the longest and hottest night of the year. She was brought by Bert Shevelove, who invited me to join them in the Ritz beforehand. Foolishly, I lost this opportunity because I was anxious to make sure that everything was ready for her arrival. More foolishly, I had sworn the staff to secrecy, and nothing is so calculated to gain attention as that. As I turned the corner that evening I was dismayed to find the street crowded with hundreds of people waiting to see her. They were not fan clubs or groups of gays, or press, for I was determined that she should not be bothered by photographers. Now I was alarmed that she might be hurt in the crush, for she was so thin that her arms and legs were like twigs. When she arrived, only an hour late, there was a gasp from the East Enders as they saw her fragility and they made way for her politely with welcoming smiles, some cheers and clapping which seemed to delight her. The pub was so crowded that I took her upstairs to the large, long room where she sat by the window with a glimpse of the river, talking animatedly. I introduced her to Ida Barr and to Annie Ross who had played her younger sister in an early film. She was nice to everyone.

An odious couple had taken over as my new managers, and when the man called 'Last Orders!' Judy Garland decided she would like to sing. Incredibly, my manager informed her that it was against the law to turn on the lights after closing time, which was news to me. He pointed to the usual two policemen waiting on the other side of the street.

'To hell with that,' said Garland. 'I'll pay the fines.' How I allowed him to I do not know, but the manager overruled me and Garland sang instead by the more romantic moonlight and the reflection from the street light outside. Another of the guests played the opening bars of 'Come Rain or Come Shine' on the pub piano, and she was off with a snap of her fingers and a lift of the chin and that ecstatic voice. When she left, she thanked me for an unforgettable evening: 'Only one thing was missing – no photographers.'

When a *Guide to British Pubs* came out, I saw that the Waterman's had more mentions in the index than any other pub in Britain. But I knew the truth. There are few easier ways of losing money than to run a pub. In my baffling way, I had achieved the impossible by making it too successful. Nothing happened until eight in the evening and then within minutes the Waterman's was so crowded that people had to push their way to the bar. Many stayed just to listen, continuing to another pub to drink. Rivals prospered, like the City Arms on the way which started to feature drag.

The eleven o'clock closing time was the killer, for it meant that we had less than three hours in which to do business. I dared not open after hours because of the constant surveillance of the police, who hoped for the trouble which never came. If the new licensing laws had been in operation then I could have made a fortune: East End pubs now stay open into the early hours if they have entertainment, and can open on Sunday afternoons. Or could I? The odds would still be against me, unless I had advisers I could trust, and I have always been unlucky there. With a large pub there are too many people with too many opportunities to cheat the licensee, and I was vulnerable because I did not live on the premises, employing managers. Yet even Queenie Watts and her husband Jim, as tough an East Ender as I have come across, were being robbed at the Ironbridge, though it took six months before they discovered the thief was the under-manager they were grooming to take over, now that Queenie was a successful actress on television.

Their accountant and closest friend was called Fred, a pinstriped, plump and pompous homosexual who had yet to 'come out'. On Queenie's advice he became my accountant, too, with the hope that he would keep a tighter rein. It took me a long time to realize he was crooked, and by then it was too late. Just as I had blinked when I got off the bus at the corner to walk up Glengarnock Avenue, and saw one of the barmen drive up in a brand new car, it puzzled me that Fred looked increasingly affluent. Years later, when he owned a Rolls-Royce and a house in Suffolk near his new friend Angus Wilson, he was still pinstriped and pompous but no longer repressed, thanking me for changing the course of his life. I could well believe it.

Accountants are not the nicest breed, but he gave them a bad name when he asked Queenie to settle her bill and she explained that it was a bad moment due to Jim's gambling debts.

'That's all right,' said Fred. 'I'll take that,' pointing to her wedding ring.

When told that he was dead, I laughed with pleasure, especially as he left massive debts of his own. I have no idea how much he took from me.

These are excuses. Fiddles were part of the East End and part of pub life. Deakin was right to call me 'Gullible Gertie', for I was tempting fate with such lavish entertainment when a broken glass wiped out the profit on a pint of beer.

Gaston Berlemont at The French Pub had no such problems, importing and selling his own wines, and not serving draught beer, and other publicans made their profit from serving food, while I gave it away at my parties upstairs. I was a fool.

❖

One morning as I lay in bed in Narrow Street, my hangover was aggravated when the bank manager phoned to inform me that my business account was £3000 overdrawn – a large amount in 1963 – and what was I going to do about it? Weakly, I told him to sell the last of the shares left me by my parents. It was time to hand in my notice to the brewers, but that was not so simple. Years later the bank manager told me I should have gone bankrupt, though his predecessor failed to suggest this at the time. It occurs to me now that I might have been able to form a company in the Waterman's name, and *that* could have gone bankrupt without the personal stigma I was anxious to avoid. 'If only' are the two saddest words in the language, but if only I had bought the Waterman's as a free house I could have sold it for a massive profit now that it was famous. Instead, the brewers screwed me down to my year's notice until they found a new tenant prepared to pay the going-in fee of £4500 which they were demanding in view of the Waterman's reputation. Now I understood the desperation of the previous landlord, forced to stay against his interest. Week after week, chequebook after chequebook, I covered my losses as if I were throwing silver in the Thames.

I should have called the brewers' bluff by walking out and telling them to whistle for their money or sue. I had earned them hundreds of thousands of pounds with my orders, and these were small beer compared to the goodwill engendered by *Time Gentlemen Please!*, an advertising agency's dream. On my own, for by now I knew that my accountant, bank manager and solicitor were useless, I did not have the guts to fight back. Prospective tenants sniffed around and were never seen again. The Isle of Dogs remained a moribund area, the price was unrealistic, and I learned afterwards that a member of the staff discouraged every applicant in the hope that Ind Coope would ask him to take over as their manager. This mad carousel became the more ridiculous when the brewers told me to apply for a new licence. Unwittingly, the police came to my rescue with the rumour that they might oppose it due to my conviction for being drunk and disorderly though they had not done so before. As this was the last publicity I needed, I roused myself at last and discovered I could play the brewers at their own game even if I could not defeat them. They, and not the law, imposed the opening times and prices. Provided it was within licensing hours, I could open when I liked and charge what I wanted. My first move was to run the pub myself. I closed it all day, opening at eight in the evening. I asked the entertainers and musicians to work for half-pay in return for what I had done for them, which they agreed to willingly. I served no draught beer and doubled the prices. Champagne was on sale for the first time and proved surprisingly popular. My intention was to shame the brewers into releasing me. Instead, for two revelatory weeks, to everyone's astonishment including mine, the Waterman's was full and the only complaint came from Ind Coope's outraged district manager. For the first time the pub made a slight profit and I was tempted to carry on, but the brewers suddenly found a tenant at a reduced asking price and I was thankful to leave.

Making the worst mistake of my life, I did so scrupulously, paying the brewers what I owed them. The self-indulgence of running a pub had cost me most of my money, yet the escapade had been extraordinary, with the extensions at Christmas and the New Year when the pub belonged to the East Enders who linked arms for a knees-up as unaffected as they were happy.

Better, perhaps, to lose like that than be wiped out on paper in a Stock Exchange swindle?

Sixteen

Time to Pay

MY DAYS on television were numbered, too. The first exhilaration had faded, which was inevitable, and the early explorations were curtailed now that the boundaries were clearly defined. Without the impetus of Rollo Gamble, I made an hour-long feature on *Courtship*, which proved surprisingly dull.

Frankly, I was stale. I had done too much too soon. It annoyed me to see how the medium was wasted by directors who used it as a stepping-stone to feature films, rarely exploiting the immediacy at which television excelled.

Then there was the vulnerability of my reputation. Elkan Allen, who devised *Out of Step* and promoted me when he was Head of Light Entertainment, asked me to lunch at Wheeler's, knowing it was my favourite restaurant, though he booked a table in one of the less sympathetic rooms upstairs. 'It will be easier to talk confidentially,' he explained, ominously. I began to suspect that the lunch had been set up as a warning. Too embarrassed to come to the point, Elkan waffled, but the points he had to make were inescapable: A-R were worried about reports of my drinking, and in a graver and lower voice, '. . . the other thing'. Oh God! not that again. It was not a happy lunch, especially as I saw Francis in full splendour when we went downstairs.

There was no single reason, there seldom is, not even the Wheeler's lunch, but I knew it was time to get out. As with the pub, I had surprising difficulty in doing so, with John McMillan refusing to let me break my contract until I resorted to a fake doctor's letter which implied a possible breakdown. This gave them no alternative, but it meant, though I was unaware of it then, that I left under a cloud of suspicion and the widespread belief that I had been sacked. No one would believe that anyone could throw up such a job of their own volition. They were right. No one in their right mind would have, especially as A-R was up for the new franchise and needed the respectability of serious documentaries. Obviously we could have reached a compromise. In the event, A-R lost the franchise and if I had stayed on I would have been paid off handsomely or offered a job at three times the salary with the new company, London Weekend.

So I left discredited. It did not occur to me to hold a farewell party and certainly it was not forthcoming from Associated-Rediffusion, who thought I had betrayed them.

Throughout that last year I had been haunted by the thought of the empty house by the sea. How sad to possess such a place and go there for only three weeks a year and the snatched weekend. I rented out 92 Narrow Street, keeping one room as a base in London, and on 1 April 1964, a date I remember because it was so important to me, Alan drove me down to Devon with the dogs in the back seat. They leapt to life when they sniffed the sea air, reviving their memories as we turned from Saunton Sands into Croyde Bay and finally down the hill to the grey stone house on the edge of Putsborough Sands.

To start with life at the Grey House was close to paradise. After the pressures of television and the stress of the pub, the relaxation was infinite. Lazy days blurred into each other as spring gave way to summer. Even when I was energetic, it was soothing: swimming in the splendid surf; planting a copse of fir trees bought from Treseders at Truro, along with plants and bushes like the evergreen escallonia which withstands the gales and acts as a windbreak; feeding the hens; searching the bracken for the eggs hidden by the nicer, humorous ducks who swam in the small pool I made by damming the stream which ran down from the hill which they climbed every afternoon, white spots in the distance.

Nothing happened at an alarming pace. Alan, enslaved by the dogs, recognized the danger of lethargy before I did, warning me that it was time to start working again. I wrote a play called *The Frighteners* for a BBC television series on London, loosely based on my own experience of the East End. Through this job I met Harry Moore, the script editor, with whom I collaborated on a musical based on Marie Lloyd. Ida Barr, who knew Marie well, had stripped off the usual whitewash, revealing her as the sacred monster she was – which made her more interesting. I took the idea to Joan Littlewood and she accepted it for the Theatre Royal, Stratford East.

As so often in my life, this was a nearly-triumph. The evening before the rehearsals began, I was asked to dinner at the splendid house in Blackheath which Joan shared with Gerry Raffles, and returned to Limehouse in a state of euphoria. I was in the theatre.

I arrived at the first rehearsal to find the stage crowded with actors doing the most extraordinary things, like a grown woman being dragged across it howling like a baby. I smiled benevolently, until it dawned on me that this was *Marie*. Not a word of our dialogue remained. No one had warned me that this was how Joan Littlewood worked.

The next morning I joined in, playing an old man in a queue in one of their games, accepted as one of Joan's 'nuts'. If I had been clever I would have gone along with that, for though she had little respect for the written word and a dislike of playwrights (including Shakespeare), she was in thrall to her actors.

Harry Moore, a gentle man with a martyred smile, arrived in the stalls and sat there white and aghast. Joan noticed him but did not speak. I had tea with some of the actors in the caff which was run by two old women who screamed incessant messages – 'Joanee! One of yer young fellers been in for yer' – which killed conversation, but I kept on smiling though I grew to hate the bubbling humour. I thought I got on well with the cast, which included Avis Bunnage as Marie – idiotically I had discouraged Joan's preference for Barbara Windsor, saying she was too young. Jimmy Perry played Marie's second husband, Alec Hurley. Nigel Hawthorne, who played a theatre manager, told me years later how it hurt him to see Joan's travesty.

My initial shock faded as words resurfaced, and Gerry Raffles, who ran the theatre, assured me I would recognize the final production. The one aspect which Joan kept to rigidly was the music, ironically the one area where it failed totally because no new music, however good, could compete with songs like 'My Old Man' and 'Oh, Mr Porter!' She took the trouble to explain points to the composer and myself and asked for a song loosely based on Fred Barnes, who was ruined after an incident involving a guardsman in Hyde Park. For once she accepted my suggestion that instead of making him a female impersonator on stage it might be funnier to have him dressed immaculately in a white suit singing butch cowboy numbers which got the bird. I wrote the lyrics, making them as dreadful as I could, and phoned them through to the composer:

I'm on my way to the great outback
And the wide open spaces
Where the men are men and yearn
For a girl's embraces.

The composer gave an elephantine bellow as we compared notes in the theatre, having misheard me on the phone, he had written, 'and yearn for a girl in braces'. I sobbed with laughter too, partly with relief that everything seemed to be going so well. Joan stopped for a second on stage and glared at us over her sinister half-specs. Studying her notes later, she beckoned me: 'It's no good. I can't go through with it. It's not going to work. I'm miserable. You're miserable.'

'But Joan,' I gulped, 'I could not be happier. I agree with everything you've done.'

'I can't work this way. I'm an egomaniac. No, it's just that I'm too old. I don't care if I break people's hearts. This is the only way I can work. I did this with Brendan and Shelagh and my other nuts and it worked. Wolf Mankowitz expected me to stick to his script but I can't work like that.'

This was said with lethal quiet. 'I don't think you know a thing about the theatre. I don't believe you can write dialogue. Norman [the composer] comes here and has the audacity to tell me what to do.' (Asked for his opinion, he had suggested one scene might be tightened up.) 'Harry sits there looking like death' (in fact he died soon afterwards) 'and upsets the actors. I can only work my way. I thought you understood that.'

The words came out like machine-gun fire, though anyone watching would have thought we were having a friendly talk. Norman sat there beaming.

Harry and I were barred from the theatre, though Norman remained because Joan was baffled by the music. In one performance during the run, she gave me a dagger-like glance as the audience roared for more during 'The Great Outback', and hissed, 'Why can't you write lyrics like that?'

'I did.'

In retrospect she was right. I did not know how to write for the theatre, and though I could have learned she demanded absolute surrender. Far better to have left the country after that dinner at Blackheath, returning for the first night.

Joan had genius. With a few strokes she achieved effects as spectacular as anything Drury Lane could do. There were moments of magic
only she could create. Her taste was astonishing. But when things
went wrong, as they did in a coffee-stall scene she inserted with some
dreadful jokes that had nothing to do with music hall, she would not
change them. One matinee everything worked so perfectly that I made
the mistake of rushing up to say how good it was, and stopped as I
realized she had cut the coffee-stall scene and another dud to save
time. They stayed in from that moment.

The critics were perceptive. Milton Shulman wrote in the *Standard*
that, 'The book seems to have been mauled in the production'; *The
Times* made a surprising reference to reports of the apparent *lack* of
disagreement between Joan Littlewood and her writers, adding, 'the
story-line is consistently sabotaged by the impulse to keep things
lively.' Frank Marcus voted it the best musical of the year. In spite of
the cold, the lovely old theatre had glowed with nostalgia as the show
gradually improved, and the one person Joan never spared was herself,
surveying the scene nightly from various concealed points in the audi-
torium like the phantom of the opera.

At least I had the chance to work with her. I returned to Devon
to lick my wounds.

◆

Associated-Rediffusion threw me a last lifeline, asking me to do a short
series of interviews as a freelance. I have forgotten the others but shall
always remember the programme with Godfrey Winn, the popular
journalist who 'shook hands with people's hearts' according to Lord
Beaverbrook.

One evening as I returned to Narrow Street from Soho I had an
argument with the taxi-driver, who drove me to Limehouse police
station. A friend arrived to collect me but by then I was even more
truculent and decided to stay in the cells. The next morning I had
my first experience of being driven in a Black Maria to the Magistrates
Court, off Commercial Road. The scene inside exploded with such
colour and vivacity that it encapsulated the spirit of the old East End,
indeed it could have been devised by Joan Littlewood at her most
abandoned, with outrageous tarts, dark-skinned bruisers, drunks,
tramps and me, charged with being drunk and disorderly. I was fined
the usual amount, a matter of ten shillings or less, and the benevolent

magistrate added that he was allowing me 'time to pay'. Smiling, I paid up smartly, raced across the square into Commercial Road, and hailed a taxi to Television House.

Godfrey Winn (nicknamed Winifred God) was in make-up when I arrived, and stayed there a long time as they adjusted his toupée. In spite of the lack of self-doubt which had spurred his vaulting ambition, making him the richest journalist in Britain, I liked him and he was always pleasant to me, constantly inviting me to dinner at the Caprice with the showbiz solicitor David Jacobs, though I always declined. He was astute enough to see that I was preoccupied, and in one of the interminable breaks asked me if everything was all right.

When I told him about my court appearance, he looked aghast. 'No, it's not that,' I assured him, 'it's the dread that it might get into the papers.' He paled even further, beneath his heavy make-up, for such an experience was beyond his ken.

When the interview was finished I headed into Soho to find Deakin, for I knew he would understand. Perhaps he had been barred from the Colony or I owed Muriel money, for we drank the afternoon away in the basement gloom of the Kismet, run by Maltese Mary for crooks, coppers and resting actors. The atmosphere was dank with failure. Far from being sympathetic, Deakin was in his 'Tough shit, kiddo' mood. Every hour I went upstairs to the news-stand at Leicester Square tube station. 'It's all right,' I assured the indifferent Deakin, 'I'm not in. I'm no longer news.'

Even so, I went up to buy the last edition, and there it was in the stop press: DAN FARSON ASKS FOR TIME TO PAY. There was no point in explaining to anyone that this was a magistrate's nonsense; it was in the paper, it was a legal phrase, therefore it must be true. After my return to Devon, a 'friend' wrote that Deakin was gloating around Soho: 'How are the mighty fallen!' Associated-Rediffusion did not ask me to appear again.

I persuaded the *Sun* newspaper to commission a series on 'Famous Men and their Mothers', starting with David Frost, who now lived in Egerton Crescent next to the house where I was born and was too busy to see me, though he filled in a written questionnaire. Godfrey Winn welcomed me in his elegant home in Pimlico, with some excellent pictures, and was so concerned by my health that he urged me to phone him whenever I thought of going 'on a bender', like a one-man Alcoholics Anonymous. It was well meant.

'You see,' Godfrey explained, 'I owe it to my public to keep fit, which is why I play tennis.'

From there to Bournemouth where Laurence Harvey was appearing in a play. I stayed in Southampton the night before and it was so cold I put the jacket of my smart suit in my case and wore my Gieves donkey-jacket to keep warm. Then I got pissed in Southampton's singularly depressing pubs. At some point my case was stolen and the police who picked me up were unusually kind and took me to a bed and breakfast where I woke in stifling flannel sheets. Surprisingly I had some money left and continued to Bournemouth in the sudden Sahara heat, yearning for my jacket which had disappeared. I knew Harvey, but he was transformed. He had clawed his way to stardom, sleeping with male producers, marrying the widows of tycoons, but was now totally relaxed for the first time, having married the model Pauline Stone, who was expecting his first child. He was so radiantly happy that he wanted to share it with the world. He was discomfited to see me sweating uncomfortably in my heavy serge jacket until I told him the truth and he hooted with laughter, taking me to a lavish lunch in the vast white rococo hotel where he was staying, plying me with Sancerre, and arranging for someone to find out the complicated relay of buses to take me back to Devon. In the last of these they had the radio on and the music was interrupted by a news flash announcing the death of the well-known writer Godfrey Winn, who had collapsed while playing tennis. Instead of my series on 'Famous Men and their Mothers', which was scrapped, the *Sun* ran my interview over two pages the next day, as a kind of obituary. So much for tennis.

Laurence Harvey's happiness was short-lived. Knowing he was dying, he asked friends to support him as he was carried into Wheeler's in Old Compton Street to say goodbye to the waiters.

'How bloody marvellous!' I exclaimed.

'No,' said one of them, 'it was rather embarrassing.' I still think it showed panache.

❖

Life resumed in Devon on a diminishing scale. The money ran out with startling speed. I am not sure exactly how long it took before there was nothing left; perhaps it was spread over ten years. Because I sold things off gradually, there was no decisive moment but an overall blur. Friends still came and went, for the Grey House was an attractive place to visit. There were brief companionships, and the house deteriorated.

Alan left to rejoin his girlfriend in London. The speedboat which had given me so much healthy walking exercise when it stuck on a sandbar, was sold at a pathetic price. Everything went in due course. I learned that when you buy, people fawn on you, but when you need to sell they exercise contempt rather than sympathy, knowing they have you at their mercy.

The Russian plates on the sideboard with the delicate hunting scenes were sent to Sotheby's. The expert in charge phoned me after the auction to inform me that they had not met the modest reserve, but he had a friend who would be prepared to buy them. I had little alternative and he knew it. Those plates and others with the Romanoff crest had been made for Tsar Nicholas II.

The paintings were the most painful to part with because I had acquired them as gifts from the artists – the rare lithograph of Maugham's head, signed by Sutherland; the rarer surgeon's head from Bacon; the two Auerbachs, and the Lucian Freud portrait of John Deakin. Paradoxically I miss Gaudier-Brzeska's lightning sketch of the tiger most of all, remembering it from my grandmother's house in Pelham Place, where I gazed at it interminably as a child.

Everything went in the end – small objects acquired with affection, the best of the furniture. I should have felt destroyed, but my perennial optimism harnessed with arrogance kept me oblivious to the harsh reality. That conceit was crucial in persuading me that I was worth survival. Also, I am a fatalist – not that I shrugged it off: it mattered terribly.

I had written the lyrics for Marie Lloyd, 'Take me or leave me, I am what I am', long before 'I am what I am' became a gay anthem, and that is how I regarded life. As a Capricorn I was the goat that scrambled to the top of the mountain and fell down the other side. Now I had reached rock bottom, stuck in a crevasse. Perhaps I should have struggled harder to extricate myself, but there were compensations in this stage of my life: at least it was preferable to crowning beauty queens in suburban cinemas.

When Cecil Beaton stayed with Billy Henderson at the end of the lane, he was shocked, as Henderson was quick to tell me afterwards, by my inactivity. But Beaton was ambitious. Actors 'rest', professors take 'sabbaticals', I was lying fallow. It would be nice to say I did this in the knowledge that the new growth would be the stronger, but there was no such thought.

❖

Throughout these years, which, perversely, I enjoyed, I had the support of three friends and six dogs. Two of the friends were ex-sailors and I assume they met through me, becoming the best of friends themselves. Both were called Bob and they were fiercely heterosexual.

Bob B. was Irish, feckless and fun. Tall, blond and handsome, he believed he would be more interesting if he lied about himself, which was the opposite of the truth. The first time we met was in London, with another ex-sailor who also had girlfriends yet seemed to prefer the company of 'queens' and took a liking to me, once sending me knickers through the post and phoning me afterwards to ask if I was wearing them. The sex was so satisfactory that we decided to live together for a time at least, for neither of us assumed that it would last. We intended to go to Devon where he could have the nominal job of driver – which suggests I still had some money and had not given the car to Alan when he left, as I should have done.

The three of us joined up one evening in a club off the Cromwell Road and continued to Narrow Street where we held an impromptu party and my other friend became so jealous of Bob B. that he drove off in a rage in the early morning to collect a girlfriend from the airport. Bob tried to phone him a few hours later and learned that he had been involved in a car crash. He was dead.

I have no idea what might have developed, though I have imagined it constantly. A few weeks later I met the camp, middle-aged queen who had been one of his closest friends.

'You must hate me,' I said. We had scarcely spoken before. To my surprise he could not have been nicer, shook his head and said that the young man was bound to come to a sticky end because he lived too fast. Though unconvinced, I was comforted.

Possibly the unmentioned and unmentionable guilt over our friend's death formed a bond with Bob. We spent an entire winter in the Grey House, walking across the sands to Woolacombe at the far end of the bay to buy our food when the shops in Braunton refused further credit. Walking back in the rain and a sensational series of rainbows, we laughed all the way. In later years when people told me that Bob was irresponsible, I remembered how uncomplaining he had been, while recognizing this was true. On one of my rare visits to London, I phoned home at nine in the morning, relieved to hear his cheerful voice with the assurance that everything was fine and the dogs looked after. An hour later I needed to phone back and he was so drunk he was virtually speechless. Returning from London without the car, Mr Symonds, the faithful taxi-driver, met me at Braunton station and let slip that while I was away he had been hired constantly by Bob and 'a fine-looking woman' to take them to the pubs. I knew of this older woman, who had embarrassed Bob by sending him Oil of Ulay when he was incarcerated in a naval glasshouse. It emerged later that they had run up a bill for £70 at the off-licence in Braunton in my name.

As Mr Symonds turned the corner at Saunton down to Croyde, I was startled to see a group of animals racing towards us. 'My God!' I exclaimed as they came nearer, 'the dogs.' What possessed them to escape is impossible to say. They looked ecstatic rather than alarmed, in spite of the danger they were in. Where were they heading, what to, what from? They were going so fast that they overtook us as we stopped but when they heard my voice calling after them they bounded back and leapt into the taxi, delirious with joy at seeing me again, gradually calming down now that they were safe. What would have happened but for this chance encounter? I could scarcely contemplate the outcome on this main road if I had not returned – they had travelled several miles already.

As for Bob, there were two things I could do – kill him or forget it. With the dogs now blissfully at home, I forgot.

Surprisingly, the house seemed remarkably in order, as if I had never been away. Relaxing by the ducks' pool the next day, I noticed bits of paper floating on the surface. When I fished them out I discovered my correspondence, which had been opened by Bob, probably in the hope of finding a cheque, and disposed of so carelessly that I was bound to find out. This was typical: he was a lousy liar and ultimately hopeless, yet a good man.

Bob K. could be equally wild. He featured in the *News of the World* when his wife sued for divorce, citing his cruelty when he returned from sea and forced her to have sex in the bath while they drank champagne. He was inundated afterwards with proposals of marriage, but unlike Bob B. he settled down, ultimately putting his life in perspective. Having built up a successful business, he lives happily as a family man yet has never lost his zest.

Then there was Peter. The thought of his recent death is still so heartbreaking that I shall try to brush over the bad times and remember him as all his friends remember him, including Francis Bacon and John Deakin, as good to look at and fun to be with. Peter could be difficult, even violent, but he was loyalty personified, trustworthy, honourable and more surprising than anyone I have known.

We met in a Manchester pub when I was writing a series on Britain for *Woman's Journal* which came to a nasty end when I described Hull as hell and the editor had to go there to apologize to the Women's Institute.

Peter was a lost soul, deeply disturbed. I took a photograph of him the next day in his shiny suit with fists clenched outside the Shambles. I believe he felt that his life was slipping away without much hope in sight. He came from a large family, born in Ashton under Lyne, four brothers in a bed, and fleas, and none the worse for it, with a mother whose weekly treat was a stout at the local and a hard-working father who liked to sing opera, emulating his idol Gigli. Peter, intensely curious, was one of those young men who know that life had more to offer, with a yearning for higher things though doubtful if he would reach them.

Strange how a life can subtly shift direction at an early stage: he went to a church school for the poor with the yearly parade through the streets when the children wore clean clothes and shoes which were put back in pawn the next day. The teachers must have been gifted, for he spoke of them often and how they kindled his interest in art and reading. My friends were startled when they learnt that his favourite book was Gibbon's *Decline and Fall of the Roman Empire*. His school arranged for the boys to join other poor children who were taken to the Hallé Orchestra in Manchester, where Sir John Barbirolli spoke to them without being patronizing, though he started with such resounding numbers as 'The Flight of the Bumble Bee' to entertain them. Peter told me that they left the hall elated.

By the time we met he was at a low ebb, turning and moaning in his sleep as if tormented. He had worked in a foundry, which he enjoyed because of the companionship, but something had gone wrong: his common-law wife had broken off their relationship and possibly through shame, he had turned his back on his family.

I often wonder if I did the right thing by befriending him. It is dangerous to open Pandora's box, but our friendship opened up his life and he was a free spirit waiting to be released. At the very least, he travelled.

We needed help to travel. The first time was one of those fraught 'freebies' when a group of journalists were flown to Rhodes and I represented *Harper's*. I sported a black eye and passed Peter off as my photographer, which would have been more convincing if he had carried a camera or even agreed to use mine. The journalists were a haughty lot, including the usual immaculately coiffed editresses who took advantage of everything on offer without ever putting a hand in their purses, maintaining a disdainful glare as if they were above such slumming.

Peter's exaltation on the plane was touching, a new experience, and we had the luck to sit at the back with Irma Kurtz where we drank such quantities of champagne that we were unaware the plane had caught fire as we landed. While the editresses teetered down the steps speechless with fear, we fell down them laughing merrily, and Peter insisted on swimming in the Mediterranean the moment we had booked in to the smart new hotel on the beach. He refused to run the gauntlet of civic receptions and smart cocktail parties, which was understandable, so I made a striking appearance with my eyepatch on my own. This was during military rule, so Rhodes was blissfully free of tourists; when we broke free from the others and lingered in Lindos it was unspoilt, with the bonus that Irma Kurtz had decided to travel independently too and provided an extra stimulus. From there, Peter and I travelled to Cos, hitched a lift on a cargo ship to Kalymnos, and an overnight ferry to Athens where I sold my Rolleiflex. Counting what money we had left, I went back to redeem it and instead of being angry the shopkeeper laughed and handed the Rollei back with a generous smile.

Another journey was less successful – a 'Peace Cruise' to Leningrad paid for by the short-lived *Mirror Magazine* whose life was almost shorter due to my bad behaviour on board the *Krupskaya*, named after Lenin's widow. It had simply not occurred to me that the passengers would be Communists, and after I toasted the anniversary of the Hungarian uprising in the bar I was branded, correctly, as a drunken trouble-maker and dissident, to be dealt with in the appropriate Soviet fashion. When a burly GPU lady tried to seize my camera, I resisted and found myself later, for the second time in my life, on the bridge being lectured by the captain. Insane with drunken rage, I thought of the authorities I had hated all my life – headmasters, officers, bank managers and brewers – and told the captain what I thought about Lenin and Communism at a time when such heresy was unheard of. Meanwhile, my volley of cables to the *Mirror Magazine* had reached the shop steward, and almost brought on a strike.

Peter had been drinking, too, and we woke in our cabin creased with hangover. When I dared emerge to find him some fruit juice, I realized I was in disgrace and we were ostracized by the other passengers except a charming elderly American couple at our table in the dining saloon who were travelling to Russia under the misapprehension that this was an ordinary cruise.

Peter and I were decanted in Copenhagen. Though so poor that I wore canvas beach shoes because I had no others, we had enough money to reassure the immigration officials, presumably expenses from the unfortunate *Mirror Magazine*. In fact they expressed their sympathy for us at being on the Soviet ship in the first place. A few minutes later we walked down the gangplank to the quayside where they saluted us as the Communist passengers watched disapprovingly from above, and drove us into the centre of this delightful town.

A lunch had been arranged in advance with my father's old friend Ejler Jørgensen, a famous restaurateur. Where most restaurants have signed photographs of film stars, the walls of Jørgensen's were lined with those of writers such as Hemingway and my father, whose books were best-sellers in Copenhagen with such titles as 'Over alle graenser' (*The Way of a Transgressor*) and 'Bag Guds ryg' (*Behind God's Back*). When my father presented Ejler with a copy of *A Mirror for Narcissus*, he inscribed it: 'Don't die until I reach you again – and we'll go to heaven with one of your Wild Ducks – and you pick the wine! SKOL!'

My father had told me about the restaurant and the dish created in his honour – 'Negley Farson's Wild Duck' – and I had had the foresight to write to Jørgensen in advance. Now an elderly man, though young in spirit, he exemplified the charm and hospitality of the Danes. He had arranged a banquet with several of his close friends, starting with fresh peeled shrimps and mayonnaise, finishing with wild strawberries, with Negley Farson's Wild Duck as the *tour de force* in between. If that was my father's favourite meal it is mine too, all washed down with whisky, to which I am usually allergic, but this was vintage malt and a different drink altogether. Learning of the débâcle on board the *Krupskaya* which I distorted so dramatically that one of the guests wrote it up in a Danish paper the next day, Jørgensen booked me into the Hotel Opera, the smallest, oldest and best in town.

I lost Peter in the Tivoli Gardens. His bed lay behind curtains on a dais at the end of the spacious, old-fashioned room, and when I parted the curtains the next morning with a merry quip about 'first orders' on the *Krupskaya* I was confronted by a middle-aged Danish woman who looked equally startled. I was not surprised that Peter had ended up with a woman, only that she was so plain, reminding me of Peter Sellers's exclamation in the film *What's New Pussycat* about his wife: 'Even *I* am prettier than she is!'

However, she proved invaluable in showing us Copenhagen, taking us to the best restaurants, where she insisted on paying. She was infatuated by Peter and would not let him out of her sight. While I drank lager in the sailors' bars in the street with the gigantic anchor at one end and porn shops in the basements, they took the boat to Malmö so she could be alone with him, though he claimed it was to bring me Alka Seltzer, which was banned in Denmark. When we took the train to England, she came too, refusing to allow us to stop off at Hamburg as I had hoped, in case Peter might escape. This was no longer amusing.

In the Colony, Muriel's intuition sensed something wrong with 'that Danish scrubber'. Peter took me aside and said we should go round the corner on some excuse, make a dash for the station and go home. Idiotically, I protested that this would be too cruel, so she came too.

By now the two Bobs had left the Grey House to live with their respective girlfriends, but they had been looking after the dogs in my absence and were eager to meet Peter's Danish 'bit', expecting a blonde beauty in her twenties rather than a middle-aged frump. Mortified, Peter ignored her completely while I wondered how to get rid of her, for he blamed me for not having left her in London. All was solved a few days later with a visit from the police, who arrested her for absconding with her employer's chequebook. The poor woman was deported to face trial for forgery. If this was her final fling I hope she remembered it as worthwhile.

◆

Somehow I came to the notice of John Anstey, editor of the weekly *Telegraph* magazine. One of the great figures of Fleet Street, he was a powerfully built man who resented subordinates, especially if they had opinions of their own. He preferred to run the supplement single-handed, which he did so successfully that when it was closed down the *Telegraph* lost 50,000 readers. He was notorious for his rapid succession of attractive secretaries, and his habit of correcting his contributors' grammar, even Graham Greene's. Kenneth Allsop was so angry when Anstey returned an article to be rewritten that he vowed he would never work for him again. I could not afford such scruples; and in any case I venerated an editor who was so punctilious that he would send a reply to a letter saying he was too busy to write at length but would do so the next day. He hated the phone as much as I did. His suggestions were constructive and he proved receptive to my ideas, which ranged from profiles and features to opinion pages, even a short story. When I suggested a feature on the art of the graveyard, to be illustrated by my own photographs, he liked the idea and suggested I should drive across Europe.

Frances, the daughter of my GI friend in Germany and nominally my god-daughter, visited the Grey House and Peter fell in love with her, a relationship I was glad to encourage. Quiet on the surface, she had an underlying humour and intelligence and the *ménage à trois* worked surprisingly well.

Somehow we had been able to buy a second-hand open Triumph, and Frances was an excellent driver, so there was no problem there. The trouble as always was money, especially as I had fallen out temporarily with my agent, who regarded Peter as a bad influence and the journey as an unnecessary jaunt. Even though she assured me that no expenses would be forthcoming, I was determined to go ahead, fuelled by optimism and Micawber's philosophy that something would turn up. Fortunately, it did. John Anstey asked me to call to discuss my plans. He poured me a drink in his sumptuous office – he had the knack of publishing features on interior decorators who might be useful – this was an honour, because he was innately shy in spite of his tough exterior. Finally he asked me, 'Don't you need some money?' He saw my expression and smiled: 'I thought you might.' Picking up the phone, he told the accounts department to arrange for a sum which seemed astounding, even though it had to cover a month's travelling through Europe. I think it was around £1000, which is why I was drinking dry martinis in the Paris Ritz a few evenings later with Peter and Frances.

Paris rarely disappoints, and everything was perfect, from the small Louisiana Hotel in the Rue de la Seine, with a market underneath my attic window and views over the roofs of the city, to the restaurant where we were allowed either spinach or gratin dauphinois with our lamb but definitely, adamantly not both. There were ample opportunities for photographs: Oscar Wilde's tomb designed by Epstein in Père Lachaise, with the balls of the winged figure broken off and a message scrawled beneath the broken stump: *Miss you Mike, love Antonio 71*. Also Brancusi's grave represented by *The Kiss*, and the elderly couple in a double bed in the cemetery at Montparnasse. Surprisingly, the most moving was the animal cemetery on an island in the Seine in the heart of Paris, where the inscriptions seemed maudlin until I appreciated that they were as heartfelt as those in Flanders.

We continued south to the quiet village of Hautrives near Lyons where the local postman, le Facteur Cheval, had built his fantasy palace over the years with a trowel, a wheelbarrow and cement, creating this edifice in the surrealist style of Gaudí, though they would not have heard of each other. He was ridiculed at the time, but the villagers now charge an entrance fee and are justifiably proud of his folly.

We coincided with the film festival at Cannes, which added to the gaiety; had drinks with Graham and Kathy Sutherland in the bungalow we found together twenty years earlier above Menton, now unrecognizable with extensions and floors of Italian marble; on to Genoa, Venice, and a climb into the mountains of Yugoslavia with the clean, fresh, memorable air of Lake Bohinsko. The next morning I looked from my bedroom window onto the same frescoed church of St James, but where was the hotel which bore the same name? There was no sign of it. I learned that it had been used as a headquarters by the Germans in the war and was burnt to the ground by the Resistance. Another change was the mountain hut of Vogel, now enlarged as a ski resort reached in minutes by a cable car, compared to the day it took us when we climbed on foot. Otherwise there was little change. They say you should never go back, but for once it was not disillusioning, though the early rapture could never be regained. I looked for the pine tree which my father made me climb that afternoon, but how could I identify it among so many, and what did it matter now?

'I didn't do much to help, did I?' said Deakin in the Golden Lion on one of my visits to London. This was as close as he came to an apology, and I laughed because it was true and there was little I could add. I understood. Apart from his insecurity, we were bound together in a mutual jealousy which defied all reason. Now that I lived in Devon – and perhaps he was envious of that – he had been vicious in my absence, pouring poison against me into Francis Bacon's ear.

Deakin had abandoned photography in favour of painting. He started with primitives, though 'sophisticates' would be more accurate for anything so calculated in its artlessness. His portraits of Queen Mary 'hung with pearls', and of tattooed sailors, were highly decorative and were bought by the Portal Gallery, but as if Deakin feared success even more than failure, he veered away the moment it was imminent and turned to collages, superimposing human eyes and mouths on arrays of vegetables and fruit with the occasional insect thrown in. Giving them titles like 'Mr Lionel Bart' or 'Miss Joan Littlewood', he explained, 'They won't be able to resist it when they see their own names'; but resist they did, though I bought one of myself, my face cut out from the cover of an Australian *TV Times*, crowned by a cauliflower, an artichoke on my chin, and several brown beetles. The one review came in the *Daily Mail*: 'I only hope that the painter's optimism will not be matched by the public's enthusiasm.' So Deakin moved on to 'Dolls' Heads', returning from the Dolls' Hospital (there really was such a place) laden with fractured and rejected heads which he decorated with transfers of bare trees so they looked like veins. At lunch in Wheeler's, where he accepted caviare because it was 'health giving' – 'Why can't you just *enjoy* it?' asked Francis, exasperated – he toyed with a bone from his poached turbot: 'I say, this would look rather good on top of one of my dolls' heads.' Francis and I groaned, but I still have that particular head, now a faded yellow. The heads were glued to plinths and cost £25, but no one was interested.

Only slightly less confident, Deakin turned to his 'Monsters,' huge Yeti-like figures made from papier-mâché and chicken wire. Gradually the Monsters, and the buckets of materials that went to their creation, filled the small upper room in Berwick Street where Deakin brought people to inspect them, including a drunken Welshman he met in the Golden Lion who promptly collapsed on the bed. Waking in the semi-darkness to find himself surrounded by the looming figures – and Deakin – he fled: 'Without so much as a thank you.' On his last visit to the Grey House, Deakin spoke affectionately of his Monsters in his new role as Dr Frankenstein, saying, 'How nice they would look dotted about in your little wood, peering through the branches.' It was too expensive to bring them down and they ended in the gutter of Berwick Street, lying in strange attitudes, for the dustmen to consign them to some rubbish dump.

When he abandoned art as he had photography, Francis came to his rescue by paying his rent and giving him money, though Deakin denied this angrily with tirades against Francis's meanness, intended as a smokescreen. He was terrified that people might suspect he had more money than he pretended, furious when he was noticed through the open door of Wheeler's enjoying some oysters at the bar on his own at twelve noon when he did not expect anyone to see him. His meanness was so integral to his façade of poverty that even the lay-abouts in the Lion were glad to flatter their downtrodden egos by buying him drinks.

My visits to London were so rare that I was not invited to the opening of the great Francis Bacon retrospective in Paris in October 1971. Perhaps he did not want me there because he was annoyed that I sold the *Surgeon's Head*, but it is more likely that I was overlooked because I was no longer around and his life was hectic. I should have liked to join the gang which set out with Muriel, Deakin, Ian and Thea Porter, especially if I had been able to go with Peter, but I did not have the funds and was scarcely aware what was happening until I received a missive from Deakin: 'A strained lunch at Wheeler's. George morose and not drinking in readiness for Paris.'

This was George Dyer, who had dominated Francis's life for the past eight years. Violent, jealous, and yet somehow pathetic, George had made intermittent suicide attempts, genuine or not, during that time; he finally succeeded just as Mme Pompidou was opening a reception held in Francis's honour.

Deakin's reaction to the tragedy was shocking. At the end of a long letter he added a PPS – 'How's about George's demise!' Was that all it meant? By then he was more concerned about himself, describing his four days in Paris as a blur of brandy, illness and purple hearts. He was going there if it killed him, and it helped to do so.

The Paris *histoire* could not have been less like your imaginings. Far from nightly dancing the *Merry Widow* at Maxim's until dawn, ospreys

On my balcony in Narrow Street overlooking the Thames at
Limehouse when the river teemed with ships.

Graham Sutherland.

Francis Bacon.

Above: With Bacon at the fair in Soho Square.

Below: At Charlie Brown's in Limehouse, with Deakin, Bacon, and dockers.

for dear Dan from his old friend, with much affection George

Gallery, the art quiz I devised for Channel 4. George Melly, Maggi Hambling and Vincent Price, our first guest.

Henry Williamson.

Jeremy Thorpe.

Right: Crossing the Caucasus in 1992. My venture on the unfortunate horse's back lasted no more than a matter of minutes.

Below: Gilbert & George at the opening of their exhibition in Moscow.

Peter Bradshaw by the pool at the Grey House.

In the peaceful backyard at Appledore.

in my hair and my throat ablaze with diamonds, it is a tear-jerker of unparalleled misery. To begin with, my illness had reached its climax – necessary details to give you the true picture, mouth and throat full of ulcers, unable to eat, big toe oozing pus, itching blisters around my arse and my prick skinned and raw. I had been having treatment for eight weeks and was due to be hospitalized but put it off until after the opening. After two weeks here now [he was writing from a homeo-pathic ward for tropical diseases in the East End] everything under perfect control and much to Francis's annoyance had nothing to do with drink, or as the doc put it so delicately, my social life.

Distrusting doctors though I do, even I was stunned when I learned that they had been giving him the wrong treatment. Deakin had lung cancer, and was sent to the Westminster Hospital where he was admit-ted to the Marie Celeste Ward, a tactless name in such circumstances, from which he wrote to me that he was holding court: 'Signed copies, champagne, the vintage port, fine champagne cognac, the endless visitors, flowers everywhere. The whole thing was out of hand and exhausting. I adored your telegram particularly after the public state-ment in The Colony "I hope to God he dies under the knife tomorrow." History does not relate what the people who do not know either of us thought. Stitches out today so not too bad.'

This was written on 11 April 1972. A later report stated: 'Successful, was an *early* cancer, all removed.' He planned to convalesce on the Greek island of Poros, where he was going to live in 'a balconied place on the harbour' arranged by an American friend who had one eye and was known as Black Patch. Francis was paying and Deakin urged me to join him: 'Now there's no need to purse your lips in bitter envy. Because all you have to do is poison all the dogs, sell Tobacco Road and live happy ever after on the proceeds. If this goes against the grain, then bring the dogs. So simple!'

This is why I flew to Athens, spending a flea-bitten night in a small hotel in Piraeus before I took the ferry to Poros. As we approached the harbour I looked eagerly for any sign of that familiar figure holding court at one of the outside tables. There was so much news to tell and to hear. There was no sign nor sound of him, so I found a room and crossed the island where I swam lengthily, submerging myself for as long as I could hold my breath to drown the Piraean bugs. Dis-appointed not to find Deakin, I went to the police station the next morning, for they were bound to have heard of a talkative little man and an American with a black eye-patch, but they knew of no one who fitted either description, and after three days of dwindling hope I flew back to England.

'Buried him this morning, deah!' cried Muriel as I opened the door. A letter had been waiting for me. 'Not a chance of Poros for a couple of months. As half the lung was taken away, I have to learn to breathe all over again. It is infuriating to be so alert and on the ball and yet so physically helpless. No plane would take me – but as soon as I can teeter up a gangplank for me to go night sleeper to Paris, on to the Orient Express for Venice – then to glide down the Adriatic in a white steamer to Piraeus where Black Patch is spending the entire summer.'

Instead, when he left hospital he was driven straight to Brighton, where Francis had arranged for his convalescence in the Ship Hotel. Playing the self-made man who has 'just come down from North', Deakin toured various pubs and met our mutual friend Rex Crutchfield, who was so pleased to see him that they continued to drink in a club until the early hours. The next afternoon Deakin rang for tea, and was dead when they brought it.

He had signed a hospital form stating that Francis Bacon was the next of kin. 'It was the last dirty trick he played on me,' said Francis, who had the unenviable task of going to Brighton to identify the body: 'They lifted up the sheet and there she was, her trap shut for the first time in her life.'

'Would that be Mr Deakin?' they asked him.

'It most certainly would.'

Francis began to laugh: 'Well, you know how it is, I can't stand those formalities. Well, they told me I needn't be next of kin after all, the state could look after him. "I know just what that means," I told them. "He'll have a pauper's funeral and everyone in Soho will say I'm the meanest man in London."'

'Oh, no,' they assured him, 'we've been in touch with Mr Deakin's bank manager and there are more than sufficient funds to give him a good send-off.'

'What?' I exclaimed, 'you mean Deakin had money all the time?'

'So it would seem,' he replied carefully. 'In fact I did give him the proceeds of one of the pictures. Seems such a waste that all of it goes to the state. Well, there it is.' For a moment he looked dejected, and I was stunned. Then we started to laugh, which is not a bad way to remember the funniest man I have known.

Seventeen

The Outcast

W HEN I WAS a boy, living with my parents in North Devon, Henry Williamson took me on an otter hunt along the remoter stretches of the River Torridge. It seemed odd that anyone should want to kill such an animal, especially the author of *Tarka the Otter*, and I was delighted when we failed to catch one. I remember my anguish as we bowled along the narrow lines with their high hedges in his open Aston Martin, and he reduced me to speechless tears with his assurance that Hitler had been a good and misunderstood man. At the end of the war, this was heresy in the eyes of a schoolboy. When I returned from my first year at Cambridge, Henry took me aside and told me with solemnity that I should be tolerant of my father: 'The old bulls and the young bulls, you know.' I did not know, and felt that Henry was trespassing. In my eyes my father had no need of tolerance. Henry played on the susceptibilities of boys and girls, especially girls, to a point that was sadistic.

Henry was the most infuriating, introspective, impatient and irascible man I have known, and he could be cruel to the many women who loved him. None of this mattered, because he was lovable too, a bad-tempered innocent. I grew to be fond of him.

Like many nature lovers, his attitude to animals was ambivalent. When Barry Driscoll arrived at Ox's Cross with his family to discuss his illustrations for a new paperback of *Tarka*, Henry crashed into the caravan at midnight to ask if they had any milk. 'I'm awfully sorry,' Barry pointed out, 'but we've only just arrived and we haven't had time to shop. Don't you have any milk?'

'No,' said Henry, looking madder than usual. 'The Jews have taken over the village and they've drunk all the milk.'

Oh *no*, thought Barry after he left, not the Jews, already. The next morning he was careful not to mention either the Jews or the milk but thought it would please Henry if he told him that he heard a grasshopper warbler in the early morning – and I thought how marvellous to hear this in your field.' Henry glared: 'I hope you haven't come here to talk about bloody animals!'

My mother said she knew when Henry was coming down the drive: she would hear the hens squawking in their coop above, the cat would leap out of the window and the dachshund squeeze under the sofa, and then the naturalist appeared.

At a dinner party when Henry failed to turn up, the conversation turned to him with comments which may have been hilarious but were made at his expense. It was a fine evening and we went outside afterwards to find the initials H.W. laid out carefully on the flagstones with twigs and grasses. We looked at them dismayed. My father broke the guilty silence. 'Tarka the rotter, that elfin son of a bitch!'

They enjoyed a love-hate relationship from the time my father attacked Henry verbally in the Savage Club, accusing him of being 'all balled up about sex'. Another time, when my father was drunk in Barnstaple on market day, when the pubs stayed open all afternoon, he pinioned Henry in one of the stalls in the Three Tuns, preventing his escape as he told him terrible truths in his whisky tirade. 'You're just trying to make a legend for yourself. Now all this stuff about your Devon forebears – you said your mother came from Ireland and now you're of old Devon stock. You're bogus, Henry, you're bogus . . .'

Ken and Betty Allsop were there too, listening to this 'incoherent stream, very drunken and blurred, and HW sat there shrivelling under it, his face stiff, his eyes big, until after making one or two vain attempts to ward it off, first to joke about it, he leaped out and said, "I'm going, I'm not going to stand any more of this."'

Outside he raged, explaining to the Allsops that he had written to my father saying that the Genealogical Society had found that his mother descended from an old Devon family now extinct, and believed this was why he was able to write about the Devon people so well – like a swallow returning to its English birthplace.

Evidently this harmless piece of information put my father in a rage in which I suspect there was a tinge of jealousy, for he knew that Henry was a fine writer. The words cascaded so thrillingly that it was a joy to read them aloud, but not when Henry did so interminably in his sepulchral, flat voice. While Ken Allsop left to have a haircut, Betty accompanied Henry to the banks of the River Taw where he decided to throw himself in, though she pointed out that as the tide was out he would only land in the mud. At this he decided to return to the Three Tuns to sue my father for slander, but when he got there he found he had been collected by taxi, depriving Henry of even that satisfaction.

Henry gained his revenge in the last volume of his *Chronicle of Ancient Sunlight*. His long-suffering editor at Macdonald was our neighbour Malcolm Elwin, a gentle, bearded literary cove who wrote biographical tomes which were heavy going, though they provided a goldmine of material to be filched by other writers who adopted a jauntier approach and became best-sellers. His wife, Eve, was an American, and Henry added to Malcolm's discomfiture by falling in love with his sixteen-year-old stepdaughter Susan. After reading *The Gale of the World*, Eve Elwin phoned me anxiously, urging me not to read it, so I bought a copy that afternoon. By this time my parents were dead.

The *Chronicle* is one of the literary achievements of the century, and the first two volumes, *The Dark Lantern* and *Donkey Boy*, evoke Edwardian London with convincing detail, though two publishers rejected them before Macdonald accepted, complaining that the 'hero' Willie Maddison, a corruption of Henry's nickname at school of Mad Willie, was unsympathetic. As Henry told me indignantly, he was not *supposed* to be 'nice.'

The Gale of the World, however, is a rum affair, with sexual descriptions which may have been influenced by Henry's infatuation with a young, bright but neurotic writer called Ann Quinn who dared to tell him that his books needed a 'modern approach', like that of her own novel *Berg* which was sexually explicit. Unfortunately, Henry's approach was bilious compared to the majesty of the early volumes, and the sex was smutty rather than salacious: 'Wanting revenge, because my father raped me when I was a child, was it punishment for coming on him when he was frigging the nanny-goat behind the hedge? If I wrote that, no one would believe it. Mother found out and I had to sleep with Granny afterwards . . .' This is Laura's memory of her abortion: 'Was it when we started to walk upright? Animals are shapely, compared with women after twenty-five. Black brassieres and French knickers – trap for John Thomas Esquire – and finally cancer of the breast from too much mauling. God I am human bait, nothing more.' Demented stuff which Kenneth Allsop found so revolting that he felt unable to review the book, though it was dedicated to him.

The moment the character of the drunken American journalist Osgood Nilsson appeared, he was unmistakably my father, with the same wound in his leg, the author of a best-seller called *Sinner's Way* (*The Way of a Transgressor*), with a grandfather who was a Confederate general whose description fits the *opéra bouffe* photograph of General Negley in uniform which I have with me now. My mother, or rather Mrs Nilsson, came of 'Irish lineage' and her father wrote 'gothic extravaganzas' (Bram Stoker, her uncle, wrote *Dracula*). She is depicted as a tiresome gossip, which was unfair, but I found the characterization of Osgood amusing, remembering my father's verbal abuse. It was Henry's libellous last laugh.

I met Henry on the sands below the Grey House the morning after he had written the last page of *The Gale of the World* and knew that the *Chronicle* was finished. He looked appalled as he told me he thought he had made a mistake, that it should have been an autobiographical work all along, and not a series of fifteen novels. I felt an instinctive sympathy, and when we coincided at Barnstaple station after the book was published, we walked across the bridge to Mugford's, chatting amiably until I felt a pang of filial loyalty and feared I was betraying my father. Over our drinks, I wondered what I could say that would hurt Henry, who was cheerfully unaware of the impending retribution.

'You know,' I remarked casually, 'what Oswald Mosley said about you?'

Caught in the headlights, he shook his head nervously.

'He said, "We do like old Henry, but he does take everything so seriously."'

I might have felled him with an axe. With my father's instinct, I had found his Achilles heel. He left ashen and stooped, leaving me aghast at my cruelty. Over the next few days he sent me a relay of letters. They began stiffly: the first was dated 9 p.m., 22 December 1969, and was posted from Ilfracombe:

Dear Dan,

I am most sorry that you felt you had to speak (almost in public) as you did in Mugford's tonight. And I can only repeat, with *truth*, that I have never had to 'get my own back' on your father Negley. I understood him. And how the alcohol disturbed his judgement, and released at times, a sense of his own social superiority: as when he produced in public General Negley's photograph in order to say to one or another of his pub-stooges 'you never had a general in *your* family, you're a no-good man.' This was repeated in many local pubs to various people near him.

This was true of Osgood Nilsson rather than my father, who never spoke like that and whose photograph of the general was large and handsomely framed, hardly something he would have carried with him on a pub crawl. Henry continued: 'I had nothing to get back. I liked Negley but loathed his remarks when drunk. So did everyone. Your mother used to apologize for them – it wasn't necessary we understood Negley. We knew how his leg sapped his vitality, year after year.'

This impression of my father as a neurotic remnant was far from the reality, but it continued over pages with a seeping bitterness: 'But when he tried to *humiliate* those whom he considered his social inferiors – as he often did when poisoned by alcohol, it was "a bit much". It was tedious. He did it to me sometimes but it was water off a duck's back. "I knew my place." And I remained overtly and inwardly *friendly*.'

I of all people, who have inherited my father's disastrous gift for alcoholic verbal abuse, can see how funny that was, for my father's closest friends in Devon were the postman and the taxi-driver, and he regarded no one as his 'social inferior'. A drunk flails verbally as he tries to find the vulnerable spot, but he is not a snob – unless he is one already. Returning to the vexed subject of Oswald Mosley, Henry wrote, 'Your remarks – or quotes – of what O.M. said to you are very sad to me. I was never really a fascist. I cared for England, I fought for England in 1914–18. I saw another war coming. And so joined the BU [British Union] as late as 1937 in Norfolk; begged to do so by Lady D [a Norfolk neighbour, Lady Downe] a Blackshirt patriot. And having joined I was always loyal to O.M. – though it led to much hardship and suffering. I'd do the same for Negley, or you if you were in trouble.' This was true. Henry was a liar, describing himself in an early story as 'a fake merchant', but his loyalty to his friends was absolute. Time and time again I heard how he sprang to my defence when I was criticized in North Devon, where gossip is a pastime.

With the sweetness which was also characteristic, he came full circle, starting a further letter:

I believe what you said re O.M. He spoke to *me* like that, once, at Nicky's wedding reception at the Savoy (1947 or 1948). [Nicholas Mosley, Lord Ravensdale was Mosley's son by his first wife, the daughter of Curzon]. I begged him NOT to form another party – 'European Union'. I wanted him to write his Memoirs instead. He was NEWS! but bad news. He let loose a sarcastic glance at me and said 'Your place in our Movement, Henry, is to stand at the Savage Club window as we go past down below, and to say 'I shouldn't be surprised if there is something in it.' Well, I didn't mind that. I'd asked for it. But twenty years later, Diana [*née* Mitford, Mosley's second wife] said 'You did advise Kit to write his Memoirs and keep quiet – I remember.' She was then white-haired and had to be sustained by pills, poor darling.

By now I was absorbed by the voluminous correspondence provoked by my remark in Mugford's, and replied in kind, prompting another letter:

Thank you for your letter, dear Dan. I'm very low – and have been for months – all 'elan' gone – and the death wish strong and constant. I was so happy, too, when I saw you in the summer. Your letter so cheering. I worried that you were so unhappy. You needn't be. I was very fond of your Papa and Mama, and remain so.
Love from Henry.

Henry's loyalty to Oswald Mosley, which explains his lasting unpopularity, needs to be seen in the context of the derelict Norfolk farm which he took over and transformed during the war, sharing Mosley's belief that farming was the backbone of British life and economy. Politically naïve, Henry was mesmerized by Hitler at the Nuremberg rallies, but this was when Germany seemed resurrected after the punitive terms of the Versailles Treaty. If Henry was seduced, he was not alone. In his contrary way, I have always thought he was a patriot. When I wrote his biography, *Henry*, I realized that everything stemmed from his experience in the trenches in the First World War, so traumatic that if you came out of them completely sane you must have been dotty to begin with. If Henry had lost an eye or a leg, his views might have been forgiven, but he was scarred inwardly. Above all, he took part in the Christmas truce, when the German soldiers and the Tommies joined together across no man's land, exchanged photos and cigarettes, played football and sang, until it was midnight and they resumed the slaughter. Discovering that the Boche thought they were fighting for a rightful cause, as he did, he was convinced that 'the two cousin nations' should never go to war again, for if they did Britain would lose her empire and become a second-rate power: which is exactly what happened. He told me that if the Germans invaded, he would have defended the farm with a pitchfork if necessary, but he alienated the locals, though they admired his wife Loetitia, and he was foolish to paint Mosley's lightning insignia on a barn door where it remains today. He was not arrested under Rule 18B, as he claimed, but he was questioned by the police after villagers reported that the white roads on his farm were pointers for the German bombers. This absurd rumour ricocheted to Devon where people said that his field at Ox's Cross was spread with lime to direct the German planes to bomb Chivenor aerodrome a few miles away. The charges were so ridiculous that Henry was released at once as a harmless eccentric, much to his indignation.

Henry had outraged his readers in 1936 with the infamous foreword to *The Flax of Dream*: 'I salute the great man across the Rhine, whose life symbol is the happy child.' He suffered for this error for the rest of his life.

When I interviewed him for television in 1975, to mark his eightieth birthday, I sat with Henry beside the breakwaters below the old lighthouse on the Torridge estuary and he spoke of Hitler again. 'Of course he was a great man, but so many great men turn out to be fiends and devils because they go too far. He wanted to avoid war with us, but went the wrong way to get it. He was a very brave soldier and he loved England.'

That Hitler was a soldier like himself had stuck in Henry's brain like a needle in the groove of an old gramophone record, confusing him to such an extent that he began to believe he had seen Hitler in the Christmas truce. A shameless liar, he embraced his lies: 'He has the truest eyes I have ever seen in a man's face, he is an ex-corporal of the Linz Regiment which opposed my regiment under Messines Hill on Christmas Day 1914. We made a truce then, which must never be broken.' A check-up revealed that Hitler had not served in the Linz Regiment, but the *List*, named after its commander. The mistake hardly matters, for if you believe in something so passionately it acquires a sort of a truth. Trying to put the matter straight, I asked him directly if he had met Hitler.

'Yes, of course,' he whispered.

'How did he strike you?' I asked unwisely, for this gave him the chance to indulge in some shadow boxing: 'He didn't strike me. I laid him flat first.' After the laughter the hushed reverence resumed with a remark about saintliness which prompted me to ask if he was comparing Hitler with Christ.

'I am in a way, of course I am, because Hitler was human and Jesus was human, he wasn't just floating about in coloured pyjamas or something like that! Hitler told me there must never be war with England; if so everything would come to an end. There were tears in his eyes. He was a very emotional man.' There were tears in Henry's eyes as well. The fantasy had taken over.

At this low period in Devon, when both of us were vulnerable, I grew fond of Henry, even loved him. Myself battling on, with the Grey House gradually being stripped of possessions like the scene in a film when the wooden carriages are broken up to fuel the engine, leaving the skeleton of a train behind; Henry growing old and forgetful, losing his battered briefcase apparently filled with money, making everyone feel guilty until it turned up again.

One morning I found him in the porch where he must have been waiting patiently for at least an hour listening to me typing. 'You should have called me,' I said. He replied that he would never disturb a fellow writer, which pleased me greatly.

Another time he came down the drive in the afternoon, exclaiming, 'I thought it was time I saw you again'. I did not have the heart to tell him he had called that morning. His physical stamina remained remarkable. Once he walked to the Grey House from Ilfracombe, a distance of ten miles: 'I hope you've got the wood for the coffin!' he gasped. Frequently on his own, he sought my company and tried to be congenial even though it went against his grain. Many people failed to appreciate his schoolboy humour, calling the Prince of Wales 'the Pragger-Wagger' and throwing bread rolls when he was taken to a restaurant. He greeted food as if unused to it, which may have been the case at this late period. 'Is this *sugared* tea?' he asked. 'It's very nice. I feel rather wan. I've gone down ten pounds.' Seeing him huddled in his overcoat, I asked if he was feeling cold and he shook his head. 'I don't feel anything. I don't expect I'd feel it if you hit me.' His looks had always been blazing; now he resembled a great grey tree in winter whose leaves are falling, leaving the branches bare.

People started to avoid him. 'Are you expecting guests?' he asked me. 'No, why?' 'Most people seem to be expecting guests when I call on them nowadays,' he sighed.

It did not suit him to be mellow. I noticed that when he stroked my dog Bonzo in an effort to please me, he ruffled her fur the wrong way, whispering, 'Poor little doggy-poggy, poor little man,' while she watched him askance.

It was painful to learn how much he was looking forward to his eightieth birthday in the belief that he would be honoured, speaking about 'the O.M. Boys' as he called Hardy, Masefield and Galsworthy, who had presented him with the Hawthornden Prize for *Tarka*, claiming that they told him he deserved the O.M. as much as they did, an unlikely remark to make to a new young writer.

His mind was going. On 9 April 1975 he wrote me a long letter from his cottage in Ilfracombe which dredged up many of the former memories, including Masefield's 'You have written more classics in the English language than any man now living,' followed by Henry's comment – 'Well, well.' The prospect of my TV programme for his eightieth birthday increased his expectation that he would be recognized at last as the greatest writer alive.

Dan, *in confidence*; I feel I am only litter left . . .
Now the son of dear Negley Farson offers a new hope. Thank you Dan! I did hope that 1 December would be kept dark: but what's the odds? *Times* and *Telegraph* keep tabs on such items. But it's rather like prophesying one's own doom – but no! Heart and lungs etc. are sound . . .

My article in the *Telegraph Magazine*, 'Recognizing Henry Williamson', was published the day before his birthday, and the response confirmed the loyalty still felt by his readers who disregarded the politics. I received close on fifty letters from strangers expressing their love for his books and admiration for the man. One wrote, 'I believe he came close to holding the key to life itself.' Henry received scores.

The television programme showed him reading aloud with sweeping views over the estuary, of Baggy Point, and walking across the old American road bordered by the Great Field of Braunton, picking up insects and flowers as he went, having a picnic with Peter,

Frances, myself and the dogs below the old lighthouse, a leisurely, lyrical film.

I was with him as he waited for the honours to arrive as they had for Hardy, disguised as Edward Driffield in Somerset Maugham's delightful *Cakes and Ale*. On Driffield's eightieth: 'I think you'd have to go a long way to find gathered together such a collection of distinguished people as got out from that train at Blackstable. It was awfully moving when the PM presented the old man with the Order of Merit.'

The only people who left the train at Barnstaple were Henry's sons. At least they gave him a celebration lunch at the Imperial Hotel but there were no honours, no Order of Merit. This was not for lack of trying. Ken Allsop pursued the suggestion and so did Victor Bonham Carter in his role as Secretary of the Royal Literary Fund. He wrote to me ruefully in 1980: 'As to the Honour, I think his pro-Hitler stance was never forgiven. I have no proof of this, but I assumed it to be the case.'

For Henry's centenary on 1 December 1995 I wrote a one-man play, and the only director to reply at length was the busiest, Richard Eyre of the National Theatre. After taking the trouble to explain where it did not work dramatically, he concluded that it was a picture of a 'cantankerous bigot', which showed how far I had failed in my intention. Cantankerous, undoubtedly, but though his views were rigid they were not due to bigotry. When Henry exclaimed that Mosley was 'a great man!' in our television film, he was expressing an absolute loyalty, a quality that is viewed with suspicion today.

Perhaps the reason for Henry's neglect, apart from the lingering stink of his politics, is simply that his qualities are those which are now condemned as old-fashioned: lyrical, loyal, romantic, compassionate – and, even, patriotic. His son Harry told me that Henry said he wanted to die by going out 'on Baggy Point at a very low tide and climb as far out on the rocks as I can and go to sleep in the sunshine and be washed off and drift out to sea'. I wish he had. Always this mention of sunlight – *A Chronicle of Ancient Sunlight*; *As the Sun Shines*; *The Sun in the Sands*. That was Henry's illusion, that he could see the sun without shadows, a clearer purity. But there are shadows and they closed in at the end. When he suffered from senile dementia his daughter Margaret placed him in the care of the monks at Twyford Abbey on the outskirts of London. By now his mind was hopelessly stuck in the First World War and he wandered about harmlessly, still upright, saluting those who visited him. One morning he escaped and was found naked on the platform of the nearest railway station; perhaps at the back of his mind he was yearning for Baggy Point once more.

Eighteen

Jeremy Thorpe and the
Queensberry Rules

THE Right Honourable Jeremy Thorpe was another subject for an HTV profile.

Jeremy had been kind to me, and my mother and father were devoted to him. Their visitors' book shows how often he stayed at the Grey House, using it as a base when he fought and finally won the North Devon constituency for the Liberals in 1959. A chameleon personality, he delighted my mother with his mimicry and gossip while holding my father's interest with his first-hand knowledge of contemporary politics as a new MP. I am sure his affection for them was genuine and not motivated by the vaulting ambition which finally o'erleapt itself. Yet I had a reservation. My father might have agreed if I had confronted him with my suspicion that there was something flawed about the man. Nearly everyone in Devon, particularly people's mothers, adored him and thought his brown suit, watch-chain and rakish trilby hat were the essence of an English gentleman, though they reminded me of a bookie at a seaside race-track. But he had the gift of making his constituents feel better when they met him. With a phenomenal memory, he not only remembered their names but those of their dogs and cats and piglets. As he leapt over the benches in Barnstaple's Pannier Market on Fridays, he greeted the stall-holders in their own peculiar language – 'Mornin' me hanse!' 'And how be you, my lover!' – which sounded patronizing to me but delighted the local women, usually as tough as their 'free-range' chickens.

I had many reasons to be grateful to him. He was the chairman of *Seconds Out* when I made my first television appearance with Frank Owen, and we both worked for *This Week*, though not together.

Though increasingly in demand as a rising political figure, he spared time to see me when I was in the doldrums and needed work, agreeing to be interviewed for a woman's magazine for an article which was never published. After taking me to lunch near his new home at Cobbaton he drove me to the top of the hill overlooking North Devon and Lundy Island to see the memorial to his first wife Caroline who had been killed in a car crash at the age of thirty-two.

By the time we made our television film, *The Man in the Middle*, he had married (in 1973) Marion, the former Countess of Harewood, and he spoke to me of the dark period in his life following the death of Caroline: 'One recovers because one has to, but I was completely numb for a year.' He thought of giving up politics, but his colleagues told him not to. He was comforted by his conviction that there must be a life after death: 'I never thought you'd be snuffed out, otherwise it would be a bad joke. You grow in stature . . . any experience which tests you must have some effect on you, whether it is good or bad is not for me to say.' When I asked him if he was the stronger for it, he replied, 'I don't know if I could go through it again – one never knows.'

This was after a general election in which the Liberal vote was the largest in living memory and he became 'the man in the middle' with his handful of Liberal MPs in the House of Commons. Desperate to form a coalition, Edward Heath invited him to Number Ten, supposedly to offer him the post of either Home or Foreign Secretary, with Scotland going to the former Liberal leader Jo Grimond. At a dinner party at Cobbaton I asked Jeremy why he had not accepted. Looking uncomfortable, he explained that he could not have carried the Liberal Party with him if he had.

I persisted: 'But if you had been seen to hold office, filmed coming in and out of Number Ten, you could have resigned on a point of principle a few months later and your position would have been strengthened.' He gave an evasive answer and joined the other guests. In the film, I asked if he would like to be prime minister and he was evasive again, though he believed he would live to see a Liberal administration. When pressed, he agreed: 'I don't think you can talk in personalities, and if you ask me if I would be the leader, I don't know.' He smiled: 'But if you ask would I *like* to be prime minister, I'll answer unequivocally – *yes!*'

At no point in the days we spent filming together did I have an inkling of the danger he was in as he and Marion played with Caroline's son Rupert on the lawn.

The permutations of politics can be bizarre. If Heath had succeeded in his attempt to form a coalition, he might have continued as prime minister and Mrs Thatcher would not have seized the leadership of the Tory party in the aftermath of its defeat. If it had not been for a dog called Rinka, Mrs Thatcher might not have gone to war over the Falklands. Thorpe gave an evasive answer regarding that coalition; so did Edward Heath when I raised the subject, telling me it was dropped because Thorpe demanded proportional representation. Both men were economical with the truth, for they knew that Thorpe was under suspicion of conspiring to murder, though Heath insisted to me that Thorpe was not under police investigation at the time. Even so, it is unthinkable that Scotland Yard, or a colleague in the cabinet, did not warn him that such a political marriage was likely to end in disaster.

The first I knew of the mayhem behind the scenes was at a party in the Haymarket to celebrate the birth of *This Week* twenty years earlier. At my low ebb, I was anxious to show that I was still around, if only to prove it to myself, so it was encouraging to meet the people I had worked with and to find them friendly. I was talking to Robert Kee and Ludovic Kennedy when Thorpe, who was guest of honour, made the welcoming speech. He had already mentioned me glowingly in an article in the *TV Times*, and in his speech too he did me proud: 'The experimentation [of early ITV] went on. Young men like Ludovic Kennedy, Robin Day, Geoffrey Johnson Smith and Chris Chataway were tried out and retained as newscasters. Dan Farson, who follows the tradition of his father Negley as a superb journalist, was launched on his first telecast in a debate with journalist Frank Owen which I chaired. He was stunned into silence through terror during a run-through and was given a pep pill. The result was such a cataract of words during the live show that Frank was struck speechless and the chairman rendered impotent. Dan is still going strong.'

That was the gist of it and I tried to look bashful as people laughed and applauded. Afterwards he led me away from a group of old friends: after such generosity I could hardly refuse his request for 'a private word'. He looked unusually strained.

Sitting down in a corner, he asked, 'Have you met my nut?'

This was the first time I heard of Norman Scott, apparently one of those odd characters who attach themselves to celebrities and make their life hell. I promised to let Jeremy know if I came across him.

In the way these things happen, as soon as I heard the name of Norman Scott it cropped up everywhere. In Barnstaple I was told he was hawking a ghosted book about Jeremy in which I was mentioned, though I could not understand why and no one seemed sure of the details. Then there was a report on 1 November in the *Somerset Free Press* of the shooting of Norman Scott's Great Dane, Rinka, on a desolate stretch of Exmoor on a cold and windy night. This was too much like Sherlock Holmes to be taken seriously, except for a surprising reference to the leader of the Liberal Party and the quote from his agent in Barnstaple, Mrs Lilian Prowse, who admitted: 'About five years ago, he [Scott] issued threats against Mr Thorpe, who took the case up with his lawyer, Lord Goodman.' This was the first time their names had been linked in public.

A few days later I found myself sitting next to Norman Scott at the bar in the Market Inn in Barnstaple. I remarked, unfeelingly, that he had probably shot the dog himself, which promptly reduced him to tears. It took a long time before I realized that the most fantastic claims in this bizarre affair were true. I wrote to Jeremy as requested, confirming that Scott seemed determined to destroy him, a letter that came back to haunt me. In fact I did not take Scott that seriously, nor his threats. He seemed far too weak to carry them through and, perversely, I rather liked his sense of humour.

The scandal broke on 31 January 1976 in the courtroom at the new civic centre in Barnstaple, where Jeremy had his constituency headquarters. The charge against Scott was trivial – obtaining £14.60 dishonestly from Social Security supplementary benefits – but it gave him the chance to seize publicity in open court. The television networks had been alerted. 'I am being hounded by people just because of my sexual relationship with Jeremy Thorpe,' he asserted. 'The whole thing gets worse and worse. I must say it, and this is why all this has happened.' He was placed on probation for two years and the accusation hit the headlines. Thorpe issued a swift denial: 'It is well over twelve years since I last saw or spoke to Mr Scott. There is no truth in his wild allegations.'

It is part of the nature of scandal that it is seldom the original offence which creates it, but the surrounding deceptions. It was Wilde's action in suing Queensberry that led to his own trial; Profumo's lie to the House of Commons led to his downfall.

I have often wondered what might have happened if Jeremy had made a statement admitting that in 1961 he had sex with Norman Scott, who had been a nuisance afterwards, and though that was regrettable it belonged to the past. Why didn't he come clean? He might have enlisted public sympathy if he had done so. I asked Douglas Potter, the genial chairman of the Torridge Council and a former mayor of Barnstaple, who replied emphatically: 'If he had made such a statement it would have been forgotten in a fortnight, and he would have sympathy. I asked him why he didn't do this, and he replied that Lord Goodman advised him not to.'

I have my doubts about Goodman, but in this I suspect he was correct. To start with, it would have been a mistake to underrate the tenacity of Norman Scott, who had all the fury of the scorned. He and Jeremy drove in harness in their persecution of each other, oblivious to the precipice ahead. It also underrates Jeremy's ambition. When Heath invited him to Downing Street the Liberals held the balance of power with a crucial six million votes. Thorpe was the man of the giddy moment as well as the man in the middle, and he was convinced that nothing and no one should prevent him in his bid for power.

When he told me that he had offered his resignation to his fellow Liberal MPs after Caroline's death, he did not mention that Norman Scott had gone to the House of Commons to confront Lord Byers, David Steel and Emlyn Hooson, and repeat his allegations. Thorpe admitted that he knew Scott 'slightly', but assured them that if there had been a homosexual relationship he would resign. They confirmed their absolute trust.

Scott was paid off in two instalments amounting to £2500 on polling day by David Holmes, the best man at Jeremy's first marriage. This did not buy his silence and he went to Tim Keigwin, the Conservative candidate, claiming that his life was in danger. Keigwin had the decency not to raise the matter during the campaign, and the £2500 did have the effect of suppressing two incriminating letters sent by Norman Scott to Peter Bessell, a former Liberal MP.

When I asked Norman why he was pursuing the vendetta, he replied that he was doing it for England – 'To prevent any possibility of Thorpe leading a coalition. Also for the sake of my son Benjamin, so that he should know that sort of man his father is, and why I did what I have done.' Startled to learn that Scott had a son, I pointed out that the boy would not thank him for dragging his name into a public scandal. I began to suspect that Scott was neurotic but sincere.

Another extraordinary aspect of the affair was the length of time it took to brew, thanks to Jeremy's smokescreen and Norman's apparent unreliability. Jeremy came to see me intermittently at the Grey House and I suspect he was trying to sound me out, unsure of how far he could go. Neither of us had ever mentioned our sexuality; though I am sure he had no doubt of mine, it had not occurred to me that he might have had the same interests. It is possible that he assumed I might be on his side for that reason.

The background he revealed was alarming. Scott had been making these charges for years, but they had been hushed up by a sympathetic press. Understandably evasive, Jeremy implied that Scott had seen Caroline at their home and confronted her with the truth of his relationship with her husband. This was shortly after the early 1970 election when the Liberals did so badly that Thorpe barely scraped home with a majority of 369 votes. Returning to London the day after Scott's confrontation, Jeremy took his son Rupert by train while Caroline drove her estate car, colliding with a lorry at a roundabout on the A30. The driver testified that she seemed to be heading directly towards him. She died in hospital soon afterwards. Inevitably there was speculation that she had committed suicide.

Scott called at Cobbaton again, in 1975, and the door was opened by Marion who went to Jeremy: 'I think it's your nut. He wants to see you.' Jeremy refused to see him, and now wondered if that had been a fatal mistake, a missed chance for a reconciliation which could have averted the tragedy. 'I believe there was still some love left,' he declared solemnly.

Surely that was all that was needed – a heart-to-heart talk over a drink to thrash it all out, with an intermediary to bring them to their senses. Except for one crucial factor, and this was why Lord Goodman was astute in telling Jeremy to deny everything about their relationship: in 1961 a homosexual act constituted a criminal offence. For the leader of the Liberal Party, it was unthinkable that he should be accused of breaking the law with a young man of twenty-one, and be liable to five years' imprisonment.

This was the fuse that set the events in process, with fantasy, rumour and truth becoming indistinguishable. To this day I have never understood the mystery of Scott's National Insurance cards, apparently held by Thorpe at one time as his 'employer', who refused to give them back. Presumably they implied proof of some relationship. Norman told me he received regular weekly retainers of £5 from the Liberal Party. When I mentioned this laughingly to Edna Friendship, who ran the Market Inn, as an example of Norman's illusions, she shook her head. 'No, I've cashed the cheques.'

Then there was the case of former MP Peter Bessell, mentioned by Jeremy at the Grey House as a crucial player in the game. Bessell was now living in America, having fled the country leaving considerable debts, and could provide evidence that Scott had been blackmailing him over an affair with a woman; that, said Jeremy, would account for the weekly retainers. I pointed out that Bessell did not sound a reliable witness, but Jeremy was clutching at anything which might discredit Scott at the forthcoming trial in Exeter where an airline pilot, Andrew Newton, would be charged with shooting the dog Rinka.

Subsequent events convinced me that Bessell had been set up. A letter he sent in confidence to Michael Barnes, Thorpe's solicitor in Barnstaple, confirming Scott's blackmail, was leaked to the press. Bessell denied it then withdrew his denial: 'I told lies to protect Thorpe,' he told the press. 'Jeremy's fear has ruined him.' Bessell had his revenge, revealing his discussion with Thorpe in the House of Commons on ways to dispose of Scott, such as dumping his body in a derelict tin mine or luring him to America, and his own dismay at such suggestions. Once again, Jeremy had misjudged his man, though the alleged murder plans were so lurid few people took them seriously.

I believe that on Jeremy's visits to the Grey House, though I was unaware of it then, I was seen as another lifeline. Fortunately I have a certain integrity like everyone else, especially when it comes to blackmail and murder, and had Peter Bradshaw to reinforce it, which he did admirably, so Jeremy dared not commit himself too far in trying to bring me out in the open. He was trespassing on my vulnerability. At one of the meetings I told him, 'Anyhow, who is going to take the word of a drunken homosexual on the skids?' and he gave a wintry smile. Even with Peter he played the role of Henry II: 'Who will rid me of this turbulent priest?'

'Should anything happen to Norman Scott,' he smiled, 'it will be "Arise, Sir Peter, new Lord Mayor of Barnstaple!"' We laughed, hollowly.

At one point he came close to warning me that it would be to my advantage if I helped him as I was involved already. 'You know there are these names mentioned at Exeter?' I nodded, having seen this mentioned in the press, but had no wish to pursue it. The entire Exeter hearing was incomprehensible, with no adequate motive alleged for killing the dog except for the allegation that Scott was blackmailing Newton over a nude photograph he had sent to a contact magazine with a view to meeting a girl. It was claimed that Scott travelled to Blackpool to blackmail him for monthly payments of £4, a fraction of the train fare, a demand so pathetic that it gave blackmail a bad name. To add to the comedy, Norman descended the court staircase singing 'I'm the queen in your copy' to the journalists assembled below. I began to warm to him.

Newton was found guilty and sentenced to two years' imprisonment on the day that Harold Wilson resigned as prime minister. There was a widely-held assumption that this was no coincidence. It also obscured the announcement that Princess Margaret's marriage to Lord Snowdon was finished. Wilson had made a startling allegation in the House of Commons of a 'strong South African participation' in the Thorpe affair. It was suggested that his resignation was timed to defuse a further outburst from Scott naming several people including two members of the royal family. Two days before the verdict, Thorpe denounced Scott's allegations as 'lies' in the *Sunday Times*, and the public were by now so confused they were on the point of believing him. They could accept his denials, but not the truth.

On a wild night a few weeks later, I was in the Grey House watching *Moby Dick* on television, with Peter and Frances. Totally engrossed, I leapt up when I heard a knocking on the window and saw a figure in the darkness outside, which proved to be the farmer who lived on the hill above. By now my phone had been cut off for non-payment, and Jeremy had rung the farmer demanding to speak to me – 'It's a matter of life and death.' Reluctantly, I missed the end of *Moby Dick* and was driven to the farmer's house where I phoned Jeremy. He asked me to come straight to London. I said this was impossible, without mentioning that I could not afford it, for I sensed that he would have brushed this aside. Stressing that it was a matter of urgency which could not be discussed over the phone, his agitation was such that I promised to see him the following week, when I had to go to London for the launch of a small book, *The Dan Farson Black and White Picture Show*. No, that was impossible, it had to be the next day.

I was equally adamant and he rang off after saying he would try to sort things out.

Next morning several overnight telegrams arrived with the post. For a moment I was mystified, for the signature was written in code – 'SMEEBERT', a combination of my father's nickname for my grandmother, 'Smee', and our old dachshund, Albert. The messages stated that Jeremy would drive down to see me; then, that this was impossible; finally, that he would be arriving at midday. It was a perfect early spring morning, cold with bright sun and clear blue skies. As Jeremy stepped from his car having driven from London, he looked like Count Dracula caught in the sunlight, the purity of the day contrasting with his haggard appearance as if it was sitting in judgement. We went into the drawing-room and I insisted that Peter stayed with us, sensing that this was an occasion when I might need a witness. Jeremy came straight to the point, for he had to return to the House of Commons to make a speech that afternoon. Explaining that there were two letters which he had written to Scott, he concluded 'They are not altogether unhelpful.'

'That's good,' I said.

'But they're not exactly helpful.'

'That's bad.'

'Lord Goodman says that if these letters can be withheld, then the whole matter will blow over and people will forget about it in six months.' If Goodman thinks that, I thought, he is an even bigger ass than I assumed. Jeremy continued, 'Now I want to get this copper-bottomed . . .' he looked round, puzzled by Peter's outburst of laughter, and repeated 'we need to get it copper-bottomed. If you will sign a statement testifying that Norman Scott poses a threat to me, then the police will not release the letters because the file will remain open. Lord Goodman gives me the assurance that your name will not be brought into it.' I have no idea if Jeremy was telling me the truth when he claimed that Goodman gave this promise.

'What exactly do you mean, that Scott poses a threat?' I asked.

'That you heard him threatening to destroy me.' Plainly this was a reference to the letter I had written about meeting Scott after the anniversary party for *This Week*.

'But everyone knows that,' I pointed out. 'He made it plain that he was determined to destroy your reputation.' I hesitated. 'You're not asking that, are you?' He shook his head. 'You're asking me to state that he threatened to destroy you physically?' He nodded.

The silence was broken by the chilling words, 'The Queensberry rules don't apply in this case.' There was nothing I could say.

I remember that the lunch Frances cooked for us was particularly revolting, not that Jeremy would have eaten much, and we said good-bye outside as he prepared to drive back to Parliament. He knew he had lost the game as far as I was concerned, but he made a last attempt: 'The moment you feel you can make such a statement, get in touch at once, but use a code.' My mind thrashed around. 'Donald?'

'No, no, that's far too close.'

This was the one of the few times that I heard Frances make a funny remark. 'What about Priscilla?' she suggested.

Peter and I clutched ourselves, laughing from the nervous release of the built-up tension. Jeremy looked at us sadly and drove away.

On Saturday morning two representatives of the *Sunday Times* arrived unexpectedly to seek my advice – was Jeremy Thorpe a man to be trusted? Even now, such a question was unthinkable in North Devon, where most of his constituents believed his assurance that 'The whole of this tissue of elaborately woven mendacity and malice is based on no more than the fact that I had met Scott in November 1961, when he called at the House of Commons.' The *Sunday Times* had seen the two compromising letters and were having doubts, but if they had looked at the facts they would have seen that Thorpe was flawed throughout. I had been surprised years earlier when he boasted that he received payment as director of various companies in Africa, and pointed out that if their interests came up in the House of Commons he was bound to be prejudiced in their favour. 'That's why they pay me!' he smiled.

Scott's outburst in the Barnstaple courtroom had obscured an issue that was basically more serious: on the same day Jeremy Thorpe was cleared by an inquiry into the collapse of the London and County Securities of which he was a former director at a salary of £5000. His association with the company, which left debts of over £50 million, was described damningly as 'an error of judgement'. The rumours had yet to surface of £10,000 allegedly paid to the Liberals by Jack Hayward, who had bought Lundy Island for the nation, into a private account in Jersey where it vanished. All these events were eclipsed by the scandal surrounding Scott.

My defences were up: I fended off the questions of the journalists and feigned an ignorance I wished I possessed, especially when the farmer's wife came down the drive, usually so silent but now a mainstream of intrigue. Anticipating another message from Jeremy and with no wish to reveal his visit, I hurried to greet her and she handed me the piece of paper on which she had written a phone message: 'Thank you very much there is now no need to come to London.'

The next day the *Sunday Times* published the two letters, which Thorpe released himself in the last desperate throw to limit the damage. 'Not unhelpful'? They were devastating, containing the affectionate but lethal phrase 'BUNNIES CAN AND WILL GO TO FRANCE', revealing that his relationship with Scott was more intimate than he maintained, and that, consequently, he was the liar. The next day he resigned as leader of the Liberal Party.

Far from abating, the storm increased. On his release from prison, Andrew Newton withdrew his absurd evidence that he was being blackmailed by Scott and claimed on the front page of the *Evening News* (19 October 1977) I WAS HIRED TO KILL SCOTT, saying he was paid a fee of £5000. Eight days later in a vain effort to squash the rumours, Thorpe called a press conference and admitted to 'affection – and nothing else'. When a journalist asked, 'Have you ever had a homosexual relationship?' his lawyer told him not to answer. But it was not until 4 August 1978 that the Right Honourable Jeremy Thorpe MP was charged with conspiracy to murder, with the subsequent charge of incitement to murder.

As I was lying in bed one morning reading the *Sunday Express*, a news item leapt out at me: the police were about to interrogate a man in the West Country who had once been famous on television. This had to be me. Like the innocent man in an Alfred Hitchcock film I found myself swept into a maelstrom of events in which I was not actually involved. For the next half-hour I lay there trying to work out if at any moment, even a drunken one, I had done anything which made me guilty. At the end, I was thankful to realize that I was blameless.

The local policeman stopped me in the street on Monday; would I visit the Bideford police station at six that evening? Foolishly, I asked him if this had anything to do with Jeremy Thorpe, but of course he was not allowed to say.

Trouble had been brewing in the locality for some time. A man who called himself a farmer had sold his story for a few pounds to the *Evening News*, describing himself extravagantly as a local Dillinger. He claimed that a Liberal lady had offered £5000 to someone at a party, with the implication that mystery lady was Marion Thorpe, the party was mine at the Grey House, and the someone was Bob K. who, much to his indignation, was taken in for questioning. The police soon realized that the informant, ironically a close friend of Bob's, lived in a fantasy world. Unfortunately, in the Thorpe affair it was hard to tell truth from lies. The man's wife appeared on Westward Television News saying, 'If he doesn't stop being silly and getting involved in things like this, I shall have to divorce him.'

Journalists descended from London, but by now I was wary. Two splendid veterans from the *Daily Mail* drank so much whisky they had to be helped into a taxi and I never read a word, presumably because they remembered nothing.

The two reporters who broke the story in the *Evening News*, Stuart Kuttner and Joanna Patyna, asked for general background information which I gave them willingly, sticking to the facts which were well-known already. Another journalist arrived with an imposing briefcase which he placed on the floor between us. Suspecting that it held a concealed microphone, I stumbled over it deliberately, apologized, and put it outside the door. To every reporter I spoke off the record, and they respected it.

My name surfaced at last in a small news item, inevitably in the *Sun*, which quoted me saying I knew nothing of the alleged offer of £5000 nor had I overheard such a conversation. I mentioned that I had met Scott and knew that Jeremy was distraught. Under my picture was the inexplicable caption DANIEL FARSON . . . A DINNER WITH THORPE. I read this with dismay in the train to London, but by the time I reached Paddington, my photo had disappeared from later editions and the story was a meaningless reference to an alleged party. Not a single person mentioned it in London, but it caused waves in Devon and had given ammunition to the police. I was involved, by name, in print.

How easily an innocent man feels guilty. When something was stolen at school I was consumed by such an embarrassment of innocence that I almost wished I had taken the wretched thing, for then I could resort to cunning. The guilty don't blush. As I waited at Bideford police station, I understood why a suspect feels the compulsion to confess to a crime he did not commit. Far from arriving flanked by solicitors, I was prepared to tell the truth and conceal nothing. My sole advantage lay in not needing to lie, but I phoned my solicitor in Barnstaple in the afternoon. Ron Prosser took it more seriously – 'I was rather surprised to see your name in the *Sun* last week' – before passing me on to a colleague who specialized in litigation. He was alarmed by my mention of Chief Inspector Magreary, whom I was about to see.

'He's fair, but he's good.'

'What do you mean by "good"? Clever?'

'Extremely clever.' He assured me I could request legal advice at any time in the interview or announce that I was leaving. It was agreed that I should phone him the moment I felt the interview was going wrong and he gave me two emergency numbers where he could be reached, with the final advice not to give 'off the cuff' answers. Knowing my volubility, this would be hard.

The River Torridge was tranquil outside and at least there were no waiting reporters or photographers. I was shown into an office with the windows firmly closed and the tables strewn with papers. Two men rose to meet me, neither friendly nor hostile. Chief Inspector Magreary took my overcoat, and I felt I might have liked him in different circumstances. The other man, Inspector Taylor from the Bristol police force, was smartly dressed in a well-cut suit, probably forty, dark-haired and handsome in a tough sort of way. I sensed at once that it would be idiotic to play games with him. We shook hands indifferently and I sat down in a chair close to the wall for protection.

'I expect you know what this is about,' said Taylor. 'The Thorpe business.' He mentioned the farmer's story and his admission that it was a pack of lies, and questioned me on the party I had been to at Jeremy's home when I was making the film for HTV. This was a preliminary skirmish. Then he informed me bluntly that I was a 'defendant' and, a moment later, 'a definite suspect' in the conspiracy to murder Norman Scott. This was the moment to explain that though I wished to speak freely I had been advised not to make 'off the cuff' statements, which Taylor brushed aside with scathing comments on the trouble solicitors can cause their clients, citing people who had held things back in 'the Thorpe business' only to return and change their stories. 'If your man advised you not to co-operate . . .'

'He did not say that,' I interrupted, but I was placed in the position of telling the whole truth or withholding it at the risk of being seen to be unco-operative. When he suggested that I had taken part in discussions to dispose of Scott, I was able to deny it; but this seemed the frame-up I dreaded. Next he asked me questions about my homosexuality which, surprisingly, had never been put to me in my life before.

'You had a lot of parties at your home, kinky parties.' More of a statement than a question. I replied that there were no parties except for friends from London at Christmas. It seemed pointless to explain that kinky parties did not appeal, nor could I afford them, as if I was defending myself. I said it was objectionable having to answer such questions.

'Yes, I can see it doesn't do your image much good,' said Taylor.

'It doesn't do *me* much good!' I exclaimed.

Then a barrage of questions about Norman Scott, my meetings, and most surprisingly of all, Scott's claim that he was going to look after my parents' dachshund Albert when they went abroad. Conceivably Jeremy had told them that Scott was a possible 'minder' for Albert, but after so many years I could not be sure.

'You had a punch-up with Scott the evening you met him,' said Magreary from across the room, wiping the incipient smile from my face.

'No.'

'Edna Friendship told me so at the time.' Ah, so she had been an informer. I admitted that I reduced Scott to tears and to my relief Magreary smiled. 'Oh yes, Scott cried all the time. You only had to say "good morning"!'

I described Scott's determination to 'destroy' Thorpe and Thorpe's visits to the Grey House, though hazy about dates as usual, which Taylor found suspicious. However, he seemed to know most of the facts already, and his aggressive approach became less hostile until he conceded that I was no longer a defendant but could be called as a witness. Then the names of the 'five famous men' came up. To this day I do not know if Thorpe raised them in the hope that the authorities would be intimidated, or if Scott had fantasized. Either way I doubted if such a list of names existed, and burst out laughing when Taylor mentioned the names of two members of the royal family, a foreign head of government – 'and yourself'.

With a whoop I cried, 'I've made the big time at last!'

'It's not funny,' said Magreary. I replied that I found it hilarious. The two men looked at me unamused. Still mystified, I let the matter drop and still have no idea how I came to be included in such illustrious company. I was starting to enjoy the interrogation, which had become surreal. Names were fired at me – 'Conway; Miller' – which meant nothing, though I was stunned by the mention of 'Deakin' and 'Le Mesurier'. John Le Mesurier, the actor, was another friend who had been to the Grey House.

At last we came to Thorpe's last, crucial, visit. I hesitated, explaining that this was not going to cast him in a favourable light.

'Just think,' snapped Taylor, resuming his former approach. 'If you didn't tell us and we found out about it when we spoke to Thorpe, that wouldn't do *you* much good, would it?' I signed my statement.

Discussing it with Magreary, Taylor added that as it was irrelevant to the main investigation, he doubted if I would be called as a witness, though it was disconcerting to learn that my statement would join forty others being sent to the Director of Public Prosecutions. It would have shown Thorpe's duplicity, though there was no proof of the conspiracy to murder and I have no idea if Thorpe was involved. When we said goodbye, I said I was glad I had been able to speak freely.

'Tell you what,' said Taylor, staring at me without returning my smile, 'If you hadn't, I'd have arrested you.'

'I don't believe you.'

'Oh yes. If you had withheld *anything*, I'd have arrested you – like that!' And he snapped his fingers.

❖

I felt such relief when I left Bideford police station that the night seemed to welcome me. I was less jolly when I woke to a day of drizzle, no newspapers due to a derailment, and a summons to see the bank manager that afternoon.

The interview in the bank began in the usual way, all fake bonhomie – 'I'm so happy to meet you, Mr Farson,' from the assistant manager, the monkey rather than the organ-grinder, though he resembled a swordfish, all teeth and pointed nose.

'Are you a married man?' I saw the dossier on the desk in front of him and thought it could not be much of a dossier if he needed to ask me that. With a sound approaching a titter, he pushed forward the recent cutting in the *Sun*. The inference was obvious, that because I was 'unmarried' I was involved in an unsavoury affair.

At some point it was inevitable that I should run into Norman Scott again, and I did so outside Mugford's in Barnstaple. He was guarded by an ugly giant, possibly supplied by a newspaper, who scowled at me grimly while Norman bounced over.

'Daniel, I do hope you're not cwoss with me.'

'Why should I be cross with you, Norman?'

'Well, I have upset some people.' The bodyguard looked at us with dislike as we burst into giggly laughter.

'Norman, you really are a shit!'

'I don't know what you mean,' he replied indignantly, looking so hurt that I feared he was about to burst into tears, but he had grown harder. When we met in the Market Inn later, he indulged in a tirade against the unfortunate Peter Bessell: 'I'm going to have that man extradited from America . . .' he stopped in mid-flow and looked at me. 'I suppose I really am a bit of a shit, you're right.'

In 1979 I saw Jeremy at the end of Appledore Quay when he fought his last election, with Marion standing grimly nearby. There were only a few to hear him and they kept their distance, but though they knew he was about to appear at the Old Bailey on a charge of conspiracy to murder, many of his constituents remained loyal. He polled an astonishing number of votes, though he lost the seat to the Conservatives. His behaviour was stoic during the long-drawn-out hearing at Minehead and then the trial at the Old Bailey, an ordeal almost beyond endurance. Marion's courage was no less and her loyalty never wavered, for if she had missed a single day of the trial her absence could have been misinterpreted. When we made our film at Cobbaton she had told me, 'Little did I think that we would have three elections in the first eighteen months of our marriage!' That was nothing compared to the hell of the trial. Scott's vengeance exposed her husband for the world to see, with detailed descriptions of all the warts and nodules on his body.

In due course Jeremy Thorpe, assisted by the astute legal team of Goodman, Napley and Carman, was acquitted. His lawyers had the wisdom to keep him and the other defendants out of the witness box, while Bessell's evidence was discredited when it emerged that the *Sunday Telegraph* had offered him £50,000 for his exclusive story, but only £8000 if there was an acquittal. This disclosure helped Thorpe's case immeasurably. As Inspector Taylor had predicted, I was not called upon to give evidence.

A few years later, at a cocktail party in North Devon I saw Marion Thorpe advancing towards me.

'Jeremy wants to see you,' she said.

I was taken to a small room where Jeremy was holding court in an armchair at the far end, a queue of people waiting for an audience as if he were royalty. I whispered to the man behind me that he was welcome to take my place as I needed to go to the lavatory, but there was no escape. Jeremy looked much the same, brown suit and watch-chain, except that his hands shook from the Parkinson's disease which afflicted him as if in final retribution. He greeted me warmly:

'Hullo, Dan. Do you remember that programme you made when your delightful grandmother, Smee, spoke of the kindness she had always received in the pen department in Harrods? Ha! Ha!' I mumbled something appropriate. It was as if nothing had happened.

Thorpe has my sympathy. He found himself in a terrible predicament, threatened by an excitable man who seemed determined to wreck his political future. It would have been wholly understandable if he had taken excessive measures to prevent this, though I am far from certain that he did. Either way, this was a tragedy for all concerned, not least for Marion Thorpe. As for myself, thank God I was able to tell the truth.

Nineteen

The Lost Decade

MERCIFULLY, time distorts the memory, erasing the hard lines etched by bitter experience. I forget how sterile life could be at the Grey House. I remember the good times.

My sights were set too low – that was a mistake. Equally, I had neither the funds nor the confidence to hitch my way to the stars. Because I needed the money, I sold objects at the wrong moment, accepting sums that would have trebled had I had time to wait. With the painful settlement of old debts and bank charges I seldom felt the gain directly.

Apart from the dogs, there was the loyal companionship of Peter, the friend I have mentioned, who never knew the best of times but remained through the worst of them, with the inevitable sulks and tantrums redeemed with laughter. And the constant solace of North Devon, the view of Baggy Point from my window with the sea pounding below at high tide. Never sounding the same, never looking the same, it was a view that never disappointed, always to look forward to on my return. It was the worst February of all, when the bank manager in London threatened to enforce the sale of the Grey House to cover the outstanding bank loan. When I saw him he made an unfortunate comparison to 'foolish old ladies in South Kensington, who hold onto their houses in reduced circumstances when they would have been better off in a flat'. His lack of understanding of these old ladies, and the blandness with which he told me to sell up and move to a smaller house, weakened my resistance at last.

Leaving a home you love is an ignominious death with all the trappings of failure – the well-known rooms suddenly strange in their emptiness, the walls denuded, possessions packed into tea-chests awaiting the arrival of the removal vans to be followed up the lane to their new destination, the point of no return, literally so in my case for I have not been back to Putsborough since then except in my dreams.

The question of where to go was resolved when we walked through Appledore and Peter heard of a cottage for sale with a derelict boat-house. It proved so right that I bought it at once. I was determined not to lose it and failed to bargain as I should have done. As no one else was interested, this was characteristically foolish: I knew I was being fleeced. Yet my instinct proved correct in one respect – the Boat House which was thrown in as a liability became the property where I live today, with the cottage on the other side of a narrow cobbled alley where smugglers are supposed to have rolled their barrels of contraband brandy brought from Lundy Island and slipped past the old Customs House.

Appledore is a fishing village dating from the Armada, on the estuary where the rivers Taw and Torridge join together and pour into the Atlantic over the turbulence of the Bideford Bar. Unlike Clovelly further down the coast, which is privately owned and quaint, Apple-dore is a thriving community with a boatyard, pubs and church. I am known as 'mazed', a West Country term for those whose behaviour is odd. The villagers find it hard to accept me, apart from the children who see me staggering down the cobbled alley next to the cottage and have been heard to say, 'There's poor Mr Farsons, going to his shed.'

There are views across the river, the sand dunes opposite and Exmoor rising in the distance, constantly changing shape and colour under the shifting skies. My backyard leans over the water and some-one who knew me in Limehouse called it 'Narrow Street on Sea'. I brought my rowboat and moored it below, learning the currents to swing me past the lifeboat, beaching at Crow Point, then walking for hours in the Braunton Burrows, the vast expanse of unspoilt sand dunes where small wild orchids appear in the spring after a fall of rain and bright blue viper's bugloss in the heat of summer. At the far end I found a natural pool surrounded by bulrushes so overgrown no one knew of it, where the dogs could drink and swim while I lay watching them or idled with a book until it was time to walk back to Crow and return with the tide. That kept me sane.

The dogs – they were the tragedy in leaving the Grey House. After Frances eloped with a young fisherman, ironically our closest friend, Peter cracked up. Desperately trying to carry on, I did the worst act of my life. Other people's dogs are as boring as other people's gardens or babies, except to those who love them, but I need to explain their importance. They were a dynasty, starting up with a beautiful black-haired mongrel in London.

'Seen yer pup?' asked Rose when I returned from filming *Sparrows Can't Sing* with Joan Littlewood. She looked embarrassed and so did the local children shoving bits of food and saucers of milk underneath the sofa. They had bought the puppy in Petticoat Lane, unable to resist her though they knew that dogs were not allowed in the Buildings. 'They want you to have her,' said Rose. The children watched my expression, willing me to weaken. When they produced the animal it was so tiny and bedraggled I doubted it would last the night.

'What's its name?' I asked.

'Trixie.' I fell into the trap. 'Oh, no it isn't . . .' I searched for something less winsome and remembered Joan that afternoon – 'Littlewood,' I declared. Their faces filled with relief, though there were cries of protest: 'That's not a dog's name.'

'After the pools,' Rose explained.

I had forgotten about the puppy when I returned home late that night and she shot from under the sofa and smothered me with kisses.

Those who have known similar companionships will understand when I say she made all the difference to my life. Those who haven't will think me maudlin. She knew the sadness of suitcases, crawling away when she sensed I was leaving, greeting me so rapturously on my return that she chewed the blanket in her ecstasy until she remembered I had left her and sulked for a moment until she could bear that no longer and leapt up with renewed joy. Though she was my dog she loved everyone she met and took to North Devon and the sea as if this were her rightful home. When she died many years later, virtually paralysed, and the vet had to 'put her down' to use that fearsome phrase, she looked at me with such kindness, barely able to lick my hand in order to reassure me. I have never known such unselfishness; that is the strength of dogs.

She had one litter in London, including a delightful half-whippet lurcher called Pencil, and more in Devon by the farmer's sheepdog on the hill above.

When we made the traumatic move to Appledore, six dogs came with us, including Frances's, Streaker, and the latest arrival, Bonzo, a black and white collie, Littlewood's granddaughter. With their adaptability, the dogs were doing their best to adjust to their new confinement in a village street in wretched contrast to the miles of sand they had raced across without restraint. Frances's departure meant there was no car to take them to the sands at Westward Ho! and Peter, whose loyalty deserved all the help I could give him, was suicidal in his unhappiness. Pencil, who chased jet planes as well as seagulls for miles along the edge of the sea, was now old and blind and it was time to call the vet again. She died in my arms after his swift injection as blissfully as if she had been waiting for such release, and I decided to kill two of the other dogs as well. One of them, Blacky, looked at me so trustingly that the image haunts me in the middle of the night. It was a terrible thing to have done and I cannot forgive myself. Surprisingly, the vet and I are good friends and have not referred to the incident. Streaker died from a natural illness a few weeks later, and the sacrifice of the others could have been avoided.

Peter recovered and in due course met a local girl who was lovely and loyal, the best thing that ever happened to him. It could have been on one of their travels to the Greek islands a few years later that he contracted a melanoma on his back which seemed so insignificant that it was cut out, probably unwisely, by the doctor at the local infirmary. A year later it moved to his groin and this time it was removed at the hospital in Barnstaple. It returned again as cancers do; one of the other doctors assured him that it was no worse, though the nurse who dressed the wound could see that it was. Anyone could see that. Finally yet another doctor sent him to the Royal Marsden in London for a proper examination. By the time he reached Paddington, Peter was in such agony that he had to crawl from the train – 'Not for the first time,' said Karen, trying to distract him – and was wheeled to the taxi-rank on a trolley. Once he reached the Marsden they kept him there discovering that it was now too late to operate.

As people so often do when faced with death, he revealed unexpected courage. All too often he had sunk to the occasion, now he rose to it nobly. In the early evening he careered around Chelsea, pushed in his wheelchair by Karen, until he had to return for his injections of morphine. Bob K. and I took him into Soho one Sunday lunchtime when Ian Board, who succeeded Muriel Belcher at the Colony, opened the annual Soho Fair. Peter's humour was no less sharp and the one time he complained with a tinge of bitterness was when he looked at me and remarked, 'I've drawn the short straw, haven't I?'

His death approached at alarming speed, though I found it impossible to accept that it would actually happen. When Karen told him he was taking it very calmly, he replied, 'You don't go screaming to the firing squad, do you?'

At the end, there was a moment when he seemed to improve, but then he had brainstorms – 'My body's getting better, now my mind's going!'

It was planned that he should be driven in a friend's car to Devon and be looked after at the Bideford Hospice where local friends could visit him. He needed a new shirt to conceal the swelling caused by the tumours and told Karen to buy him one in the King's Road that was bright and colourful. Knowing how choosy he could be, she was worried in case he disliked it but he was delighted, quoting Rizzo as he made his bus journey in the film *Midnight Cowboy*: 'I'm going to Florida.' He kept his laughter.

An extraordinary thing happened when he was due to leave and I arrived with the friend to take him home. The doctors gathered around Peter's bed in the early morning. By now it was plain that he was dying, but they asked him if he wanted to leave and when he said yes, they agreed, though they knew of the bureaucracy involved. I told him I would see him at the other end but he died in the ambulance on the way home, on 27 July 1992 wearing his Rizzo shirt. Karen was with him.

One of the more bizarre aspects of grief is the short-lived reaction which is near elation, like the famous photograph by Weegee of a street scene in New York just after a man has been murdered, his body surrounded by a circle of onlookers who seem to be laughing. This is a form of release, yet it seems odd to remember that we sat outside in Appledore, with Karen and her father, her sister, and the friend who came to London, drinking as if in celebration. The Irish have the right idea with their wakes when they lose their inhibitions.

The next few days were torment, and the clergyman was exemplary except for telling Karen that a local woman had said she assumed the man had died from AIDS. Not only was this untrue, but cruel, considering Peter's almost old-fashioned sense of fidelity. People say such things when they are unhappy themselves, but the clergyman should not have repeated it. The clichés of death meant more than I would have suspected, with the letters and the banks of flowers for his grave sent by friends in London. The funeral in the church at Appledore only a few yards away had a touching dignity, though I found it difficult to complete the reading of 'Sea Fever' by John Masefield, one of Peter's favourite poets:

I must go down to the seas again, to the vagrant gypsy life,
To the gull's way and the whale's way where the wind's like a
   whetted knife;
And all I ask is a merry yarn from a laughing fellow rover,
And a quiet sleep and a sweet dream when the long trick's over.

What did I give him? Not so much as I should have wished, but most people feel that. At least I did not try to change him into something he was not. Looking back on someone close, one remembers the best moments, like the journey Karen, Peter and myself made by boat along the Black Sea to Trabzon, over the Alps and down through Turkey to Mersin and up the Mediterranean coast; or the time we went to the recently excavated city of Aphrodisias where his knowledge and interest in the Ancient World was fulfilled; or the lunch on Easter Sunday at the Temple de la Gloire in Paris with Diana Mosley who kept me enthralled with the accounts of her internment in the war under Rule 18B, and such visitors as her sister Unity who had been in love with Hitler. 'Oh,' exclaimed Diana Mosley, 'how kind of you!' 'I thought it was grouse which she brought me and put on the radiator, but they were her *gloves*.'

Lady Diana found so much in common with Peter that the next day the elderly American who had been the other guest at luncheon tracked me down by telephone to the Deux Magots where I was drinking with Peter and Karen. 'Lady Diana would like a word,' he told me. 'Oh yes,' I preened. 'No, not with you, with Mr Bradshaw.' Peter returned beaming twenty minutes later. 'I suppose she wanted to talk about Hitler and all that?' He nodded. 'Did she have a message for me?' He shook his head. 'Not a word?' I asked incredulously. 'Not a mention!' I can recall with pleasure how we shook with laughter, drinking in the spring sunlight – Easter in Paris.

Francis Bacon respected his intelligence. Peter spoke to him with directness, telling me I took Francis too lightly – 'You don't realize what a serious person he is,' – but it was the humour which forged the rapport. At the second retrospective at the Tate, Peter found Francis looking forlorn behind a table piled high with bottles and catalogues, and asked him to sign one which Francis did with his usual

'Best wishes'. 'Surely you can do better than that?' asked Peter. 'What about "Thank you for the trade"?' 'You're not making me look common,' said Francis.

Returning once from Turkey, we stopped in Soho and Peter hurried from the Colony to see me in The French Pub: 'Francis is up there and I think it's bad news, but I told him to tell you himself.' A few weeks earlier Francis was on the point of agreeing to help me write his official biography, but now he had changed his mind as I guessed he would, though he rewarded me with some prints later. There was just Francis, John Edwards, Karen, Peter and myself at the bar, and Ian behind it. Francis was in a genial mood but could not resist telling Ian, 'You know why Muriel said you were the best barman she had? Because you cheated her less than the others.' Then he remembered it was his birthday and took us to L'Escargot, to Ian's evident relief, where he examined my noisettes of lamb in their rich wine sauce and exclaimed: 'I do hope I don't have *gravy* with mine,' investing that word with all the horror of the Dickensian workhouse. It was a phrase that stuck in Peter's mind, using it constantly to the surprise of the people he was with, regardless of the food, 'I do hope I don't have *gravy* on mine!'

Peter was lazy. He enjoyed painting and should have tried harder. I did my utmost to encourage him, even by subterfuge. When he joined a painting course run by a mutual friend, Tony Smith, near Montpellier, I warned Tony that he needed to be tough, but Peter simply enjoyed himself, for which he had a greater aptitude. When the others staged a small exhibition afterwards, they liked him so much that they reserved a corner in his honour which they filled with contributions of their own.

One of the good moments was due to Keith Waterhouse. I took Keith's photo in the Groucho Club one afternoon when he was wearing a bright red v-neck sweater and Peter was galvanized into painting a massive portrait. When I showed a photograph of the picture to Keith a few weeks later he exclaimed, 'Oh, I like that. I do like that.'

'Why don't you buy it?' I suggested. At that moment Jeffrey Bernard came up and I feared he would damn it, but Peter Bowles arrived in time to save the day, having plainly enjoyed a good lunch: 'No, *I* want to buy it,' he declared. That settled it. I suggested a price of £1000 and agreed on £750 when Keith said he would invite Peter,

Karen and myself to lunch at the Ivy for the unveiling, with himself and his ladyfriend. He did so in style, starting with champagne. With their understanding of northern humour, he got on well with Peter, his ladyfriend was welcoming to Karen, celebrities came in and out and were introduced, and at the end of this triumphant meal the brown paper was stripped from the portrait by Peter like a conjuror completing a trick. For a split second I could sense Keith's amazement; plainly it was not what he expected, but this was so fleeting that no one else noticed and we left the Ivy arm-in-arm leaving the picture to be collected later, one of the best days in Peter's life.

Francis detested possessions, particularly paintings by other people. When I showed him an advance copy of one of my books, he would hurl it on the floor with a dismissive 'Very nice, I'm sure,' so I feared the worst when in 1986 Peter asked me to take a painting to London which he had done especially for him. It was based on the film still from Eisenstein's 1925 classic *Battleship Potemkin* of the nurse on the Odessa steps, her glasses shattered by a bullet, blood running from her eyes, her mouth open in a scream as the pram slips from her grasp and bounces down the steps. The scream was a constant image in Bacon's work: he made the surprising admission, 'I always thought that I could make the scream as beautiful as a late Monet landscape, but I never succeeded.' Though he had painted a full-length version of the nurse in the film, he had never attempted a close-up of the face as Peter had done. I flinched from his reaction as I climbed the steep, narrow stairs at Reece Mews, but as Francis took the picture which Peter had wrapped so carefully and tore away the brown paper with the glee of a schoolboy on his birthday, it occurred to me that people seldom gave him anything because he had so much. I was prepared for the usual dismissive comment when he saw the painting; instead he studied it in silence while I held my breath and said nothing. Almost a minute must have passed as he drew away from it and came closer. Then he gave an emphatic gesture '*That's* what I've always wanted to achieve – the colour of the mouth.'

Though I knew him so well this revealed a modesty I had not suspected; or perhaps the strength of genius knowing it is still possible to learn. He wrote to Peter, dispensing as always with punctuation:

Dear Peter, I love the painting I think it is beautifully done and it is marvellous to see it in colour Thank you so much for giving it to me

it is something I really love to have – do hope to see you soon and
thank you again for such a marvellous present – All very best wishes
Love Francis

Far from throwing it away as I feared, Francis gave the painting to
his heir, John Edwards, who was kind enough to return it to me as
a present for Karen. I look at the picture constantly, and whether by
a lucky chance or not it is magnificent. At least Peter did that.

If Francis had been alive when Peter was in the Marsden, I am sure
he would have visited him regularly for the hospital was only a few
minutes walk from Reece Mews, but he had died on 22 April 1992,
three months earlier. We had one last glorious morning when he was
in such amazing form that the years peeled away and we laughed as
we had when I first entered Soho, playing against each other like
musical instruments. I had been trying to persuade him to take part
in a television documentary on John Deakin, but he had turned against
the idea, claiming to the director that he scarcely knew Deakin. This
was a final attempt to lure him to the Bibendum, his favourite restaurant nearby, where the crew would be waiting to film him over
lunch. Clasping an expensive bottle of iced Krug, I arrived at Reece
Mews soon after nine. There was a long silence after I knocked, then
a sudden commotion on the balustrade above which always reminded
me of Juliet's balcony, and Francis appeared with the indignant cry,
'I'm not being filmed!'

Prepared for that, I called back, 'Of course not!' brandishing the
Krug like a badly-cast Romeo. 'I want to apologize for all the trouble
you've been put to.'

A moment of familiar glare followed by the familiar smile. 'All right
then, I suppose you'd better come up.'

Knowing how he liked to be provoked, I seized the initiative with
some deliberately aimed volleys. 'I hear you've seen the Max Ernst.
There isn't much excitement, is there?'

'*Nothing.*'

'George Melly says it's outstanding.'

'Dear George is obsessed by Ernst, but he doesn't really know
anything about anything, does he?' We were away. I was startled to
find him so radiant. I asked him about his asthma, and he explained
that at times it left him gasping, but this was one of the good days.
Though photographs would have proved otherwise, he seemed as

young as he had the first day we met in The French Pub forty years earlier. Always ageless, he once told Peter, 'They say I look twenty years younger, but even if I was twenty years younger I'd still be an old man.' Never did he seem old.

Searching for something to drink, he found that his own champagne was warm so we opened the impressively-shaped Krug, which justified its price. As I led him on, he demolished every artist mentioned, partly for my benefit, and when I made a point pretentiously, and sometimes deliberately, he waved his glass and replied jeeringly, 'Now you're a leading art critic, you really must be more careful not to talk such *rubbish*! Cheerio!' He glistened. Freud was too 'careful'; Auerbach had gone off; and he had doubts concerning Michael Andrews. When I said I was not entirely happy with Andrews's use of acrylic and spray gun in his pictures of Ayers Rock, Francis looked at me knowingly and replied slowly, 'As a matter of fact I use a spray gun and acrylic myself.'

'You do?' I exclaimed, genuinely surprised.

'Yes, but I use them less obviously,' he beamed.

Jasper Johns was dismissed as 'a dainty little lady. I saw quite a lot of her in Paris. I *hated* her.' When I dared to criticize Johns's picture of the metal coat-hanger, he brushed that aside in his impatience: 'That came from Duchamp. Did you know that Jasper Johns and Rauschenberg were lovers? And though much nicer than Johns, I can't do with De Kooning either.'

Showing him the striking cover for my new book *With Gilbert and George in Moscow*, which the artists had designed, he had the grace to examine it for a few seconds before he threw it on the floor. 'Oh, yes! There they are – why do they always have to stand like that? I did see their room in the Tate when I went to see mine, but it's not any good, is it?'

'You need to have space to see them,' I suggested. 'The Tate is too cramped.'

Curiosity getting the better of contempt, he asked if they used a stencil and I explained that every few years they took as many as thirty thousand photographs, enlarged the details which interested them and assembled a composition in panels which they coloured in vivid dyes.

'They don't actually paint them?'

'No, but the technique is astonishing, more interesting than Warhol.'

'Oh, yuss,' said Francis, unconvinced. 'But do you know Warhol's early "accidents"? They were marvellous. Mind you, all those Marilyns and Jackies are rubbish.'

Mentioning the Buhrle Collection at the Royal Academy, and knowing of his admiration for *Madame Moitessier*, I praised the first portrait as you entered the exhibition, saying it was so sublime that I went back to see the name of the artist – 'And of course it was Ingres!' Stumped for a second, Francis gave me his basilisk stare, then – 'You do realize that Ingres could be *really* bad. He did some very bad things.' I moved on swiftly to the Manets and the painting of the suicide with the man sprawled across the bed holding a revolver. He gave a snort of contempt – 'Well, of course you would mention the *worst*.' And he was right.

He was so exuberant that I dared to raise the film at last in the hope that he might change his mind, but he interrupted fiercely. 'Deakin was a horrible little man and not a very good photographer. I used him only because he was there and needed the money. Anyhow, photography is of no importance.' I let this pass.

If Francis had greeted me with suspicion, this had gone. For the next two hours we laughed and confided so warmly that I knew I should not waste a second, though I thought guiltily of the film crew waiting at Bibendum. At last he mentioned his friendship with the Spaniard, of whom I had heard though few people had met him. I knew he had some connection with a bank in London and by some absurd reasoning concluded that he was a dark, middle-aged, saturnine and abstemious banker, severe and unsympathetic. In other words, I had no idea what he was like until Francis produced two colour photographs he had taken when they were on holiday. Neither the chiselled looks of a male model, nor the swept-back black hair I had imagined, but a young man whose vigour was such that he seemed to be flying in mid-air though his feet were firmly on the ground. Thirty-five years old, he was one of those Spaniards with tawny-coloured hair, a shock of it, and blue eyes. His mouth was open, laughing with the enjoyment of someone being photographed in a ski resort in brilliant weather.

'My God!' I exclaimed. 'You've done it at last.'

'What have I done?' Francis asked, evidently pleased at my open-mouthed reaction.

'You've found the Nietzsche of the football team,' his declared ambition many years ago. He looked at me with a fleeting hint of respect for once, and laughed.

'Oh, I have, have I?' He laughed again. 'You may be right.'

'How has John taken it?'

'He says he's only after my money.'

'Did that hurt you?'

'Not really. You see he has money of his own. Anyhow, all my life people have only wanted to know me because of my money or my paintings.' He gave his inimitable shrug of resignation – 'So there it is.'

He explained that the Spaniard had written to him constantly after the second Tate retrospective, but he had not bothered to reply. 'You know how boring that can be.' Then they met at a party – 'And one night we drank so much that we came back and went to bed together.' Pacing his words stealthily, he added, 'But now I'm afraid that the physical side of our relationship has come to an end after two years.'

'Oh, come on, Francis, can't you be grateful for what you've had and enjoy his friendship?'

'*No!* I want *more*.'

Francis was eighty-two. Our laughter could have been heard in the mews outside.

A few nights later I met the Spaniard for the first and only time. Francis was leaving the Groucho Club as I was going in, with a lack-lustre couple who were collecting their coats and hats. They did not seem to have enjoyed their dinner, except for the Spaniard who ran over to shake my hand warmly as if he had always wanted to meet me, though I was surprised that he knew who I was. The photographs had not lied and maybe Francis felt a twinge of jealousy as he glowered from the doorway like a satanic doll. 'You're always so drunk,' he muttered, which was incontestable. That was the last time I saw either of them, though I still hope I might meet the Spaniard again for I am sure, from what I have heard, that he loved Francis and made him happy. With a family and a job of his own, he made no demands.

Against the advice of his doctor, Francis left for Spain a few weeks later, in the middle of April 1992, to see the Spaniard and an exhibition of his work at the new Marlborough Gallery in Madrid. Pneumonia, aggravated by a severe attack of asthma, brought him to hospital where he died alone of a heart attack six days later. There were no friends and no service at his cremation, no notice taken whatsoever except for a wreath sent by Noel and Lesley Botham from The French Pub, who had been alerted to the news by a friend in Madrid. Only a few Spanish journalists and photographers gathered round the coffin, one of them taking a macabre photo of Francis inside, a bandeau across his forehead bearing his name.

It was not so much a death as a disappearance, everything he wanted. 'When I'm dead, put me in a plastic bag and throw me in the gutter,' he once told Ian Board. He was triumphant to the end.

Twenty

A Critic for all Occasions

SOMETIMES before and after the move to Appledore, I knew what I was doing; too often I bluffed my way, desperate to make money. Never more so than when I was appointed the first food writer for the *Sun* after submitting an outline of my plans which was so brilliant that I was unable to sustain it. After eighteen months the *Sun* and I agreed to part, and when I look at those columns today I can only marvel at my sleight of hand. The *Sun* continues in a state of shock as far as food is concerned: the subject has never been referred to since.

In 1986 I joined *Sunday Today* as profile writer for the ebullient editor, Peter McKay, an exceptionally funny and canny Scot. This job paid expenses, which enabled me to visit London, where I enjoyed researching the column, though the paper's circulation was so small that few people read my pieces. There was constant surprise: Quintin Hogg, who had written so warmly forty years earlier when he sold an article to Guy L'Estrange, was now unrecognizable as Lord Hailsham, bloated from the fat of his high office as Lord Chancellor. As he perched on a throne-like chair in his magnificent office overlooking the Thames, his Head of Information sat close beside me ready to leap to his lordship's defence should I try to stab him, out of some pent-up grievance against the law. Already I had been frisked and searched by security officers on my way in. Hailsham made no sign that he noticed my arrival and when I asked, smilingly, if he remembered me, he replied with a curtness worthy of the Duke of Wellington: 'No sir, I do not.'

That was immaterial; what shocked me was his apparent uninterest in prison reform – 'Nothing to do with me at all. It's Home Office business' – and his reply when I asked what he did to judges who misbehaved – 'Nothing!' When I mentioned AIDS, he remarked that 'People should be more moral and responsible.' When I referred to the government's campaign for the use of condoms this produced a welcome levity. 'In my day we called them French letters,' he chuckled, which prompted me to quote my mother who had been to a literary dinner in Chicago where Balzac was referred to as 'a giant in French letters'. The Lord Chancellor wheezed like a pair of bellows: 'I have no doubt he was.'

Edward Heath was another odd one, seeing me alone in his comfortable home in Belgravia, guarded by a solitary, miserable policeman outside. Heath offered me a drink and, although shocked when I failed to recognize the name of some Far Eastern company he was associated with, was friendly enough to invite me to see his pictures in the Close at Salisbury. But when I mentioned the name of Mrs Thatcher he went out of focus, slumping across the sofa like a wounded mammoth. Stressing that Churchill had included Chamberlain in his government (surely in very different circumstances), he spoke with unconcealed anger. 'This is the first time a Prime Minister has attempted to denigrate one's predecessor. Mrs Thatcher has never offered me ANYTHING except,' and he cast the words contemptuously, 'the post of Ambassador to Washington.' At least he was not going gentle into the good night. I liked him.

Michael Foot lunched with me at the Gay Hussar in Soho wearing the infamous 'donkey-jacket' which he placed beside him on the banquette as if it were a dog. 'Look,' he said affectionately, 'as the Queen Mother told me after the service at the Cenotaph, "What a *sensible* coat to wear on a cold day like this."' But on his way home, the car radio informed him that an MP – 'Of course he was Labour!' – had accused him of insulting the nation by appearing at the ceremony improperly dressed, and the nation never forgave him.

Victoria Wood arrived at the Groucho Club looking so vulnerable that I asked if anything was wrong. She told me that £100 had been stolen from her handbag in her BBC dressing-room. 'Would champagne make it better?' 'Oh, yes, please!' which launched us on an evening in Soho when it would have been easy to fall in love with her. 'How wonderful it's been,' she sighed when we emerged at last from Kettner's. 'I have enjoyed myself and no one recognized me.' At that moment a woman stopped us. 'You're my favourite, Pam, I know your poems by heart.' Victoria signed the proffered paper with a flourishing 'Love from Pam Ayres'.

The new editor asked me to interview a TV personality, Sarah Kennedy. She could only see me in the evening, instead of over my usual lunch at the Hussar, and by then I was so drunk that we took an instant dislike to each other and I remembered little afterwards. There was only one way out, to search the library files for clippings to fill the empty space in my mind. To my surprise one of the first quotes was my own when I was a TV critic reviewing a show called *Sixty Minutes*: 'Like nanny to the rescue, Sarah Kennedy has bounced into *Sixty Minutes* to nurse that wounded programme back into life . . . she is a product of the TV age. Like the children today who make faces at the camera, the medium holds no mystery for her. Sadly, Sarah and Co are frankly lightweight.' Crikey! No wonder she told me, 'Shut up, Farson, you talk too much.' Somehow, deciphering my few notes, stretching my imagination as it had never been stretched before, I produced a piece for the editor who had watched me the evening before as I floundered in the wine bar in Victoria, before Sarah terminated the interview with an abrupt, 'Sarah is jolly good! But you, my dear, are a mess!' All too true, but as she fixed her baby blues on me she softened for a moment. 'Whatever you do, don't grow on me,' which prompted me to write a piece in her favour, at my expense. This was given a spread with her photograph on the front page and the headlined caption GUESS WHO CALLED DANIEL FARSON A BLUSTERING OLD TWIT? So it ended well. Unfortunately the job came to an end after six months because *Sunday Today* closed down.

I was caught in the familiar trap, too broke to go to London where I could find some work. In the spring of 1983 I noticed that the *Mail on Sunday* were using guest TV critics, and I was determined to land the job. After a few trial columns I joined the staff. This was luck: I could do the job from home and all I needed was a chair, a TV set in the corner and an eye to watch it.

It was familiar territory, but I made two disastrous mistakes. I took the job too seriously, which is foolish when you review programmes which have already been seen, in a column which will be forgotten tomorrow. The best you can do is to write entertainingly and confirm the viewers' prejudice. The greater mistake was being lulled into such complacency that I took my entire month's holiday a year later in order to go to Turkey, where I hoped to buy a piece of land. Now that I was on a handsome salary, I could just afford it. Alan Coren was chosen as guest critic when I was away and I asked George Melly if there was any danger that he might be after my job.

'I shouldn't think so,' he laughed. 'After all, he's very important and editor of *Punch*, he wouldn't be bothered.' But bother he did.

Stewart Steven let me go, graciously, and I learned the cardinal rules of criticism: do advance research, see previews, never leave your post for more than two weeks, and choose your deputy. In the event, I lost my land in Turkey too, but that is another story.

I rejoined the *Mail on Sunday* as their Art Correspondent in 1990, thanks to *Gallery*, the television art quiz I devised with the help of Peter Bradshaw. It was a good idea because it was simple: two panels were shown the detail of a painting which they had to identify, and then discuss. I chose George Melly as the 'host', with the artist Maggi Hambling on one team, and the art historian Frank Whitford on the other. Our guests included Vincent Price and Roald Dahl on the first programme, who fell out when we showed a Francis Bacon: 'I'm sorry,' said Price in his melting butterscotch voice, 'but I find Mr Bacon theatrical, fussy . . .'

'Now, now,' interrupted Dahl, 'we can't have that.'

'Do you know Mr Bacon?' Price asked innocently.

'As a matter of fact, I do. I own several of his paintings.'

'I knew it, I knew it!' Price exclaimed, and Dahl was so furious that he walked out of the studio afterwards, refusing to pose for photographs with the others.

'That Mr Dahl,' said Price as we stood next to each other at the urinal afterwards, 'he's not a nice purrson, is he?' But I knew it was good television.

Gallery lasted for four series, covering an amazing spectrum of art. In search of suitable paintings, it took me across Britain to parts of the country which were new to me – a Van Gogh in Walsall, a Goya in Glasgow, El Greco at Barnard Castle, the Pre-Raphaelites in the Lady Lever Museum at Port Sunlight outside Liverpool. I learned to look again. David Attenborough, one of our guests, told me that when he stood in front of Piero's *Baptism* he felt 'blessed'. I went to the National Gallery the next week, and understood. The job as art correspondent continued to reveal an aspect of life I was scarcely aware of before. I had no training in art and no knowledge but I developed an eye.

Henry Irving, on his farewell tour of England, included in his address at the Royal Hotel in Bristol a passage which I find particularly moving:

> Without opening a book, or listening to music, or sitting at the play, or meditating at a picture gallery, you can lead a blameless, prosperous and even energetic life. But it will be a very dry, narrow and barren life, cut off from some of the world's greatest treasures. It will be a life of defective growth from the imaginative side.

My life had been enriched immeasurably by the arts. I had the luck as an art critic to coincide with an extraordinary moment in British art when it was important to learn a new visual language and accept that if I was shocked and bewildered, it was reason to look again.

Above all, I had the extraordinary good fortune to meet the most interesting British artists of the second half of this century, and not only to know them but to know them well, especially Francis Bacon who was a friend for forty years.

Gilbert & George became two of my closest friends after inviting me to fly out with them in the spring of 1991 for the opening of their exhibition in Moscow. Their arrival in identical tweed suits, misinterpreted as the quintessence of the British aristocracy, caused a sensation, celebrated with a cascade of banquets as we floated on a sea of vodka, with the Russian hosts seizing any excuse for a toast and a further influx of alcohol. Courteous to everyone they met, George would murmur: 'How kind, very sweet,' echoed by Gilbert – 'Extraordinary!'

I saw their exhibition take root in the New Tretyakov Gallery opposite Gorky Park as their team assembled the panels which had been driven across Europe. With their flair for publicity and far-sightedness, they ploughed back their profits to mount the show like a military exercise, with a small army of assistants armed with lavish catalogues, posters, G&G badges, even stickers for the Muscovite taxis. Most prized of all were the G&G tee-shirts, of a quality unknown in Russia, which changed hands at high prices as luxurious status symbols from the West. I saw young Russians wearing them day after day, reluctant to take them off.

❖

I met Damien Hirst at the 1992 Turner Prize dinner in the Tate Gallery. After chatting amiably a cloud crossed his ragamuffin face and he asked who I was. He recoiled: 'Not that nasty man who writes those horrible things about me?' As I had just described him as a taxidermist trying to emulate a pop star, this was unanswerable, though I reminded him that I had written asking to hear his point of view and he had not replied. But he hurried away; and cried when he lost the prize.

Our next meeting took place a couple of years later in the Serpentine Gallery, where he curated a mixed show called 'Some Went Mad, Some Ran Away'. He was accompanied by an American artist, Ashley Bickerton, who had flown in from New York that morning with a twelve-foot rubber shark as his exhibit, while Hirst displayed the notorious pickled lamb, vandalized by a man with an inkpot, which added to the publicity.

Ashley was studiously dressed in frayed cotton shorts and an orange cap, explaining, as he caught me looking at him, 'If I put on my best clothes and daub my skin with facial cream, I flop. When I look real scummy, I score.' Plainly he was out to score. When he was overcome by a vertigo-hangover as he tried to suspend his shark from the ceiling, I knew how he felt and suggested we move to The French Pub where Damien, for we were on first-name terms by now, ordered champagne and we forgot about lunch. Later we moved up the street to the Colony and by now we were friends. This was consolidated the week before the Turner Prize in 1995 when I pursued him for a newspaper profile which involved the difficulty of finding him in the first place, for he seemed to change addresses nightly. I would wait hours for him to turn up, and we would consume amounts of alcohol when he did which were excessive even for me. None of the delays and missed appointments mattered the moment I was in his company, for it was brilliant with his legendary high spirits, usually vodka, whisky and champagne, and his generosity which is becoming as legendary as Bacon's. Hirst is in that exuberant tradition and one of his pictures hangs beside a Bacon reproduction behind the bar at the Colony. 'I feel the same delight when he opens the door,' said the owner, Michael Wojas, who succeeded Ian Board, 'as I did with Francis.'

For the sake of the newspaper column, I had to ask Hirst about his preoccupation with dead animals, suggesting that many people saw him as a con-artist who had the last laugh with the shock of his exhibits and the prices they fetch. Surprisingly hurt, Hirst demanded to know if I had seen his entry for the Turner Prize, the dissected cow and calf called *Mother and Child Divided*. I said I had, but he knew I was lying. The next day I went to see it for myself, which few of the editors who were condemning it as 'scandalous' had done. I understood why he was so insistent, for no reproduction, not even on film, prepared me for the animals cut in half, apparently suspended in space. It has the haunting beauty of a *vanitas* still-life conveying the transience of life — a poignant contemporary *memento mori*. Damien's mother, Mary Brennan, a splendid lady who had travelled from Leeds to see it, told me, 'Damien's piece made me cry. It's very close to home. I know how it feels. He deserves to win, but he's a winner, so it doesn't matter.'

Win he did.

On the last morning of that visit to London, finding that the digital clock in my hotel bedroom was an hour and a half slow so that I missed my train, I stumbled downstairs to catch the next one. I was handed a message from Damien asking me to call on him at yet another new address before I left. I moaned, exhausted from the week's excess, unable to take more, yet equally unable to resist such a request. There was no phone number.

I climbed down the basement steps to find Mary Brennan in bed with her baby grandson, Connor, whom Damien had carried so proudly round Soho, and Damien himself emerged from the back looking as if he had just gone to sleep, as he probably had. He handed me an envelope.

'This is for you,' he said, 'to launch your photographic exhibition.'

During the hours we drank together, I mentioned that I hoped to mount a major retrospective in my photographs, and was aghast to discover the cost involved in printing, mounting and so on. Without intending it as a hint, I concluded that I would have to look for several people prepared to back me. Damien was the first, his envelope stuffed with Deutschmarks. I caught the next train back to Devon with infinite relief.

Twenty-One

Across the Caucasus

'S.O.B.' said my doctor when I told him I hoped to climb the Caucasus.

He was known as forthright but I thought this was uncalled for. 'Son of a bitch?' I murmured reproachfully.

'No. Short of breath.'

Subsequently Dr Hunt sent me a letter advising me to go ahead: 'Yes, you are overweight and your blood pressure could be a problem. You are certainly not in serious danger, but it is a very difficult thing to itemize exactly as in my experience people with your abominably unhealthy lifestyle tend to go on for years longer in defiance of all the laws of nature.' That was good news. He added: 'It would be an advantage if you could get into some gentle training, preferably by cutting down the bottle to a certain extent.' Wise advice to be noted, tested and abandoned.

My desire to cross the Caucasus was inspired by my father's attempt as he explained in the splendid opening to *Caucasian Journey* 1951:

> In the spring of 1929 I set out to ride horseback over the western Caucasus with Alexander Wicksteed, an old English eccentric who, for six years, had been trying to live like a Russian in Red Moscow. Our intentions were to get the first pair of horses at Kislovodsk, then to proceed by easy stages, camping out on the northern spurs of the Caucasus wherever we liked a place, or I found some good trout fishing; finally to try and take our horses over the snow-clad Klukhor Pass (9200 feet) and ride down beside the foaming River Kodor to the melon beds of Sukhum on the shores of the Black Sea.

These images had thrilled me for years. Ultimately, my father failed and I wanted to find out why. There seemed no chance to follow in his footsteps until Gilbert & George invited me to Moscow for their exhibition in the spring of 1990. When they flew back to London, I stayed on with James Birch, who had instigated the show, to watch the May Day parade. There used to be two: the display of military might on the ninth, commemorating victory over Germany in 1945, preceded on the 1st by healthy, muscular girls in short skirts and twirling hoops. On 1 May 1990 it was nothing like that.

As we joined the crowds surging towards Red Square I saw a procession with flags and a banner of the crucified Christ carried by a priest, heading up the hill. Running ahead to take photographs we were caught up in the movement and swept into the square, where the procession halted opposite Lenin's tomb with the Soviet leaders on the podium above it, Gorbachev unmistakable in a grey hat. Only then did I realize this was not a peaceful procession – we were in the centre of a demonstration with flags from the dissenting republics of the Soviet Union – but I was in the very position I was hoping for.

Lines of police in plain clothes kept us isolated, staring at us with unconcealed fury as the demonstration erupted. One dissident shouted abuse at the Soviet leader, his face contorted, while another led the rest in a chant which grew louder and fiercer all the time. In the background, Red Square reverberated from the din of martial music intended to enhance the occasion but which heightened the tension.

A woman next to me clutched her ears against the noise; the nervous young policeman facing me developed a tic, his cheeks fluttering as if they concealed the wings of a small bird; a man, who was not one of the demonstrators, turned towards me and shook his head. I asked if he spoke English and he did so haltingly: 'They are shouting for freedom – they are telling "Gorbachev resign." There has been nothing in our history like it.' He wiped his face with his glove.

The most powerful men in Russia watched us from only yards away. Suddenly Gorbachev's patience ran out and he gave the signal to leave, his fingers drumming on the ledge. As we left the square we saw tanks and water-guns but I learned that Gorbachev had given orders there should be no violence in spite of the affront to his authority. The outside world recognized this at once, amazed by the photos and newsreel of the few around us who had dared insult the president. The first crack had appeared.

The next morning I flew to Tblisi in a filthy Aeroflot plane, the seat beside me vacant because it contained someone's vomit, and a few days later I flew over the great range of the Caucasus which stretch from the Black Sea to the Caspian, dividing Europe from the East. There are twelve mountains higher than Mont Blanc, with Elbruz the highest at 18,784 ft. Between Elbruz and Mount Kazbek there are 125 miles of snowfields and glaciers, and seeing these from above it was easy to believe that some of the former tribes in their remote valleys could be reached only at certain times of year. It was this isolation which had made the Caucasus the refuge for the outlawed over the centuries, from Tsarist and Soviet oppression.

Your first approach to the Caucasus is something you never forget. I experienced a sudden, overwhelming sensation of happiness as irrational yet as powerful as if I were a young soldier returning home. The train crossed a countryside of lilac woods in heavy spring blossom, with headscarved women tending immaculate plots while others sunbathed on the green banks. When my father was in the mountains he felt that elation – 'It is seldom, as we get on, that one feels the sudden unaccountable, bubbling happiness of youth. But I had a burst of it' – and so did I, even inside the rattling, overcrowded train. It is a sensation you are lucky to have a few times in your life, and it lasts for seconds, and there is nothing like it.

There is a moment in Tolstoy's *The Cossacks*, when the world-weary young officer Olenin, who has been posted to the Caucasus after his life has been tarnished by gambling debts and debauchery, sees the mountains for the first time:

> seeming to run along the horizon, their rosy tips gleaming in the rays of the rising sun. All his Moscow recollections, his shame and his regrets, all his trivial dreams of the Caucasus, departed and never returned again. 'Now it has begun!' a sort of triumphant voice said to him.

My own approach by train could hardly have been more mundane, but I understood Olenin's emotion. Every mountain range is different: some are threatening, others have the softness of pillows, the Caucasus welcome you as if you belong.

In Kislovodsk I was met by my interpreter Yuri and his girlfriend, and we were joined by a powerful Karachaite mountaineer, Ali, perpetually smiling, who would act as a guide in the region where Russian was not always spoken. My objective was the village of Khassaut where my father bought his horses, having failed to do so in Kislovodsk which the Soviets had penetrated in 1929, bringing with them all the restrictions of Communist bureaucracy.

As soon as we drove out of Kislovodsk, ignoring the warning that foreigners were not allowed to do so without a permit from the militia, the atmosphere changed. We entered a green valley where black sheep fed beside a river, tended by a solitary shepherd as he would tend them day after day, year after year against attack from wolves and bears. A few small wild horses romped across the hills.

I had brought a copy of *Caucasian Journey* which I showed to Ali, for Khassaut was a Muslim village in Karachay, photographed by my father in 1929 with a mosque and minaret, fine houses with cupolas, and clusters of villagers in the square. Altogether there were 600 households. When we entered Khassaut sixty-one years later we found a village in ruins with fewer than twenty people. The minaret had vanished and all that was left of the mosque was a skeletal base. The elegant houses had gone. We fell silent until a few women came running to greet us and cried out with excitement when Ali showed them the photograph in the book.

'They say, "Bless the gentleman from England".'

'Why?'

'Because for the first time they know what their village looked like.'

As we drove back we passed the same shepherd and it seemed he had not moved. The light was fading and we stopped at the top of a mountain pass to look back on the smouldering, tumbling shapes in colours that shifted from rose to violet to darkest gentian, with details exposed in final shafts of sunlight. Echoes reached us of distant dogs barking in a valley far below, and as I raised my eyes again I gasped from that heart-stopping moment when you see the peaks of the snow mountains *above* the clouds.

What had happened to Khassaut?

This was why I planned to return a year later, learn the answer and complete my father's journey, if I could, by crossing the Klukhor Pass.

I envisaged a restful cruise down the Volga, much as my father had enjoyed on a little paddle steamer when he left Moscow in 1929, eating sterlet all the way, with treats of caviare for breakfast. After ten days I would reach Astrakhan, take a train along the Caspian to Baku, a bus to Tblisi, and from there by car over the Georgian military highway tantalizingly described by my father as 'one of the most

sensationally beautiful mountain highways in the world'. From Kislovodsk I would set out with horses into Karachay, find out who the
Karachaites were, of whom I knew so little, and what had happened
to Khassaut. In the Caucasus I would sleep in a tent beside a surging
river after an evening meal of trout cooked on a wood fire. The
Klukhor Pass would be the climax. All very romantic.

❖

'I think I'm going mad,' I said to James Birch, my travelling companion
on the ghastly boat from Moscow called the *Clara Tsepkin* after
Lenin's revolutionary German comrade. I rechristened her the *Pipkin*.

Having paid a bribe of $400 in advance to secure a luxury cabin,
we were confronted by a cell barely able to contain one of us, let
alone two. '*Nyet!*' cried the furious first mate when we complained.
Russians do not complain, nor did a suite or luxury cabins exist. In
the end, bribing a woman with the usual Marlboro, we secured a
second cabin and headed for the saloon which looked promisingly
prow-shaped, with curtains around the windows and a solitary plastic
carnation on each table.

'Vodka,' I beamed at the waitress, having found a table at the far
end which overlooked the foredeck. Things were looking up.

'*Nyet!*' she replied with the hostility and appearance of a pugilist.

I tried again. 'Cognac?'

'*Nyet*,' with greater satisfaction.

Desperate by now to quench my thirst, I asked for *mineral-vodiye*,
which is sold in bottles, but even that received an emphatic *nyet*.

'*Nichevo?*' I said faintly, meaning 'Nothing whatsoever!'

'*Nichevo!*' she declared with all the pomp of the Russians.

'I think I'm going mad,' I announced.

'How do you mean?' asked James.

'Well, we're in the ship's saloon but there's no food and nothing
to drink.'

'And have you noticed something very odd?' He nodded towards
the passengers sitting in phlegmatic silence at the other tables. 'They've
given their orders to the two waitresses, but nothing is being
served.'

'And now they're leaving,' I pointed out, 'but they can't have eaten
because there isn't any food. It doesn't make sense. Unless . . .' an
uneasy thought occurred to me, 'there really isn't any food.' We

laughed at such absurdity, and when the waitress with the boxer's face returned we mimed as if we wanted to eat. She shook her head, smiling as she shoved the menu in front of us and produced a pencil and paper to take our order. As there was nothing to order this seemed a cruel charade.

'This is surreal,' I said to James. 'A restaurant with neither food nor drink, not even water.'

He sighed with impatience, as he was wont to do over the next few weeks: 'Don't you understand anything? This is Russia. Nothing makes sense.'

'What in God's name are we doing?' I moaned, 'sailing on a dry ship down the Volga?' – a silly remark, for I knew exactly, though I had not expected it to be like this. The idea of a boat trip always seems deceptively idyllic, but the reality had never been as harsh as this, not because of the discomfort, which was immaterial, nor the lack of food, though that was alarming, but because the *Pipkin* threatened to be the most boring ship that ever sailed.

We were saved by a mysterious young Russian called Vladimir who had the courage to come over and introduce himself when he heard us talking in English, knowing a few words himself and eager to learn more. The mystery was due to his refusal of Marlboro cigarettes because he did not smoke, nor did he drink. Also there was something odd about his description of himself as a 'philosopher', and when I asked if he was on holiday he replied, 'Every day is holiday for me, and every day leetle work. Unofficial. Everything in Russia today has to be unofficial.' Over the next few days we wondered constantly if his proclaimed hatred of Communism meant that he was a Communist agent planted to inform on us, or one of the young who were growing rebellious. He was travelling all the way to Astrakhan in spite of the cholera epidemic which prevented us from going further than Volgograd. His slight knowledge of English was a godsend and when we spoke slowly he was quick to understand.

It was dark outside and though we were sailing down a canal there was the sense of cocooned limbo which envelops every ship at night. The imaginary second sitting was over and the two waitresses relaxed: Lou, the older pugilist, and the younger Nina, who took a fancy to James and Vladimir and my Marlboro. Suddenly Lou produced a plate of coarsely cut salami, never to be seen on board again, with a sliced tomato and some marmalade sweets. This unexpected treat was surpassed by a small bottle of fiery cognac at a cost which was derisory with the rate of exchange so unfairly in our favour. I would have paid a king's ransom for this concession from Lou, who had taken pity on us. It had to be drunk neat for we remained waterless. Later Vladimir discovered a tap two decks below where boiled water, probably from the filthy canal, dripped into the stained decanter I brought from my dismal cabin. After our first stop at a small town called Uglich, with a church lined by golden panels, Vladimir knocked on my cabin and thrust five bottles of mineral water into my arms, more welcome than champagne. With a beaming smile of satisfaction at my delight, he wished me goodnight. In such ways is friendship formed.

Over the alleged breakfast next morning, worth attending for the cup of tea, Lou was called away and returned with the lop-sided smile which people assume when they have witnessed an accident. '*Odin*,' she announced, holding up a finger, and spoke to Vladimir who explained that the Kapitan had commanded us to appear on the bridge in an hour's time. Though we were guiltless, this made no difference in Russia and I feared we might be dumped at the next port and detained.

When we reported to the bridge, insisting that Vladimir accompany us as interpreter, the first mate glared, I smiled graciously, pretending I was the Duke of Devonshire, and James looked docile. Then the Kapitan started to harangue us. Thick-set, slightly balding, he seemed pleasant enough until he became transformed, rambling hysterically for several minutes, giving Vladimir no chance to interpret, while the first mate interrupted the tirade with unintelligible yells of his own.

When the violence abated, I spoke with the authority of a district officer calming a native uprising, and produced my article in the *Sunday Telegraph* the previous year on Gilbert & George in Moscow, with the statue of Vera Mukhina's *Industrial Worker and Collective Farm Girl* behind them, and various other bits and pieces purely as a distraction.

This provoked the Kapitan to further rage, turning our passports upside down in case they revealed a forgery, though it was plain he could not understand a word. I blessed my friend in London who had arranged for visas for every port we stopped at along the Volga; having married a Russian girl he knew how important such precautions could be.

'He asks why two Englishmen are on board his ship,' Vladimir translated. I was tempted to say for the delicious food, but even the Kapitan could not have swallowed that.

'We are on board the *Pipkin* . . .' I began, stopped by a yell as he turned to Vladimir who translated impassively, 'He says what is this *Pipkin*, I say you mean *Tsepkin*.'

'We are on board your beautiful ship,' I continued, 'because we wish to see the Volga which my father did in 1929, the true Russia in all her glory and nobility . . .' Vladimir had a tough time translating this rigmarole and it was obvious that the Kapitan found it inconceivable that anyone should travel on his ship for pleasure. There had to be an ulterior motive. Finally he was reduced to demanding two hundred more roubles for the second cabin, and seemed disappointed when James handed them over instantly.

'No problem!' I beamed.

As we were waved away, Vladimir told us, 'That is crazy man. He says he will report you to the KGB, he thinks you are spies.' I was surprised to find I was trembling with anger.

As the Volga expanded it was more like a coastline than a river, with ports along the way: Yaroslavl, strangely deserted, and Kostroma, where we raced back to the *Pipkin* at seven in the evening with the panic of passengers who fear they might be left behind. Vladimir retired to his cabin to listen to his high-powered radio while I lay down on my bunk and shared the interminable suffering of Sholokhov's *And Quiet Flows the Don*, a book I began to hate. The day had been invigorating, but Vladimir looked unhappy when he joined us for dinner.

'Is anything the matter?'

'I heard announcement on radio,' he confided softly. 'They say Gorbachev is ill, but I do not think so. It is all confusing, but I think he has been overthrown by Politburo. It is finished.' He pushed away his plate with disgust, not only at the food, and gave a great sigh: 'From now on, dictatorship again.'

This was the first we heard of the attempted coup. When the Kapitan threatened to report us to the KGB he might have been bluffing; now he had a reason for suspecting western observers.

The *Pipkin* sailed on, cocooned in her complacency, impervious to the turbulence outside. Seagulls joined us as the Volga widened even further and I caught glimpses of small beaches like those my father swam from when the paddlesteamer stopped and the water was clean.

There was a sweep of chocolate water lined by green hillocks and trees on the European side, with an occasional glimpse of a tent hiding in woods, and low, endless plains on the Asian side opposite. Huntsmen lived beyond the law in these woodlands, trapping and fishing for survival, and were known as 'trolls'. As the sun set I was elated by the faded splendour of a low-lying white monastery which stretched to the water's edge, recognizing it as the Dead Monastery photographed by my father. It still looked dead; that it was there at all was reassuring.

And all the while the passengers munched their revolting food, talking in whispers, with no outward recognition of the coup which would change their lives if it succeeded, for these were the people who received the perquisites of the regime, officers and their wives, staunch supporters of the Communist Party. I could not like them, but understood that they must detest me as someone who had no right to be on board their ship. For them this was a luxury cruise because they were escaping from the drab monotony of their lives in Moscow and the confinement of overcrowded one-room apartments. For them, this was a holiday! Also, the fulfilment of a lifelong ambition to sail down Mother Volga. This accounted for the constant changes of clothes, with the rows of medals transferred from one garment to the other by the older men. I was startled at first by the number of one-armed passengers until I realized it was the same man in different outfits. He was married to a malevolent woman who wore a bright red hairpiece surrounded by her own grey hair, as bizarre a top-knot as I have seen.

At dinner Vladimir waited until we were alone. 'The news is now very bad. There is state of emergency and curfew in Moscow. Now all Russia is quiet, waiting.' He paused, turning the pages of our dictionary with startling speed in order to find the words he was looking for. 'The West are accused of making trouble. This could be bad with the Kapitan and you.' It meant also that Vladimir was putting his head on the block by remaining with us, though he had a street-wise sense of survival.

When we docked at the Tartar capital of Kazan it promised romance, but the modern city proved depressing with the usual dereliction and filthy buses bumping over potholes. It brightened the further we went, and after a dutiful visit to a Tartar mosque, the first Vladimir had seen, we found a church of unexpected charm, Dutch or German in style, with carved decorations of fruit and flowers in contrast to the oppressive ornamentation of the Orthodox churches laden with gilt. In the covered market, where peasant women walked down the middle with a shopping basket suspended at either end of a wooden yoke as if they were oxen, I pounced on a jar of honey and downed a glass of fresh goat's milk on the spot.

As we neared the town centre it was seething with people as if in the wake of a big parade. The atmosphere of tension was tangible as people asked each other what was happening. Soon we had to squeeze through the crowds outside the office of a newspaper where Vladimir tried to get close enough to read the latest bulletin on handwritten placards pinned beside blown-up portraits of Gorbachev and Yeltsin. He dived into the scrum, emerging to tell us, 'Everyone is asking, "Where is our President?", "Is he alive?", "What is happening to us?"' He added that one news-sheet claimed that Yeltsin had been branded as a criminal by the new regime. Caught up in the provincial reaction to the coup, I had a different view from the press corps in Moscow. It was a unique moment to be sailing down the Volga.

The KGB came on board as we were due to sail. There was a sharp knock on my cabin door as I was changing, and I was confronted by a smartly suited young man and three impassive, unsmiling colleagues behind him. He studied me intently as I struggled into a clean shirt, and then shoved his identification card in my face. At least he had the grace to say '*Strasvitye*', the Russian equivalent of 'how do you do', followed by a demand for documents. This time he seemed to recognize the visas, though he turned the pages of my passport with the usual bewilderment. Presumably the crazed Kapitan had radioed ahead asking that two British agents should be interrogated, possibly in view of the Western opposition to the coup. Smiling amiably, I produced my jar of honey and placed it on the table as proof of my harmless time on shore. The KGB man hesitated. Then with an emphatic gesture he handed the passport back and left.

James had been questioned as well and had just seen the first mate, who glared at him: 'If looks could kill!' Vladimir confirmed, 'The passengers ask me if you are Western spies.'

When I smugly mentioned my jar of innocent honey, James shook his head pityingly: 'That will really make them think you're up to something, like showing your wretched articles to the captain. Nothing is that straightforward in Russia. Have you asked yourself

how they knew we would be in our cabins at that moment? And
have you noticed that the fourth KGB man was the *Pipkin*'s sailor
who flirts with our waitress? That's rather suspicious.'

'You mean *he's* a spy?' That way lay paranoia.

'I mean that our innocence has nothing to do with anything in
Russia. I've had other brushes with the KGB,' he revealed surprisingly,
'but never in such terrifying circumstances as this. Now they're bound
to deport us from Volgograd.'

'I think James is nervous, yes?' smiled Vladimir.

'Decidedly,' I agreed.

'Absolutely,' said James.

As a distraction I produced my last bag of Maltesers and offered
one to Nina, the more attractive waitress, the one the KGB sailor
flirted with. I mimed to James aghast when she withdrew her hand.
'I noticed,' he whispered. 'Her hands are covered in sores. She
wouldn't be allowed to wait on table in England.'

'Not *that*,' I exclaimed impatiently. 'She took the lot!'

The Volga might have widened but my cabin seemed to have
narrowed. I thought I was hallucinating until I realized that a very
large lady had boarded the *Pipkin* at Kazan and had moved into the
adjacent cabin. Every time she leant against the dividing partition, it
buckled and my ledge narrowed.

We reached Ulianovsk at eleven that evening and as there was only
a half-hour stop I did not bother to go ashore. Instead, the KGB came
on board to see us. This time there was no courtesy from an unpleasant,
slant-eyed official who tried to bully us. While he cross-examined
James in the saloon, the nicer middle-aged lady who was translating
whispered to me urgently, 'Things are bad in Moscow,' with the
alarming gesture of slitting her throat, turning away before her colleague could see us. So, the coup did implicate us, especially if the
Kapitan had declared our presence illegal. It was lucky that we had
not gone ashore, for our visas did not include the small port of
Ulianovsk, where they could have arrested us on some pretext. Instead
they had to let us continue, though with muttering and obvious
reluctance.

A blare of martial music assaulted us from loudspeakers as we sailed
from Samara the next day and I felt for the animals caged in the small,
atrocious zoo near the landing stage with the music at full blast, their
food probably stolen by the keepers as in other zoos in Russia. There

was another knock on the door and I braced myself, but this time it was Vladimir straight from his radio. 'Great news!' he crowed. 'This is very important day. Now we have big changes.' He laughed with joy as he revealed that Gorbachev was back in Moscow. 'This,' he declared emotionally, 'is second Russian Revolution!'

There was a new sense of peace as the ship glided over the water with scarcely a murmur from her engines. The river was wide again, several miles across, and so smooth that the bow caused just a ripple as she cut through. Occasionally a patch of ruffled water creased the surface as if disturbed by some mysterious element below. The steppes were stupendous, stretching 'without border' as Vladimir put it, on either side, with no sign of humanity. They were not flat but undulating, dust-coloured with occasional clumps of trees, once inhabited by the fox, ermine and sable which drove the hunters eastwards as the animals were exterminated for their pelts – the 'soft gold' which prompted the colonization of Siberia.

Vladimir and I leaned over the rail, absorbing the view in silent rapport. Our journey would have been frightening without his sense of humour to restore the balance, always convulsed by my reference to the *Pipkin*, which became a private joke. His reflective mood, induced by the dusk and passing shorelines, changed as two Russian girls joined him and he started to flirt outrageously. I was pleased to know that he would have their company on the journey back, and left him laughing. That is how I remember the *Pipkin* at her best, sailing down the Volga jauntily as if she were heading for the open sea.

Our last supper was uneventful so I went to my cabin at eleven. James told me that after I left, a passenger arrived in the dining-room and started to flirt with Nina, the sexy waitress with the sores. Lou was staggering from drink and Vladimir was dancing with the two girls to their transistor on the deck, oblivious to the bridge above them. When the Kapitan descended in his habitual fury, he found Lou slumped in a chair, with Nina smoking our Marlboro on the knees of the passenger, who had brought a bottle of cognac, the first sign of alcohol aboard apart from our nightly treat. Speechless, the Kapitan then caught sight of Lou's little 'passengers' book' which I had signed earlier. Glaring at it suspiciously, he called for Vladimir to translate: I SHALL ALWAYS REMEMBER MY LOVELY CRUISE DOWN THE VOLGA. THE PIPKIN IS UNFORGETTABLE.

'The *Pipkin*!' shrieked the Kapitan, exasperated to hear this word again. 'What is this *Pipkin*?'

Lost for an explanation, Vladimir tried to calm him down: 'I think the Englishman is mad!'

❖

Rumbles of the new revolution echoed in Volgograd, the old Stalingrad, where they celebrated wildly on the Saturday night, and in Baku, that town on the salt-impregnated Caspian, where oil derricks nodded in suburban back gardens with their small slicks of filthy oil. I was arrested in the main square the morning after our arrival as I photographed Lenin's statue with a crane drawn up beside the outstretched arm, I assumed to clean it. A limousine swept up and several policemen converged on James and myself, while others jumped out of bushes. Like the Kapitan, the senior policeman was hysterical with rage, though we were plainly harmless. The more he gibbered, the more I nodded benevolently in order to enrage him further. After the KGB this was child's play in an increasingly silly game, until I was grabbed from behind by two plain-clothes men and hustled into the back of the limousine with darkened windows so that no one could see what was happening, though the square was empty anyway. James surrendered his film, but I refused and they started to shake me like a cocktail.

'For god's sake,' James muttered, 'give them the film. Why do you always have to cause trouble?'

'No,' I replied emphatically. 'It might be interesting to see the inside of a Russian prison.' Recognizing a potential troublemaker, the senior man denied me this experience by seizing my Konika, ripping out the half-exposed film. There was now no point in protesting further, so I left the limousine with as much disdain as I could muster and returned furiously to the hotel at the end of the square, followed by James who was equally though differently angry: 'If you think it would be fun in a Russian prison, you really are mad!'

Going onto my balcony on the fifteenth floor later in the morning I saw crowds gathering in the square, which proved to be a demonstration against the Soviet-backed regime in Azerbaijan. I returned to the square, this time with my faithful Rolleiflex for the Konika had jammed. Police were lined up with helmets and riot shields in front of Lenin's statue, about to be pulled down like the statues in Moscow which had been toppling all week. That is why the crane was there.

By mid-afternoon there were ten thousand people in the square and the police abandoned any attempt to control them as the tanks rolled in; when I crossed the line of riot shields there was no more interference.

Paradoxically, the atmosphere softened with the arrival of the army as the demonstrators thrust carnations into the gun barrels of the tanks and the baby-faced soldiers helped to pull the children on top, or stood laughing with their arms around each other's shoulders. Then the leaders of the demonstration surged forward and tore down the flimsy barricades which blocked the steps and started to demand the independence of Azerbaijan from the Kremlin. Briefly a separate state in 1918–20, when British troops entered the town at the end of the First World War, the Azerbaijanis were now proudly nationalistic, as so many of the former Soviet republics became. The speakers were apparently demanding the dismissal of the president, a hard-line Communist who had see-sawed his allegiance. Caught up in the excitement, people were anxious to talk when they realized I was English, though I felt an imposter when a hush fell on the square and they raised their right arms in solidarity and I did so too. It seemed rude not to join in.

That night, under the cover of darkness, the crane went into action and Lenin fell. When I looked out from my balcony in the morning there were just a few bricks from the plinth and a mound of dust.

Eventually we arrived at Kislovodsk, where we rejoined Yuri and Ali and set out in an overcrowded jeep a few days later to collect our horses in a remote valley. How can I describe the Caucasus? There are details which look familiar, but the whole is on such a majestic scale that even the Rift Valley in East Africa is dwarfed by comparison.

Yet it is not the size but the infinite variety that is so attractive: a ridge of land which resembled the rocky formation in Crete overlooking the inlet where Zorba danced; the black, hornless cattle dubiously descended from Aberdeen Angus, suggesting the Scottish Highlands; lawn-like slopes reminding me of the other Highlands in Kenya; while woods with wild flowers in the denser grass might have been in North Devon except that these were patrolled by wolves and bears. Ali claimed they were harmless except to wandering sheep, adding the universal lament that the only enemy in the Caucasus is *man*.

These are the twin joys of the Caucasus: the tranquillity of the foothills belied by the sweeping panoramas on every side. Yet neither these nor the range of mountains which peel back in layers are daunting.

'Have you seen gorges or canyons like this?' cried Ali's cousin, Khopay. Translated by Yuri, he continued, 'It is a pity not many people know such a beautiful place exists. You must tell people in the West that the tribes have always been independent and are proud of this. Hard work is the most important quality, very dignified. If you have Karachaite friend he is very reliable.'

After the radiant start the mists came down and the shepherd with our horses was nowhere to be found when we reached the remote rendezvous. This did not surprise me: Ali's arrangements seemed tenuous from the start, though we were paying him handsomely, but this was Russia where nothing works to rule though rule is everything. There was no alternative but to make our way to Khassaut where we were welcomed back by the woman with the smiling face.

There is no hospitality to equal that of simple people, more civilized than those who live in towns, and that in the mountains is special. It is instinctive, the peasant family takes a pride in it, and it is lavish. The smiling woman whom I met on my visit the year before was the second wife of Ali's uncle, if he was his uncle, and considerably younger. She seemed to do all the work, showing us to a room upstairs with rough beds and giant pillows where we could sleep. After I stacked my equipment I went outside to absorb the warm-hearted moment at dusk when the village stirred briefly from its torpor as women came back from the fields carrying pails of red berries, and Ali's alleged uncle returned from hunting, and two horsemen cantered in as they herded cattle and calves along the road while tethered dogs barked in a frenzy of frustration.

I sat with Ali's uncle on a rickety bench against the wall of his house as the last survivors of Khassaut paid their respects to him as headman of the village, one man with a kiss, a nephew with a smile of obeisance, and a girl with a dutiful shake of the hand, all of which he accepted impassively. Ramazan might have been carved from granite except for his massive hands which shook convulsively; though this did not prevent him from hunting, I felt his aim must be erratic. His eyes were narrow, his mouth, unaccustomed to disagreement, was hard. It was only when we sat down to dinner that I began to appreciate him. First he broke his silence to make a short speech saying how pleased he was to learn that I was following in my father's footsteps and was paying him such respect. He declared, as if he meant it, that I was an honoured guest in his house and wished me health and a safe journey when I left. I felt inadequate as I attempted to respond.

His was the best of the few remaining houses. It looked nothing from the outside, but the single room was decorated with high kitsch – plastic flowers, kewpie dolls, and posters of inquisitive kittens and a circus troupe in elaborate make-up. These contrasted with fine carpets on the walls, the skin of a jackal whose snout was pierced by an eagle's feathers, dried white thistles, and the uncle's hat suspended on antlers.

The most astonishing object was a framed portrait of Shamil, who fought the Tsarist troops when they tried to conquer the Caucasus from 1834 to 1859 with extraordinary courage and religious conviction. I asked the smiling woman why they had a picture of Shamil, for he had defended the eastern Caucasus rather than here.

'Because he was the Muslim defender of *all* the Caucasus against the Russians,' Yuri translated, complaining to me afterwards, 'She says these things against the Russians, but I am Russian.' I was enthralled by this confirmation that we were outside Russia, with this lingering echo of the great rebellious past.

Ramazan shot lynx, bear, wolf, wild goat and jackal. Once he was out hunting when a young bear emerged from the trees and attacked him – so much for the claim that they never attacked man. As they fought, they rolled down the hill with no time for Ramazan to seize his gun. As the bear tore off his clothes in the struggle, he managed to reach his knife, wedged the handle against himself and thrust the blade into the animal's breast, remaining locked in this bizarre embrace until the bear died fifteen minutes later. A nerve had been severed; that explained Ramazan's shaking hands, which were not due to Parkinson's disease as I assumed.

During the few days we waited for Ali to procure our horses, I learned the history of the Karachaites from Ramazan, who had been living in the nearby village of Hurzuk when the Germans invaded in 1942. Karachay covered 11,000 square miles and the Russians had been their traditional enemies since 1828, when General Emmanuel occupied the region with a company of Tsarist troops. After the Revolution the Communists moved in, proving even worse, though the tribes retained an independence in the furthest valleys. Compared to the Soviets, even the Germans were preferable, which is why, when they invaded in 1942, the leading Karachaite family presented the German general with the gift of a stallion, a saddle embroidered with local silver and a golden sabre. The Germans were welcomed as liberators. 'They did not harm anyone,' Ramazan assured me, 'except for the Communists and the Jews.' The anti-Semitism in the mountains was startling.

When the Germans withdrew, many of the Karachaites went with them. Those who remained were surrounded and bombed by heavy artillery and planes. At the end of the summer of 1943, the Soviets seized Khassaut after marching from Kislovodsk and Stalin took his revenge.

'Stalin punished the whole Karachaite nation,' Yuri translated. 'It was so unfair. He destroyed everything and all their records so that no trace of the Karachaites should exist, which is why we know so little of their history. Stalin even destroyed their books.' In November 1943 they were forced into exile.

'Couldn't they resist?' I asked naïvely.

Yuri shrugged: 'What use is a dagger against a machine gun?'

They were given no warning. Ramazan's father had to run carrying his boots to the Studebaker lorry supplied by American Lend-Lease, and put them on inside. Within twenty-four hours everyone had been taken to the nearest railway station where his family was sent to Kazakhstan rather than Siberia. Ramazan was fourteen years old, which suggests he was younger than myself. He was a strong boy, but though his father survived that first winter he did not recover from the disease and excessive heat of the following summer. The rest of the family worked hard and were such superb shepherds that the authorities hoped they would stay when Khrushchev allowed them to return to their homes. Instead, they found their villages empty, the houses not only looted but blown apart by explosives in case something of value had been hidden. Now Khassaut was forgotten; not even the reverberations of the coup had reached them here.

This was why it looked so contented when I woke at six-thirty and walked with a towel and sponge bag along the path to the Narzan spring, where I washed thoroughly, shaved, brushed my teeth and drank the sparkling water, watched by two dogs, a friendly black mongrel with a wagging stump of tail and her lean, brown friend who sloped back with me as I walked along the Khassaut river whose water was as pure as could be.

We set out with our horses on a peerless morning a few days later, accompanied by the two dogs. I led a horse which was known as 'tricky', though it seemed docile apart from the irritation of stopping every few yards to munch wild flowers by the roadside. It would be difficult to start a day more radiantly, walking with dogs and horses beside a sparkling river with a zing in the air as fresh as my last gulp from the Narzan spring. After two hours we reached a solitary farm-holding where several Caucasian guard-dogs surrounded us, barking furiously until they were called off by their owner. Not as savage as they liked to pretend, they scared the lean dog which slunk away, but respected Hadji, as I called the mongrel with the stump of a tail, as if she were royalty in shabby disguise. Though Ali threw stones at her to make her go back with her companion for her own safety, she had decided to be our protector and was not to be deterred.

We climbed a hill which was so steep it was almost vertical, with nothing to grip on as I zig-zagged my ascent in the long grass, peppered with wild flowers, a cluster of blue gentian, and a coiled black snake which slithered harmlessly away. I was relieved that James was equally out of condition and I did not protest when Ali came back to carry my camera case, pointing excitedly to the left. There was Elbruz, its twin snow-covered peaks shining in the sunlight; I knew from my father's experience that bad weather could obscure them for weeks on end. Elbruz was eighteen miles away in this spectacular panorama, with a ridge of rock to the right and the illusion that a vast sea stretched behind it. Ahead of us successive jagged peaks were just as I imagined mountains when I was a child. In this expanse not a building could be seen; as for signs of life, I noticed a solitary horseman, then a shepherd guarding a hillside flock, and one other – that was all in the hundreds of miles surrounding us.

After six miles we stopped to eat at a hut where shepherds stayed in the summer. We were approaching a plateau which promised flat going, but proved a series of hills which left me gasping. As we crossed a field, a handsome black stallion came charging towards us, stamping his hooves as he tried to keep his frightened mares in order, though this frightened them all the more.

'Very hostile, I can tell you,' said Yuri severely. 'He protects his wives.'

He looked startled when I replied, 'And quite right too.'

Hadji was equally protective of us and charged back, snapping at the stallion's forelegs while keeping at a safe distance. I noticed that Ali regarded her with new admiration.

As we continued across the hilly plateau, three Karachaite horsemen swept down and one of them slid effortlessly from his saddle to shake my hand, a gold tooth glistening in the afternoon sun. He was not the most magnificent specimen of mankind, and his crooked smile suggested craftiness. He was intensely curious and nodded approvingly as all the Karachaites had done when Yuri explained that I was following in my father's tracks.

Did I like the Caucasus? It was easy to answer that with enthusiasm.

What was life like in England? That was more difficult. I tried to describe how we had more food in the shops and more entertainment in the larger cities. 'But there is a wisdom in the mountains. You have a freedom denied to us.' This high-falutin' response baffled him, as well it might.

Had I drunk the Narzan water? We were on safer ground and I told him enthusiastically, 'Oh yes, in Khassaut, this morning.'

Was I happy to be there? I tried to convey my feelings, ending with the simple truth: 'This is probably the happiest day of my life.'

Satisfied at last, he slipped back in the saddle, shook my hand, and with a cry of '*Dosvidanya, Danyl*!' he flung out his arms in farewell.

I watched the three Karachaite horsemen gallop up the hill pursued by their barking dogs. At the top they twirled and twisted their horses, showing off in their exuberance. A second of stillness as they stood out in silhouette, a final echoing cry, and they poured over the other side and were gone.

❖

The rest of the journey, strolling through the Caucasus with our pack-horses, was not the idyllic experience I had been looking forward to. There was no nightly bartering for lambs to be roasted with sour cream over open fires, nor trout from the 'foaming' rivers, though I had brought the identical flies my father used when he fished the Kuban. Instead we ate tins of so-called ham, which James identified as 'donkey dick'. We slept in a tent in the pouring rain by a raging river, though even this was not as rough as I had hoped. By now I was so fit that I slept blissfully, woken once when Hadji barked furiously outside, apparently to ward off a bear glimpsed by Ali in the undergrowth.

Our horses collapsed, which did not surprise me for they were wretched specimens, and Ali put them in the care of a farmer who was busy sending dozens of sheep to market. Hadji was left behind as well, with Ali's promise to collect her with the horses on his way back to Kislovodsk. As we hitched a lift on a lorry, I heard a piercing howl behind me and looked back in remorse only to see that Hadji had nipped the Alsatian admirer who had come too close, and was wagging her tail in glee, a born survivor and the nicest Russian of them all.

Our porters deserted us when we left Dombai a few days later, as they had the great mountaineer Douglas Freshfield who had climbed Mount Elbruz in 1886, nine years after the Tsar subdued Shamil. We were driven to our starting-point, where Ali told me to go ahead while he reassembled our equipment, leaving the tents and sleeping-bags behind.

'Ali is angry,' Yuri confided. 'These men tell him, "Ali, we respect you but this is madness. It is too difficult. Why should we risk our lives?"'

Freshfield's Teberdine guides had deserted him on the grounds that if the pass was impassable for horses it was impassable for them too. He had to turn back on 27 June 1886, which made it all the stranger that my father, who knew this, attempted his climb on 27 June 1929. My timing was ridiculed by my friends. I had chosen 12 September 1991 – because the late Patric Walker in his horoscope at the start of the year wrote that Capricorns could do anything they wanted on that particular day.

To start with the climb was easy, partly because Ali had submitted us to an endurance test two days earlier in order to make or break us; also because of the remnants of the zig-zag track used by tribes over the centuries trying to cross to the Black Sea since long before the birth of Christ, improved later as a short-lived road for the Tsarist army in their invasion of the Caucasus until it became too steep and the Sukhumi Military Road was abandoned. Eroded by ice and wind, it had not been used for sixteen years when my father followed it, then it was used again by the Germans in the last war until they were forced back by the Russian outposts. Now it was derelict again, though there were just enough traces for us to recognize it.

True to the beckoning treachery of mountains, the next ridge revealed another and then another until I turned a corner and found I was looking down on Lake Klukhor, a sickly green with a smaller blacker lake beyond with ice-floes dripping into it. The lake was evil. This was where Freshfield's guides deserted him among 'a group of wild precipitous peaks, such as is seldom met with even in the Caucasus'.

I recognized it too from my father's description in *Caucasian Journey*, when he endured a night of freezing hell after he sent his Karachaite guide back to Teberda with the horses who could go no further, constantly floundering up to their bellies in the soft snow.

And there it was. A few pools on its mottled surface were beginning to turn slushy green. Water poured through a broken gap in the snow shelf at its mouth and fell over the ledge in a sheer drop of a thousand feet or so. Over this mouth, with a gap between them of only some twenty feet, projected two shelves of snow and ice. They looked strong enough to bear the weight of a man, and the water at the mouth was shallow enough to wade; but it was too tricky a spot to risk horses. We were stymied – 400 feet below the Klukhor Pass.

Ali arrived and pointed to the outline of a track which reached the far side of the lake. '*Pass . . .*' and made a downward gesture to indicate our descent. I pressed on, but as Freshfield and my father discovered, the manoeuvring around the lake was the worst part, with overhanging rocks dripping down, falls of rock and landslides of stones which were almost invisible from a distance but blocked the way every few yards. Every time I thought I had clambered over the last landslide, there came another. No horse could have managed it, for the ledge grew so narrow that I had to place my feet exactly, using my staff, and at one moment I nearly slipped as my father had done, and would have gone over except for the grip of my mountain boots. Though I doubt if the fall would have killed me, to be injured in such a place did not bear thinking of.

Recent falls of snow presented the problem of deciding whether I would fall straight through or whether there would be rock underneath. The only solution was to find out, and the snow proved firm enough to support me. There was one aspect mentioned by my father that I recognized instantly – the din. The basin of the lake served as an echo-chamber, and the hundreds of dripping streams united in a single, complaining shudder which reverberated round the walls of rock.

At 9100 feet I crossed beyond the lake to the top of the Klukhor Pass, which was marked by memorials to dead Soviet soldiers, and I experienced a sense of anticlimax which was melancholy compared to the consummation I expected. I recovered by the time the others arrived and congratulated James, suggesting we took photographs of each other on the summit as if we were proper mountaineers.

'For God's sake,' he muttered. 'Can't you ever keep quiet? After what we've just been through.' Then we sat on the ground exhausted.

Why had my father failed? He had simply timed it badly, or been unlucky in a year when the snow had not yet melted, even in June, but was deep and dangerously soft, impassable for his horses. Yet he *had* climbed the Pass. He *had* reached the same point. 'But the other side of the Pass held disillusionment. There was no trail and the snows went to the cliff edge and then dropped sheer into a valley that was as white as a bowl.'

He and his Karachaite guide Yusuf, as faithful to him as Ali was to us, had found a foothold of rock and began to test their luck: if they slid into the bowl-like valley, that would not be so bad in spite of my father's gammy leg. But if they went over that ledge directly below them, it could be fatal. They selected two boulders: the first, gaining momentum, thundered down the slope, splashed the snow like spray and rolled the entire way across the valley at the bottom. Impressive, but comforting. The next started on the same course, but shot over the cliff – an experiment which settled the argument.

'It is better to live,' said Yusuf in a low voice. My father's sense of failure was so acute that he flung himself down on a cot on his return to Teberda. It was Wicksteed, his companion down the Volga, who roused him: 'Bless my soul, what are you so surly about? Man proposes and God disposes – don't you know you can't just "buy a railroad ticket" over the Caucasus?'

'Listen, Wicker,' said the father, 'I am now going to arise and buy as many bottles of that strong Caucasian purple wine as I can get hold of – and get thoroughly plastered.'

'Wait a minute,' said Wicksteed, 'I'll come with you.' Later, seated among the shimmering trees in their 'local', Wicker announced: 'I have come to the conclusion that the happiness or the oblivion that one gets from alcohol is not altogether illegitimate.'

No wonder my father dedicated *Caucasian Journey* to Wicksteed.

Now, looking below me, I appreciated how deceptive this must have looked to my father in heavy snow, but there was no time for euphoria as we finished off the last of the donkey-dick and turned the corner to see the whole, terrible terrain stretching far below us with the mountains closing in now that the clouds had surrounded us. I was about to learn once more that descents are nastier.

Three days later I was swimming in the Black Sea off Sukhumi. Yuri was still with us, but I had said farewell to Ali after we reached the scattering of houses known as Sumi after making our way from a shepherd's hut where we spent the night. I gave him my first aid kit with the hypodermic needles which fetched large prices in Russia at the time, and I had brought his mountain boots and a colourful Scottish sweater from London. Ali was undemonstrative. He grinned as usual but did not thank me, nor did I want him to, though he indicated there was one object he would really like – the cheap little khaki cap I had bought from a surplus store in North Devon. His only emotion was his anxiety to leave as quickly as possible, for he belonged to the Karachaites who had been Muslim since the sixteenth century, while the Georgians were early Christian, and their outlooks were opposed: the Karachaites regarded the Caucasus as holy, the Georgians turned their faces towards the Black Sea.

We continued into a different land, Abkhazia, with well-tended orchards and pleasant gardens in front of scattered chalets painted in gentian blue with carved wooden balustrades, and stairs leading to the first floor because of the winter snow, though it was now as hot, and the vegetation as lush, as the Mediterranean.

Since then there has been civil war. When I arrived the holiday resort of Sukhumi was basking in the autumn sun. I picked tangerines in Stalin's garden, and the beach where I swam had yet to be littered with tank tracks and the detritus of war. I wondered if there was a single word to apply to Russia. Cynicism is too easy, ennui is too obvious, paradox is inadequate. Perhaps Churchill came closer with his 'riddle wrapped in a mystery inside an enigma'. Probably there is no single word, just as there is no single truth about Russia, but a thousand lies. There is a terrible irony that in finding their freedom, the Russians have torn themselves apart like sharks in bloodstained water.

The Black Sea was cleaner than I expected and soothed the muscles which had been strained over the recent weeks. The elation had not hit me until then. If I had learned anything it was my own inadequacy, and I had a shrewd idea of that before. I had crossed the Klukhor Pass, but I could not have done so without Ali. There was no mountaineering skill involved, my father's endurance on that ledge during that freezing night made my achievement puny. Yet there can be a greater vanity in denigrating oneself too far. I *had* achieved what I set out to do, and it was a journey that few can make today. Furthermore, thanks to his forbearance, I am still on speaking terms with James.

One morning after a night in Soho after my return when I must have mentioned where I had been, I woke to find a paper napkin stuffed in my pocket with a message. I do not know who wrote it, nor can I trace the quotation, but it said everything for me: LIFE IS AN ADVENTURE ALWAYS TO BE GAINED.

Twenty-Two

Return to Dalyan

AFTER MY turbulent start in Istanbul, I took the Taurus Express to Adana in the east, to discover the train had no restaurant, no buffet, no food, no water. Confronted by the disaster of a dry train, two years after a dry ship down the Volga, I bolted into the station bar at Haydarpasa across the Bosphorus and hurried back with a glass, a plastic container of water and a bottle of raki. Most unwise.

The carriages did not connect and the few other passengers were there because of an airline strike, for the Turks despise trains as a last, inferior resort. I had a narrow, filthy compartment to myself with a hard bunk, and emerged to join the others who stared disconsolately at the strange landscape which resembled gigantic cow-pats in the desert for hours on end, the cost of the journey just a couple of pounds.

A friendly woman with the complexion of pigskin offered me an apple, and though she refused my raki with much gentility she studied the brochure of the hotel I was heading for, the last stop before Syria, with nods of approval.

We reached Adana after twenty hours at six in the morning, before the heat of the city descended, and I sipped coffee at a nearby bar, joined by some of the stragglers off the train including the pigskin woman; I paid for her tea with my new graciousness. Then another train took me across the plain of Issus, where Alexander the Great defeated Darius of Persia in 333 BC, hilltops still crowned with castles. A friendly conductor examined my bottle of raki, now a quarter full, and threw it out of the window to my infinite relief, helping me find a taxi in Iskenderun, once Alexandretta – Iskender means Alexander – which as so often in life looks jollier in photographs than it does in reality. After a half-hour drive I reached the small fishing village of Arsuz where I relaxed at last, recovering from my debaucheries thanks to the kindness of the gigantic young Turk who ran the hotel. On my third night he invited me to a banquet, starting with Iskenderun prawns caught in the bay outside. Drinking beforehand in the comfortable lounge which was open to the sea a few yards away, I was startled to see the pigskin lady in the opposite corner and hurried over to greet her.

'What an extraordinary coincidence!' I told Sedat when I returned, explaining we had met in the train. He shook his head.

'I do not think so.'

Sedat's disapproving expression said it all. She had followed me, possibly hoping for an affair. Poor, misguided pigskin lady. Sedat spoke to her and she did not reappear. He knew her reputation.

❧

In travelling to Aleppo on my way to Damascus I was not entirely motivated by the search for new experience. Having heard of changes, I was postponing my return to Dalyan on the Mediterranean coast, a place I had fallen in love with.

I remember my emotion on a spring morning in 1982 in Ecincek Bay when I was collected from the pilot boat which had moored for the night, having sailed from Marmaris in one of the first flotillas along this coast. The Turk who fetched us was Abidin Kurt whose healthy ambition had brought him to London, where he worked in a Bayswater hotel receiving large tips from the Arabs despised by the other porters. By the time he returned to Dalyan he spoke English and had saved enough to buy his own boat.

I knew none of this that first morning, just that the water was pure, pierced by two vaulting dolphins who seemed to leap with ecstasy. As we turned the bay I saw the sandbar of Iztuzu stretching for several miles up to the hills at the far end. Enhancing this natural beauty, and making it even more extraordinary, were the wooden shacks dotted in ramshackle disarray along the beach, rising above it in the early shimmering sunlight as if on stilts. This apparition lasted for a minute or two before Abidin swept us through the narrow entrance too shallow for yachts with keels, in his flat-bottomed caique, past the brackish lagoon on the other side, into the Dalyan delta lined with reeds, though not tall enough to prevent glimpses of the cotton fields with the brightly coloured shawls of peasant women at work, and low mauve hills beyond. Terrapins scurried into the roots of the reeds, kingfishers darted. We moored beneath a hill, and Abidin led us up to the ancient city of Caunus, with the remnants of an amphitheatre and a view over miles of marshland where the sea had retreated. Below us Turkish archaeologists, assisted by convicts, had dredged up a jaunty white marble lion, its paw resting with delightful arrogance on the head of a bull. Back on the caique we passed the wooden barriers, raised and lowered to catch the local mullet – Dalyan means fishery – and then another exhilaration: the group of Lycian tombs carved high in the cliffs by an early form of scaffolding, cream in colour, shaped like gigantic doors and long since looted. Past the village into the river sheltered with trees on either side, the splash of a large fish jumping ahead of us, into the expanse of Lake Koyeciz where we swam in the fresh water, returning to Dalyan for lunch at the simple Denizati (Sea Horse) restaurant on the water's edge. I had known no morning so surprising. Everyone should have a second country, and now Turkey was mine. I left to continue my journey vowing to return, as I did the following year, and for years after that.

I stayed with Aly Aktas, the only pension in the village on my next visit, woken by the gentle chugging of the boats piled high with bales of cotton on their way upriver. I walked to the Denizati every morning, writing my notes while the smiling waiter, Ismet, sought my help with his English phrase-book. Otherwise we sat and smiled in silence, and I realized that language can be a dreadful barrier to understanding. At night I ate my dinner, which Ismet would not allow me to pay for, as the sun slid down behind the hills opposite, and the mosquitoes came out, always the curse of Dalyan's marshland which bred the malaria which led to the downfall of Caunus.

After that I stayed with Abidin Kurt in his wooden shack on the sandbar, which he had built himself six years earlier. There was no light apart from oil-lamps and moonlight through the open squares with flaps which served as windows. Water was brought up with buckets from cement barrels sunk in the sand. A kilim on the floor served as my bed; we had breakfast on the wooden verandah, with tea boiled on a butane-gas bottle, and an occasional meal cooked over a wood fire.

Abidin left early to collect his yachtsmen from Ecincek while I walked along the edge of the gentle, subsiding surf as tiny crabs scuttled into holes in the sand. Here was the grace of life that my father found in Bohinsko. For me it was the height of simple luxury.

The wooden huts were known as *barakas*. There were as many as fifty at their peak, used by local Turks who came downriver for the fresh air and no mosquitoes. There was no road. Incredibly, there was even a restaurant, two in mid-summer, one of them run by people from Istanbul, with high-backed wooden chairs though still open to the elements on either side. In the spring when there were no visitors, I shared the sandbar with the loggerhead turtles who lumbered ashore at night to lay as many as two hundred eggs the size of ping-pong balls. Exhausted by the effort, after covering the nest with their flippers they crawled back to the safety of the sea a few yards away. Reluctant to intrude with a flashlight, I contented myself with the discovery of their tracks the next morning, like tiny tanks, sometimes heading in the wrong direction before they sensed their mistake and turned back. As many as three hundred turtles came to Iztuzu as they had done for thousands of years, the last of a dwindling breed, increasingly vulnerable to progress. When the eggs hatched, Abidin and his fishermen friends scooped up the babies and carried them to the sea before the birds attacked or they blistered to death on the scorching sand. That image of Abidin, as strong as the lion he resembled, delighted me especially as the fishermen resented the adult turtles for snaring their nets. Abidin was a natural conservationist, loving the area so much that when we sailed up or down the river at dusk, and he pointed to the distant village where he grew up, there were tears in his eyes. Turks have an unabashed pride in their country which we have forgotten.

In the late 1970s a remarkable woman arrived at Iztuzu, June Hai-moff, soon to be known along the coast as Kaptan June, who came ashore with her current lover, a young Swiss ski-instructor, in tow as her crew. She was one of those English lady adventurers who descended on the Middle East in broad-brimmed hats, disturbing the natives with their femininity. Travelling ever further east in her search for a summer haven, she thought she might have found it here. Returning eight years later, with neither Swiss nor boat, she planned her own *baraka*, drawing the outlines in the sand with a piece of driftwood and conscripting the local men to build it. The following spring she was handed her keys. A few yards from the sea, her confrontation with the turtles was destined. The effect on Kaptan June was traumatic: 'If you save the turtles, you are involved in a philosophy which ties in with the rest of nature. It's a primeval instinct. Kill them and you destroy the protection of motherhood.' The threat they lived under was confirmed by plans to build a large German complex at the far end of Iztuzu. I suspect she saw this as a threat to her own solitude as well, but the plight of the turtles became a national concern as she enlisted the support of Green parties all over the world. She told me of the day in 1987 when the foundation stone was laid for the new hotel: 'A group of musicians with alp-horns were flown in wearing Bavarian costume, with dancers dressed in leather and officials in suits. They had their lunch, leaving the beach to their bulldozers, and no one looked at the sea, no one felt the wind, and no one thought of the turtles.'

I was looking for land of my own, and found it opposite Dalyan, under the Lycian tombs. It never occurred to me to build a *baraka* on the beach, probably because I hoped for something permanent, a home rather than a summer shack. It was Abidin who pointed out the plot of land which he had heard was for sale. We tied up and I walked across the rough, hard earth covered with yellow ragwort, my imagination planting it with an orchard of lemon, orange, apricot and plum trees stretching down to the river. This wistful daydream was strengthened by the sight of an old mulberry tree beside the water, a solitary male – which looked forlorn, as if it needed a young female mulberry to be planted for companionship – and several established trees near the track at the back used by tractors, also a poplar, a massive palm, an overgrown fig, with a cactus and a grapevine, which was where I envisaged my house, surrounded by hibiscus and bougainvillaea, with space under the roof for swallows. Crucially, there was even a disused well which could be restored to irrigate the land, for the water from the river was too brackish. I planned a line of delicate eucalyptus to mark the boundary and whisper in the breeze, and several Corsican pine. I tracked down the owner of the land to Dalaman, where he was a teacher. With Abidin acting as interpreter, the owner explained that his family wanted to retain a strip of the land for themselves, but this would still leave me 5000 square metres. I went to Koycegiz to consult a lawyer who told me I might have to buy the land in Abidin's name, which was no problem, and stopped at the governmental farm where I could buy my trees and shrubs – by now I was thinking of avocado too, unknown in the district. When I mentioned oleander, Abidin recoiled: 'They are everywhere, we need special trees.' He was starting to plant the garden too.

At Muğla, the civic capital of the province, I spent weary hours signing forms needed by the notary to give Abidin the power of attorney, and returned to Dalaman where I beat the owner down with a bargaining skill I did not know I possessed, exploiting my concession over the strip of land. Finally we reached a compromise and shook hands on the deal – around £11,000. Bar the signing, I had the land! I was overjoyed.

I should have followed the advice given to my father when he was in Turkey in the 1920s by the Greek ambassador: 'There are three things, M'sieur, a man should not do: have a wife in Romania, a ship in the Black Sea, or own land in Turkey – he will lose all three.' I had neither wife nor ship, but I lost the land when the owner's three nephews convinced him to change his mind, and though I had paid a deposit there was little I could do. In the event, I lost my job as the *Mail on Sunday*'s television critic as well. I had been absent for too long, and while I was away my deputy, Alan Coren, took witty advantage of a sudden upsurge of programmes after months of dross: the shooting of J.R. in *Dallas*, the death of *Coronation Street*'s Elsie Tanner. I was out of work once more.

Armed with a generous pay-off from the *Mail on Sunday*, I returned a few months later intending to buy the land outright as I had heard from Abidin that the nephews had changed their mind – but this proved a false hope.

Abidin asked me to join him at a wedding party in Candir, the village where he was born, no more than a cluster of houses on the other side of Caunus. It was a perfect night, with more shooting stars than I had seen since Lake Bohinsko. As we approached we could hear drums reverberating in the stillness. This was the feast before the next day's ceremony: it was simple, traditional and charming – I was the only visitor. Groups of men were dancing or sitting on planks which were balanced on empty beehives, with tables strewn with plates of chicken and white beans mixed with oil and herbs, and bottles of raki. Other men sprawled across kilims laid on the earth, below the only modern house in the village, which had two floors and a flat roof which was crowded with women, kept apart, for no woman would dare to dance in front of the men. They stood there watching intently like birds in a tree.

The headman of the village joined us and I realized that the men below were the sons, their fathers keeping out of the way for once in order not to spoil their fun. Usually the sons did not drink in front of their elders.

'They will get very drunk,' said Abidin severely, 'and feel very brave and fight each other.' That sounded all right to me. The musicians were gypsies from Ortega. Two were outstanding, thwacking their drums with a persistent beat which grew in violence while the other two played instruments which resembled wooden flutes but sounded surprisingly like bagpipes. The younger men came over to welcome Abidin and myself, including the groom, a young man of twenty-six with a humorous face, wearing a brown suit. He had spoken to his wife at the formal ceremony two weeks earlier, but they had never touched, everything being fixed by the families. He asked me to dance and I accepted eagerly, deluding myself that I was good at Turkish dancing. There were subtleties I was unaware of, but the jumping about with arms in the air part was something even I could imitate. A few minutes later he appeared with Turkish lira notes pinned to the lapels of his jacket. I had no large notes to contribute, so I tried to pin a clutch of smaller ones which swung around him like a college scarf.

Encouraged by the raki, Abidin and I got down to the basic truths of life, one of the hazardous advantages of alcohol. Thinking of the land I had lost, I told him he was blessed to live in such surroundings. 'If you have a clean heart, then life is good,' he replied, which made me wonder why bad people prosper. He told me that when he married he would have a traditional wedding too, with a dozen gypsies and a feast which would last for days. The night began to spin, and the dancing grew frenzied. Like young bloods capering in front of a bull the dancers taunted the drum, sinking to their knees in front of it while the gypsy advanced, beating it to death, daring the dancer to attack. Suddenly, the party erupted, the groom was seized, covered with a striped sheet and beaten as if he were a drum himself. For a split second I thought they had sliced his hand, or worse. In fact a red-dyed bandage had been knotted around his wrist. It would be removed a few hours later, and the hand would be stained by the paste of henna for two weeks. The same ritual was taking place with the bride at Ortega, symbolic of the coming loss of her virginity. If the groom had any doubts about that, she would be returned to her family in disgrace.

I woke next morning in Abidin's father's home. The drums were still beating, on their way to collect the bride, the young men still gyrating as they followed, the women packed into separate carts behind. Later in the day at the Denizati I saw the wedding party on their way back, the musicians still playing though the women were animated now, waving from their separate caiques, the bride among them, her face covered, as they crossed the river. The groom had gone ahead to greet her at the entrance to their new home. A goat or sheep would be slaughtered and the meat distributed while the couple disappeared to the bedroom, where the groom would lift the bride's veil. They would touch for the first time.

It was an event of unalloyed optimism. Even as an outsider, with the variance of my own state of mind, I appreciated the warmth of their welcome, and I could swank that I had danced with the groom. I felt a deep tenderness towards Dalyan.

Then everything changed. The government ordered that the huts on the beach should be pulled down because they were a shanty town. June Haimoff moved to a small house on the outskirts of Dalyan, resurrecting her *baraka* in the garden. She had created such a rumpus at Iztuzu that the hotel complex was abandoned due to pressure from the German Green Party. Immediately the village turned against her. The Minister for Tourism complained that development should not be sacrificed for 'a few tortoises'. More serious for Kaptan June was the fury of the young Turks, who accused her of depriving them of their livelihood. She was denounced as a Greek spy, the ultimate insult. The local police took an exquisite revenge, impounding her passport and then letting the whole village know her real age. One shopkeeper shouted at her that she was a whore who had slept with every man in the village. 'Except for you,' she shouted back, seething inwardly, 'Which shows I have some taste.'

Defiantly, she held a party to announce her engagement to 'The Wolf', a penniless, homeless, illiterate young man of twenty-six. They exchanged rings, bought by herself, she sang and everyone cheered. Then he left her.

How many people had tried to kill her, I asked. She thought this over. 'To my knowledge, only one.' This was a caretaker who had fed her poisoned mushrooms. Did she sack him? 'No. If they try to kill you and fail, then you have them in your power afterwards.'

Then everything changed again. The German Greens paid Dalyan a handsome compensation for their lost hotel development, enabling the villagers to invest in small hotels and pensions of their own. Suddenly, turtles were the rage. Fishermen who had resented them before realized their tourist potential, and several hundred boats carried visitors down the delta to the beach. Turtle souvenirs along the quay, turtle tee-shirts, turtle pizzas . . . Hundreds of coaches disgorged thousands of tourists every day, and June Haimoff, popular once again as 'Madame Turtle', warned me in a letter: 'I fear you will be disillusioned to see it now, an ugly mess of concrete imposing itself upon the distant, beautiful skyline, winking lights and flashing neon signs like a lovely woman degraded, despoiled, a poor man's Las Vegas.'

I was reluctant to return, but as the godfather to Abidin's first son, I felt I had to see them. Approaching the village I saw changes at once, a new road, new buildings, but these were perhaps inevitable. It was Dalyan itself which proved such a shock.

The road which led through it was choked with people, the traffic could hardly move, and charabancs filled the square where a statue had been erected – apparently of turtles copulating, though a closer look revealed a mother and her babies. It was the start of Ramadan when the Turks, demented by celibacy and sobriety, run amok, surging towards the coast to celebrate. The atmosphere was so jolly that I joined in, grateful now for the new restaurants and bars. I found myself missing the hustle-bustle when the Turks returned to the cities and Dalyan was left to the daily invasion of tourists and I began to take stock of the changes. There was much to be grateful for: outboard engines were forbidden on the river, and new buildings were restricted to two storeys; the top of the new post office, intended as apartments for top officials, was lopped off. Several of the new hotels were attractive, if impersonal. Yet the heart seemed to have gone out of the lazy village. The little Denizati had been destroyed to make way for a promenade along the river's edge. 'They'll make it like the concrete marina at Fethiye,' I exclaimed.

'Exactly,' said Abidin. 'That is everything they admire.' Even Ismet's bakery had gone, and he now worked in one of the shops selling garments, smiling less often than before. I was booked into a hateful modern hotel where nothing worked. The Wolf had absconded with a buxom German. 'He was the only one,' sighed June. Her victory had proved hollow, and she now believed that the German hotel might not have been so disastrous after all.

I took the bus to Iztuzu along a fine new road lined with oleander, the panorama of the sandbar below still amazing. The restaurants had gone, along with the shanty settlement, and though there is a kiosk where you can buy a soft drink or an Efes beer it is not the same.

I walked along the edge of the lapping surf. It was pleasant enough, but when I returned to the village in the afternoon I found myself killing time – killing time in Turkey! Something I had never done before – but I had changed, as, surely, had the place. The bars caught alight in the evening, one of them attracting a group of outsiders as weird and lost as myself, where I drank too much raki in the search for oblivion, having learnt nothing in the past two years.

I thought myself lucky that I had lost my land. If the turtles survive it will be due to June Haimoff, yet, as she admits, in saving them she has helped destroy Dalyan. That love affair was over.

❖

But no, I cannot leave it like that. As I said at the beginning of this book, you should not take me too seriously. I must not end with the smack of defeat. Having reached my seventies, I expect less; my sexuality scarcely seems to matter now, though it ruled my life before. The only intolerance comes from gays. As for the demon drink, that remains a serious problem. It is just too bad if others cannot forgive, but sad when it leads to the loss of friendship. My problem is not to live without guilt, as analysts advise, but to live *with* it.

In *Victory*, Conrad writes of Mr Heyst that he had 'perceived the means of passing through life without suffering and almost without a single care in the world – invulnerable because elusive'. I could hardly be more different. I am exposed, I strive to live on different levels, always vulnerable, ever the self-deceiver. And none of it matters. See yourself as others do – why? Their views hardly matter and are probably wrong. See yourself as you know you are, and forgive. As Brendan Behan put it: 'Fuck the begrudgers!'

When I was twenty-one I chose to be British, and would do so again, though I am dismayed to find young people sleeping rough in Soho's doorways, a tiny hand emerging from a zipped-up sleeping bag, a girl with a shivering dog, a boy shambling past with a blanket draped over his shoulders. It seems we have become a mean country, with the assumption that such people have failed in lives that have hardly begun.

When the Turks ask me about life in England, I dare not tell them of our child abuse or the rape of old ladies, for they would not understand. On my last visit to Turkey in 1996 when I drove inland, I saw solitary children returning home from school down remote country roads, and reflected that few parents would take such a risk in Britain today. Yet every time I take the train from Paddington to Devon I am elated by the freshness of the English countryside, the vivid greens of the fields dotted with black and white cattle. I rejoice in where I live, overlooking the estuary of the rivers Taw and Torridge which join up opposite and flow out to sea over Bideford Bar. Hardly a day passes without surprise: the turns of the tide which goes out a hundred yards, advancing again to lap against my sea-wall and sometimes flood my back yard; the return of the salmon fishermen with their nets at low ebb; the occasional seal or porpoise; cormorants winging their way upriver and diving for fish. Sometimes a distant sweep of Exmoor which I have never seen before is revealed by a sudden shaft of sunlight. There are coves towards Hartland Point which are so isolated it takes an effort to reach them, but when you do you are rewarded by the sense of having stepped back a thousand years in time.

My back yard is filled with plants and shrubs, honeysuckle and clematis climbing up the cherry tree grown from a stone by Peter, the fig tree brought from the Grey House reaching to my balcony. Karen lives next door with her companion, who has filled the old row-boat with earth and planted it. He has painted one wall in Grecian blue so the yard is lush and Mediterranean on a sunny day.

We are happy enough in our different ways, with a collie dog who is even happier. This morning I took Heidi along the Cannons where the estuary turns into the Atlantic, with Lundy Island on the horizon. A hot day in June, the sands extending for miles, and no one in sight. I was tempted to swim naked. Life today is a matter of such moments.

In two days' time I take the Shuttle to Paris for the Francis Bacon exhibition at the Pompidou Centre, like others of his friends who are travelling from America and Tangier. Life is still an adventure always to be gained. Far from becoming mellow, there are times when I feel that I have only just begun.

There is no deceiver like the self-deceiver.

Index